A
Heartwarming
ROMANCE
COLLECTION

3 Romances from a *New York Times* Bestselling Author

A
Heartwarming
ROMANCE
COLLECTION

Wanda E. Brunstetter

BARBOUR BOOKS
An Imprint of Barbour Publishing, Inc.

Print ISBN 978-1-64352-535-8

eBook Editions:
Adobe Digital Edition (.epub) 978-1-64352-537-2
Kindle and MobiPocket Edition (.prc) 978-1-64352-536-5

For more information about Wanda E. Brunstetter, please access the author's website at: www.wandabrunstetter.com

Cover Photograph: Sandra Cunningham / Trevillion Images

Published by Barbour Books, an imprint of Barbour Publishing, Inc., 1810 Barbour Drive, Uhrichsville, OH 44683, www.barbourbooks.com

Our mission is to inspire the world with the life-changing message of the Bible.

Member of the
Evangelical Christian
Publishers Association

Printed in Canada

Talking for Two

To my son, Richard Jr.,
who first suggested I learn ventriloquism.
To my daughter, Lorine,
the best ventriloquist student I ever had.
To Clinton Detweiler,
a talented ventriloquist:
Much thanks for all your helpful insights.

Chapter One

"Miss Johnson, will you make Roscoe talk to us again?" Four-year-old Ricky Evans squinted his pale blue eyes and offered up a toothy grin so appealing that Tabitha knew it would be impossible for her to say no.

She pulled the floppy-eared dog puppet from its home in the bottom drawer of her desk and quickly inserted her hand. Thankful she was wearing blue jeans and not a dress today, she dropped to her knees and hid behind the desk, bringing only the puppet into view. Roscoe let out a couple of loud barks, which brought several more children running to see the program. Then Tabitha launched into her routine.

"Did you know I used to belong to a flea circus?" the scruffy-looking puppet asked. The children now sat on the floor, completely mesmerized, waiting for what was to come next.

"Really and truly?" a young girl called out.

Roscoe's dark head bobbed up and down. "That's right, and before long, I ran away and stole that whole itchy show!"

The children giggled, and Roscoe howled in response.

Tabitha smiled to herself. She was always glad for the chance to entertain the day care kids, even if she was doing it behind a desk, with a puppet that looked like he'd seen better days.

Five minutes and several jokes later, she ended her routine and sent all the children to their tables for a snack of chocolate chip cookies and milk.

"You're really good with that goofy puppet," came a woman's soft voice behind her.

Tabitha turned to face her coworker and best friend, Donna Hartley. "I enjoy making the kids laugh," she said, pushing an irritating strand of hair away from her face. "It makes me feel like I'm doing something meaningful."

7

Always confident, always consoling, Donna offered her a bright smile. "Just helping me run Caring Christian Day Care is meaningful."

Tabitha blinked. "You really think so?"

Donna pulled out a chair and motioned Tabitha to do the same. "You know what you need, Tabby?"

Tabitha took a seat and offered up a faint smile, relishing the warm, familiar way her friend said her nickname. Donna began calling her that when she and her parents moved next door to the Johnsons, nearly twenty-three years ago. That was when Tabitha had been a happy, outgoing child. That was when she'd been an only child.

Shortly after she turned six, her whole life suddenly changed. The birth of blond-haired, blue-eyed sister Lois had turned talkative, confident Tabby into a timid, stuttering, introverted child. Her father, who'd once doted on her, now had eyes only for the little girl who looked so much like him. Tabby's mother was a meek, subservient woman; rather than stand up to her controlling husband and his blatant acts of favoritism, she had merely chosen to keep silent while Tabby turned into a near recluse.

"Are you listening to me?" Donna asked, jerking Tabby's thoughts back to the present.

"Huh? What were you saying?"

"Do you know what you need?"

Tabby drew in a deep breath and blew it out quickly. "No, but I'm sure you can't wait to tell me."

Donna snickered. "Okay, so I'm not able to keep my big mouth shut where you're concerned. Old habits die hard, you know."

Tabby tapped her foot impatiently. "So, what do I need?"

"You need to attend that Christian workers' conference we heard about a few weeks ago."

"You know I don't do well in crowds," Tabby grumbled. "Especially with a bunch of strangers. I stutter whenever I talk to anyone but you or the day care kids, and—"

"But you won't be in a crowd," Donna reminded. "You'll be in a workshop, learning puppetry. You can hide behind a puppet box."

Tabby shrugged, letting her gaze travel to the group of happy children sitting at the table across the room. "No promises, but I'll think about it."

Seth Beyers had never figured out why anyone would want to buy an ugly dummy, but the customer he was waiting on right now wanted exactly that.

"The uglier the better," the young man said with a deep chuckle. "The audiences at the clubs where I often perform seem to like ugly and crude."

Seth had been a Christian for more than half of his twenty-six years, and he'd been interested in ventriloquism nearly that long as well. It just didn't set right with him when someone used a God-given talent to fill people's heads with all kinds of garbage. While most of Seth's customers were Christians, a few secular people, like Alan Capshaw, came to his shop to either purchase a ventriloquist dummy or have one repaired.

"Okay, I'll do my best for ugly," Seth said with a slight nod. "How does Dumbo ears, a long nose, and lots of freckles sound?"

"The big ears and extended nose is fine, but skip the freckles and stick a big ugly wart on the end of the dummy's snout." Alan grinned, revealing a set of pearly white teeth.

The dummy may turn out ugly, but this guy must really attract women, Seth mentally noted. Alan Capshaw not only had perfect teeth, but his slightly curly blond hair, brilliant blue eyes, and muscular body made Seth feel like he was the ugly dummy. He never could figure out why he'd been cursed with red hair and a slender build.

Seth waited until the self-assured customer placed a sizable down payment on his dummy order and sauntered out the door—and then he allowed himself the privilege of self-analysis. Sure, he'd had a few girl-friends over the past several years, and if he were really honest with himself, he guessed maybe he wasn't too bad looking, either. *At least not compared to the ugly dummy I'll soon be constructing.*

Whenever Seth went anywhere with his little buddy, Rudy Right, folks of all ages seemed to flock around him. Of course, he was pretty sure it was the winking dummy to whom they were actually drawn and not the hopeful ventriloquist.

Seth scratched the back of his head and moved over to the workbench. This was the place where he felt most comfortable. This was where he could become so engrossed in work that his troubles were left behind. He'd started fooling around with a homemade sock puppet and a library book on ventriloquism soon after he was old enough to read. When he turned twelve, his parents enrolled him in a home-study course on ventriloquism. In no time at all, Seth Beyers, normal, active teenager, had turned into a humorous, much sought-after ventriloquist. It wasn't long after that when he began performing at local fairs, school functions, and numerous church programs. About that time, he also decided he would like to learn how to make and repair dummies for a living. He'd always been good with his hands, and with a little help from a couple of books, it didn't take long before he completed his first ventriloquist figure.

Seth now owned and operated his own place of business, and people from all over the United States either brought or sent their ventriloquist figures to him for repairs. When he wasn't performing or teaching a class on ventriloquism, Seth filled special orders for various kinds of dummies. All but one of Seth's goals had been reached.

He wanted a wife and family. He'd been raised as an only child and had always longed for brothers and sisters. Instead of playing with a sibling, Seth's best friend was his sock puppet. Then Mom and Dad had been killed in a plane crash when he was fourteen, and he'd been forced to move from Seattle to Tacoma to live with Grandpa and Grandma Beyers. He loved them both a lot, but it wasn't the same as having his own family. Besides, his grandparents were getting on in years and wouldn't be around forever.

Seth groaned and reached for a piece of sandpaper to begin working on a wooden leg. "What I really need is to find someone who shares my love for Christ and wants to serve Him the way I do." He shook his head. "I wonder if such a woman even exists."

The telephone rang, pulling him out of his reflections. He reached for it quickly, before the answering machine had a chance to click on. "Beyers' Ventriloquist Studio." Seth frowned as he listened. "Glen Harrington's had a family emergency and you want me to fill in?" There was a long pause. "Yeah, I suppose I could work it into my schedule."

Seth wrote down a few particulars, then hung up the phone. The last thing he needed was another seminar to teach, but he didn't have the heart to say no. He'd check his notes from the workshop he'd done in Portland a few months ago, and if everything seemed up to date, maybe there wouldn't be too much preliminary work. Since the seminar was only for one day, he was sure he could make the time.

He closed his eyes briefly as his lips curled into a smile. *Who knows, maybe I'll be able to help some young, talented kid hone his skills and use ventriloquism as a tool to serve the Lord.*

Tabby stared dismally out the living room window in the converted garage apartment she shared with Donna. It was raining again, but then this was late spring, and she did live in the suburbs of Tacoma, Washington. Liquid sunshine was a common occurrence here in the beautiful Evergreen State.

Normally the rain didn't bother her much, but on this particular Saturday it seemed as though every drop of water falling outside was landing on her instead of on the emerald grass and budding trees. She felt as if it were filling up her soul with agonizing depression and loneliness.

Tabby wrapped her arms tightly around her chest, as a deep moan escaped her lips. "Maybe I should have gone to Seattle with Donna and her parents after all." She shivered involuntarily. Tabby disliked crowds, and there was always a huge flock of people at the Seattle Center. No, she was better off here at home, even if she was lonely and miserable.

A sharp rap on the front door brought Tabby's musings to a halt. She moved away from the window and shuffled toward the sound. Standing on tiptoes, she peered through the small peephole, positioned much too high for her short stature.

Tabby's heart took a dive, and her stomach churned like whipping cream about to become butter. She didn't receive many surprise visits from her sister. Maybe this one would go better than the last. At least she hoped it would. Tabby drew in a deep breath, grasped the door handle, then yanked it open.

A blond-haired, blue-eyed beauty, holding a black, rain-soaked umbrella and ensconced in a silver-gray raincoat, greeted her with a wide smile. "Hi, Timid Tabitha. How's everything going?"

Tabby stepped aside as Lois rushed in, giving her umbrella a good shake and scattering droplets of cold water all over Tabby's faded blue jeans. Lois snapped the umbrella closed and dropped it into the wrought-iron stand by the front door. With no invitation, she slipped off her raincoat, hung it on the nearby clothes tree, then headed for the living room. Sitting carefully on the well-worn couch, she hand-pressed a wrinkle out of her pale blue slacks.

Tabby studied her sister. It must be nice to have her good looks, great taste in clothes, and a bubbling personality besides. Compared to Lois's long, carefully curled, silky tresses, Tabby knew her own drab brown, shoulder-length hair must look a mess.

"So, where's your roommate?" Lois asked. "On a rainy day like this, I figured the two of you would probably be curled up on the couch watching one of your favorite boring videos."

"Donna w–went to S–Seattle with her f–folks, and *L–Little W–Women* is not b–boring." Tabby glanced at the video, lying on top of the TV, then she flopped into the rocking chair directly across from her sister. "The b–book is a c–c–classic, and s–s–so is the m–movie."

"Yeah, yeah, I know—little perfect women find their perfect happiness, even though they're poor as scrawny little church mice." Lois sniffed, as though some foul odor had suddenly permeated the room. "The only part of that corny movie I can even relate to is where Jo finally finds her perfect man."

"You've f–found the p–p–perfect man?" Tabby echoed.

Lois nodded. "Definitely. Only mine's not poor. Mike is loaded to the gills, and I'm about to hit pay dirt." She leaned forward, stuck out her left hand, and wiggled her ring finger in front of Tabby's face.

"Wow, w–what a r–r–rock! Does th–this m–m–mean what I th–th–think?"

"It sure as tootin' does, big sister! Mike popped the all-important question last night, right in the middle of a romantic candlelight dinner at Roberto's Restaurant." Lois leaned her head against the back of the couch and sighed deeply. "Six months from now, I'll be Mrs. Michael G. Yehley, lady of leisure. No more humdrum life as a small potatoes secretary. I plan to spend the rest of my days shopping till I drop."

"You're g–getting m–married that s–soon?"

"Don't look so surprised, Shabby Tabby." Lois squinted her eyes. "And for crying out loud, stop that stupid stuttering!"

"I—I c–can't h–h–help it." Tabby hung her head. "I d–don't d–do it on p–purpose, you—you know."

"Give me a break! You could control it and get over your backward bashfulness if you really wanted to. I think you just do it for attention." Lois pursed her lips. "Your little ploy has never worked on me, though. I would think you'd know that by now."

"I d–do not d–do it for a–attention." Tabby stood up and moved slowly toward the window, a wisp of her sister's expensive perfume filling her nostrils. She grimaced and clasped her trembling hands tightly together. *Now I know I should have gone to Seattle. Even a thousand people closing in around me would have been easier to take than five minutes alone with Lois the Lioness.*

"Are you going to congratulate me or not?"

Tabby forced herself to turn and face her sister again. Lois was tapping her perfectly manicured, long red fingernails along the arm of the couch. "Well?"

"C–c–congratulations," Tabby mumbled.

"C–c–congratulations? Is that all you've got to say?"

"Wh–wh–what else is th–there to s–say?"

"How about, 'I'm very happy for you, Lois'? Or, 'Wow, sis, I sure wish it were me getting married. Especially since I'm six years older and quickly turning into a dried-up, mousy old maid.'"

Lois's cutting words sliced through Tabby's heart, and a well of emotion rose in her chest, like Mount Saint Helens about to explode. How could anyone be so cruel? So unfeeling? She wished now she had never opened the front door. This visit from her sister wasn't going any better than the last one had. Blinking back unwanted tears, Tabby tried to think of an appropriate comeback.

"Say something. Has the cat grabbed your tongue again?" Lois prompted.

Tabby shrugged. "I–I th–think you'd better just g–g–go."

Her sister stood up quickly, knocking one of the sofa pillows to the floor. "Fine then! Be that way, you little wimp! I'm sorry I even bothered to stop by and share my good news." She swooped her raincoat off the clothes tree, grabbed the umbrella with a snap of her wrist, and stormed out the front door without so much as a backward glance.

Tabby stood staring at the door. "My little sister doesn't think I'll ever amount to anything," she muttered. "Why does she treat me that way?"

"Lois is not a Christian," a small voice reminded.

Tabby shuddered. Why was it that whenever she felt sorry for herself, the Lord always came along and gave her a nudge? Tabby's parents weren't churchgoers, either. In fact, they had never understood why, even as a child, Tabby had gotten herself up every Sunday morning and walked to the church two blocks from home. Without Jesus' hand to hold, and the encouragement she got from Donna, she doubted if she would even be working at the day care center.

With a determination she didn't really feel, Tabby squared her shoulders and lifted her chin. "I'll show Lois. I'll show everyone." But even as the words poured out of her mouth, she wondered if it was an impossible dream. What could she, Timid Tabitha, do that would prove to her family that she really was a woman of worth?

Chapter Two

"I still can't believe I let you talk me into this," Tabby groaned as she settled herself into the passenger seat of Donna's little red car.

Donna put the key in the ignition, then reached over to give Tabby's arm a reassuring squeeze. "It's gonna be fine. Just allow yourself to relax and have a good time. That's what today is all about, you know."

A frown twisted Tabby's lips. "That's easy enough for you to say. You're always so laid back about everything."

"Not always. Remember that blind date my cousin Tom fixed me up with last month? I was a nervous wreck from the beginning to the end of that horrendous evening."

Tabby laughed. "Come on now. It couldn't have been all that bad."

"Oh yeah?" Donna countered as she pulled out into traffic. "How would you have felt if the most gorgeous guy you'd ever met took you on a bowling date, only because your matchmaking cousin set it all up? I didn't mention it before, but the conceited creep never said more than three words to me all night."

Tabby shrugged. "That would never happen to me, because I'm not about to go on any blind dates. Besides, have you thought maybe the poor guy was just shy? It could be that he wasn't able to conjure up more than three words."

Donna gave the steering wheel a slap with the palm of her hand. "*Humph!* Rod Thompson was anything but shy. In fact, he spent most of the evening flirting with Carol, my cousin's date."

Tabby squinted her eyes. "You're kidding."

"I'm not. It was probably the worst night of my life." Donna wiggled her eyebrows. "It was nearly enough to throw me straight into the arms of our preacher's son."

"Alex? Has Alex asked you out?"

"Many times, and my answer is always no."

"Why? Alex Hanson is cute."

Donna released a low moan. "I know, but he's a PK, for crying out loud! Nobody in their right mind wants to date a preacher's kid."

Tabby's forehead wrinkled, and she pushed a lock of hair away from her face. "Why not? What's wrong with a preacher's kid?"

Donna laughed. "Haven't you heard? The pastor and his entire family live in a fish bowl. Everyone expects them to be perfect."

"If Alex is perfect, then what's the big problem?"

"I said, he's supposed to be perfect. Most of the PKs I've ever known are far from perfect."

Tabby chuckled. "I have a feeling you really like Alex."

"I do not!"

"Do so!"

"Do not!"

Their childish banter went on until Tabby finally called a truce by changing the subject. "Which workshop are you going to register for at the seminar?" she asked.

Donna smiled. "Chalk art drawing. I've always been interested in art, and if I can manage to use my meager talent in that form of Christian ministry, then I'm ready, able, and more than willing."

Tabby glanced down at the scruffy little puppet lying in her lap. "I sure hope I won't have to talk to anyone. Unless I'm behind a puppet box, that is." She slipped Roscoe onto her hand. "If I'm well hidden and can talk through this little guy, I might actually learn something today."

"You're just too self-conscious for your own good. You've got such potential, and I hate to see you waste it."

"Potential? You must have me mixed up with someone else."

Donna clicked her tongue. "Would you please stop? You'll never build your confidence or get over being shy if you keep putting yourself down all the time."

"What am I supposed to do? Brag about how cute, smart, and talented I am?" Tabby grimaced. "Take a good look at me, Donna. I'm the plainest Jane around town, and as I've reminded you before, I can barely say two words to anyone but you or the day care kids without stuttering and making a complete fool of myself."

"You want people to accept you, but you don't think you can ever measure up. Am I right?"

Tabby nodded.

"That will all change," Donna insisted. "Just as soon as you realize your full potential. Repeat after me—I can do it. I can do it. I can do it!"

Tabby held Roscoe up and squeaked, "I can do it, but that's just because I'm a dumb little dog."

The foyer of Alliance Community Church was crammed with people. Tabby gulped down a wave of nausea and steadied herself against the sign-up table for the puppet workshop. She was sure that coming here had been a terrible mistake. If not for the fact that Donna was already in line at the chalk art registration table, she might have turned around and bolted for the door.

"Sorry, but this class is filled up," said a soft-spoken older woman behind the puppet registration table.

"It—it—is?" Tabby stammered.

"I'm afraid so. You might try the ventriloquist workshop." The woman motioned toward a table across the room. "If you like puppetry, I'm sure you'd love to try talking for two."

Tabby slipped quietly away from the table, holding Roscoe so tightly her hand ached. There was no more room in the puppet workshop. Now she had a viable excuse to get out of this crowded place. She turned toward the front door and started to run. Pushing her way past several people, she came to a halt when she ran straight into a man.

"Whoa!" his deep voice exclaimed. "What's your hurry?"

Tabby stared up at him in stunned silence. She was rewarded with a wide smile.

Her plan had been to make a hasty exit, but this young man with soft auburn hair and seeking green eyes had blocked her path.

He nodded toward the puppet she was clutching. "Are you signed up for my class?"

Her gaze was drawn to the stark white piece of paper he held in his hand. "I—uh—th–that is—"

"I hope you're not self-conscious about using a hand puppet instead of a dummy. Many ventriloquists use puppets quite effectively."

Tabby gulped and felt the strength drain from her shaky legs. The guy thought she wanted to learn ventriloquism, and apparently he was the teacher for that workshop. The idea of talking for two and learning to throw her voice did have a certain measure of appeal, but could she? Would she have the nerve to sit in a class with people she didn't even know? Could she talk for her puppet without a puppet box to hide behind? *Maybe I could just sit quietly and observe. Maybe I'd never have to say a word.*

As she studied the handout sheet she'd just been given, Tabby wondered what on earth had possessed her to take a ventriloquist class, of all things! She felt about as dumb as a box of rocks, but as she pondered the matter, an idea burst into her head. Maybe she could do some short ventriloquist skits for the day care kids. If they liked Roscoe popping up from behind a desk, how much more might they enjoy seeing him out in plain view? If she could speak without moving her lips, the kids would think Roscoe really could talk.

From her seat at the back of the classroom, Tabby let her gaze travel toward the front. The young man with short-cropped auburn hair had just introduced himself as Seth Beyers, owner and operator of Beyers' Ventriloquist Studio. He was holding a full-sized, professional ventriloquist figure with one hand.

"I'd like to give you a little rundown on the background of ventriloquism before we begin," Seth said. "Some history books try to date ventriloquism back to biblical times, citing the story of Saul's visit to the witch of Endor as a basis for their claim." He frowned. "I disagree with this theory, though. As a believer in Christ, I take the scriptural account literally for what it says. In fact, I don't think the Bible makes any reference to ventriloquism at all.

"Ventriloquism is nothing more than an illusion. A ventriloquist talks and creates the impression that a voice is coming from somewhere other than its true source. People are often fooled into believing the ventriloquist is throwing his voice. Ventriloquism has been around a long time. Even the ancient Greeks did it. Romans thought ventriloquists spoke from their stomachs. In fact, the word ventriloquism comes from two Latin roots—*venter*—meaning belly, and *loqui*—the past participle of the verb *locuts*, which means to speak."

Seth smiled. "So, the word ventriloquism is actually a misnomer, for there is really no such thing as stomach talking. A ventriloquist's voice comes from only one place—his own throat. Everything the ventriloquist does and says makes the onlooker believe his voice comes from someplace else."

Positioning his foot on the seat of an empty folding chair, Seth placed the dummy on top of his knee. "Most of you will probably start by using an inexpensive plastic figure, or even a hand puppet." Gesturing toward the dummy, Seth added, "Later on, as you become more comfortable doing ventriloquism, you might want to purchase a professional figure like my woodenheaded friend, Rudy."

Suddenly it was as though the dummy had jumped to life. "Hi, folks! My name's Rudy Right, and I'm always right!"

A few snickers filtered through the room, and Seth reprimanded his little friend. "No way, Rudy. No one but God is always right."

"Is that so? Well, in the dummy world, I'm always right!" Rudy shot back.

Tabby leaned forward, watching intently. Seth's lips didn't move at all, and the sound supposedly coming from Rudy Right was nothing like the instructor's deep voice. If common sense hadn't taken over, she might have actually believed the dummy could talk. *A child would surely believe it. Kids probably relate well to what the dummy says too.*

Yanking her wayward thoughts back to the happenings at the front of the room, Tabby giggled behind her hand when Rudy Right accused his owner of being a bigger dummy than he was.

"Yep," spouted Rudy, "you'd have to be really dumb to wanna be around dummies all the time." With the wink of one doeskin eye, the woodenhead added, "Maybe I should start pullin' your strings and see how you like it!"

When the laughter died down, Seth made Rudy say goodbye, then promptly put him back in the suitcase from which he'd first appeared. With a muffled voice from inside the case, Rudy hollered, "Hey, who turned out the lights?"

In the moment of enjoyment, Tabby laughed out loud, temporarily forgetting her uncomfortable shyness. Everyone clapped, and the expert ventriloquist took a bow.

"I see a few of you have brought along a puppet or dummy this morning," Seth said. "So, who would like to be the first to come up and try saying the easy alphabet with the use of your ventriloquist partner?"

When no one volunteered, Seth pointed right at Tabby. "How about you, there in the back row?"

Her heart fluttered like a bird's wings. She bit her bottom lip, then ducked her head, wanting to speak but afraid to do so.

Seth took a few steps toward her. "I'm referring to the young woman with the cute little dog puppet."

If there had only been a hole in the floor, Tabby would have crawled straight into it. She felt trapped, like a caged animal at the Point Defiance Zoo. She wanted to tell Seth Beyers that she wasn't ready to try the easy alphabet yet. However, she knew what would happen if she even tried to speak. Everything would come out in a jumble of incoherent, stuttering words, and she'd be completely mortified. Slinking down in her chair, face red as a vine-ripened tomato, she merely shook her head.

"I guess the little lady's not quite up to the task yet," Seth responded with a chuckle. "Is there someone else brave enough to let us critique you?"

One hand from the front row shot up. Seth nodded. "Okay, you're on!"

An attractive young woman with long red hair took her place next to Seth. She was holding a small boy dummy and wearing a smile that stretched from ear to ear. "Hi, my name's Cheryl Stone, and this is my friend Oscar."

"Have you done any ventriloquism before?" Seth questioned.

Cheryl snickered. "Just in front of my bedroom mirror. I've read a book about throwing your voice, but I haven't mastered all the techniques yet."

"Then you have a bit of an advantage." Seth flashed her a reassuring smile.

Tabby felt a surge of envy course through her veins. Here were two good-looking redheads, standing in front of an audience with their dummies, and neither one looked the least bit nervous. Why in the world did she have to be so paralyzed with fear? What kept her locked in the confines of "Timid Tabitha"?

"Okay, let's begin with that easy alphabet," Seth said, breaking into Tabby's troubling thoughts. "All the letters printed on the blackboard can be said without moving your lips. I'll point to each one, and Cheryl will have her dummy repeat after me."

Cheryl nodded. "We're ready when you are."

Seth moved toward the portable blackboard positioned at Cheryl's left. "Don't forget to keep your mouth relaxed and slightly open, biting your top teeth lightly down on the bottom teeth." Using a pointer-stick, Seth began to call out the letters of the easy alphabet.

Cheryl made Oscar repeat each one. "A C D E G H I J K L N O Q R S T U X Y Z."

She'd done it almost perfectly, and Seth smiled in response. "Sometimes the letter Y can be a problem, but it's easy enough if you just say ooh-eye."

"What about the other letters in the alphabet?" an older man in the audience asked. "What are we supposed to do when we say a word that has B, F, M, P, V, or W in it?"

"That's a good question," Seth replied. "Those all get sound substitutions, and we'll be dealing with that problem shortly."

Oh, no, Tabby groaned inwardly. *This class is going to be anything but easy.*

"Let's have Cheryl and her little friend read some sentences for us," Seth continued. Below the easy alphabet letters he wrote a few lines. "Okay, have a go at it."

"Yes, I can do it." Cheryl opened and closed her dummy's mouth in perfect lip sync. "She had a red silk hat, and that is no joke!"

Everyone laughed, and Cheryl took a bow.

Seth erased the words, then wrote a few more sentences. "Now try these."

"I ran across the yard, heading to the zoo. I need to get a key and unlock the car."

Tabby wrestled with her feelings of jealousy as Cheryl stood there

21

looking so confident and saying everything with no lip movement at all. Tabby sucked in her bottom lip and tried to concentrate on learning the easy alphabet. After all, it wasn't Cheryl's fault she was talented and Tabby wasn't.

"That was great, Cheryl!" Seth gave her a pat on the back.

She smiled in response. "Thanks. It was fun."

The next few hours flew by, with only one fifteen-minute break for snacks and use of the restrooms. Tabby's plan had been to sneak out during this time and wait for Donna in the car. The whole concept of ventriloquism had her fascinated, though, and even if she wasn't going to actively participate, she knew she simply couldn't leave now.

By the time the class finally wound down, everyone had been given a video tape, an audiocassette, and several handouts. Everything from the easy alphabet to proper breathing and sound substitutions had been covered. Now all Tabby had to do was go home and practice. Only then would she know if she could ever learn to talk for two.

Chapter Three

Y ou're awfully quiet," Donna said, as they began their drive home from
the seminar. "Didn't you enjoy the puppet workshop?"

"I never went," Tabby replied.

"Never went?"

"Nope. The class was filled up."

"If you didn't go to the workshop, then where have you been all morning, and why are you holding a bunch of handouts and tapes?"

"I was learning ventriloquism."

Donna's dark eyebrows shot up. "Ventriloquism? You mean you took
the workshop on how to throw your voice?"

"Yeah, and I think I threw mine away for good."

"It went that badly, huh?"

Tabby's only reply was a slow sweep of her hand.

"What on earth possessed you to take something as difficult as ventriloquism?" Donna questioned. "I'm the adventuresome type, and I'd never
try anything like that."

Tabby crossed her arms. "Beats me."

"Did you learn anything?"

"I learned that in order to talk for two, I'd need talent and nerves of
steel." Tabby groaned. "Neither of which I happen to have."

Donna gave the steering wheel a light rap with her knuckles. "Tabitha
Johnson, will you please quit putting yourself down? You've got plenty of
talent. You just need to begin utilizing it."

"You didn't say anything about nerves of steel, though," Tabby
reminded. "Being shy is definitely my worst shortcoming, and without
self-confidence, I could never be a ventriloquist."

"I wouldn't be so sure about that."

"Right! Can't you just see it? Timid Tabitha shuffles on stage, takes one look at the audience, and closes up like a razor clam." She wrinkled her nose. "Or worse yet, I'd start to speak, then get so tongue-tied every word would come out in a jumble of uncontrollable stuttering."

Donna seemed to be mulling things over. "Hmm. . ."

"Hmm. . .what?"

"Why don't you practice your ventriloquism skills on me, then put on a little program for the day care kids?"

"I've already thought about that. It's probably the only way I could ever talk for two." Tabby shrugged. "Who knows—it might even be kind of fun."

"Now that's the spirit! I think we should stop by the Burger Barn and celebrate."

"You call that a place of celebration?"

Donna laughed. "Sure, if you love the triple-decker cheeseburger—and I do!"

Tabby slipped Roscoe onto her hand. "Okay, girls; Burger Barn, here we come!"

In spite of the fact that he'd lost a whole morning of work, Seth had actually enjoyed teaching the ventriloquism workshop. With the exception of that one extremely shy young woman, it had been exciting to see how many in the class caught on so quickly. The little gal holding a scruffy dog puppet had remained in the back row, scrunched down in her seat, looking like she was afraid of her own shadow. She never participated in any way.

Seth had encountered a few bashful people over the years, but no one seemed as self-restricted as that poor woman. Whenever he tried to make eye contact or ask her a question, she seemed to freeze. After a few tries he'd finally given up, afraid she might bolt for the door and miss the whole workshop.

A muscle twitched in his jaw. *I really wish I could have gotten through somehow. What was the point in her taking the class, if she wasn't going to join in? But then, who knows, the shy one might actually take the tapes and handouts home, practice like crazy, and become the next Shari Lewis.*

He chuckled out loud. "Naw, that might be stretching things a bit."

Gathering up his notes, Seth grabbed Rudy's suitcase. He needed to get back to the shop and resume work on Alan Capshaw's ugly dummy. There would be another full day tomorrow, since he was going to be part of a Christian workers' demonstration at a church in the north end of Tacoma.

Seth didn't get to worship at his home church much anymore. He was frequently asked to do programs for other churches' Sunday schools, junior church, or special services that might help generate more interest in Christian ministry. Between that and his full-time business, there wasn't much time left for socializing. Seth hoped that would all change some day. Not that he planned to quit serving the Lord with the talents he'd been generously given. No, as long as the opportunity arose, he would try to follow God's leading and remain faithfully in His service.

What Seth really wanted to modify was his social life. Keeping company with a bunch of dummies was not all that stimulating, and even performing for large crowds wasn't the same as a meaningful one-on-one conversation with someone who shared his interests and love for God.

"Well, Rudy Right," Seth said, glancing at the suitcase in his hand, "I guess it's just you and me for the rest of the day."

The Burger Barn was crowded. Hoping to avoid the mass of people, Tabby suggested they use the drive-thru.

"Part of the fun of going in is being able to check out all the good-looking guys," Donna argued.

Tabby wrinkled her nose. "You do the checking out, and I'll just eat."

A short time later they were munching their food and discussing the workshop.

"Tell me about the chalk art class," Tabby said. "Did you learn anything helpful?"

Donna's face lit up. "It was wonderful! In fact, I think I'm gonna try my hand at black light."

"Black light?"

"You hook a thin, black light over the top of your easel. The pictures you draw with fluorescent chalk almost come to life." Donna motioned with her hand, as though she were drawing an imaginary illustration. "I wish you could have seen some of the beautiful compositions our instructor put together. She draws well anyway, but under the black light, her pictures were absolutely gorgeous!"

Tabby smiled. "I can see she really inspired you to use your artistic talent."

"I'll say. I thought maybe you and I could combine our talents and put on a little program during Sunday school opening sometime."

"You're kidding, right?"

"I'm not kidding at all. I could do a chalk art drawing, and you could put on a puppet show. You might be able to use that old puppet box down in the church storage room." Donna gulped down her lemonade and rushed on. "It's not like you'd have to try your new ventriloquist skills or anything. You could hide behind the puppet box, and—"

Tabby held up one hand. "Whoa! In the first place, I have no ventriloquist skills. Furthermore, I've never done puppets anywhere but at the day care. I'm not sure I could ever do anything for church."

"Sure you could," Donna insisted. "Tomorrow, during our morning worship service, we're going to be entertained and inspired by some of the best Christian education workers in the Puget Sound area."

Tabby's interest was piqued. "We are? I hadn't heard. Guess I've been spending too much time helping out in the church nursery lately."

Donna smiled. "There will be a puppet team from Edmonds, Washington, a chalk artist from Seattle, a ventriloquist, who I hear is a local guy, and several others."

Tabby stared out the window. *Hmm. . .seeing some professionals perform might be kind of interesting. No way does it mean I'll agree to Donna's harebrained idea of us performing at Sunday school, though. I'll just find a seat in the back row and simply enjoy the show.*

The church service would be starting soon, and Seth hurried through the hall toward the sanctuary. Someone had just come out of the ladies' restroom, head down and feet shuffling in his direction. *Thump!* She bumped straight into his arm, nearly knocking little Rudy to the floor.

From the startled expression on her face, Seth could tell she was just as surprised to see him as he was to see her. "Oh, excuse me!" he apologized.

"It's—it's o–o–okay," the young woman stammered. "It w–w–was probably m–m–my fault."

Seth smiled, trying to put her at ease. "I was the instructor at the ventriloquism workshop you took yesterday; do you remember?"

She hung her head and mumbled, "Y–y–yes, I kn–kn–know who y–y–you are. S–s–sorry for g–g–getting in the w–way."

"Naw, it was all my owner's fault," Seth made his dummy say in a high-pitched voice. "He's got two left feet, and I guess he wasn't watchin' where he was goin'." The vent figure gave her a quick wink, then added, "My name's Rudy Right, and I'm always right. What's your name, sister?"

"My name's Tabitha Johnson, but you can call me Tabby." She reached out to grasp one of the dummy's small wooden hands.

Seth grinned. By talking to her through his partner, Tabby seemed much more relaxed. She was even able to make eye contact—at least with the dummy. *I should have tried that in the workshop yesterday. She might have been a bit more receptive.*

Seth had used his ventriloquist figure to reach frightened, sick, and even a few autistic children on more than one occasion. They had always been able to relate better to the dummy than they had to him, so maybe the concept would work as well on adults who had a problem with shyness. He also remembered recently reading an article on stuttering, which seemed to be Tabby's problem. One of the most important things a person could do when talking to someone who stuttered was to be patient and listen well. He thought he could do both, so Seth decided to try a little experiment. "It was nice having you in my workshop," he said, speaking for himself this time.

Tabby's gaze dropped immediately to the floor. "It w–w–was good."

"Did ya learn anything?" This question came from Rudy.

Tabby nodded, looking right at the dummy, whose eyes were now flitting from side to side.

"What'd ya learn?" Rudy prompted.

"I learned that ventriloquism is not as easy as it looks."

No stuttering at all this time, Seth noted. *Hmm. . .I think I may be on to something here.*

"Are you gonna be a ven-trick-o-list?" Rudy asked, giving Tabby a wink.

Tabby giggled. "I'd like to be, but I'm not sure I'd have the nerve to stand up in front of people and talk."

"Aw, it's a piece of cake," Rudy drawled. "All ya have to do is smile, grit your teeth, and let your dummy do most of the talkin'." The figure's head cranked to the left. "Of course, ya need to find a better-lookin' dummy than the one I got stuck with!"

At this, Rudy began to howl, and Tabby laughed right along with him.

Seth's experiment had worked, and he felt as if he'd just climbed to the summit of Mount Rainier.

"I'm surprised to see you here today," Tabby said, directing her comment at Rudy.

The dummy's head swiveled, and his blue eyes rolled back and forth again. "My dummy was asked to give a little demonstration during your worship time. I just came along to keep him in line."

"And to be sure I don't flirt with all the cute women," Seth added in his own voice.

Tabby's face flushed. "I—uh—it's been n–nice t–t–talking to you. I th–think I sh–should g–go find a s–seat in the s–s–sanctuary now."

"Maybe I'll see you later," Seth called to her retreating form.

Tabby slid into a back-row pew, next to Donna.

"What took you so long? I thought I might have to send out the Coast Guard, just in case you'd fallen overboard or something."

Tabby groaned at Donna's tasteless comment. "I ran into the ventriloquist who taught the workshop I took yesterday."

"You did? What's he doing here?"

"He's part of the demonstration. He brought along his cute little dummy."

"I guess he would, if he's going to do ventriloquism." Donna sent a quick jab to Tabby's ribs with her elbow. "Did he talk to you?"

28

"Who?"

Another jab to the ribs. "The ventriloquist, of course."

"Actually, it was the dummy who did most of the talking. He was so funny too."

Donna nodded. "I guess in order to be a ventriloquist, you'd need a good sense of humor."

Tabby twisted her hands together in her lap. How in the world did she think she could ever talk for two? Humor and wisecracking didn't come easy for someone like her. She was about to relay that to Donna, but the church service had begun. She turned her full attention to the front of the room instead.

Mr. Hartung, the middle-aged song leader, led the congregation in several praise choruses, followed by a few hymns. Announcements were given next, then the offering was taken. After that, Pastor Hanson encouraged the congregation to use their talents to serve the Lord, and he introduced the group who had come to inspire others to use their talents in the area of Christian ministry.

The first to perform was Mark Taylor, a Christian magician from Portland, Oregon. He did a few sleight-of-hand tricks, showing how sin can seriously affect one's life. Using another illusion, he showed the way to be shed of sin, through Jesus Christ.

Next up was Gail Stevens, a chalk artist from Seattle. She amazed the congregation with her beautiful chalk drawing of Christ's ascension into heaven, adding a special touch by using the black light Donna had been so enthusiastic about. This illuminated the entire picture and seemed to bring the illustration to life, as Jesus rose in a vibrant, fluorescent pink cloud.

There were oohs and ahs all around the room, and Donna nudged Tabby again. "That's what I want to be able to do someday."

Tabby nodded. "I'm sure you will too."

A group of puppeteers put on a short musical routine, using several Muppet-style puppets, who sang to a taped version of "Bullfrogs and Butterflies." Tabby enjoyed their skit but was most anxious for the upcoming ventriloquist routine.

Joe Richey, a Gospel clown from Olympia, did a short pantomime, which he followed with a demonstration on balloon sculpting. He made a simple dog with a long body, a colorful bouquet of flowers, and ended the routine by making a seal balancing a ball on the end of its nose. Everyone clapped as Slow-Joe the Clown handed out his balloon creations to several excited children in the audience.

Seth Beyers finally took his place in the center of the platform.

"There he is," Tabby whispered breathlessly. "And that's his cute little dummy, Rudy."

Seth had already begun to speak, and Tabby chose to ignore her friend when she asked, "Who do you really think is cute? The funny-looking dummy or the good-looking guy who's pulling his strings?"

"I would like you all to meet my little buddy, Rudy," Seth boomed into the microphone.

"That's right—I'm Rudy Right, and I'm always right!"

"Now, Rudy, I've told you many times that no one but God is always right."

Rudy's glass eyes moved from side to side. "Is that so? I guess we must be related then!"

"The Bible says that God made people in His own image, and you're certainly not a person."

There was a long pause, as if Rudy might be mulling over what the ventriloquist had said. Finally, the dummy's mouth dropped open. "I may be just a dummy, but I'm smart enough to pull your strings!"

Seth laughed, and so did the audience.

Donna leaned close to Tabby. "This guy's really good. His lips don't move at all."

Tabby smiled. "I know." Oh, how she wished she could perform like that, without stuttering or passing out from stage fright. What a wonderful way ventriloquism was to teach Bible stories and the important lessons of life.

A troubling thought popped into Tabby's head, pushing aside her excitement over the ventriloquism routine. *What would it feel like to have someone as good-looking, talented, and friendly as Seth Beyers be interested in someone as dull and uninteresting as me?*

Chapter Four

Wasn't that program great?" Donna asked, as she steered her car out of the church parking lot. "Could you believe how gorgeous the chalk art picture was under the black light?"

"Uh-huh," Tabby mumbled.

"And did you see how quickly Gail Stevens drew that picture? If I drew even half that fast, I'd probably end up with more chalk on me than the paper."

"Hmm. . ."

Donna glanced Tabby's way. "Is that all you've got to say? What's wrong with you, anyway? Ever since we walked out the door, you've been acting like you're a million miles away."

Tabby merely shrugged her shoulders in reply.

"Since my folks are out of town this weekend, and Mom won't be cooking us her usual Sunday dinner, should we eat out or fend for ourselves at home?"

Tabby shrugged again. "Whatever you think. I'm not all that hungry anyway."

"What? Tabitha Johnson not hungry?" Donna raised her eyebrows. "Surely you jest!"

Tucking a thumbnail between her teeth, Tabby mumbled, "I've never been much into 'jesting.'"

Donna reached across the short span of her car to give Tabby's arm a quick jab. "I've seen the little puppet skits you put on for the kids at our day care. I think they're quite humorous, and so do the children."

Tabby felt her jaw tense. "You're just saying that to make me feel better."

"Uh-uh, I really do think your puppet routines are funny."

"That's because I'm well out of sight, and only the silly-looking dog is in the limelight." Tabby grimaced. "If I had to stand up in front of an

31

audience the way Seth Beyers did today, I think I'd curl up and die right on the spot."

"You know, Tabby, ventriloquism might be the very thing to help you overcome your shyness."

"How can you say that, Donna? I'd have to talk in front of people."

"Yes, but you'd be talking through your dummy."

"Dummy? What dummy? I don't even have a dummy?"

"I know, but you could get one."

"In case you haven't heard—those lifelike things are really expensive. Besides, I'm only going to be doing ventriloquism for the kids at day care. Roscoe's good enough for that." She inhaled deeply. "Of course I have to start practicing first, and only time will tell whether I can actually learn to talk for two."

As Seth Beyers drove home from church, a keen sense of disappointment flooded his soul. The realization that he hadn't seen Tabby Johnson after the morning service didn't hit him until now.

During his little performance with Rudy, he'd spotted her sitting in the very back row. After the service he had been swarmed by people full of questions about ventriloquism and asking for all kinds of information about the dummies he created and repaired.

Tabby had obviously slipped out the door while he'd been occupied. He would probably never see her again. For reasons beyond his comprehension, that thought made him sad.

He reflected on something Grandpa had recently told him: *"Everyone needs to feel as if they count for something, Seth. If you recognize that need in dealing with people, you might be able to help someone learn to like themselves a bit more."*

Seth knew his grandfather's advice was good, and as much as he'd like to help Tabby, he also knew all he could really do was pray for the introverted young woman. He promised himself he would remember to do so.

Tabby had been practicing ventriloquism for several weeks. She'd often sit in front of the full-length mirror in her bedroom, completely alone except for Roscoe Puppet. Not even Donna had been allowed to see her struggle through those first few difficult attempts at talking for two. If Tabby were ever going to perform for the day care kids, it wouldn't be until she had complete control of her lip movement and had perfected those horrible sound substitutions. There was *th* for v and f, *d* for b, and *n* for m. It was anything but easy, and it was enough to make her crazy!

Tabby took a seat in front of the mirror, slipped Roscoe onto her hand, and held him next to her face. "What do you think, little buddy? Can we ever learn to do ventriloquism well enough to put on a short skit for the kids?"

Manipulating the puppet's mouth, she made him say, "I think we can. . . I think we can. . . I think I have a bang-up plan. You throw your voice, and let me say all the funny stuff."

Tabby smiled triumphantly. "I did it! I said the sound substitutions without any lip movement!" She jumped to her feet, jerked open the door, and bolted into the living room. Donna was there, working on a chalk drawing taped to her easel. Tabby held Roscoe in front of her face. "I think I'm finally getting the hang of it!"

Donna kept on drawing. "The hang of what?"

Tabby dropped to the couch with a groan. "I'm trying to tell you that I can talk without moving my lips."

Donna finally set her work aside and turned to face Tabby. "That's great. How about a little demonstration?"

Tabby swallowed hard, and a few tears rolled unexpectedly down her cheeks.

Donna was at her side immediately. "What's wrong? I thought you'd be thrilled about your new talent."

"I am, but I wonder if I'll ever have the nerve to actually use it." She swiped at the tears and sniffed. "I really do want to serve God using ventriloquism, but it seems so hard."

"God never promised that serving Him in any way would be easy," Donna said. "And may I remind you of the acts you already do to serve the Lord?"

Tabby sucked in her bottom lip. "Like what?"

"You teach the day care kids about Jesus. You bake cookies for the residents of Rose Park Convalescent Center. You also read your Bible, pray, and—"

Tabby held up one hand. "Okay, okay. . .I get the picture. What I want to know is, are you saying I should be content to serve God in those ways and forget all about ventriloquism?"

Donna shook her head. "No, of course not. You just need to keep on trying and never give up. I believe God wants all Christians to use their talents and serve Him through whatever means they can."

Running a hand through her hair, Tabby nodded. "All right. I'll try."

With fear and trembling, Tabby forced herself to do a short ventriloquist routine the following day for the day care kids. Fifteen little ones sat cross-legged on the carpeted floor, looking up at her expectantly.

Tabby put Roscoe on one hand, and in the other hand she held a small bag of dog food. Drawing in a deep breath, she began. "R–R–Roscoe wants to tell you a little st–st–story today."

Tabby couldn't believe she was stuttering. She never stuttered in front of the kids. *It's only my nerves. They'll settle down in a few minutes.*

Several children clapped, and one little freckle-faced, redheaded boy called out, "Go, Roscoe! Go!"

Tabby gulped. It was now or never.

"Hey, kids—what's up?" the puppet said in a gravelly voice.

So far so good. No lip movement, and Roscoe's lip sync was right on.

"We just had lunch," a young girl shouted.

Tabby chuckled, feeling herself beginning to relax. "That's right," she said to the puppet. "The kids had macaroni and cheese today."

Pointing Roscoe's nose in the air, Tabby made him say, "I think I smell somethin' else."

"They had hot dogs too. That's probably what you smell."

"Hot dogs? They had hot dogs?"

Tabby nodded. "That's right. Now it's time for your lunch."

"Oh, boy! I get a nice, big, juicy hot dog!"

"No, I have your favorite kind of dog food." Tabby held the bag high in the air.

Roscoe's furry head shook from side to side. "No way! I hate dog food! It's for dogs!"

The children laughed, and Donna, standing at the back of the room, gave Tabby an approving nod.

Tabby's enthusiasm began to soar as she plunged ahead. "But, Roscoe, you are a dog. Dogs are supposed to eat dog food, not people food."

"That's easy for you to say," Roscoe croaked. "Have you ever chomped down on a stale piece of dry old dog food?"

"I can't say as I have."

"Dog food makes me sick," Roscoe whined.

"I never knew that."

Roscoe's head bobbed up and down. "It's the truth. In fact, I was so sick the other day, I had to go to the vet."

"Really?"

"Yep! The vet took my temperature and everything."

"What'd he say?" Tabby prompted.

"He said, 'Hot dog!' " The puppet's head tipped back, and he let out a high-pitched howl.

By the time Tabby was done with her routine, Donna was laughing so hard she had tears rolling down her cheeks. As soon as the children went down for their afternoon naps, she took Tabby aside. "That was great. You're really good at talking for two."

"You think so?"

"Yes, I do. Not only have you mastered lip control and sound substitutions, but your routine was hilarious. Where did you come up with all those cute lines?"

Tabby shrugged. "Beats me. I just kind of ad-libbed as I went along."

Donna gave Tabby a quick hug. "Now all you need is a good ventriloquist dummy."

With an exasperated groan, Tabby dropped into one of the kiddy chairs. "Let's not get into that again. I can't afford one of those professional figures, and since I'll only be performing here at the day care, Roscoe will work just fine!"

∞

Seth was nearly finished with the ugly dummy he was making for Alan Capshaw. While it had turned out well enough, it wasn't to his personal liking. A good ventriloquist didn't need an ugly dummy in order to captivate an audience. A professional ventriloquist needed talent, humor, and a purpose. For Seth, that purpose was sharing the Gospel and helping others find a meaningful relationship with Christ.

In deep concentration at his workbench, Seth didn't even hear the overhead bell ring when a customer entered his shop. Not until he smelled the faint lilac scent of a woman's perfume and heard a polite "Ahem" did he finally look up from his work.

A young, attractive woman with short, dark curls stood on the other side of the long wooden counter.

Seth placed the ugly dummy aside and skirted quickly around his workbench. "May I help you?"

"Yes. I was wondering if you have gift certificates for the dummies you sell."

Seth smiled. "Sure. For what value did you want it?"

"Would three hundred dollars buy a fairly nice dummy?"

He nodded. "Prices for ventriloquist figures range anywhere from one hundred dollars for a small, inexpensive model to seven hundred dollars for one with all the extras."

"I'd like a gift certificate for three hundred dollars then."

Seth went to his desk, retrieved the gift certificate book, accepted the young woman's check, and in short order the business was concluded.

"Are you a ventriloquist?" he asked when she put the certificate in her purse and started to turn away.

She hesitated, then pivoted to face him. "No, but a friend of mine is, and she's got a birthday coming up soon."

"You're giving her a professional figure?"

"Sort of. She'll actually be the one forced to come in here and pick it up."

"Forced?" Seth's eyebrows arched upwards. "Why would anyone have to be forced to cash in a gift certificate for a ventriloquist dummy?"

"My friend is extremely shy," the woman explained. "It's hard for her to talk to people."

"Your friend's name wouldn't happen to be Tabby Johnson, would it?"

"How did you know that?"

"I thought I recognized you when you first came in. Now I know from where." Seth extended his right hand. "I'm Seth Beyers. I saw Tabby sitting with you during the Christian workers' program at your church a few weeks ago."

"I'm Donna Hartley, and Tabby and I have been friends since we were kids. She said she spoke with you. Well, actually, I guess it was more to your dummy."

Seth nodded. "I could hardly get her to make eye contact."

"That's not surprising."

"Whenever she talked to me, she stuttered." His forehead wrinkled. "She could talk a blue streak to my little pal, Rudy, and never miss a syllable."

Donna shrugged. "To be perfectly honest, besides me, the day care kids are the only ones she can talk to without stuttering."

"Day care kids?"

"Our church has a day care center, and Tabby and I manage it. It's about the only kind of work Tabby can do. Her self-esteem is really low, and I seriously doubt she'd ever make it around adults all day."

Seth couldn't begin to imagine how Tabby must feel. He usually didn't suffer from low self-esteem—unless you could count the fact that he hadn't found the right woman yet. Occasionally he found himself wondering if he had some kind of personality defect.

"Do you think ventriloquism might help Tabby?" Donna asked, breaking into his thoughts.

He shrugged. "Maybe."

"Tabby did a short routine at the day care the other day. It went really well, and I think it gave her a bit more confidence."

Seth scratched the back of his head. He felt like taking on a new challenge. "Hmm. . . Maybe we could work on this problem together."

Donna's eyebrows furrowed. "What do you mean?"

"You keep encouraging her to perform more, and when she comes in to pick out her new dummy, I'll try to work on her from this end."

Donna's expression revealed her obvious surprise. "You'd do that for a complete stranger?"

" 'Whatever you did for one of the least of these brothers and sisters of mine, you did for me,'" Seth quoted from the book of Matthew.

"I like your Christian attitude," Donna said as she turned to leave. "Thanks for everything." After the door closed behind her, Seth let out a piercing whoop. He would soon be seeing Tabby again. Maybe he could actually help her. Maybe this was the answer to his prayers.

Chapter Five

"I wish you weren't making such a big deal over my birthday," Tabby grumbled as she and Donna drove home from the grocery store one evening after work. This time they were in Tabby's blue hatchback, and she was in the driver's seat.

"It's just gonna be a barbecue in my parents' backyard," Donna argued. "How can that be labeled a big deal?"

Tabby grimaced. "You ordered a fancy cake, bought three flavors of ice cream, and invited half the city of Tacoma!"

"Oh, please! Your folks, Lois, her boyfriend, your grandma, me, and my folks—that's half of Tacoma?" Donna poked Tabby on the arm. "Besides, your folks live in Olympia now."

"I know, but being with my family more than twenty minutes makes me feel like it's half of Tacoma," Tabby argued.

"It isn't every day that my best friend turns twenty-five," Donna persisted. "If I want to throw her a big party, then it's my right to do so."

"I don't mean to sound ungrateful, but you know how things are between me and my family," Tabby reminded.

Donna nodded. "Yes, I do, and I know your parents often hurt you by the unkind things they say and do, but you can't pull away from them and stay in your cocoon of shyness. You don't have to like what they say and do, but you've got to love your family anyway." She sighed. "What I'm trying to say is, you've gotta love 'em, but you can't let them run your life or destroy your confidence, the way you've been doing for so long. It's high time for you to stand up and be counted."

"Yeah, right. Like that could ever happen."

"It could if you gained some self-confidence and quit letting Lois overshadow you."

"Fat chance! Just wait till you see the size of her engagement ring. It

39

looks like Mount Rainier!"

Donna laughed. "How you do exaggerate."

"She's only marrying this guy for his money. Did I tell you that?"

"Only about a hundred times."

"I think it's disgusting." Tabby frowned. "I'd never marry anyone unless I loved him. Of course, he'd have to be a Christian," she quickly added.

"I'm beginning to think neither of us will ever find a husband," Donna said. "You're too shy, and I'm too picky."

"I can't argue with that. Unless I find a man who's either just a big kid or a real dummy, I'd never be able to talk to him."

"Maybe you can find a ventriloquist to marry, then let your dummies do all the talking."

Tabby groaned. "Now there's a brilliant idea. I can see it now—me, walking down the aisle, carrying a dummy instead of a bouquet. My groom would be waiting at the altar, holding his own dummy, of course."

Donna chuckled. "You are so funny today. Too bad the rest of the world can't see the real Tabitha Johnson."

The birthday party was set to begin at six o'clock on Saturday night, in the backyard of Donna's parents, Carl and Irene.

"I still say this is a bad idea," Tabby grumbled, as she stepped into the living room, where Donna waited on the couch.

"Should we do something special with your hair?" Donna asked. "We could pull it away from your face with some pretty pearl combs."

Tabby wrinkled her nose. "I like it plain. Besides, I'm not trying to make an impression on anyone." She flopped down next to Donna. "Even if I were, it would never work. Dad and Mom won't even know I'm alive once Lois shows up with her fiancé."

"I've got a great idea!" Donna exclaimed. "Why don't you bring Roscoe to the barbecue? After we eat, you can entertain us with a cute little routine."

Tabby frowned. "You're kidding, right?"

"No. I think it would be a lot of fun. Besides, what better way to show your family that you really do have some talent?"

"Talent? What talent?"

"There you go again." Donna shook a finger in Tabby's face. "Self-doubting will never get you over being shy."

Tabby stood up. She knew Donna was probably right, but it was time to change the subject. "Do you think this outfit looks okay?" She brushed a hand across her beige-colored slacks.

"Well, now that you asked. . .I was thinking you might look better in that soft peach sundress of mine."

"No thanks. I'm going like I am, and that's final."

The warm spring evening was a bit unusual for May in rainy Tacoma, but Tabby wasn't about to complain. The glorious weather was probably the only part of her birthday that would be pleasant.

The smoky aroma of hot dogs and juicy burgers sizzling on the grill greeted Tabby as she and Donna entered the Hartleys' backyard. Donna's father, wearing a long, white apron with a matching chef's hat, was busy flipping burgers, then covering them with tangy barbecue sauce. He stopped long enough to give both girls a quick peck on the cheek but quickly returned to the job at hand.

His petite wife, who looked like an older version of Donna, was setting the picnic table with floral paper plates and matching cups.

"Is th–there anything I can d–do to help?" Tabby questioned.

Irene waved her hand toward the porch swing. "Nope. I've got it all covered. Go relax, birthday girl."

"That's a good idea," Donna agreed. "You swing, and I'll help Mom."

Tabby didn't have to be asked twice. The Hartleys' old porch swing had been her favorite ever since she was a child. Soon she was rocking back and forth, eyes closed, and thoughts drifting to the past.

She and Donna had spent many hours in the quaint but peaceful swing, playing with their dolls, making up silly songs, and whispering shared secrets. *If only life could have stayed this simple. If only I could always feel as contented as when I'm in this old swing.*

"Hey, big sister. . .Wake up and come to the party!"

Lois's shrill voice jolted Tabby out of her reverie, and she jerked her eyes open with a start. "Oh, I–I d–didn't kn–know you w–w–were here."

"Just got here." Lois gave Tabby an appraising look. "I thought you'd be a little more dressed for tonight's occasion."

Tabby glanced down at her drab slacks and pale yellow blouse, then she lifted her face to study Lois's long, pastel blue skirt, accented by a soft white silk blouse. By comparison, Tabby knew she looked like Little Orphan Annie.

Lois grabbed her hand and catapulted her off the swing. "Mom and Dad aren't here yet, but I want you to meet my fiancé, the successful lawyer, whose parents have big bucks."

Tabby was practically dragged across the lawn and over to the picnic table, where a dark-haired, distinguished-looking young man sat. A pair of stylish metal-framed glasses were perched on his aristocratic nose, and he was wearing a suit, of all things!

"Mike, honey, this is the birthday girl—my big sister, Tabitha." Lois leaned over and dropped a kiss on the end of his nose.

He smiled up at her, then turned to face Tabby. "Hi. Happy birthday."

"Th–th–thanks," she murmured.

Michael gave her an odd look, but Lois grabbed his hand and pulled him off toward the porch swing before he could say anything more.

Donna, who had been pouring lemonade into the paper cups, moved toward Tabby. "Looks like your sister brought you over here just so she could grab the old swing."

Tabby watched her beautiful, self-assured sister swagger across the lawn, laughing and clinging to Michael like she didn't have a care in the world. She shrugged. "Lois can have the silly swing. She can have that rich boyfriend of hers too."

"Oh, oh. Do I detect a hint of jealousy?"

Tabby knew Donna was right, and she was about to say so, but her parents and grandmother had just come through the gate, and she figured it would be rude to ignore them.

"So glad you two could make it." Donna's father shook hands with Tabby's parents, then turned to her grandmother and planted a noisy kiss on her slightly wrinkled cheek. "You're sure lookin' chipper, Dottie."

"Carl Hartley, you still know how to pour on the charm, don't you?"

Grandma Haskins raked a wrinkled hand through her short, silver-gray hair and grinned at him.

Up to this point, no one had even spoken to Tabby. She stood off to one side, head down, eyes focused on her beige sneakers.

Grandma Haskins was the first to notice her. "And here's our guest of honor. Happy twenty-fifth, Tabitha."

Tabby feigned a smile. "Th–thanks, Grandma."

"Yes, happy birthday," Mom added, placing a gift on one end of the table.

Tabby glanced up at her mother. She knew she looked a lot like Mom. They had the same mousy brown hair, dark brown eyes, and were both short of stature. That was where the similarities ended, though. Mom was much more socially secure than Tabby. She was soft-spoken, but unlike Tabby, her words didn't come out in a mumble-jumble of stammering and stuttering.

Tabby's gaze went to her father then. He was still visiting with Donna's dad and never even looked her way. Lois got her good looks from him, that was for sure. His blond hair, though beginning to recede, and those vivid blue eyes were enough to turn any woman's head. *No wonder Mom fell for Dad.*

Donna's mother, Irene, the ever-gracious hostess, instructed the guests to be seated at the picnic table, while she scurried about to serve them all beverages.

Even though Tabby was the only one in her family who professed Christianity, they all sat quietly through Carl's prayer. When he asked God to bless Tabby and give her many good years to serve Him, she heard Lois snicker.

Tabby had a compelling urge to dash back home to her apartment—where she'd be free of Lois's scrutiny and her dad's indifference. She knew it would be rude, and besides, the aroma of barbecued meat and the sight of several eye-catching salads made her feel as if she were starving. The promise of cake, ice cream, and gifts made her appreciate the special party Donna had planned too. It was more than her own family would have done. With the exception of Grandma, she doubted whether any of them even cared that today was her birthday.

"Please don't sing 'Happy Birthday' and make me blow out the dumb candles," Tabby whispered when Donna set a huge cake in front of her a short time later. It was a beautiful cake—a work of art, really—German chocolate, Tabby's favorite, and it was covered with thick cream-cheese frosting. Delicate pink roses bordered the edges, and right in the middle sat a giant-sized heart with the words *"Happy Birthday, Tabby."*

"Don't spoil everyone's fun," Donna said softly.

Tabby bit back a caustic comeback, forcing herself to sit patiently through the strains of "Happy Birthday."

"Okay, it's time to open the presents." Donna moved the cake aside, then placed the gifts directly in front of Tabby. The first one was from Lois. Inside a gold-foil-wrapped gift box was a pale green silk blouse and a makeup kit. It was filled with lipstick, blush, eyeliner, mascara, and a bottle of expensive perfume.

At Tabby's questioning look, Lois said, "I thought it might spark you up a bit. You always wear such drab colors and no makeup at all."

Tabby could have argued, since she did wear a touch of lipstick now and then. "Th–thanks, L–Lois," she mumbled instead.

Grandma Haskins reached over with her small gift bag. "Open mine next."

Tabby read the card first, then removed a small journal from the sack.

"I thought you might enjoy writing down some of your personal thoughts," Grandma explained. "I've kept a diary for many years, and I find it to be quite therapeutic."

Tabby and her maternal grandmother exchanged a look of understanding. Despite the fact that Grandma, who'd been widowed for the last ten years, wasn't a Christian, she was a good woman. Tabby felt that Grandma loved her, in spite of all her insecurities.

"Thank you, Grandma. I th–think it'll be f–fun."

"This one's from your folks," Donna said, pushing the other two gifts aside.

There was no card, just a small tag tied to the handle of the bag. It read: *"To Tabitha, From Mom and Dad."*

Tabby swallowed past the lump lodged in her throat. *They couldn't even write "love." That's because they don't feel any love for me. They only wanted me until Lois came along; then I became nothing but a nuisance.*

"Well, don't just sit there like a dunce. Open it!" her father bellowed.

Tabby ground her teeth together and jerked open the bag. Why did Dad always have to make her feel like such an idiot? As she withdrew a set of white bath towels, edged with black ribbon trim, her heart sank. Towels were always practical, but white? What in the world had Mom been thinking? She was sure it had been her mother's choice because Dad rarely shopped for anything.

"Th–thanks. Th–these will go g–good in our b–b–bathroom," she stuttered.

"I was hoping you'd put them in your hope chest," Mom remarked.

Tabby shook her head. "I d–don't have a h–hope chest."

"It's high time you started one then," Dad roared. "Lois is only nineteen, and she's planning to be married soon."

As if on cue, Lois smiled sweetly and held up her left hand.

"Your engagement ring is beautiful," Donna's mother exclaimed. "Congratulations to both of you."

Michael beamed and leaned over to kiss his bride-to-be.

Tabby blushed, as though she'd been kissed herself. Not that she knew what it felt like to be kissed. The only men's lips to have ever touched her face had been her dad's, when she was young, and Carl Hartley's, whenever he greeted her and Donna.

Donna cleared her throat. *"Ahem!* This is from Mom, Dad, and me." She handed Tabby a large white envelope.

Tabby's forehead wrinkled. Donna always went all out for her birthday. A card? Was that all she was giving her this year?

"Go ahead, open it," Donna coached. She was smiling like a cat who had just cornered a robin. Carl and Irene were looking at her expectantly too.

Tabby shrugged and tore open the envelope. She removed the lovely religious card that was signed, *"With love, Donna, Irene, and Carl."* A small slip of paper fell out of the card and landed on the table, just missing the piece of cake Grandma Haskins had placed in front of Tabby. Tabby picked it up, and her mouth dropped open. "A gift certificate for a ventriloquist dummy?"

"Ventriloquist dummy?" Lois repeated. "What in the world would you need a dummy for?"

Before Tabby could respond, Donna blurted out, "Tabby's recently learned how to talk for two. She's quite good at it, I might add."

If ever there had been a time when Tabby wanted to find a hole to crawl into, it was now. She swallowed hard and said in a high-pitched squeak which sounded much like her puppet, "I—I'm just l—l—learning."

By the time Tabby and Donna returned to their apartment, Tabby's shock over the surprise gift certificate had worn off. It had been replaced with irritation. She knew Donna's heart was in the right place, and Tabby didn't want to make an issue out of it, but what in the world was she going to do?

Tabby placed her birthday gifts on the kitchen table and went out to the living room. Donna was busy closing the mini-blinds, and she smiled when she turned and saw Tabby. "I hope you enjoyed your party."

Tabby forced a smile in response. "It was nice, and I really do appreciate the expensive gift you and your folks gave me."

Donna nodded. "I sense there's a 'but' in there someplace."

Tabby flopped into the rocking chair and began to pump back and forth, hoping the momentum might help her conjure up the courage to say what was on her mind. "It was an expensive birthday present," she said again.

Donna took a seat on the couch, just opposite her. "You're worth every penny of it."

Tabby shrugged. "I don't know about that, but—"

"There's that 'but.'" Donna laughed. "Okay, let me have it. What don't you like about the idea of getting a professional ventriloquist dummy?"

Tabby stopped rocking and leaned forward. "I—uh—"

"Come on, Tabby, just spit it out. Are you mad because my folks and I gave you that certificate?"

"Not mad, exactly. I guess it really would be kind of fun to own a dummy, even if I'm only going to use it at the day care."

"That's exactly what I thought," Donna said with a satisfied smile.

"The gift certificate says it's redeemable at Beyers' Ventriloquist Studio."

"That's the only place in Tacoma where ventriloquist dummies are bought, sold, and repaired."

"I know, but Seth Beyers owns the business, and he—"

"Oh, I get it! You have a thing for this guy, and the thought of being alone with him makes you nervous."

Tabby bolted out of the rocking chair, nearly knocking it over. "I do not have a thing for him! I just can't go in there and talk to him alone, that's all. You know how hard it is for me to speak to anyone but you or the kids. Wasn't that obvious tonight at the party?" She began to pace the length of the living room. "I couldn't even get through a complete sentence without stuttering and making a complete fool of myself. No wonder my family thinks I'm an idiot."

Donna moved quickly to Tabby's side and offered her a hug. "You're a big girl now, Tabby. I can't go everywhere with you or always be there to hold your shaking hand."

Donna's words stung like fire, but Tabby knew they were spoken in love. "What do you suggest I do—call Seth Beyers and see if I can place an order over the phone?"

Donna shook her head. "Of course not. You need to take a look at what he's got in stock. If there isn't anything suitable, he has a catalog you can look through."

"But I'll stutter and stammer all over the place."

Donna stepped directly in front of Tabby. "I suppose you could always take little Roscoe along for added courage," she said with a teasing grin.

Tabby's face brightened. "Say, that's a great idea! I don't know why I didn't think of it myself!"

Chapter Six

Tabby knew there was no point in procrastinating. If she didn't go to Beyers' Ventriloquist Studio right away, she'd have to endure the agony of Donna's persistent nagging. Since today was Friday, and she had an hour off for lunch, it might as well be now.

Tabby slipped Roscoe into the pocket of her raincoat, said goodbye to Donna, and rushed out the door. She stepped carefully to avoid several large puddles, then made a mad dash for her car, because, as usual, it was raining.

"Why couldn't it have done this last night?" she moaned. "Maybe then my birthday party would have been canceled." She slid into the driver's seat, closed the door with a bang, and pulled Roscoe out of her pocket. "Okay, little buddy, it's just you and me. I'm counting on you to get me through this, so please don't let me down."

Seth had been up late the night before, putting the finishing touches on a grandpa dummy someone in Colorado had ordered from his catalog. He'd had trouble getting the moving glass eyes to shift to the right without sticking. Determined to see it through to completion, Seth had gone to bed shortly after midnight. Now he was feeling the effects of lost sleep and wondered if he shouldn't just close up shop for the rest of the day. He didn't have any scheduled customers that afternoon, and since it was raining so hard, it wasn't likely there would be any walk-ins, either.

Seth was heading over to put the CLOSED sign in the window, when the door flew open, nearly knocking him off his feet. Looking like a drenched puppy, Tabby Johnson stood there, holding her purse in one hand and a small, scruffy dog puppet in the other.

"Come in," he said, stepping quickly aside. "Here, let me take your coat."

"My—my c—coat is f—fine. It's w—w—waterproof."

Seth smiled, hoping to make her feel more at ease, but it didn't seem to have any effect on the trembling young woman. "I've been expecting you," he said softly.

"You—h—have?"

"Well, maybe not today, but I knew you'd be coming in sometime soon."

Tabby slipped Roscoe onto her hand and held him in front of her face. "How did you know Tabby would be coming here?" she made the puppet say.

Seth had no idea what she was up to, but he decided to play along. "Tabby's friend was in the other day," he answered, looking right at the puppet. "She bought a gift certificate for a dummy and said it was for Tabby's birthday."

Tabby's hand slipped slightly, and Roscoe's head dropped below her chin.

Now Seth could see her face clearly, and he had to force himself to keep talking to the puppet and not her. "Say, what's your name, little fellow?"

"Woof! Woof! I'm Roscoe Dog!"

She's actually doing ventriloquism, Seth noted. *Doing a pretty good job at it too. Should I compliment her? Maybe give her a few encouraging words about her newfound talent? No, I'd better play along for a while and see if I can gain her confidence.*

Seth moved over to the counter where he usually did business with customers. He stepped behind it and retrieved one of his catalogs from the shelf underneath. "Are you planning to help Tabby pick out a dummy?" he asked, again directing his question to the puppet.

Roscoe's head bounced up and down. "Sure am. Have ya got anything on hand?"

"You don't want to look at the catalog?" This time Seth looked right at Tabby.

She squirmed under his scrutiny, but in a well-spoken ventriloquist voice she made the puppet say, "I'd rather see what you've got first."

Seth frowned. Tabby seemed unable to carry on a conversation without either stuttering or using the puppet, and she still hadn't looked him in the eye when he spoke directly to her. What was this little woman's problem, anyhow?

Tabby tapped the toe of her sneaker against the concrete floor as she waited for Seth's response to her request.

"Okay, I'll go in the back room and see what I can find," he finally mumbled. When Seth disappeared, she took a seat in one of the folding chairs near the front door. She didn't know what had possessed her to use Roscoe Puppet to speak to Seth Beyers. He probably thought she was out of her mind or acting like a little kid. If she'd tried to talk to him on her own, though, she'd have ended up stuttering like a woodpecker tapping on a tree. Tabby knew it was stupid, but using the puppet helped her relax, and she was able to speak clearly with no stammering at all. *Guess this little experience will be something to write about in my new journal,* she thought with a wry smile.

The telephone rang sharply, causing Tabby to jump. She glanced around anxiously, wondering whether Seth would hear it ringing and return to answer it. For a fleeting moment she thought of answering it herself but quickly dismissed the idea, knowing she'd only stutter and wouldn't have the foggiest idea of what to say.

She was rescued from her dilemma when Seth reappeared, carrying a large trunk, which he set on one end of the counter. "Be right with you," he said, reaching for the phone.

Tabby waited impatiently as he finished his business. She was dying to know what was inside that huge chest.

Five minutes later, Seth finally hung up. "Sorry about the interruption. That was a special order, and I had to be sure of all the details."

Tabby moved back to the counter, waiting expectantly as Seth opened the trunk lid. "I didn't know if you wanted a girl, boy, or animal figure, so I brought a few of each," he explained. Tabby's eyes widened as Seth pulled out several dummies and puppets, placing them on the counter for her inspection.

"They all have open-close mouths and eyes that move from side to side. Would you like to try one?"

Roscoe was dropped to the counter as Tabby picked up a small girl dummy dressed in blue overalls and a pink shirt. The figure's moving glass eyes were blue, and her brown hair was braided. Tabby held the figure awkwardly with one hand, unsure of what to say or do with it. The telltale sign of embarrassment crept up the back of her neck, flooding her entire face with familiar heat. "H—how do you w—work it?"

"Here, let me show you." Seth moved quickly around the counter until he was standing right beside Tabby. She could feel his warm breath against her neck, and she shivered when his hand brushed lightly against her arm. She wondered if she might be coming down with a cold.

Seth pulled the slit on the dummy's overalls apart, so Tabby could see inside the hollow, hard plastic body. "See here. . .that's where the wooden control stick is hidden. You turn the rod to the right or left for the figure's head to move." He demonstrated, while Tabby held the dummy.

"When you want to make her talk, you need to pull sharply down on this." He gave the small metal handle a few tugs. "The right lever makes the eyes move from side to side."

When Tabby nodded, Seth stepped away, allowing her access to the inside of the figure's body. "Okay, now you try it."

The control stick felt stiff and foreign beneath Tabby's trembling fingers, and it took a few tries before she got the hang of it. "Hi, my name's Rosie," she made the dummy say in a high-pitched, little-girl voice. "Will you take me home with you?"

Tabby pretended to whisper something into the figure's ear.

"She wants to know how much I cost," Rosie said to Seth.

His sudden frown made Tabby wonder if the girl dummy cost a lot more than the value of her gift certificate.

"This little game has been fun," Seth said kindly, "but if we're gonna do business, I think Tabby should speak for herself."

Seth's words hadn't been spoken harshly, but they still had an impact, causing Tabby to flinch, as though she'd been slapped.

"I'm sorry, but I get in enough dummy talk of my own," he apologized. "I'd really like to speak to you one-on-one."

Tabby lifted her gaze to finally meet his, and their eyes met and held. "I—I h—have a ph—phobia about sp—speaking in p—public or to p—people

I–I'm uncomfortable w–w–with."

Seth grinned, but his eyes remained serious. "I know all about phobias."

"Y–you do?"

"Yep. I studied them in one of my college psychology classes." He pointed at Tabby. "Your phobia is called phonophobia—fear of speaking aloud. I think everyone has at least one phobia, so it's really not such a big deal."

"W–we do? I m–mean, other p–people have ph–phobias too?"

"Oh, sure. In fact, I believe I'm plagued with one of the worst phobias of all."

Tabby shot him a quizzical look. "R–really? W–what's your ph–ph–phobia?"

"It's arachibutyrophobia—peanut butter, sticking to the roof of my mouth."

She giggled, in spite of her self-consciousness. "Y–you're m–making that up."

He shook his head. "No, that's the correct terminology for my phobia."

Tabby eyed him suspiciously.

He raised his hand. "I'm completely serious. I really do freak out every time I try to eat peanut butter. If it gets stuck to the roof of my mouth, which it usually does, I panic."

If Seth was trying to put her at ease, it was working, because Tabby felt more relaxed than she had all day. She tipped her head toward Rosie. "So, h–how much does she cost?" she asked, stuttering over only one word this time.

"Three hundred dollars. Your gift certificate should pretty well cover it."

"W–what about tax?"

He rewarded her with a quick wink. "My treat."

"Oh no, I c–couldn't let you do th–that."

Seth shrugged. "Okay. You treat me to a cup of coffee and a piece of pie, and we'll call it even."

"I—I have to get b–back to w–w–work," she hedged, beginning to feel less relaxed and fully aware that she was stuttering heavily again.

"You can give me your address and phone number, which I'll need for my customer records anyway," Seth said with a grin. "I'll come by your house tonight and pick you up."

Tabby's heartbeat picked up considerably. "P–p–pick me u–up?" Her knees felt like they could buckle at any moment, and she leaned heavily against the counter for support.

Seth's grin widened. "How's seven o'clock sound?"

She was keenly aware of his probing gaze, and it made her feel even more uneasy. All she could do was nod mutely.

"Great! It's a date!"

"How'd it go? Did you get a dummy? Where is it, and how come you don't look overjoyed?"

"You'd better go take your lunch break," Tabby said as she hung her wet raincoat over the back of a chair. "We can talk later."

Donna shook her head. "I ate with the kids, and now they're resting. We have plenty of time to talk."

With a sigh of resignation, Tabby dropped into one of the little chairs.

Donna pulled out the chair next to her and took a seat too. "Don't keep me in suspense a moment longer. Where's the dummy?"

"Right here," Tabby said, pointing to herself. "I'm the biggest dummy of all."

Donna's forehead wrinkled. "I don't get it."

"I'm supposed to take Seth Beyers out for pie and coffee tonight." Tabby's lower lip began to tremble, and her eyes filled with unwanted tears.

"You've got a date with Seth Beyers, and you're crying about it? I sure hope those are tears of joy."

Tabby dropped her head into her hands and began to sob.

"Please don't cry," Donna said softly. "I would think you'd be thrilled to have a date with someone as good-looking and talented as Seth."

Tabby sniffed deeply. "It's not really a date."

"It's not? What is it then?"

"He covered the tax for Rosie, so I owe him pie and coffee."

Donna shook her head. "I have absolutely no idea what you're talking about. Who's Rosie?"

Tabby sat up straight, dashing away the tears with the back of her hand. "Rosie's my new dummy. She's out in the car."

"Okay, I get that much. What I don't get is why you would owe Seth pie and coffee."

"I just told you. He covered the tax. My gift certificate was the right amount for the dummy, but not enough for the tax. Seth said if I treated him to pie and coffee, he'd call it even."

Donna smiled smugly. "Sounds like a date to me."

Seth had spent the better part of his day thinking about the pie and coffee date he'd made with Tabby. He wasn't sure why the thought of seeing the shy young woman again made his heart pound like a jackhammer. His mouth felt as though he'd just come from the dentist's office after a root canal. Maybe his interest in Tabby went deeper than a simple desire to help her climb out of the internal cell that obviously held her prisoner. If Seth were being completely honest, he'd have to admit that he was strangely attracted to Tabby. She might not be a beauty queen, but she was a long way from being ugly. In fact, he thought she was kind of cute. Even so, it wasn't her looks that held him captive. *What is it then?* he wondered.

Seth shrugged into a lightweight jacket and started out the door. "Guess I'll try to figure it all out tonight, over a piece of apple pie and a cup of coffee."

Tabby passed in front of her full-length bedroom mirror and stopped short. For a fleeting moment she thought she saw a smiling, beautiful woman staring back at her. No, that wasn't possible, because she was ugly. *Well, maybe not actually ugly,* she supposed. *Just ordinary. Shy and ordinary.* How could timid, stuttering Tabitha Johnson with mousy-colored brown hair and doe eyes ever look beautiful? Tabby's navy blue cotton dress slacks with matching blue flats weren't anything spectacular. Neither was the red-and-white pin-striped blouse she wore. She'd curled her hair for a change, and it fell in loose waves across her shoulders. It was nothing compared to her sister's soft, golden locks, though. What, then, had caused her to think she looked beautiful?

Tabby studied her reflection more closely. A hint of pink lipstick was all the makeup she wore. However, her cheeks glowed, and her eyes sparkled with. . .what? Excitement? Anticipation? What was she feeling as she prepared for this outing with Seth Beyers?

"Nervous, that's what I'm feeling!" Tabby exclaimed, pushing that elusive lock of hair away from her face. She reached for the doorknob. "Guess there's no turning back now. A promise is a promise," she muttered as she stepped into the living room. She began to pace, wondering if the butterflies, so insistent on attacking her insides, would ever settle down.

"Would you please stop pacing and sit down? You're making me nervous!" Donna patted the sofa cushion beside her. "Have a seat."

Tabby flopped onto the couch with a groan. "I hate waiting."

When the doorbell rang, Tabby jumped up like someone who'd been stung by a wasp. "Do you think I look okay?"

"You're fine. Now go answer that door."

As soon as Tabby opened the front door, her mouth went dry. Seth stood there, wearing a beige jacket, an off-white shirt, and a pair of brown slacks. His auburn hair looked freshly washed, and his green eyes sparkled with the kind of happiness she so often wished for. "Hope I'm not late," he said in a jovial tone.

"I–I th–think you're r–right on time."

"Are you ready to go?"

Tabby hesitated. "I—uh—let me g–get my d–dummy first."

Seth's eyebrows shot up. "I thought this was a pie and coffee thing." Without waiting for an invitation, he pushed past Tabby and sauntered into the living room. His gaze went to Donna, sitting on the couch. "You're Tabby's friend, right?"

She nodded. "Last time I checked."

"Can't you talk some sense into her?"

Donna shrugged and gave him a half-smile. "She's your date."

"Quit talking about me like I'm not even in the room!" Tabby shouted. "I need the dummy so I don't stutter."

Seth and Donna were both grinning at her. "What? What's so funny?" she hollered.

"You're not stuttering now," Seth said, taking a seat in the overstuffed chair nearest the door.

"I–I was angry," Tabby shot back. "I usually d–don't stutter when I'm mad."

Seth chuckled and gave Donna a quick wink. "Guess maybe we should keep her mad at us."

Donna wiggled her eyebrows. "You think that might be the answer?"

Tabby dropped to the couch. "Would you please stop? This is no l–laughing m–matter."

Donna looked at Seth and smiled, then she glanced back at Tabby. "Can't you see yourself sitting at the pastry shop, holding your dummy and talking for two?" She grabbed a throw pillow and held it against her chest, making a feeble attempt at holding back the waves of laughter that were shaking her entire body.

"You never know," Seth said with a chuckle. "We might draw quite a crowd, and Tabby could become famous overnight. I'd probably drum up some ventriloquist business in the process too."

Tabby didn't know whether to laugh or cry. She sat there several seconds, watching her best friend and so-called date howling at her expense. When she'd had all she could take, Tabby jumped up and stormed out of the living room. Jerking open her bedroom door, she stalked across the carpet and flung herself on the bed. "I may never speak to Donna again," she wailed. "Forget about the dumb old tax. Seth Beyers can buy his own pie and coffee!"

Chapter Seven

A stream of tears ran down Tabby's face, trickling toward her ears. She jumped off the bed, fully intending to go back into the living room and give Seth and Donna a piece of her mind, but she stopped short just after she opened the door.

"Tabby has real potential," she heard Donna say. "She's just afraid to use her talents."

"She needs lots of encouragement," Seth responded. "I can see how shy she is, but I didn't think taking the dummy along on our date would help her any. In fact, if someone were to laugh at Tabby, it might make things even worse. I really do want to help her be all she can be, but I'm not sure how to go about it."

"I think you're right," Donna said. "Taking the dummy along would be a bad idea."

Tabby peered around the corner. She could only see the back of Seth's head, but Donna was in plain view. She ducked inside her room. Now probably wasn't a good time to reappear. Not with the two of them talking about her.

Tabby crawled onto her bed again and stared at the ceiling. When she heard a knock at the door, she chose to ignore it. The door opened anyway, but she turned her face to the wall.

"Tabby, I'm sorry." The bed moved under Donna's weight, and Tabby felt a gentle hand touch her trembling shoulder. "Seth and I were wrong to laugh at you. It was all in fun, and we didn't expect you to get so upset."

Tabby released a sob and hiccupped. "Seth must think I'm a real dummy."

"I'm sure he doesn't. He only wants to help you."

Tabby rolled over, jerking into an upright position. "Help me? You mean he thinks I'm some kind of neurotic nut who needs counseling?" She swiped the back of her hand across her face. "Is he still here, or has he split by now?"

"He's still here."

Tabby bit her lip and closed her eyes with the strain of trying to get her emotions under control. "Just tell him the pie and coffee date is off."

Donna hopped off the bed and started for the door. "He's your date, not mine, so you can tell him yourself."

Tabby grabbed one of her pillows and let it sail across the room, just as the door clicked shut.

Seth paced back and forth across the living room—waiting, hoping, praying Tabby would come out of her room. He needed to apologize for his rude behavior. The last thing he wanted was to hurt Tabby's feelings.

"Maybe I should have kept my big mouth shut and let her drag the dumb dummy along on our date. The worst thing that could have happened is we'd be the laughingstock of the pastry shop," he mumbled. "It sure wouldn't be the first time I've been laughed at. Probably not the last, either."

When Tabby's bedroom door opened, Seth snapped to attention. His expectancy turned to disappointment when Donna stepped from the room without Tabby. Seth began to knead the back of his neck. "She's really hoppin' mad, huh?"

Donna nodded. "Afraid so. She wouldn't even listen to me."

"Will she talk to me?"

Donna shrugged and took a seat on the couch. "I doubt it, Seth. She wanted me to tell you that the date is off, but I told her she'd have to tell you yourself."

Seth chewed on his lower lip. "And?"

"She threw a pillow at me, but it hit the door instead."

Seth groaned. "She may be shy, but she's obviously got quite a temper."

Donna shook her head. "Not really. In fact, I've never seen her this angry before. She usually holds in her feelings. She must have it pretty bad."

Seth lowered himself into a chair. "Have what pretty bad?"

Donna opened her mouth to reply, but was stopped short when

Tabby stepped into the room.

Seth could see she'd been crying. Her eyes were red, and her face looked kind of swollen. It made him feel like such a heel. He jumped up from his chair and moved swiftly toward her. "Tabby, I—"

She raised her hand, and he noticed she was holding a checkbook. He fell silent. It was obvious that a simple apology was not going to be enough.

Tabby shifted from one leg to the other, wondering what to say. She was keenly aware of Seth's probing gaze, and it made her feel uneasy. She was sure he already thought she was an idiot, so it shouldn't really matter what she said at this point. After tonight, Seth would probably never want to see her again anyway.

Tabby continued to stand there, shoulders hunched, arms crossed over her chest. She felt totally defeated. "Y–you h–hurt me," she squeaked. "You h–hurt me b–bad."

Seth nodded. "I know, and I'm sorry for laughing at you. It's just that—"

"You d–don't have to—to explain," Tabby said with a wave of her hand. "I know it w–would embarrass you if I t–took my d–dummy, but I can't t–talk right w–without her."

Seth took a few steps toward Tabby, which brought his face mere inches from hers. "Your stuttering doesn't bother me, but if you'd be more comfortable bringing Rosie, then I'm okay with it."

Tabby gulped and drew in a deep breath. She was sure Seth was only trying to humor her. Taking the dummy into the pastry shop would be even dumber than taking her puppet to Seth's place of business earlier that day. She held out her checkbook. "Let's forget about pie and coffee, okay? I'll write you a check to cover the tax due on Rosie."

Combing his fingers through his hair, Seth frowned. "You don't want to go out with me?"

She glanced at him anxiously, then dipped her head, afraid of the rejection she might see on his face. "I d–don't w–want to embarrass y–you."

"Look, if it would make you feel more at ease, we can get our pie and coffee to go. We could take it to the park and eat it in the car."

Tabby shifted uneasily. She really did want to go, but—

Donna, who'd been sitting silently on the couch, spoke up. "Would you just go already? You two are driving me nuts!"

"I th–think she w–wants to get rid of me," Tabby said, giving Seth a sidelong glance.

He wiggled his eyebrows playfully. "Her loss is my gain."

Tabby's heartbeat quickened at his sincere tone. He did seem to be genuinely sorry. "Okay, l–let's go. Without R–Rosie, though. One d–dummy is enough for y–you to h–handle."

"I hope you're not referring to yourself," he said with a puckered brow.

"She is," Donna said, before Tabby had a chance to answer. "She's always putting herself down."

Tabby shot her friend a look of irritation before retrieving her raincoat from the hall closet. "We'll talk about this later."

Donna shrugged. "You two have fun!"

"We will," Seth called over his shoulder.

"I was impressed with your ventriloquism abilities when you were in my shop today," Seth said. He and Tabby were sitting in his black Jeep, at a viewpoint along the five-mile drive in Point Defiance Park.

Tabby took a sip of her mocha latte. "I'm just a beginner, and I know I still have lots to learn."

"But you're a quick learner. I saw no lip movement at all."

She shrugged. "That's what Donna's been telling me. She thinks I should do a ventriloquist routine for our Sunday school opening sometime."

Seth's face broke into a smile. "That's a terrific idea!"

"Oh, I couldn't."

"Why not?"

"I stutter."

Seth chuckled. "Not when you're really mad. . .or doing ventriloquism." He snapped his fingers. "Do you realize that you haven't stuttered once since we pulled into this parking spot? I don't know if it's the awesome sight of the lights on Narrows Bridge that has put you at ease, or if you're just beginning to feel more comfortable around me."

Tabby contemplated that for a few seconds. Seth was right; she hadn't been stuttering. For the first time all evening Tabby didn't feel nervous. In fact, she felt more relaxed than she had all day. Donna and the day care kids were the only people she'd ever felt this comfortable around. Maybe Seth could be her friend. Maybe. . .

Tabby grimaced. Who was she kidding? Seth was confident, good-looking, and talented. He'd never want someone like her as a friend. In his line of work, he met all sorts of people. Probably had lots of close friends. She was sure none of them stuttered or turned cherry red every time someone looked at them. Why did she allow herself to hope or have foolish dreams? Would she spend the rest of her life wishing for the impossible?

"Tabby, did you hear what I said?" Seth's deep voice broke into her thoughts, and she forced herself to look at him.

"Huh?"

He rested his palm on her trembling hand. "You don't have to be nervous around me. I'm just plain old Seth Beyers, fearful of eating sticky peanut butter."

Tabby swallowed hard. Seth's gentle touch made her insides quiver, and she looked away quickly, hoping to hide the blush she knew had come to her cheeks. At this moment, she felt as though *her* mouth was full of gooey peanut butter. How could she not be nervous when he was touching her hand and looking at her with those gorgeous green eyes? She closed her own eyes and found herself wondering how Seth's lips would feel against her own.

"My fear may not affect my relationship with people," Seth continued, "but it's real, nonetheless." He trailed his thumb across her knuckles, marching a brigade of butterflies through her stomach. "I'd like to be your friend, Tabby. I want to help you overcome your shyness. You have potential, and if you'll let Him, I know the Lord can use you in a mighty way."

Tabby blinked away stinging tears. How she wished it were true. She'd give anything to face the world with confidence. It would make her life complete if she could serve God without fear or bashfulness—even if it wasn't in a mighty way, like Seth was doing with his ventriloquist skills.

"Will you allow me to help?" Seth asked.

Tabby felt drawn to his compassionate eyes, and she sensed he could see right through her. *I could drown in that sea of green.*

"Tabby?"

She nodded. "I–I'm not expecting any big m–miracles, but yes, I w–would like your help."

For the next several days Seth's offer of help played itself over and over in Tabby's mind. When he dropped her off at the apartment that night, after pie and coffee, he'd said he would give her a call, but he never explained how he planned to help her. Would he offer to get her speech therapy? If so, that would never work. Her parents had sent her for all kinds of therapy when she was growing up. Nothing helped. There wasn't a thing wrong with Tabby's speech. If there had been, she would have stuttered all the time, not just in the presence of those who made her feel uncomfortable. It was her low self-esteem and shyness that caused her to stutter, and she was sure there wasn't anything that could be done about it.

"You're awfully quiet today," Donna remarked, pulling Tabby out of her musings.

Tabby glanced over at her friend in the passenger seat. They took turns driving to work, and today they'd taken Tabby's car.

Tabby gave the steering wheel a few taps. "I was just thinking."

Donna laughed. "Thinking's okay, as long as you pay attention to where you're going."

"I am."

"Oh, yeah? Then how come you drove right past the church?"

Tabby groaned as she glanced to the left and saw the corner of Elm Street. She cranked the wheel and made a U-turn.

"Oh, great, now you're trying to get yourself a big, fat ticket," Donna complained. "What's with you this morning?"

"Nothing. I'm just preoccupied." Tabby pulled into the church parking lot and turned off the ignition.

"Thinking about Seth Beyers, I'll bet."

Tabby opened her mouth, but before she could get any words out, Donna cut her off. "I think that guy really likes you."

"Seth's just friendly. He likes everyone." Tabby didn't like where this conversation was going, and she'd have to steer it in another direction soon, or they might end up in an argument.

"I know Seth is friendly," Donna persisted, "but I think he's taken a special interest in you. You should have seen how upset he was when you ran into your room the other night."

"How about this weather? Can you believe it hasn't rained in the last half hour? We'd better get inside before it changes its mind and sends us another downpour."

Donna clicked her tongue. "You're trying to avoid the subject, and it won't work. I have something to say, and you're gonna hear me out."

"We'll be late for work."

Donna glanced at her watch. "We're ten minutes early. So, if you'll quit interrupting, we still have plenty of time to talk."

Tabby drew in a deep breath and let it out in a rush. "Okay, get whatever it is off your chest. I really want to get on with my day."

Donna gave her a reproachful look. "What I have to say isn't all that bad."

"All right then, let me have it."

Donna blinked. "My, my, you're sure testy. It's Seth, isn't it?"

Tabby remained silent.

"I really do think the guy likes you."

Tabby wrinkled her nose. "You already said that. I think Seth's the type of person who's kind to everyone. It's obvious that he takes his relationship with Christ seriously."

Donna raised her dark eyebrows. "And you don't?"

Tabby shrugged. "I try to, but I'm not outgoing and self-confident the way he is. I don't think I'm a very good Christian witness."

"You could be, Tabby. You have a wonderful new talent, which you should be using to serve the Lord."

"I–I still don't feel ready to do ventriloquism in front of a crowd."

"Maybe you need to take a few more lessons. I'm sure if you asked, Seth would be more than willing to help you."

Tabby drew in another long breath, and this one came out as a shuddering rasp. "He said he'd help, and I even agreed."

"That's great. I'm glad to hear it."

"I've thought it over thoroughly," Tabby said. "I like Seth too much to expect him to waste his time on someone like me."

Donna shook her head. "Now that's the most ridiculous thing I've ever heard. If you like the guy, then why not jump at any opportunity you have to be with him?"

"Aren't you getting this picture? I don't stand a chance with someone like Seth Beyers. He's totally out of my league."

Donna held up both hands. "I give up! You don't want to see your potential or do anything constructive to better yourself, so there's nothing more I can say." She jerked open the car door and sprinted off toward the church.

Tabby moaned and leaned against the headrest. "Maybe she's right. Maybe I need to pray about this."

Chapter Eight

Seth had been thinking of Tabby for the past few days. In fact, he couldn't get her out of his mind. The other night she'd told him where she worked, and he had decided to stop by the day care for a little visit. One of the fringe benefits of being self-employed was the fact he could pretty much set his own hours and come and go whenever he felt like it. Today he'd decided to take an early lunch and had put a note in his shop window saying he wouldn't be back until one.

Seth pulled his Jeep into the church parking lot, turned off the engine, and got out. He scanned the fenced-in area on one side of the building. There were several children playing on the swings, so he figured that must be part of the Caring Christian Day Care.

He ambled up the sidewalk, and was about to open the gate on the chain-link fence, when he caught sight of Tabby. She was kneeling on the grass, and a group of children sat in a semicircle around her, listening to a Bible story. The soft drone of her voice mesmerized him, as well as the kids, who were watching Tabby with rapt attention. She wasn't stuttering at all, he noticed. It was uncanny, the way she could speak so fluently with these children, yet stutter and hang her head in embarrassment whenever she was with him.

"And so, little ones," Tabby said as she closed the Bible, "Jonah truly learned his lesson that day."

"He never went on a boat again, right, Teacher?" a little red-haired, freckle-faced boy hollered out.

Tabby smiled sweetly, and Seth chuckled behind his hand. She still didn't know he was watching her, and he decided to keep it that way for a few more minutes.

"Jonah's lesson," Tabby explained, "was to obey God in all things. He could have drowned in that stormy sea, but God saved him by bringing the big fish along in time."

"I wonder if the fishy had bad breath," a little, blond-haired girl piped up.

Tabby nodded. "The inside of that fish probably smelled pretty bad, but Jonah was kept safe and warm for three whole days. When the fish finally spit him out on dry land, Jonah was happy to be alive."

"And I'll bet he never went fishing after that," said the freckle-faced boy.

Tabby laughed softly. Her voice sounded like music to Seth's ears. How could anyone so introverted around adults be so at ease with children? *She'll make a good mother some day,* Seth found himself thinking. *She has a sweet, loving spirit, and the kids seem to relate really well to her.*

Seth opened the gate and stepped inside the enclosure just as Tabby stood up. She brushed a few blades of grass from her denim skirt, and the children all stood too.

"It's time to go inside," she instructed. "Miss Donna is probably ready for us to bake those cookies now."

A chorus of cheering voices went up, and the kids, including those who had been swinging, raced off toward the basement door.

Tabby started to follow, but Seth cleared his throat loudly, and she whirled around to face him. "Oh, you—you sc–scared me. I d–didn't know you w–were h–here. How l–long have you–you been st–standing there?"

Seth grinned at her. "Just long enough to hear the end of a great story. The biblical account of Jonah and the big fish is one of my favorites."

"It's m–my favorite too," she murmured.

"You're really good with the kids," he said, nodding in the direction of the disappearing pack of children.

"Th–thanks. I love w–working w–with them."

"It shows."

There was a moment of silence, as Seth stood there staring at Tabby, and she shifted from one foot to the other.

"Wh–what br–brings you here?" she finally asked.

"I came to see you," he said with a wide smile.

Her only response was a soft, "Oh."

"But now that I'm here, I think maybe I should follow the kids into the day care and see what kind of cookies they'll be making." Seth offered her a wink, and she blushed, dropping her gaze to her white sneakers.

"We're m–making chocolate ch–chip," Tabby said. "We'll be t–taking them to R–Rose Park Convalescent C–Center tomorrow m–morning."

He nodded. "Ah, so you're not only a great storyteller, but you're full of good deeds."

Her blush deepened, and she dipped her head even further. "It's n–nothing, really."

"I think you're too modest," Seth replied, taking a few steps toward her. When he was only inches away, he reached out and gently touched her chin. Slowly, he raised it, until her dark eyes were staring right into his. "There, that's better. It's kind of hard to carry on a conversation with someone who's staring at her feet."

Tabby giggled, obviously self-conscious, and it reminded him of one of her day care kids. "Wh–what did you w–want to see m–me about, Se–Se–Seth?"

"I thought maybe we could have lunch and talk about something," he answered, stepping away. "I saw a little deli just down the street, and I'm on my lunch hour, so—"

"Th–that would be nice, but I've got c–cookies to b–bake," she interrupted. "D–Donna and I w–will pr–probably be baking l–long after the k–kids go down for their n–naps."

Seth blew out his breath. "Okay, I guess I can call you later on. Will that be all right?"

She nodded. "Sure, th–that will be f–fine. Do y–you have m–my ph–phone number?"

"It's on the invoice I made out for your dummy purchase the other day."

"Oh." She turned toward the church. "I–I'd better g–get inside now. T–talk to you l–later, Seth."

He waved to her retreating form. "Yeah, later."

"You're wanted on the phone, Tabby!"

Tabby dried her hands on a towel and left the kitchen. When she entered the living room, Donna was holding the receiver, a Cheshire-cat grin on her pixie face.

"Who is it?"

"Seth."

Taking in a deep breath, Tabby accepted the phone, then motioned Donna out of the room.

Donna winked and sauntered into the kitchen.

"H–hello, Seth," Tabby said hesitantly. Her palms were so moist, she hoped she could hold onto the receiver.

"Hi, Tabby. How are you?"

"I'm o–okay."

"I'm sorry we couldn't have lunch today, but I said I'd call later. Is this a good time for you to talk?"

She nodded, then realizing he couldn't see her, she squeaked, "Sure, it's—it's f–fine."

"Good. You see, the reason I wanted to talk to you is, Saturday afternoon I'll be doing an advanced ventriloquism class," Seth said. "I was hoping you'd agree to come."

Tabby twirled the end of the phone cord between her fingers. "I—uh—really c–can't, Seth."

"Can't or won't?"

She flinched, wondering if Seth could read her mind.

"Tabby?"

"I–I wouldn't feel comfortable trying to do v–v–ventriloquism in front of a b–bunch of strangers," she answered truthfully. "You know h–how bad I stutter. They'd probably l–laugh at me."

There was a long pause, then, "How 'bout I give you some private lessons?"

"P–private lessons?"

"Sure. We could meet once a week, either at your apartment or in my shop."

"Well. . ."

"I'd really like to see your talent perfected. Besides, it would be a good excuse to be with you again."

He wants to be with me. Tabby squirmed restlessly. Did Seth really see

68

her in some other light than a mere charity case? Could he possibly see her as a woman? An image of little Ryan O'Conner, the freckle-faced boy from day care, flashed through her mind. He had a crop of red hair, just like Seth. *I wonder if our son would look like that?*

"Tabby, are you still there?" Seth's deep voice drew Tabby back to their conversation.

"Yes, I'm—I'm h–here," she mumbled, wondering what on earth had been going on in her head. She hardly knew Seth Beyers, and fantasizing about a child who looked like him was absolutely absurd!

"Are you thinking about my proposal?" Seth asked, breaking into her thoughts a second time.

"Pro–proposal?" she rasped. Even though she knew Seth wasn't talking about a marriage proposal, her heart skipped a beat. They'd only met a short time ago. Besides, they were exact opposites. Seth would never want someone as dull as her.

"So, what's it gonna be?" he prompted.

She sent up a silent prayer. *What should I do, Lord?* A few seconds later, as if she had no power over her tongue, Tabby murmured, "O–okay."

"Your place or mine?"

Tabby caught a glimpse of Donna lurking in the hallway. "You c–could come here, but we'll p–probably have an audience."

"An audience?"

"Donna—my r–roommate."

Seth laughed. "Oh, yeah. Well, I don't mind, if it doesn't bother you."

Actually, the thought of Donna hanging around while Seth gave her lessons did make Tabby feel uncomfortable. It was probably preferable to being alone with Seth at his shop, though. "When do you w–want to b–begin?" she asked.

"Is tomorrow night too soon?"

She scanned the small calendar next to the phone. Tomorrow was Friday, and like most other Friday nights, she had no plans. "Tomorrow n–night will be f–fine. I d–don't get home till six-thirty or seven, and I'll need t–time to change and eat d–dinner."

"Let's make it seven-thirty then. See you soon, Tabby."

Seth hung up the phone and shook his head. He could just imagine how Tabby must have looked during their phone conversation. Eyes downcast, shoulders drooping, hair hanging in her face.

His heart went out to her whenever she stuttered. He felt a hunger, a need really, to help the self-conscious little woman. He wanted to help her be all she could be. Maybe the advanced ventriloquism lessons would enable her to gain more confidence.

Seth turned away from the phone. *If I work hard enough, Tabby might actually become the woman of my dreams.* He slapped his palm against the side of his head. "Now where did that thought come from? I can't possibly be falling for this shy, introverted woman."

Back when he was a teen, Seth had made a commitment to serve God with his ventriloquist talents. He'd also asked the Lord for a helpmate—someone with whom he could share his life and his talent. Since he'd never found that perfect someone, maybe he could make it happen.

He sighed deeply. The way Tabby was now, he knew she'd only be a hindrance to his plans. He could just imagine what it would be like being married to someone who couldn't even talk to a stranger without stuttering or hiding behind a dummy. Unless he could draw her out of that cocoon, there was no possibility of them ever having a future together.

"What am I saying?" Seth lamented. "I hardly even know the woman, and I'm thinking about a future with her!" He shook his head. "Get a grip, Seth Beyers. She's just a friend—someone to help, that's all. You'd better watch yourself, because you're beginning to act like one of your dummies."

"I don't know what you're so nervous about. You've already mastered the basic techniques of ventriloquism, so the rest should be a piece of cake," Donna said with a reassuring smile.

Tabby nodded mutely as she flopped onto the couch beside Donna. The truth was, she was a lot more nervous about seeing Seth than she was about perfecting her ventriloquism skills. She liked him—a lot. That's what frightened her the most. She'd never felt this way about a guy before. She knew her childish fantasies about her and Seth, and children who looked like him, were totally absurd, but she just couldn't seem to help herself.

"Tabby, the door!"

Donna's voice broke through Tabby's thoughts, and she jumped. She hadn't even heard the doorbell. "Oh, he's here? Let him in, okay?"

Donna grinned. "Since he's come to tutor you, don't you think *you* should answer the door?"

Tabby felt a sense of rising panic. "You're not staying, I hope."

"If you're gonna do ventriloquism, then you'll need an audience," Donna said.

The doorbell rang again, and Tabby stood up. When she opened the front door, she found Seth standing on the porch, little Rudy cradled in the crook of one arm and a three-ring binder in his hand. "Ready for a lesson?"

She nodded, then motioned toward the living room. "We h–have our audience, j–just as I expected."

"That's okay. It's good for you to have an audience," Seth answered. "It'll give you a feel for when you're on stage."

Tabby's mouth dropped open. "On st–st–stage?"

Seth laughed. "Don't look so worried. I'm not suggesting you perform for a large crowd in the next day or two. Someday you might, though, and—"

"No, I won't!" Tabby shouted. "I'm only d–doing this so I can per–perform better for the kids at the d–day care."

Seth shrugged. "Whatever." He followed her into the living room. "Where's your dummy?"

"In my room. I'll go get her." Tabby made a hasty exit, leaving Seth and Donna alone.

"She's a nervous wreck," Donna remarked as Seth placed the notebook on the coffee table, then took a seat on the couch.

"Because you're here?"

She shook her head. "I think you make her nervous."

"Me? Why would I make Tabby nervous?"

"Well, I'm pretty sure. . ."

"I–I'm ready," Tabby announced as she entered the room carrying Rosie.

Seth stood up. "Great! Let's get started."

"Sh–should I sit or st–stand?"

"However you're the most comfortable." Seth nodded toward the couch. "Why not sit awhile, until you're ready to put on a little performance for us?"

"I–I may never be r–ready for that."

"Sure you will," Seth said with assurance. He wanted her to have enough confidence to be able to stand up in front of an audience, but from the way she was acting tonight, he wondered if that would ever happen.

"Tabby, show Seth how you can make Rosie's head turn backwards," Donna suggested.

Tabby dropped to the couch and held her dummy on one knee. She inserted her hand in the opening at the back of the hard plastic body and grabbed the control stick. With a quick turn of the stick, Rosie was looking backwards. "Hey, where'd everybody go!" the childlike voice squealed.

Not one stuttering word, Seth noted, as he propped one foot on the footstool by Donna's chair. *Talking for two seems to be the best way Tabby can converse without stammering.* "We're right here, Rosie. Come join the party." This came from Rudy Right, who was balanced on Seth's knee.

"Party?" Rosie shot back. "We're havin' a party?"

"Sure, and only dummies are invited." Rudy gave Tabby a quick wink.

She giggled, then made Rosie say, "Guess that means we'll have to leave, 'cause the only dummies I see are pullin' someone else's strings."

Seth chuckled. "I think we've been had, Tabby." He scooted closer to her. "Would you like to learn a little something about the near and far voice?"

"Near and far? What's that?" The question came from Donna.

"The near voice is what you use when your dummy is talking directly to you or someone else. Like Tabby and I just did with our two figures," Seth explained. "The far voice would be when you want your audience to believe they're hearing the dummy talking from someplace other than directly in front of them." He pointed to the telephone on the table by the couch. "Let's say you just received a phone call from your dummy, and you want the audience to hear the conversation." Seth reached over and grabbed the receiver off the hook.

"Hi, Seth, can I come over?" A far-sounding, high-pitched voice seemed to be coming from the phone.

"Sure, why don't you?" Seth said into the receiver. "We're having a party over at Tabby and Donna's tonight, so you're more than welcome to join us."

"That's great! I love parties!" the far voice said. "Be right there!"

Seth hung up the phone and turned to face Tabby. "Do you have any idea how I did that?"

"You used the power of suggestion," Donna said, before Tabby had a chance to open her mouth. "We saw a phone and heard a voice, so it makes sense that we thought the sound was coming from the receiver."

Seth looked at Tabby. "What do you think?"

"I–I'm not sure, but I think m–maybe you did something different in your th–throat."

Seth grinned. "You catch on fast. I tightened my vocal chords so my voice sounded a bit pinched or strained. There's an exercise you can do to help make this sound."

"Oh, great! I love to exercise," Donna said, slapping her hands together.

Seth could tell from Tabby's expression that she was more than a bit irritated with Donna's constant interrupting. He wished there was some way to politely ask her well-meaning friend to leave.

"Actually, Donna, it's not the kind of exercise you're thinking of. It's only for ventriloquists, so. . ."

Donna held up both hands. "Okay, I get the picture. You want me to keep my big mouth shut, right?"

"You are kind of a nuisance," Tabby replied.

Wow, she can get assertive when she wants to. Seth wondered what other traits lay hidden behind Tabby's mask of shyness.

"I'll keep quiet," Donna promised.

Tabby raised her eyebrows at Seth, and he grinned in response. "Now, let's see. . . . Where were we?"

"An exercise." Donna ducked her head. "Sorry."

"The first thing you do is lean over as far as you can," Seth said as he demonstrated. "Try to take in as much air as possible, while making the *uh* sound."

Tabby did what he asked, and he noticed her face was turning red. How much was from embarrassment and how much from the exercise, he couldn't be sure, but he hoped it wouldn't deter her from trying.

"Now sit up again and try the same amount of pressure in your stomach as you make the *uh* sound." He placed one hand against his own stomach. "You'll need to push hard with these muscles as you speak for your far-sounding voice. Oh, and one more thing. It's best to keep your tongue far back in your mouth, like when you gargle. Doing all that, try talking in a high, whisper-like voice."

"Wow, that's a lot to think about all at once!" The comment came from Donna again, and Seth wondered if Tabby might be about to bolt from the room.

"There is a lot to think about," he agreed, "but with practice, it gets easier." He leaned close to Tabby and whispered, "Ready to try it now?"

She sucked in her bottom lip and nodded. "Hi, I'm glad you're home. I was afraid nobody would answer the phone."

Seth grabbed her free hand and gave it a squeeze. "That was awesome, Tabby! You catch on quick. A natural born ventriloquist, that's what you are."

A stain of red crept to her cheeks, but she looked pleased. "Th–thanks."

Seth pulled his hand away and reached for the notebook he'd placed on the coffee table. "I have some handout sheets to give you. Things for you to practice during this next week and a few short distant-voice routines to work on."

Tabby only nodded, but Donna jumped up and bounded across the room. "Can I see? This has all been so interesting! I'm wondering if maybe

I should put away my art supplies and come back to your shop to look at dummies." She grinned at Tabby. "What do you say? Should I take up ventriloquism so we can do some joint routines?"

Chapter Nine

By the time Tabby closed the door behind Seth, she felt emotionally drained and physically exhausted. Tonight's fiasco would definitely be recorded in that journal Grandma had given her. Donna had done nothing but interrupt, offer dumb opinions, and flirt with Seth. At least that's how Tabby saw it. Her best friend was obviously interested in the good-looking ventriloquist. What other reason could she have for making such a nuisance of herself?

Well, she's not going to get away with it, Tabby fumed. She headed for the living room, resolved to make things right. *Friend or no friend, I'm telling Donna exactly what I think.*

Donna was sitting on the couch, fiddling with the collar on Rosie's shirt. "You know what, Tabby? I think your dummy might look cuter in a frilly dress. You could curl her hair and—"

"Rosie looks just fine the way she is!" Tabby jerked the ventriloquist figure out of Donna's hands and plunked it in the rocking chair. "I'd appreciate it if you'd mind your own business too."

Donna blinked. "What's your problem? I wasn't hurting Rosie. I was only trying to help."

Tabby moved toward the window, though she didn't know why. It was dark outside, and there was nothing to look at but the inky black sky. "I've had about enough of your opinions to last all year," she fumed.

Donna joined Tabby at the window. "I thought your lesson went really well. What's got you so uptight?"

Tabby turned to face her. "I'm not uptight. I'm irritated."

"With me?"

Tabby nodded. "You like him, don't you?"

"Who?"

"Seth. I'm talking about Seth Beyers!"

76

Donna tipped her head. "Huh?"

"Don't play dumb. You know perfectly well who I mean, and why I think you like him."

"I think Seth's a nice guy, but—"

"Are you interested in him romantically?"

"Romantically?" Donna frowned. "You've gotta be kidding."

Tabby sniffed deeply. "No, I'm not. You hung around him all night and kept asking all sorts of dumb questions."

Donna's forehead wrinkled. "You're really serious, aren't you?"

"I sure am."

"I think we'd better have a little talk about this. Let's sit down." Donna motioned toward the couch.

Tabby didn't budge. "There's nothing to talk about."

"I think there is."

"Whatever," Tabby mumbled with a shrug.

Donna sat on the couch, but Tabby opted for the rocking chair, lifting Rosie up, then placing the dummy in her lap after she was seated.

"I'm not trying to steal your guy," Donna insisted. "He's not my type, and even if he were, you should know that I'd never sabotage my best friend."

The rocking chair creaked as Tabby shifted, then she began to pump her legs back and forth. "Seth is not my guy."

A smile played at the corner of Donna's lips. "Maybe not now, but I think he'd like to be."

Tabby folded her arms across her chest and scowled. "Fat chance."

"There might be, if you'd meet him halfway."

"Like you did tonight—with twenty questions and goofy remarks?"

"I was only trying to help."

"How?"

"Before Seth arrived, you said you were nervous."

"And?"

"I was trying to put you at ease."

"By butting in every few minutes?" Tabby gulped and tried to regain her composure. "How was that supposed to put me at ease?"

Before Donna could say anything, Tabby stood up. "All you succeeded in doing tonight was making me more nervous."

"Sorry."

Donna's soft-spoken apology was Tabby's undoing. She raced to the couch, leaned over, and wrapped her friend in a bear hug. "I'm sorry too. I–I'm just not myself these days. I think maybe I. . ." Her voice trailed off, and she blinked away tears threatening to spill over. "Let's forget about tonight, okay?"

Donna nodded. "Just don't let it ruin anything between you and Seth."

Tabby groaned. "There's nothing to ruin. As I said before, there isn't anything going on. Seth and I are just friends—at least I think we are. Maybe our relationship is strictly business."

Donna shrugged. "Whatever you say."

"I think I'll take my next ventriloquist lesson at Seth's shop," Tabby said as she started toward her room. "Tonight made me fully aware that I'm not even ready for an audience of one yet."

Seth wasn't the least bit surprised when Tabby called the following week and asked to have her next lesson at his place of business. Her friend Donna had turned out to be more than a helpful audience, and he was sure that was the reason for the change of plans. The way he saw it, Donna had actually been a deterrent, and it had been obvious that her constant interruptions made Tabby uptight and less able to grasp what he was trying to teach her. Even though they might be interrupted by a phone call or two, Beyers' Ventriloquist Studio was probably the best place to have Tabby's private lessons.

A glance at the clock told Seth it was almost seven. That was when Tabby had agreed to come over. His shop was closed for the day, so they should have all the privacy they needed.

"She'll be here any minute," he mumbled. "I'd better get this place cleaned up a bit."

Not that it was all that dirty, but at least it would give him something to do while he waited. If things went really well, he planned to ask her on a date, and truthfully, he was more than a little anxious about it. What if she turned him down? Could his male ego take the rejection, especially when he'd planned everything out so carefully?

Seth grabbed a broom out of the storage closet and started sweeping up a pile of sawdust left over from a repair job he'd recently done on an all-wooden dummy brought in a few weeks ago.

As he worked, he glanced over at Rudy Right, sitting in a folding chair nearby. "Well, little buddy, your girlfriend, Rosie, ought to be here any minute. I sure hope you're not as nervous as I am."

The woodenheaded dummy sat motionless, glass eyes staring straight ahead.

"So you're not talking today, huh?" Seth said with a shake of his head. "I'll bet you won't be able to keep your slot jaw shut once Tabby and her vent pal arrive."

Talking to Rudy like this was nothing new for Seth. He found that he rather enjoyed the one-way conversation. It was good therapy to talk things out with yourself, even if you were looking at a dummy when you spoke. He was glad there was no one around to witness the scene, though. If there had been, he might be accused of being a bit eccentric.

Seth chuckled. "Maybe I am kind of an oddball, but at least I'm having fun at my profession."

The bell above his shop door jingled, disrupting his one-way conversation. He grinned when Tabby stepped into the room, carrying Rosie in her arms. "Hi, Tabby."

"I–I hope I'm not l–late," she said. "Traffic was r–really bad."

Seth glanced at the clock again. "Nope, you're right on time."

"Are—are you r–ready for my l–lesson? You l–look kind of b–busy."

"Oh, you mean this?" Seth lifted the broom. "I was just killing time till you got here. My shop gets pretty dirty after I've been working on a dummy."

She nodded. "I g–guess it w–would."

Seth put the broom back in the closet and turned to face Tabby. "Are you ready for lesson number two?"

"I–I th–think so."

"Let's get started then." He motioned toward one of the folding chairs. "Have a seat and I'll get my notes."

∞

Tabby watched as Seth went to his desk and shuffled through a stack of papers. *Why is he taking time out of his busy schedule to work with me?* she asked herself. *I'm sure he has much better things to do than give some introverted, stuttering woman private ventriloquist lessons.*

"Okay, all set." Seth dropped into a chair and graced her with a pleasant smile. "Did you get a chance to practice your near and far voices?"

"I p–practiced a little."

"How about a demonstration then?"

"N–n–now?"

"Sure, now's as good a time as any." Seth pointed at Rosie. "If it would be any easier, you can talk through her instead of a pretend object or the telephone."

"How c–can I do th–that?" Tabby asked. "If I t–talk for R–Rosie, won't that be m–my near v–voice?"

Seth scratched his head. "Good point. I'll tell you what—why don't you set Rosie on a chair across the room, then talk for her. Make it sound as though her voice is coming from over there, and not where you're sitting."

Tabby bit down on her bottom lip and squeezed her eyes tightly shut. She wasn't sure she could do what Seth was asking, and she certainly didn't want to make a fool of herself. She'd already done that a few times in Seth's presence.

"You can do this," Seth urged. "Just give it a try."

Tabby opened her eyes and blew out the breath she'd been holding. "All r–right." She stood up and carried Rosie and a chair across the room, then placed the dummy down and returned to her own seat. "Hey, how come you put me way over here?" she made Rosie say in a childlike voice.

"You're in time-out."

"That's not fair, I'm just a dummy. Dummies should never be in time-out."

"Oh, and why's that?"

"Dummies are too dumb to know how to behave."

Tabby opened her mouth, but Seth's round of applause stopped her. She turned to look at him and was surprised when he gave her "thumbs-up."

"D–did I do o–okay?"

He grinned from ear to ear. "It was more than 'okay.' It was fantastic, and you never stuttered once. I'm proud of you, Tabby."

Tabby could feel the warmth of a blush as it started at her neckline and crept upward. She wasn't used to such compliments and was unsure how to respond.

"In all the years I've been teaching ventriloquism, I don't think I have ever met anyone who caught on as quickly as you," Seth said sincerely. "You mastered the basics like they were nothing, and now this—it's totally awesome!"

"You really th–think so?"

"I know so. Why, you—"

Seth's words were cut off when the shop door opened, jingling the bell. In walked Cheryl Stone, the attractive redhead who had demonstrated her talents at Seth's beginning ventriloquism workshop, where Tabby first met him.

Cheryl gave Seth a smile so bright Tabby was sure the sun must still be shining. "Hi, Seth, I was in the neighborhood and saw your lights on. I was wondering if you've finished that new granny figure for me yet?"

Seth gave Tabby an apologetic look. "Sorry about the interruption," he whispered. "I wasn't expecting anyone else tonight, and I forgot to put the closed sign in my window."

"It's o–okay," Tabby murmured. "I'll j–just w–wait over th–there with R–Rosie w–while you take c–care of b–business." She was stuttering heavily again, and it made her uncomfortable.

Seth nodded. "This will only take a minute."

Tabby moved quickly toward Rosie, hoping Cheryl wouldn't stay long. She watched painfully as the vibrant young woman chatted non-stop and batted her eyelashes at Seth. *She likes him, I can tell. I wonder if they've been seeing each other socially.*

Tabby shook her head. It was none of her business who Seth chose to see. Besides, if she were being totally honest, she'd have to admit that Seth and Cheryl did make a striking pair. They were both redheads, had bubbling personalities, and could do ventriloquism. What more could Seth ask for in a woman?

Chapter Ten

It was nearly half an hour later when Cheryl finally walked out the door. Seth gave Tabby an apologetic look. "Sorry about that. Guess she's a little anxious to get her new dummy." He offered Tabby one of the most beautiful smiles she'd ever seen. "Before we continue with your lesson, I'd like to ask you a question."

Her heart quickened. Why was he staring at her that way? She swallowed against the tightening in her throat. "What question?" she squeaked.

Seth dropped into the seat beside her. "I have to go to Seattle tomorrow, to pick up an old dummy at the Dummy Depot. I was wondering if you'd like to go along."

Tabby's mouth went dry. He was asking her to go to Seattle. Was this a date? No, it couldn't be. Seth wouldn't want to go out with someone as plain as her. Why didn't he ask someone like cute Cheryl Stone? From the way the redhead kept flirting with him, Tabby was sure she would have jumped at the chance.

"Tabby?" Seth's deep voice cut into her thoughts.

"H–huh?"

"Are you busy tomorrow? Would you like to go to Seattle?"

She blinked. "Really? You w–want m–me to go along?"

He nodded. "I thought after I finish my business at the Dummy Depot we could go down by the waterfront. Maybe eat lunch at Ivar's Fish Bar and check out some of the gift shops along the wharf. I think it would be fun, don't you?"

Tabby gazed at the floor as she mulled this idea over. Tomorrow was Saturday. She wouldn't be working, and she had no other plans. She hadn't been to the Seattle waterfront in ages. Despite the amount of people usually there, it wasn't closed in the way so many of the buildings in Seattle Center were. The waterfront was open and smelled salty like the sea. Besides, it was an opportunity to spend an entire day with Seth.

"Tabby?"

She looked up. "Y–yes. I'd l–like to go."

Tabby didn't sleep well that night. Excitement over spending a whole day with Seth occupied her thoughts and kept her tossing and turning. She was sure Seth wouldn't appreciate her taking Rosie to talk through, but she was concerned about her stuttering. Seth had told her several times that her speech impediment didn't bother him. It bothered her, though—a lot. She'd have given nearly anything to be confident and capable like normal people.

"If only God hadn't made me so different," she wrote in her journal before turning off the light by her bed.

Tabby let her head fall back as she leaned into the pillow. *Maybe it wasn't God who made me different. It's all Lois's fault. If she just wasn't so beautiful and confident—everything Mom and Dad want in a daughter—everything I'm not.* She squeezed her eyes tightly shut. *Guess I can't really blame Lois, either. She can't help being beautiful and confident. It would take a miracle to make Mom and Dad love me the way they do her. They think I'm a failure.*

The thrill of her upcoming date with Seth was overshadowed by pain. She needed to work on her attitude. It wasn't a good Christian example, not even to herself. She released a shuddering sigh, whispered a short prayer asking God to help her accept things as they were, then drifted off to sleep.

When Tabby entered the kitchen the following morning, she found Donna sitting at the table, sketching a black-and-white picture of a bowl of fruit.

"All ready for your big date?"

Tabby shrugged. "It's not a real date."

"What would you call it?"

"I'd call it a day in Seattle to—" She giggled. "Maybe it is kind of a date."

Donna laughed too. "You came home last night all excited about going, and it sure sounded like a date to me. I'm kind of surprised, though."

"About what?"

"I didn't think you liked Seattle."

Tabby dropped into a chair. "I don't like the Seattle Center, or shopping downtown, but we're going to the waterfront. I love it there, even with all the people."

Donna grinned. "I think you'd go to the moon and back if Seth Beyers was going."

"Don't even go there," Tabby warned. "I've told you before, Seth and I are just friends."

Donna shrugged. "Whatever you say."

Tabby glanced at the clock above the refrigerator. "Seth will be here in an hour, and I still need to eat breakfast, shower, and find something to wear." She reached for a banana from the fruit bowl in the center of the table.

"Hey! You're destroying my picture! Why don't you fix a fried egg or something?"

Tabby pulled the peel off the banana and took a bite. "Eggs have too much artery-clogging cholesterol. Fruit's better for you." She glanced at Donna's drawing. "Besides, you've already got some bananas sketched, so you shouldn't miss this one."

Donna puckered her lips. "You never worry about cholesterol when you're chomping down a burger or some greasy fries."

Tabby gave her a silly grin. "Guess you've got me there."

"How'd the lesson go yesterday? You never really said," Donna asked.

Tabby was tempted to tell her about Cheryl's interruption and how much it had bothered her to see the two redheads talking and laughing together. She knew it would only lead to further accusations about her being interested in Seth.

She flicked an imaginary piece of lint from the sleeve of her robe and replied, "It went fine."

"Great. I'm glad."

Tabby felt a stab of guilt pierce her heart. She was lying to her best friend. Well, not lying exactly, just not telling the whole story. "Seth got an unexpected customer, and we were interrupted before we really got much done."

"But you continued on with the lesson after they left, didn't you?"

Tabby grabbed an orange from the fruit bowl and began to strip away the peel. "The customer was a redheaded woman named Cheryl. I think Seth likes her."

"But it's you he invited to Seattle," Donna reminded.

"He probably feels sorry for me."

Donna dropped her pencil to the table. "Is there any hope for you at all?"

Tabby sighed. "I wish I knew. Sometimes I think there might be, and other times I'm so full of self-doubts."

"What makes you think Seth likes this redhead, anyway?" Donna asked.

"She's cute, talented, and outgoing. What guy wouldn't like that?" Tabby wrinkled her nose. "They looked like a pair of matching bookends."

Donna snickered. "Well, there you have it! If Seth can look at this redheaded gal and see himself, then he's bound to fall head over heels in love with her."

Tabby pushed away from the table. "Seth and Cheryl make a perfect couple, and I'm just a millstone around Seth's neck."

"If he saw you as a millstone, he sure wouldn't be asking you out. Normal people don't go around asking millstones to accompany them to Seattle for the day."

Tabby stared off into space. "Maybe you're right."

Seth arrived on time. Not wishing to give Donna the chance to say anything to him, Tabby raced out the front door and climbed into his Jeep before he even had a chance to get out.

"I was planning to come in and get you," Seth said as she slid into the passenger seat.

She smiled shyly. "That's okay. I was r–ready, so I f–figured I may as w–well s–save you the b–bother."

Seth smiled. "You look nice and comfortable."

Tabby glanced down at her faded blue jeans and peach-colored sweat-shirt, wondering if she was dressed too casually. Maybe she should have chosen something else. She considered Seth for a moment. He was wearing a pair of perfectly pressed khaki-colored pants and a black polo shirt. His hair was combed neatly in place, parted on the left side. He looked way too good to be seen with someone as dowdy as her.

"So, w—where exactly is th—this Dummy Depot, and w—what kind of d—dummy are you b—buying there?" she asked, hoping to drag her thoughts away from how great Seth looked today.

Seth pulled away from the curb. "The Dummy Depot sells mostly used dummies. Harry Marks, the guy who runs the place, recently got one in that needs some repairs. He asked if I'd come get it, since his car isn't running and he didn't want to catch a bus to Tacoma. I thought it might be kind of nice to mix a little pleasure with business," Seth said, giving Tabby another one of his heart-melting smiles.

Tabby nodded. "Makes sense to me." She leaned her head against the headrest and released a contented sigh. Maybe he really did want to be with her. Maybe there was a chance that. . .

"Have you known Donna long?" Seth asked, breaking into her thoughts.

"Huh?"

"How long have you and Donna been friends?"

"Ever since we w—were kids. Her folks m—moved next-door to us when we were b—both two."

"Tell me a little about your family," he pried.

"There's nothing m—much to tell."

"There has to be something." Seth tapped the steering wheel with his long fingers. "Do your folks live nearby? Do you have any brothers and sisters?"

Tabby swallowed hard. The last thing she wanted to do was talk about her family. This was supposed to be a fun day, wasn't it? "My—uh—p–parents live in Olympia, and I h—have one s—sister. She l—lives in a high-rise apartment in d—downtown Tacoma, and sh—she's a secretary. There's n—nothing m—more to tell."

"You're lucky to have a sister," Seth commented. "I grew up as an only child. My folks were killed in a car wreck when I was fourteen, and my grandparents took me in."

"I'm so s—sorry," she murmured.

"Grandma and Grandpa Beyers were good to me, though. They taught me about Christ and helped me learn to use my talents for Him." Seth smiled. "I'll never forget the day Grandpa informed me that when he and Grandma were gone, the house would be mine."

Tabby knew the house he was referring to was the one he lived in now. The basement had been converted into his ventriloquist shop. Seth had told her that much when she'd had her lesson the evening before. What he hadn't told her was that the house had been his grandparents', or that they'd passed away.

"I'm s–sorry your g–grandparents aren't l–living anymore. It must be h–hard not to h–have any family," she said with feeling. As much as she disliked many of the things her own family said or did, she couldn't imagine what it must have been like growing up as an only child or not having her parents around at all, even if they did make her feel like dirt most of the time.

Seth chuckled. "Grandma and Grandpa aren't dead yet."

"They're n–not?"

"No, they moved into a retirement home a few years ago. Said the old house was too much for them to handle." Seth cast her a sidelong glance. "Grandpa thought the place would be well suited to my business, not to mention a great place to raise a bunch of kids someday."

Tabby wasn't sure how to respond to that statement. She'd always dreamed of having a big family herself, but the possibility didn't seem very likely.

"There sure is a l–lot of traffic on the f–freeway today, isn't there?" she said, changing the subject again.

Seth nodded. "Always is a steady flow of cars on I–5, but the weekends are even worse. Things will level off a bit once we get away from the city."

Tabby turned to look out the passenger window. They had just entered the freeway and were traveling over a new overpass. As busy as the freeway was here, she knew it would be even worse once they got closer to Seattle. It made her thankful Seth was driving. She'd be a ball of nerves if she were in the driver's seat.

"Mind if I put a cassette in the tape player?" Seth asked.

"Go a–ahead."

When the soft strains of a familiar Christian song came on, Tabby smiled. Seth liked the same kind of music she did. She closed her eyes and felt her body begin to relax. She wasn't sure if it was because of Seth's rich baritone accompanying the tape, or simply the fact that she was with him today. Tabby was glad she'd accepted Seth's invitation to go to Seattle.

Seth glanced over at Tabby. Her eyes were shut, and she was sitting silent and still. He wished he could read her mind. Find out what thoughts were circling around in her head. *She reminds me of a broken toy. She didn't have much to say about her family. I wonder if something from her past is the reason for her terrible shyness. If she's hurting, then maybe her heart can be mended. There's even a chance she could actually be better than new.*

The only trouble was, Seth wasn't sure how to find out what kind of pain from the past held Tabby in its grip. She was a mystery he wanted to solve. Since Tabby seemed so reserved and unable to communicate her feelings to him, maybe he should talk to Donna about it. Tabby said they'd been friends most of their lives. Surely Donna would know what made Tabitha Johnson tick. A little bit of insight might help him know what direction to take in making her over into his perfect woman.

Seth hugged the knowledge to himself and smiled. *As soon as I get the chance, I'll get together with Donna and find out what gives.*

Chapter Eleven

The Dummy Depot was located in downtown Seattle, in a small shop near the busy shopping area. While Seth talked business with the owner, Tabby walked around the room studying all the figures for sale. It didn't take long to realize she could have bought a used dummy for half the price she'd paid for Rosie. She consoled herself with the fact that most of the figures looked well-used and had lost their sparkle. Rosie, on the other hand, was brand new, without a scratch, dent, or paint chip on her entire little body. Besides, she'd purchased the dummy with the birthday gift certificate from Donna and her parents. They'd wanted her to have a new one or else they wouldn't have given it to her.

"Ready to go?" Seth asked suddenly.

"Sure, if y–you are."

Holding the damaged dummy under one arm, Seth opened the shop door with his free hand. "I don't know about you, but I'm getting hungry. I think I can actually smell those fish-and-chips wafting up from the waterfront."

Tabby's mouth watered at the mention of eating succulent cod, deep-fried to perfection, and golden brown fries, dipped in tangy fry sauce. "Guess I'm kinda h–hungry too," she admitted.

Ten minutes later they were parking in one of the huge lots near the waterfront. Seth reached for Tabby's hand as they crossed the street with the light.

Her hand tingled with his touch. *This does feel like a date,* she thought, though she didn't have a whole lot to gauge it by, considering she'd only been on a couple of dates since she graduated from high school. Those had been set up by Donna, and none of the guys had held her hand or acted the least bit interested in her. Of course, she hadn't said more than a few words, and those had come out in a mishmash of stammering and stuttering.

Groups of people were milling about the waterfront. Tabby clung tightly to Seth's hand, not wishing to get separated. As they headed down the sidewalk toward one of the fish bars, she spotted a young man walking a few feet ahead of them. He had two sizable holes in the back of his faded blue jeans, and long, scraggly brown hair hung halfway down the back of his discolored orange T-shirt. That was not what drew her attention to him, however. What made this man so unique was the colorful parrot sitting on his shoulder. With each step the man took, the parrot would either let out an ear-piercing squawk or imitate something someone had just said.

"I'm hungry! I'm hungry!" the feathered creature screeched. "The ferry's coming! The ferry's coming! Awk!"

Tabby glanced to her left. Sure enough, the Vashon Island ferry was heading toward one of the piers. Enthusiastic children jumped up and down, hollering that the ferry was coming, and the noisy parrot kept right on mimicking.

"I don't know who's more interesting—that guy with the long hair or his obnoxious bird," Seth whispered to Tabby.

She giggled. "The b–bird has my vote."

"I heard this story about a guy who owned a belligerent parrot," Seth remarked.

She looked up at him expectantly. "And?"

"The parrot had a bad attitude, not to mention a very foul mouth."

"So, what h–happened?"

"The guy tried everything from playing soft music to saying only polite words in front of the bird, but nothing worked at all."

"Did he s–sell the parrot then?"

Seth shook his head. "Nope. He put him in the freezer."

Tabby's mouth dropped open. "The freezer?"

"Yep, for about five minutes. When he opened the door again, the parrot calmly stepped out onto the guy's shoulder, a changed bird."

"He didn't use b–bad words anymore?"

"Nope. In fact, the parrot said, 'I'm truly sorry for being so rude.' Then the colorful creature added, 'Say, I saw a naked chicken in that icebox. What'd that poor bird do?'"

Tabby laughed, feeling happy and carefree and wishing the fun of today could last forever.

Seth sobered, nodding toward the edge of the sidewalk. "You see all kinds down here."

Tabby watched with interest as a group of peddlers offered their wares to anyone who would listen. Everything from costume jewelry to painted T-shirts was being sold. Several men lay on the grass, holding signs announcing that they were out of work and needed money. An empty coffee can sat nearby—a place for donations. Tabby thought it sad to see people who were homeless or out of a job, reduced to begging. These few along the waterfront were just the tip of the iceberg too.

"It's hard to distinguish between who really needs help and who's merely panhandling," Seth whispered in her ear.

She nodded, wondering if he could read her mind.

"Ivar's has a long line of people waiting to get in," Seth said. "Is it okay with you if we try Steamer's Fish Bar instead?"

Tabby glanced at the restaurant he'd mentioned. The aroma of deep-fried fish drifted out the open door and filled her senses. "One fish-and-chips place is probably as good as another," she replied.

They entered the restaurant and placed their orders at the counter, then found a seat near a window overlooking the water. Tabby watched in fascination as several boats pulled away from the dock, taking tourists on a journey through Puget Sound Bay. It was a beautiful, sunny day—perfect weather for boating.

"Would you like to go?"

Seth's sudden question drew Tabby's attention away from the window. "G–go? But we j–just got here," she said, frowning.

Seth grinned. "I didn't mean go home. I meant, would you like to go for a ride on one of those tour boats you're watching so intently? We could do that after we eat, instead of browsing through the gift shops."

"Do w–we have t–time for th–that?"

Seth glanced at his watch. "I don't see why not. My shop's closed for the day, and I don't have to be back at any set time. How about you?"

Tabby shook her head. "I have all d–day."

"Then would you like me to see about getting a couple of tour-boat tickets?"

Tabby felt the tension begin to seep from her body as she reached for her glass of lemonade. "Actually, if I h–had a choice, I think I'd r–rather take the ferry over to V–Vashon, then ferry from there b–back to Tacoma."

Seth's face brightened. "Now that's a great idea! I haven't ridden the ferry in quite a while."

Tabby hung tightly to the rail as she leaned over to stare into the choppy waters of Puget Sound Bay. The wind whipped against her face, slapping the ends of her hair in every direction. It was exhilarating, and she felt very much alive. Seagulls soared in the cloudless sky, squawking and screeching, as though vying for the attention of everyone on board the ferry. It was a peaceful scene, and Tabby felt a deep sense of contentment fill her soul.

Seth was standing directly behind Tabby, and he leaned into her, wrapping his arms around her waist. "Warm enough?" he asked, his mouth pressed against her ear.

Tabby shivered, and she knew it was not from the cool breeze. "I'm fine."

Seth rested his chin on top of her head. "This was a great idea. I've had a lot of fun today."

"Me too," she murmured.

"It doesn't have to end when we dock at Point Defiance."

"It doesn't?"

"Nope. We could have dinner at the Harbor Lights."

Tabby glanced down at her outfit and grimaced. "I'm not exactly dressed for a fancy restaurant, Seth."

He chuckled. "Me neither, but I don't think it matters much. A lot of boaters pull into the docks at the restaurants along Tacoma's waterfront. I'm sure many people will be dressed as casually as we are."

Tabby shrugged. She was having such a good time and didn't want the day to end yet. "Okay. . .if you're sure."

"I'm positive," Seth said, nuzzling her neck.

She sucked in her breath. If this was a dream, she hoped it would last forever.

Seth sat directly across from Tabby, studying her instead of the menu he held in his hands. She was gazing intently at her own menu, which gave him the perfect opportunity to look at her without being noticed. When had she taken on such a glow? When had her eyes begun to sparkle? He shook his head. Maybe it was just the reflection from the candle in the center of the table. Maybe he was imagining things.

Tabby looked up and caught him staring. "What's wrong?" she asked with furrowed brows. "Don't you see anything you like?"

Seth's lips curved into a slow smile.

"What's so funny?"

He reached across the table and grasped her hand. "Two things are making me smile."

She gave him a quizzical look.

"You haven't stuttered once since we left Seattle."

Tabby's face turned crimson, making Seth wonder if he should have said anything. "I didn't mean to embarrass you. It makes me happy to know you're finally beginning to relax in my presence."

She returned his smile. "I do feel pretty calm tonight."

He ran his thumb across the top of her hand and felt relief when she didn't pull it away.

"You said there were two things making you smile. What's the second one?"

He leaned farther across the table. "Just looking at you makes me smile."

A tiny frown marred her forehead. "Am I that goofy looking?"

Seth shook his head. "No, of course not! In fact, I was sitting here thinking how beautiful you look in the candlelight."

"No one has ever c–called me b–beautiful before," she said, a blush staining her cheeks.

Great! Now she's stuttering again. So much for making her feel relaxed. Seth dropped her hand and picked up his menu. "Guess I'd better decide what to order before our waiter comes back. Have you found anything you like yet?"

Tabby nodded. "I think I'll have a crab salad."

"You can order whatever you want," Seth said quickly. "Lobster, steak, or prime rib—just say the word."

"Crab salad is all I want," she insisted.

Seth was about to comment when the waiter returned to their table.

"Have you two decided?" the young man asked.

"I'll have prime rib, and the lady wants a crab salad." Seth handed both menus back to the waiter. "I think we'll have two glasses of iced tea as well."

As soon as the waiter left, Seth reached for Tabby's hand again. "I didn't mean to make you blush a few minutes ago. How come you always do that, anyway?"

"Do what?"

"Turn red like a cherry and hang your head whenever you're paid a compliment."

Her forehead wrinkled. "I–I don't know. I'm not used to getting compliments. You don't have to try and make me feel good, you know."

"Is that what you think—that I'm just trying to make you feel good?"

"Well, isn't it?"

His throat tightened. "I don't pass out false compliments so someone will feel good, Tabby."

Her gaze dropped to the tablecloth. "Let's forget it, okay?"

Seth offered up a silent prayer. *Should I let this drop, Lord, or should I try to convince her that I'm really interested in her as a woman, and that. . .* He swallowed hard. What did he really want from this relationship? When he'd first met Tabby, he'd felt sorry for her. He could sense her need for encouragement and maybe even a friend, but when had he started thinking of her as a woman and not just someone to help? There was a great yearning, deep within him, and he wondered if it could be filled by a woman's love. Tabby might be that woman. He had thought about her nearly every day since they first met. That had to mean something, didn't it?

Seth felt a sense of peace settle over him as he heard the words in his head say, *Go slow, Seth. Go slow.*

Chapter Twelve

I can't believe you were gone all day!" Donna exclaimed when Tabby entered their apartment.

Tabby dropped to the couch beside her and released a sigh of contentment. "Today was probably the best day of my life."

Donna's eyebrows shot up. "Did Seth kiss you?"

"Of course not!"

"You're turning red like a radish. He must have kissed you." Donna poked Tabby in the ribs. "Tell me all about it, and don't leave out one single detail."

Tabby slid out of Donna's reach. "Don't get so excited. There's not that much to tell."

"Then start with when Seth picked you up this morning and end with a detailed description of his kiss."

Tabby grimaced. "I told you, there was no kiss!" Her inexperience with men was an embarrassment. If she'd been more coy, like that cute little redhead, Cheryl, maybe Seth would have kissed her.

"Then what has you glowing like a Christmas tree?" Donna asked, pulling Tabby out of her musings.

"Seth is a lot of fun, and I had a good time today," she mumbled.

Donna released a sigh. "That sure doesn't tell me much."

Tabby leaned her head against the back of the couch. "Let's see. . . We drove to Seattle, and freeway traffic was terrible." A long pause followed.

"And?"

"When we got to Seattle, we went to the Dummy Depot to pick up a ventriloquist figure Seth needs to repair." Another long pause.

"Then what?"

"We went down to the waterfront, where we had a great lunch of fish-and-chips."

"You must have done more than that. You've been gone all day."

Tabby glanced at her watch and wrinkled her nose. "It's only a little after eight. Besides, you're not my mother, and I'm not on any kind of a curfew."

Donna squinted her eyes. "You look like you're on cloud nine, so I figure you must have done something really exciting today."

Tabby grinned. "We did. We rode the ferry from Seattle to Vashon Island, then we caught another one to Point Defiance." She closed her eyes and thought about Seth's arms around her waist and his mouth pressed against her ear. She could still feel his warm breath on her neck and smell his woodsy aftershave lotion. That part of the day had been the most exciting thing of all. She wasn't about to share such a private moment with Donna—even if she was her best friend.

"What'd you do after you left Point Defiance?" Donna asked.

"We went to dinner at the Harbor Lights."

Donna let out a low whistle. "Wow! Things must be getting pretty serious between you two. The Harbor Lights costs big bucks!"

Tabby groaned. "It's not that expensive. Besides, going there doesn't mean anything special."

Donna gave her a knowing look. "Yeah, right."

"It's true," Tabby insisted. "I'm the queen of simplicity, so why would a great guy like Seth be attracted to someone like me?"

Donna clicked her tongue. "Are you ever going to see your true potential?"

Crossing her arms in front of her chest, Tabby shrugged. "I don't know. Maybe I do have some worth."

After their day in Seattle, Tabby had hoped Seth might call and ask her out again. That would have let her know if he really was interested in seeing her on a personal level or not. However, the week went by without a single word from him. Today was Thursday, and she had another, previously scheduled ventriloquism lesson that evening. Thinking about it had very little appeal, though. If only Seth had called. If only. . .

As she drove across town, Tabby forced her thoughts away from

Seth and onto the routine she'd been practicing with Rosie. She was determined to do her very best this time. Even if Seth never saw her as a desirable woman, at least she could dazzle the socks off him with her new talent.

When she arrived at Seth's, Tabby was relieved to see he had no customers. The thought of performing before an audience held no appeal whatsoever.

Seth greeted her with a warm smile. "I'll be with you in just a minute. I have to make a few phone calls."

Tabby nodded and took a seat, placing Rosie on her lap. Mentally, she began to rehearse the lines of her routine, hoping she had them memorized so well she wouldn't have to use her notes. Watching Seth as he stood across the room talking on the phone was a big enough distraction, but when the bell above the shop door rang, announcing a customer, Tabby froze.

In walked Cheryl Stone carrying her dummy, Oscar. She hurried past Tabby as though she hadn't even seen her and rushed up to Seth just as he was hanging up the phone. "Seth, you've got to help me!" she exclaimed.

"What do you need help with?" Seth asked.

"Oscar's mouth is stuck in the open position, and I can't get it to work." Cheryl handed him the dummy. "I'm supposed to do a vent routine at a family gathering tonight, and I was hoping you'd have time to fix Oscar for me."

Seth glanced at Tabby. "Actually, I was just about to begin teaching a lesson. Why don't you use your new dummy tonight—the one you recently bought from me?"

Cheryl shook her head. "I haven't gotten used to that one yet. Besides, Oscar's so cute, he's always a hit wherever I perform."

"Have a seat then," Seth said, motioning toward the row of chairs along the wall where Tabby sat. "I'll take Oscar in the back room and see what I can do."

Cheryl smiled sweetly. "Thank you, Seth. You're the nicest man."

The chocolate bar Tabby had eaten on her drive over to Seth's suddenly felt like a lump of clay in her stomach. Cheryl obviously had her eye on Seth. For all Tabby knew, he might have more than a passing interest in the vibrant redhead too.

Cheryl took a seat next to Tabby, opened her purse, withdrew a nail file, and began to shape her nails. The silence closing in around them was broken only by the steady ticking of the wall clock across the room and the irritating scrape of nail file against fingernails.

Should I say something to her? Tabby wondered. Just sitting here like this felt so awkward. Given her problem with stuttering, she decided that unless Cheryl spoke first, she would remain quiet.

Several minutes went by, and then Cheryl returned the nail file to her purse and turned toward Tabby. "Cute little dummy you've got there."

"Th–thanks."

"Are you here to see about getting it repaired?"

Tabby shook her head. "I–I'm t–taking l–lessons." She glanced toward the back room, hoping Seth would return soon. There was something about Cheryl's confidence and good looks that shattered any hope Tabby might have of ever becoming a successful ventriloquist, much less the object of Seth's affections.

Cheryl tapped her fingers along the arm of the chair. "I wonder what's taking so long? Seth must be having quite a time with Oscar's stubborn little mouth." She eyed Tabby curiously. "How long have you been taking ventriloquism lessons?"

"Not l–long."

"Guess you'll be at it for a while, what with your stuttering problem and all." Cheryl offered Tabby a sympathetic smile. "It must be difficult for you."

Hot tears stung Tabby's eyes as she squirmed in her seat, then hunkered down as if succumbing to a predator. She bit her lower lip to stop the flow of tears that seemed insistent on spilling onto her flaming cheeks. She was used to her family making fun of her speech impediment, but seeing the pity on Cheryl's face was almost worse than reproach.

Dear Lord, she prayed silently, *please help me say something without stuttering.*

With newfound courage, Tabby stuck her hand into the opening at the back of Rosie's overalls, grabbed the control stick, opened her own mouth slightly, and said in a falsetto voice, "Tabby may have a problem with shyness, but I don't stutter at all." It was true, Tabby noted with satisfaction. Whenever she did ventriloquism, the voice she used for her dummy never missed a syllable.

Cheryl leaned forward, squinting her eyes and watching intently as Tabby continued to make her dummy talk.

"My name's Rosie; what's yours?"

"Cheryl Stone, and my dummy, Oscar, is in there getting his mouth worked on." Cheryl pointed toward the room where Seth had disappeared.

Tabby smiled. She could hardly believe it, but Cheryl was actually talking to her dummy like it was real. Of course, Cheryl was a ventriloquist, and people who talked for two did seem to have the childlike ability to get into the whole dummy scene.

"How long have you been doing ventriloquism?" little Rosie asked Cheryl.

Cheryl smiled in response. "I learned the basics on my own a few years ago. Since I met Seth, he's taught me several advanced techniques."

I wonder what else he's taught you. Tabby opened Rosie's mouth, actually planning to voice the question, but Seth entered the room in the nick of time.

"I think Oscar's good to go," he said, handing the dummy to Cheryl.

Cheryl jumped up. "How can I ever thank you, Seth?" She stood on tiptoes and planted a kiss right on Seth's lips!

Tabby wasn't sure who was more surprised—she or Seth. He stood there for several seconds, face red and mouth hanging open. Finally, he grinned, embarrassed-like, then mumbled, "I'll send you a bill."

Cheryl giggled and gave his arm a squeeze. "You're so cute." As she started for the door, she called over her shoulder, "See you on Saturday, Seth!" The door clicked shut, and Cheryl Stone was gone.

Tabby wished she had the courage to ask Seth why he'd be seeing Cheryl on Saturday, but it didn't seem appropriate. Besides, she had no claim on him, and if he chose to date someone else, who was she to ask questions?

"Sorry about the interruption," Seth said in a businesslike tone of voice. "We can begin now, if you're ready."

Tabby swallowed hard. Cheryl was gone, but the image of her lovely face rolled around in Tabby's mind. She'd been more than ready for a lesson when she came into Seth's shop, but now, after seeing the interchange between Seth and Cheryl, the only thing she was ready for was home!

Chapter Thirteen

Seth eased into a chair and leaned forward until his head was resting in his hands. He couldn't believe how terrible Tabby's lesson had gone. Beside the fact that there had been an air of tension between them ever since Cheryl left, Tabby seemed unable to stay focused. What had gone wrong? Was he failing as a teacher, or was she simply losing interest in ventriloquism? Did she have any personal feelings for him, or had he read more into their Seattle trip than there actually was? Tabby seemed so relaxed that day, and when he'd held her hand, she hadn't pulled away. In fact, as near as he could tell, she'd enjoyed it as much as he had.

Seth groaned and stood up again. He wasn't sure how or even when it happened, but Tabitha Johnson definitely meant more to him than just someone to help. After seeing the way she was with her day care kids the other day, and after spending time with her in Seattle, he really was beginning to hope she was the woman he'd been waiting for. If he could only make Tabby see what potential she had. If she could just get past all that shyness and stuttering, he was sure she'd be perfect for him.

He moved toward the telephone. Tabby wouldn't be home yet. Maybe it was time for that talk with her friend.

Donna answered on the second ring. Seth quickly related the reason for his call, and a few minutes later he hung up the phone, happy in the knowledge that he'd be meeting Donna for lunch tomorrow. Between the two of them, maybe Tabby could become a confident woman who would use all her abilities to serve the Lord.

"I am so glad this is Friday," Tabby murmured, as she prepared to eat her sack lunch at one of the small tables where the day care kids often sat.

"Me too," Donna agreed. She grabbed her sweater and umbrella and started for the door. "See you later."

"Hey, wait a minute," Tabby called. "Where are you going?"

"Out to lunch, and I'd better hurry."

"Say, why don't I join you?"

"See you at one." Donna waved and disappeared out the door before Tabby could say another word and without even answering her question.

Tabby's forehead wrinkled. Donna hardly ever went out to lunch on a weekday. When she did, she always arranged for one of their helpers to take over the day care so Tabby could come along. What was up, anyway?

Tabby snapped her fingers. "Maybe Donna has a date and doesn't want me to know about it. I'll bet there's a mystery man in my friend's life."

"Who are you talking to, Teacher?"

Tabby jerked her head at the sound of four-year-old Mary Stevens's sweet voice.

"I—uh—was kind of talking to myself."

Mary grinned. "Like you do when you use Roscoe or little Rosie?"

Tabby nodded. "Something like that." She patted the child on top of her curly blond head. "What are you doing up, missy? It's nap time, you know."

The child nodded soberly. "I'm not sleepy."

"Maybe not, but you need to rest your eyes." Tabby placed her ham sandwich back inside its plastic wrapper and stood up. "Come on, sweetie, I'll walk you back to your sleeping mat."

Seth tapped the edge of his water glass with the tip of his spoon as he waited impatiently for Donna to show up. She'd promised to meet him at Garrison's Deli shortly after noon. It was only a few doors down from the church where she and Tabby ran their day care center. It shouldn't take her more than a few minutes to get here.

He glanced at his watch again. Twelve-twenty. Where was she anyway? Maybe she'd forgotten. Maybe she'd changed her mind. He was just about to leave the table and go to the counter to place his order, when he saw Donna come rushing into the deli.

She waved, then hurried toward his table. Her face was flushed, and her dark curls looked windblown. "Sorry I'm late," she panted. "Just as I was leaving the day care, Tabby started plying me with all sorts of questions about where I was having lunch, and she even suggested she come along. I chose to ignore her and hurried out of the room. Then I got detained a few more minutes on my way out of the church."

Seth gave her a questioning look as she took the seat directly across from him.

"One of the kids' parents came to pick him up early. She stopped me on the steps to say Bobby had a dental appointment and she'd forgotten to tell us about it," Donna explained.

Seth nodded toward the counter. "I was about to order. Do you know what you want, or do you need a few minutes to look at the menu?"

"Chicken salad in pita bread and a glass of iced tea sounds good to me," she replied.

"I'll be right back," Seth said, pushing away from the table. He placed Donna's order first, then ordered a turkey club sandwich on whole wheat with a glass of apple juice for himself. When he returned to the table, he found Donna staring out the window.

"Looks like it could rain again," he noted.

She held up the umbrella she'd placed on one end of the table. "I came prepared."

Seth decided there was no point in wasting time talking about the weather. "I was wondering if we could discuss Tabby," he blurted out. "That day you came into my shop to get the gift certificate for Tabby's dummy, we agreed that we'd work together to help her. I've really been trying, but to tell you the truth, I kind of feel like a salmon swimming upstream."

Donna giggled. "How can I help?"

"I have a few questions for you," he answered.

"What do you want to know?"

"I've never met anyone quite as shy as Tabby," he said. "Can you tell me why that is and what makes her stutter?"

Donna drew in a deep breath and exhaled it with such force that her napkin blew off the table. "Whew. . .that's kind of a long story." She bent down to retrieve the napkin, then glanced at her watch. "This will have to be a scaled down version, because I have to be back at work by one."

Seth leaned forward with his elbows on the table. "I'm all ears."

"I've known Tabby ever since we were little tykes," Donna began. "Up until she turned six, Tabby was a fun-loving, outgoing child."

"What happened when she turned six?"

"Her sister was born." Donna grimaced. "Tabby's dad favored Lois right from the start. I can't explain why, but he started giving Tabby put-downs and harsh words. She turned inward, became introverted, and began to lack confidence in most areas of her life." She drummed her fingers along the edge of the table. "That's when she began stuttering."

Seth was about to reply, but their order was being called. He excused himself to pick up their food. When he returned to the table, Seth offered a word of prayer, and they both grabbed their sandwiches. "Do you think you can eat and talk at the same time?" he asked.

"Oh, sure, I've had lots of practice," Donna mumbled around her pita bread.

"I've noticed that Tabby stutters more at certain times, and other times she hardly stutters at all."

Donna nodded. "It has to do with how well she knows you, and how comfortable she feels in your presence."

"So, if Tabby felt more confident and had more self-esteem, she probably wouldn't stutter as much—or at all."

Donna shrugged. "Could be. Tabby's worst stuttering takes place when she's around her family. They intimidate her, and she's never learned to stand up for herself."

Seth took a swallow of apple juice, and his eyebrows furrowed. "Tabby doesn't stutter at all when she does ventriloquism. It's almost like she's a different person when she's speaking through her dummy."

Donna shrugged. "In a way, I guess she is."

"Just when I think I've got her figured out, she does something to muddle my brain."

"Like what?"

"Last night was a good example," Seth answered. "Tabby arrived at my shop for another lesson, and I thought she was in a good mood, ready to learn and all excited about it."

"She was excited," Donna agreed. "She's been enthusiastic about everything since the two of you went to Seattle."

Seth brightened some. "Really? I thought she'd had a good time, but I wasn't sure."

Donna grinned. "Tabby was on cloud nine when she came home that night." Her hand went quickly to her mouth. "Oops. . . Guess I wasn't supposed to tell you that."

Seth felt his face flush. That was the trouble with being fair skinned and redheaded. He flushed way too easily. *Tabby must have some feelings for me. At least she did until. . .*

"Tell me what happened last night to make you wonder about Tabby," Donna said, interrupting his thoughts.

He took a bite of his sandwich, then washed it down with more juice before answering. "As I said before, Tabby was in a good mood when she first came in."

"And?"

"Then an unexpected customer showed up, and after she left, Tabby closed up like a razor clam."

"Hmm. . ."

"Hmm. . .what?"

Donna frowned. "Tabby was in kind of a sour mood when she came home last night. I asked her what was wrong, and she mumbled something about not being able to compete with Cheryl." She eyed Seth speculatively. "Cheryl wouldn't happen to be that unexpected customer, would she?"

"Afraid so. Cheryl Stone is a confident young woman with lots of talent as a ventriloquist."

"Is she pretty?"

He nodded. Cheryl was beautiful, vivacious, and talented. *That perfect woman you've been looking for,* a little voice taunted. *If Cheryl is perfect, then why do I think I need to remake Tabby?*

"Will you be seeing Tabby again?" Donna asked.

He swallowed hard, searching for the right words. Did he love her? Did she love him? He enjoyed being with her, that much he knew. Was it love he was feeling, though? It was probably too soon to tell.

"I–I don't know if we'll see each other again," he finally answered. "Guess that all depends on Tabby."

"On whether she wants more lessons?" Donna asked.

Seth shrugged. "That and a few other things."

Donna didn't pry, and he was glad. He wasn't in the mood to try to explain his feelings for Tabitha Johnson, or this compelling need he felt to make her into the woman he thought he needed.

"Well," Donna said a few minutes later, "I really do need to get back to work." She finished her iced tea and stood up. "Thanks for lunch, Seth. I hope some of the things we've talked about have been helpful. Tabby's my best friend, and I care a lot about her." She looked at him pointedly. "She carries a lot of pain from the past. I don't want to see her hurt anymore."

Seth stood up too. "My car's parked right out front. I'll walk you out," he said, making no reference to the possibility that he might add further hurt to Tabby's already battered mental state. He was so confused about everything right now, and some things were better left unsaid. Especially when he hadn't fully sorted out his feelings for her and didn't have a clue how she really felt about him.

With a bag of trash in her arms, Tabby left Gail, their eighteen-year-old helper, in charge of the day care kids while she carried the garbage out to the curb. The garbage truck always came around three on Friday afternoons, which meant she still had enough time to get one more bag put out.

Tabby stepped up beside the two cans by the curb and had just opened the lid of one, when she heard voices coming from down the street. She turned her head to the right and froze in place, one hand holding the garbage can lid, the other clutching the plastic garbage bag.

She could see a man and woman standing outside Garrison's Deli. She'd have recognized them anywhere—Seth for his red hair, Donna for her high-pitched laugh. What were they doing together? Tabby's mouth dropped open like a broken hinge on a screen door. Her body began to sway. She blinked rapidly, hoping her eyes had deceived her. Seth was actually hugging her best friend!

Chapter Fourteen

Tabby dropped the garbage sack into the can, slammed the lid down, whirled around, and bolted for the church. She didn't want Donna or Seth to see her. She had to think. . .to decide the best way to handle this little matter. Would it be better to come right out and ask Donna what she was doing with Seth, or should she merely ply her with a few questions, hoping the answers would come voluntarily?

Tabby returned to the day care center with a heavy heart. Were Seth and Donna seeing each other socially? Was he Donna's lunch date? Was he the mystery man in her best friend's life? As much as the truth might hurt, she had to know.

Tabby was setting out small tubs of modeling clay when Donna sauntered into the room humming "Jesus Loves Me." She looked about as blissful as a kitten with a ball of string, and not the least bit guilty, either.

"How was lunch?" Tabby asked after Donna had put her purse and umbrella in the desk drawer.

"It was good. I had pita bread stuffed with chicken salad."

"What did your date have?"

Donna spun around, and her eyebrows shot up. "My date?"

"Yeah, the person you met for lunch."

"Did I say I was meeting someone?"

Tabby shrugged. "Not in so many words, but you acted kind of secretive. Are you seeing some guy you don't want me to know about?"

Donna lowered herself into one of the kiddy chairs, keeping her eyes averted from Tabby's penetrating gaze. "Let's just say I'm checking him out. I need to see how well we get along. I want to find out what he's really like."

Tabby opened one of the clay lids and slapped it down on the table. "Why didn't you just ask me? I know exactly what he's like!"

Donna's forehead wrinkled, and she pursed her lips. "Since when do you have the inside scoop on our pastor's son?"

"Who?"

"Alex Hanson."

"Alex? What's Alex got to do with this?"

"I had lunch with Alex the Saturday you and Seth went to Seattle," Donna explained.

Tabby's insides began to quiver. What was going on here, anyway? "That's fine. I'm happy you finally agreed to go out with Alex, but what about today? Did you or did you not have lunch with someone over at Garrison's Deli?"

Donna's face grew red, and little beads of perspiration gathered on her forehead. "Well, I—"

"You don't have to hem and haw or beat around the bush with me." Tabby grunted. "I know perfectly well who you had lunch with today."

"You do?"

Tabby nodded. "I took some garbage outside a little while ago. I heard voices, and when I looked down the street, there stood Seth—with his arms around my best friend!" She flopped into a chair and buried her face in her hands.

Donna reached over and laid a hand on Tabby's trembling shoulder, but Tabby jerked it away. "How could you go behind my back like that?"

"You're wrong. Things aren't the way they appear."

Tabby snapped her head up. "Are you going to deny having lunch with Seth?"

"No, but—"

"Was it you and Seth standing in front of the deli?"

"Yes, but—"

"You can't argue the fact that he was hugging you, either, can you?"

Donna shook her head. "No, I can't deny any of those things, but I'm not the least bit interested in Seth. We've been through all this before, Tabby, and—"

"Just how do you explain the secret lunch. . .or that tender little embrace?"

Donna's eyes filled with tears. "I didn't want you to know I was meeting

Seth, because I didn't want you to think we were ganging up on you."

Tabby bit her bottom lip, sucking it inside her mouth when she tasted blood. "In what way are you ganging up on me?"

"Can't we talk about this later? The kids will be up from their naps soon," Donna said, glancing toward the adjoining room.

Tabby lifted her arm, then held it so her watch was a few inches from Donna's face. "We still have three minutes. I think you can answer my question in that amount of time, don't you?"

Donna pulled a tissue from her skirt pocket and blew her nose. "Guess you don't leave me much choice."

Tabby's only response was a curt nod.

"It's like this. . .Seth was concerned about your actions last night. He said you didn't do well at your lesson, and that you seemed kinda remote. He's trying hard to help you overcome your shyness, and perfect your—"

"So the two of you are in cahoots, trying to fix poor, pitiful, timid Tabitha!" Tabby could feel the pulse hammering in her neck, and her hands had begun to shake.

Donna's eyelids fluttered. "Calm down. You'll wake the kids."

Tabby pointed to her watch. "It's almost time for them to get up anyway."

"That may be true, but you don't want to scare the little tykes with your screeching, do you?"

Tabby sniffed deeply. "Of course not. But I'm really upset right now, and I'm not sure who I should be angrier with—you or Seth."

Donna grimaced. "Sorry. I didn't mean to get you all riled up. I just thought—"

Donna's sentence was interrupted when a group of children came trooping into the room, chattering and giggling all the way to the table.

Donna gave Tabby a look. For now, this conversation was over.

Seth hung up the phone, wondering why he'd ever agreed to recruit another ventriloquist to perform with him at the Clearview Church Family Crusade. The female ventriloquist who'd originally been scheduled to perform had just canceled out. Now they were asking him to find a replacement.

Seth knew plenty of ventriloquists. The trouble was, it was so last-minute. The crusade was set for next Friday night, and finding someone at this late date would be next to impossible. If only he could come up with...

The bell above his shop door rang sharply as a customer entered the shop. It was almost closing time, and the last thing Seth needed was one more problem he didn't know how to fix. He glanced up, and his heart seemed as though it had quit beating. It was Tabby, and she didn't look any too happy.

"Hi," Seth said cheerfully. "I'm glad to see you. You never called about having another lesson, and—"

Tabby held up one hand. "I've decided I don't need any more lessons."

"Then why are you here? You're not having a problem with Rosie, I hope."

She shook her head. "No, I w—wanted to talk about—"

Seth snapped his fingers, cutting her off in midsentence. "Say, you just might be the answer to my prayers!"

She furrowed her brows and turned her hands, palm up. "I d—don't get it."

He motioned toward a folding chair. "Have a seat, and I'll tell you about it."

When Tabby sat down, Seth took the chair next to her.

"Well, h—how am I an answer t—to your prayers?" she asked.

He reached for her hand. This was not going to be easy. Only a God-given miracle would make Tabby willing to do what he asked.

Tabby was tempted to pull her hand from Seth's, but she didn't. It felt good. In fact, she wished she'd never have to let go. She stared up at him, searching his face for answers.

"I—uh—will be doing a vent routine at Clearview Community Church next Friday night," Seth began slowly.

"What's that got to do with me?"

"I'm getting to that." He smiled sheepishly. "The thing is, Sarah McDonald, the other ventriloquist who was originally scheduled, has had a family emergency and was forced to bow out." Seth ran his thumb along the inside of Tabby's palm, making it that much harder for her to concentrate on what he was saying. "I was hoping you might be willing to go with me next week—to fill in for Sarah."

Tabby's throat constricted, and she drew in a deep, unsteady breath. Did Seth actually think she could stand up in front of an audience and talk for two? He should be smart enough to realize she wasn't ready for something like that. The truth was, even though she had gained a bit more confidence, she might never be able to do ventriloquism for a large audience.

"I know it's short notice," Seth said, jerking her thoughts aside, "but we could begin practicing right now, then do more throughout the week. I'm sure—"

The rest of Seth's sentence was lost, as Tabby closed her eyes and tried to imagine what it would be like to perform before a crowd. She could visualize herself freezing up and not being able to utter a single word. Or worse yet, stuttering and stammering all over the place.

"Tabby, are you listening to me?" Seth's mellow voice pulled her out of the make-believe situation, and she popped her eyes open.

"I c–can't d–do it, Seth."

He pulled her to her feet, then placed both his hands on her shoulders. "You can do it, so don't be discouraged because you believe you have no ability. Each of us has much to offer. It's what you do with your abilities that really matters. Now, repeat after me. . .'I can do everything through Christ, who gives me strength.'"

In a trembling voice, Tabby repeated the verse of scripture from Philippians 4:13. When she was done, Seth tipped her chin up slightly, so they were making direct eye contact. "I know you can do this, Tabby."

She merely shrugged in response.

"You're a talented ventriloquist, and it's time to let your light shine," Seth said with feeling. He leaned his head down until his lips were mere inches from hers. "Do this for me, please."

Tabby's eyelids fluttered, then drifted shut. She felt the warmth of Seth's lips against her own. His kiss was gentle like a butterfly, but as intense as anything she'd ever felt. Of course, her inexperience in the kissing department didn't offer much for comparison. Tabby knew she was falling for Seth Beyers, and she wanted desperately to please him. She'd come over here this evening to give him a piece of her mind, but now all such thoughts had melted away, like spring's last snow. She reveled in the joy of being held in Seth's arms and delighted in the warmth of his lips caressing her own.

When they pulled apart moments later, Tabby felt as if all the breath had been squeezed out of her lungs.

"Kissing is good for you, did you know that?" Seth murmured against her ear.

Numbly she shook her head.

"Yep. It helps relieve stress and tension. Just think about it—when your mouth is kissing, you're almost smiling. Everyone knows it's impossible to smile and feel tense at the same time."

Tabby leaned her head against his shoulder. She did feel relaxed, happy, and almost confident. In a voice sounding much like her dummy's, she rasped, "Okay, I'll do it. Rosie and I will p–perform a vent routine."

He grinned and clasped his hands together. "Great! I know you'll be perfect."

Chapter Fifteen

Tabby awoke the following morning wondering if she'd completely lost her mind. What in the world had come over her last night? Not only had she not told Seth what she thought about him trying to change her, but she'd actually agreed to do a vent routine next week—in front of a large audience, no less!

"It was that kiss," Tabby moaned as she threw back the covers and crawled out of bed. "If only he hadn't kissed me, I could have said no."

She winced as though she'd been slapped. Would she really rather he hadn't kissed her? In all honesty, if Seth would offer another of his sweet kisses, she'd probably say yes all over again.

Feeling more like a dummy than a ventriloquist, Tabby padded in her bare feet over to the window and peered through the mini-blinds. The sun was shining. The birds were singing. It was going to be a beautiful day. Too bad her heart felt no joy. She turned and headed for the kitchen, feeling as though she was part of a death march.

Discovering Donna sitting at the table, talking on the cordless phone, Tabby dropped into a chair. When Donna offered her a warm smile, she only grunted in response.

By the time Donna's conversation was over, Tabby had eaten an orange, along with a handful of grapes, and she was about to tackle a banana. "Good morning, sleepyhead. I thought you were never going to get up."

"I got in late last night," Tabby mumbled as she bit into the piece of fruit.

"Tell me about it!" Donna exclaimed. "I finally gave up waiting for you and went to bed. You said you had an errand to run after work. Where were you anyway?"

Tabby swallowed the chunk of banana and frowned. "I'm afraid my errand turned into more of an error."

Donna's eyebrows lifted in question.

"I went to Beyers' Ventriloquist Studio, planning to put Seth in his place for trying to run my life."

"And did you?"

Tabby sucked in her bottom lip and squared her shoulders. "Afraid not. I ended up promising to do a vent routine at the Clearview Church Family Crusade next Friday."

Donna slapped her hand down on the table, and Tabby's banana peel flew into the air, landing on the floor. "Awesome! That's the best news I've had all year. Maybe even in the last ten years!"

Tabby shook her head. "Don't get so excited. I haven't done it yet."

"Oh, but you will," Donna said excitedly. She pointed to the phone. "That call was from Alex Hanson. He asked me to go out with him again, and guess where we're going?"

"Please don't tell me it's the crusade," Tabby said, already knowing the answer.

"Okay, I won't tell you. I'll just let you be surprised when you look out into the audience and see your best friend and your pastor's son cheering you on."

Tabby gazed at the ceiling. "I think I need a doctor to examine my head more than I need a cheering section." She groaned. "I can't believe I let Seth talk me into such a thing!"

"You'll do just fine," Donna said with an assurance Tabby sure didn't feel. "I imagine you and Seth did some practicing last night?"

Yeah, that and a few other things. Tabby wasn't about to discuss Seth's kiss. Donna would probably go ballistic if she knew that had happened. "We had a bite of supper at the café near Seth's shop, then we worked on my routine till almost midnight." Tabby grimaced. "I'm lucky I even have any voice left after all that talking. Maybe I could get out of this if I had laryngitis or something. Seth asked me to do him a favor by filling in for someone else, and—"

"And you love the guy so much, you couldn't say no," Donna said, finishing Tabby's sentence.

Tabby's eyes filled with tears. "He wants me to be something I'm not."

"Which is?"

"Confident, talented, and ready to serve the Lord."

Donna reached across the table and patted Tabby's hand. "I've seen you do ventriloquism, so I know how talented you are. I also know you want to serve the Lord."

Tabby nodded and swiped at her face with the backs of her hands.

"The confident part will come if you give yourself half a chance," Donna assured her. "If you wallow around in self-pity the rest of your life, you'll never realize your full potential."

Tabby released a shuddering breath. "I know you're right, but I still stutter when I'm nervous or with people I don't know well. How can I become truly confident when I can't even talk right?"

"Philippians 4:13: 'I can do everything through Christ, who gives me strength,'" Donna reminded.

Tabby sniffed. "Seth quoted that same verse last night."

"See," Donna said with a smile. "The Lord wants you to lean on Him. If you keep your focus on Jesus and not the audience, I know you can do that routine next week."

Tabby smiled weakly. "I hope so." Her eyes filled with fresh tears. "I owe you an apology for the other day. We've been friends a long time, and I should have known you'd never try to make a play for Seth behind my back."

Donna nodded. "You're right; I wouldn't. And you are forgiven."

Tabby and Seth met every evening for the next week to practice their routines for the crusade. Not only was it helpful for Tabby to memorize her lines and work on her fear of talking for two in public, but it was an opportunity to spend more time with Seth. Sometimes, after they were done for the night, he'd take her out for pie and coffee, and a few times they just sat and talked. They were drawing closer, there was no doubt in Tabby's mind, but much to her disappointment, Seth hadn't tried to kiss her again. Maybe he thought it best to keep things on a strictly business basis, since they were preparing to do a program and shouldn't be playing the game of romance when they needed to be working.

As she entered the Clearview Community Church that Friday night, carrying Rosie in a small suitcase, Tabby's heart thumped so hard she was sure everyone around could hear it. The driving force that enabled her to make the trip across town was the fact that Seth was counting on her, and she didn't want to let him down.

She spotted Seth talking to a man in the foyer. When he noticed Tabby, he motioned her to come over.

"Tabby, I'd like you to meet Pastor Tom Fletcher," Seth said, placing his arm around her waist. "He's heading up the program tonight."

"It's nice to meet you," the pastor said, reaching out to shake her hand.

She nodded and forced a smile. "N—nice to m—meet you too."

"Seth was just telling me that you've graciously agreed to fill in for Sarah McDonald. I sure do appreciate this."

Tabby cringed, wishing she could tell Pastor Fletcher the truth—she wasn't graciously filling in. She'd been coerced by Seth's honeyed words and his heart-melting kiss.

"Tabby's new at ventriloquism," Seth said to the preacher. "She's got lots of talent, though. Doesn't move her lips at all."

Right now I wish my lips were glued shut, she fretted. *I wish Seth would quit bragging about me. It'll only make the pastor expect more than I'm able to give.*

"Why don't we go backstage now?" Seth suggested, giving Tabby a little nudge.

She let herself be led along, feeling like a sheep heading straight for the slaughterhouse. If she lived through this ordeal, she'd be eternally grateful. She caught sight of Donna and her blond-haired date as they were entering the sanctuary. Donna waved, and Alex gave her a thumbs-up. She managed a weak smile, but the truth was, she felt like crying.

As though he could read her mind, Seth bent down and whispered, "Relax. You'll do fine."

"I wish everyone would quit telling me that."

Seth offered her a reassuring smile. "Do you realize that your last sentence was spoken without one bit of stuttering?"

She shook her head. Right at this moment she could barely remember what her last sentence had been about, much less focus on the fact that she hadn't stuttered.

Seth led her through a door, and a few minutes later they were in a small room with several other performers. Tabby recognized a few of them who'd been part of the demonstration for Christian workers at her own church a few months ago. There were Mark Taylor, the magician from Portland, Oregon, and Gail Stevens, the chalk artist from Seattle. Tabby knew Donna would be glad to see her. She'd probably be practicing her chalk art in earnest after tonight's performance. Slow-Joe the Clown was busy practicing his animal twisting skills, and some puppeteers were lining up to do their puppet skit. Tabby envied them. . .partly because they were going first and could get their routine over with, but mostly because they had the advantage of a puppet box to hide behind. If only she didn't have to face that crowd out there in the sanctuary!

"Now remember," Seth said, pulling Tabby aside, "I'll go out first and do my routine with Rudy; then you'll come out with Rosie, and we'll do a little bantering with our dummies. By then your confidence should be bolstered, so I'll just bow out, and you'll be on your own."

She looked up at him with pleading eyes. "That's the part that has me so worried, Seth. Couldn't you stay by my side the whole time?"

He shrugged. "I suppose I could, but I think the audience will appreciate your talent more if they see you perform solo."

Who cares if the audience appreciates my talent? I just want to get through this ordeal and live to tell about it. Tabby's heart fluttered like a frightened baby bird, and she fidgeted with the bow on Rosie's new pink dress. Donna would be glad to see she'd taken her advice and dressed the dummy up a bit.

Seth reached for her hand and squeezed it. "Your fingers feel like icicles, Tabby. Take a deep breath, and try to relax."

"That's easy enough for you to say," she muttered. "You're an old pro at this."

It seemed like no time at all that Seth was being announced by Pastor Fletcher. He grabbed Rudy and his stand, blew Tabby a kiss, and walked confidently onto the stage.

Tabby stood as close to the stage door as she could without being seen. She didn't want to miss her cue and end up embarrassing both Seth and herself. Seth was doing a bang-up job with his routine, but she was too nervous to appreciate any of it. All too soon, Seth announced her.

Holding Rosie with one hand and balancing the metal stand Seth had given her with the other, Tabby swallowed the panic rising in her throat and moved slowly across the stage. Applause sounded from the audience, and she felt her face flame.

"Rudy and I both needed dates for tonight," Seth told the crowd. "This is my friend, Tabitha Johnson, and I'll let her introduce her little pal."

Tabby opened her mouth, but nothing came out. She just stood there, feeling like some kind of frozen snow woman, unable to remember her lines and too afraid to speak them if she had.

Coming quickly to her rescue, Seth opened Rudy's mouth. "I think Tabby's waiting for me to introduce her friend. After all, she is my date, so it's probably the right thing to do." The dummy's head swiveled to the left, and one of his doe eyes winked at Rosie. "This is Rosie Wrong, but someday I hope to right that wrong and make her my bride. Then she'll be Rosie Right, who's always right, because she married me—Rudy Right!"

The audience roared and clapped their approval. Tabby felt herself begin to relax a little, and she was even able to make her dummy say a few words.

"What makes you think I'd marry a dummy?" Rosie announced. "Do I look stupid?"

"No, but you sure are cute!" Rudy shot back.

More laughter from the audience. This was fun—almost. What was Tabby going to do once Seth and Rudy left the stage? So far, she'd only spoken for Rosie. How would things go when she was forced to speak herself?

Rudy and Rosie bantered back and forth a bit longer, then finally Seth said the words Tabby had been dreading. "Well, folks, I think it's time for Rudy and me to say goodbye. I'll leave you in the capable hands of Tabby and her friend, Rosie. I'm sure they have lots of fun up their sleeves." With that, Seth grabbed Rudy and his stand and marched off the stage. The audience clapped, and Tabby nearly panicked. She forgot to pray, and in her own strength, she tried to concentrate on her routine. Everything Seth had told her seemed like ancient history. She couldn't think of anything except trying to please the audience and the paralyzing fear that held her in its grip.

"Say, R–Rosie, h–have you h–heard any good elephant j–jokes lately?" she finally squeaked.

"Oh, sure. Would you like to hear them?" Rosie responded.

Tabby only nodded. One less sentence to stammer through.

"Why do elephants have wrinkles?" Rosie asked.

"I d–don't know."

"Well, for goodness' sake, have you ever tried to iron one?"

A few snickers came from the audience, but it was nothing compared to the belly laughs Seth had gotten. This did little to bolster Tabby's confidence, and she struggled to remember the rest of her performance.

"I sure wish I had enough money to buy an elephant," Rosie said.

"Why w–would you—you w–want an el–elephant?"

"I don't. I just want the money."

Tabby paused, hoping the audience would catch on to the little joke, but they didn't. Not even Donna laughed. Tabby felt like a deflated balloon. So much for the confidence she thought she might have gained. She was failing miserably at entertaining this audience, much less bringing any glory to God through her so-called talent. Then there was Seth. What must he think of his star pupil now? He was probably as mortified as she was, and she couldn't blame him one little bit.

"M–money isn't everything, R–Rosie," Tabby said.

"It's all I need."

"Do y–you know w–what the Bible says about m–money?"

"No, do you?"

Tabby did know what it said, but for the life of her, she couldn't remember. In fact, she had no idea what to say or do next. The audience looked bored with her routine, and she'd done nothing but tell stale jokes and stutter ever since Seth took his leave. Her hands were shaking so badly she could hardly hold Rosie still, and her legs felt like two sticks made of rubber. If she didn't get off this platform soon, she would probably pass out cold.

Tabby drew in a deep breath, grabbed Rosie up in one quick swoop, and darted off the stage.

Chapter Sixteen

Tabby was sobbing hysterically by the time she reached the room off-stage. With all Seth's encouragement, she'd almost begun to believe she did have some talent, but she'd blown it big time. She had let God down, disappointed Seth, and made a complete fool of herself in front of nearly two hundred people! How could she have let this happen? Why hadn't she just told Seth no? All she wanted to do was go home, jump into bed, and bury her head under the covers.

She felt Seth's arms go around her waist. "It's okay, Tabby," he murmured against her ear. "This was your first time, and you were a little nervous, that's all. It's happened to everyone, and it will get easier with time and practice." He slid his hand up to her back and began patting it, as though that would somehow bring her comfort. "You'll do better next time, I'm sure of it."

Tabby pulled away sharply. "There won't be a next time, Seth! Except for the day care kids, I'll never have another audience."

"Yes, you will. You could be perfect if you'd give yourself half a chance. Please, let me help you. . . ."

It seemed as though Seth was asking her to be perfect at ventriloquism, but some of the things she'd heard him say to both Donna and herself made Tabby wonder if what Seth really wanted was for her to be perfect.

"You've helped me enough!" she cried. "Thanks to you, I made myself look like a total idiot out there!"

Before Seth could offer a rebuttal, Tabby jerked the door open. "Find someone else to help," she called over her shoulder. "I'll never be perfect, and I'm not the woman you need!" Slamming the door, she dashed down the hall. Despite the tears blinding her eyes, Tabby could see someone standing by the front door of the church. It was Donna.

Tabby shook her head. "Don't even say it. I don't want your pity or any kind of sappy pep talk about how things will go better next time."

Donna opened her mouth to say something, but Tabby yanked on the door handle, raced down the steps, and headed straight for her car. All she wanted was to be left alone.

The next few weeks were filled with mounting tension. Tabby barely spoke to anyone, and Donna kept trying to draw her into a conversation. Seth phoned several times, but Tabby wouldn't accept any of his calls. He even dropped by the day care on two occasions, but she refused to talk to him. It pained her to think she'd fallen in love with a man who couldn't accept her for the way she was. If he wanted "perfect," then he might be better off with someone like Cheryl Stone. Why hadn't he asked her to fill in for the ventriloquist who couldn't do the routine for the crusade? At least Cheryl wouldn't have humiliated herself or Seth in front of a church full of people.

A phone call from her parents a week later threw Tabby into deeper depression. On Friday night they would be hosting an engagement party for Lois. Tabby was expected to come, of course. She had always been obligated to attend family functions, even if no one seemed to notice she was there. If she didn't go, she'd probably never hear the end of it, but it irked her that they waited until the last minute to extend an invitation. There was hardly enough time to buy a suitable gift.

The party was set for six-thirty, and it was a good forty-five-minute drive from Tacoma to Olympia. That was barring any unforeseen traffic jams on the freeway. Tabby knew she'd have to leave for Olympia by five-thirty. The day care was open until six-thirty, but Donna said she and their helper could manage alone for an hour.

Seth was fit to be tied. His phone calls to Tabby and his trips to the day care had been for nothing. No matter how much he pleaded, she still refused to talk to him. He could understand her being upset about the routine she'd botched at the crusade. That didn't excuse her for staying mad at him, though.

Sitting at his workbench, mechanically sanding the arm of a new vent figure, Seth sulked. At first he'd only thought of Tabby as someone who needed his help. Then he began to see her as a friend. Finally, he realized he could love her, but she just didn't fit his mold for the "perfect" wife.

Even though they hadn't known each other very long, Seth cared a lot about Tabby and only wanted the best for her. She'd accused him of trying to change her. Maybe it was true. If he were being totally honest, he'd have to admit he did want her to be different—to fit into his special design and become the kind of person he wanted her to be. Tabby might be right. Perhaps he should find someone more suited to him. Maybe Cheryl Stone would be a better match. She had talent, confidence, and beauty. There was just one problem. . . . He wasn't in love with Cheryl. The truth of this revelation slammed into Seth with such force, it left him with a splitting headache. Until this very moment, he'd never really admitted it. He was actually in love with Tabby Johnson, and not for what she could be, but rather for who she was—gentle and sweet-spirited with children, humble and never bragging, compassionate and helpful—all the qualities of a true Christian.

Seth left his seat and moved toward the front door of his shop. He put the Closed sign in the window, then turned off the lights. What he really needed was a long talk with God, followed by a good night's sleep. Maybe he could think things through more clearly in the morning.

"Are you sure you don't want me to go with you tonight?" Donna asked Tabby as she prepared to leave the day care center.

Tabby shook her head. "This shindig is for family members only—our side and the groom's. Besides, you've got another date with Alex, remember?"

Donna shrugged. "I know how much you dread being with your family. If I were there, it might buffer things a bit. I could call Alex and cancel."

"Not on your life! It's taken you forever to get past your fear of dating a PK. Don't ruin it by breaking a date when it's totally unnecessary." Tabby waved her hand. "Besides, I'm a grown woman. As you've pointed out many times, it's high time I learn to deal with my family without having someone there to hold my hand."

Donna squeezed Tabby's arm. "Okay, try to have fun tonight, and please, drive carefully."

Tabby wrinkled her nose. "Don't I always?"

"It's not your driving I'm worried about. It's all those maniacs who exceed the speed limit and act as if they own the whole road."

"I'll be careful," Tabby promised as she went out the door.

Tabby was glad she'd left in plenty of time, because the freeway was terrible this night. She was tempted to take the next exit and travel the back roads, but the traffic was so congested, she wasn't sure she could even move over a lane in order to get off. By the time she finally pulled off at the Olympia exit, Tabby was a bundle of nerves.

She knew part of her apprehension was because she was about to enter the lions' den. At least, that's the way it always felt whenever she did anything that involved her family. If only Mom and Dad could love and accept her the way they did Lois. If only she was the kind of daughter they wanted. What exactly did they want? Beauty. . .brains. . .boldness? Lois had all three, and she'd been Dad's favorite ever since she was born. But what parent in their right mind would love one child more than another?

Tabby clenched her teeth. Everyone wanted her to change. Was there anyone willing to accept her just the way she was? Donna used to, but lately she'd been pressing Tabby to step out in faith and begin using her talents to serve the Lord. *If I ever have any children of my own, I'll love them all the same, no matter how different they might be.*

Then there was Seth. Tabby thought at first he just wanted to help her, but she was quite sure now he'd been trying to make her over ever since they first met. Was she really so unappealing the way she was? Must she become a whole new person in order for her family and friends to love and accept her?

A verse of scripture from 2 Corinthians popped into her mind: *"Therefore, if any man be in Christ, he is a new creature: old things are passed away; behold, all things are become new."*

Tabby had accepted the Lord at an early age. She knew she'd been cleansed of her sins, which made her a "new creation." Her stuttering problem and lack of confidence had made her unwilling to completely surrender her life to Christ and let Him use all her talents, though. If she were really a new creation, shouldn't she be praying and asking the Lord's help to become all she could be? She hadn't prayed or kept her focus on Jesus the other night at the church program. Instead, she'd been trying to impress the audience.

"I'll think about this later," Tabby murmured as she turned into her parents' driveway. Her primary concern right now was making it through Lois's engagement party.

Seth was tired of dodging his problems. With Bible in hand and a glass of cold lemonade, he took a seat at the kitchen table, determined to relinquish his own selfish desires and seek God's will for his life.

The first passage of scripture he came to was in Matthew. Jesus was teaching the Beatitudes to a crowd of people. Seth read verse five aloud. " 'Blessed are the meek, for they will inherit the earth.' "

He propped his elbows on the table and leaned his chin against his palms. "Hmm. . .Tabby fits that category, all right."

He jumped down to verse eight. " 'Blessed are the pure in heart, for they will see God.' " How could he have been so blind? Purity seemed to emanate from Tabby. Morally, she seemed like a clear, crisp mountain stream, untouched by the world's pollution.

Seth turned to the book of Proverbs, knowing the thirty-first chapter addressed the subject of an honorable wife. " 'A wife of noble character who can find? She is worth far more than rubies.' " He scanned the rest of the chapter, stopping to read verse thirty. " 'Charm is deceptive, and beauty is fleeting; but a woman who fears the Lord is to be praised.' "

Praised. Not ridiculed, coerced, or changed into something other than what she was. Seth placed one hand on the open Bible. He knew he'd found a good thing when he met Tabitha Johnson. Even though she was shy and couldn't always speak without stuttering, she had a generous heart and loved the Lord. Wasn't that what he really wanted in a wife?

Seth bowed his head and closed his eyes. "Dear Lord, forgive me for wanting Tabby to change. You love her just as she is, and I should too. Please give me the chance to make amends. If she's the woman You have in mind for me, then work out the details and make her heart receptive to my love. Amen."

Unexpected tears fell from Seth's eyes, and he sniffed. He had to talk to Tabby right away, while the truth of God's Word was still fresh on his heart. Praying as he dialed the telephone, Seth petitioned God to give him the right words.

When Donna answered, Seth asked for Tabby.

"She's not home," Donna said. She sounded as though she was either in a hurry or trying to put him off. Was Tabby still too angry to speak with him? Had she asked Donna to continue monitoring her phone calls?

"I really do need to speak with her," Seth said with a catch in his voice. "It's important."

"I'm not giving you the runaround, Seth. Tabby isn't home right now."

"Where is she?"

"She left work a little early and drove to Olympia."

"Why'd she go there?"

"It's where her parents live. They're having an engagement party for her sister, Lois."

"Oh." Seth blew out his breath. If Tabby was in Olympia, she probably wouldn't get home until late. There would be no chance of talking to her until tomorrow.

"I'd like to talk more, Seth, but my date just arrived," Donna said.

He groaned. "Yeah, okay. Tell Tabby I'll call her tomorrow." Seth hung up the phone and leaned his head on the table. Why was it that whenever he made a decision to do something, there always seemed to be some kind of roadblock? If only he'd committed this situation to God a bit sooner.

"Guess all I can do is put things in Your hands, Lord...which is exactly where they should have been in the first place."

Chapter Seventeen

Tabby's mother greeted her at the door with a frown. "You're late. Everyone else is here already."

Tabby glanced at her watch. It was ten minutes to seven. She was only twenty minutes late. She chose not to make an issue of it, though, merely shrugging and handing her mother the small bag she was holding. "Here's my g–gift for L–Lois."

Mom took the gift and placed it on a table just inside the living room door. "Come in. Everyone's in the backyard, waiting for your father to finish barbecuing the sirloin steaks."

Tabby grimaced. Apparently Dad was going all out for his favorite daughter. *If I were engaged, I doubt I'd even be given an engagement party, much less one with all the trimmings. And even if there were a party in my honor, Dad would probably fix plain old hamburgers, instead of a select, choice cut of meat.*

"How was the freeway tonight?" Mom asked as she and Tabby made their way down the hallway, leading to the back of their modest but comfortable split-level home.

"Bad. R–really bad. That's w–why I'm l–late," Tabby mumbled.

Mom didn't seem to be listening. She was scurrying about the kitchen, looking through every drawer and cupboard as if her life depended upon finding whatever it was she was searching for.

"C–can I help w–with anything?" Tabby asked.

"I suppose you can get the jug of iced tea from the refrigerator. I've got to find the long-handled fork for your father. He sent me in here five minutes ago to look for it."

Tabby crossed the room, opened the refrigerator, grabbed the iced tea, and started for the back door.

"Wait a minute," Mom called. "I found the fork. Would you take it out to Dad?"

"Aren't you c–coming?" Tabby took the fork from her mother and waited expectantly.

"I'll be out in a minute. I just need to check on my pan of baked beans."

Tabby shrugged and headed out the door, wishing she could be anywhere else but here.

About twenty people were milling around the Johnsons' backyard. Some she recognized as aunts, uncles, and cousins. Then there was Grandma Haskins, Dad, Lois, and her sister's wealthy fiancé, Michael Yehley. Some faces were new to her. She assumed those were people related to the groom.

"I see you finally decided to join us," Dad said gruffly, when Tabby handed him the barbecue fork. "Ever since you were a kid, you've been slow. Yep, slower than a turtle plowing through peanut butter. How come you're always late for everything?"

Peanut butter, Tabby mused. *That's what Seth has a fear of eating.* It seemed that lately everything made her think about Seth. She wouldn't even allow Dad's little put-down to rattle her as much as usual. She was too much in love. There, she'd finally admitted it—at least to herself. *For all the good it will do me. Seth doesn't have a clue how I feel, and even if he did, it wouldn't matter. He sees me only as a friend—someone to help out of her shell.* She frowned. *Besides, I'm still mad at him for coercing me into doing that dumb vent routine.*

"Are you just going to stand there like a dummy, or is there some justification for you being so late?" Dad bellowed, snapping Tabby out of her musings.

"I w–wasn't l–l–late on pur–pur–purpose," she stammered. She always stuttered worse around Dad. Maybe it was because he was the one person she wanted most to please. "Tr–traffic was r–really h–h–heavy."

"Why didn't you take off work early so you could get here on time?" Dad said, jerking the fork out of Tabby's hand.

She winced. "I—I d–did l–leave early." Tears hung on her lashes, but she refused to cry.

Dad turned back to the barbecue grill without saying anything more. Tabby pirouetted toward her grandmother, knowing she would at least have a kind word or two.

Grandma Haskins, cheerfully dressed in a long floral skirt and a pink ruffled blouse, greeted Tabby with a peck on the cheek. "It's good to see you, dear." She tipped her silver-gray head to one side. "You're looking kind of peaked. Are you eating right and getting plenty of sleep? You're not coming down with anything, I hope."

Tabby couldn't help but smile. Grandma was always worrying about something. Since she saw Tabby so seldom, it was only fitting that she'd be her target tonight. Tabby didn't really mind, though. It felt kind of nice to have someone fussing over her. Ever since she'd made a fool of herself at the crusade, she had been wallowing in self-pity. Maybe a few minutes with Grandma would make her feel better. "I'm f–fine, Grandma, r–really," she mumbled.

Tabby and Grandma were about to find a place to sit down, when Lois came rushing up. Her face was flushed, and she looked as though she might have been crying.

"What's wrong, Lois?" Grandma asked in a tone of obvious concern.

Lois sniffed deeply and motioned them toward one of the empty tables. As soon as they sat down, she began to cry.

Tabby gave her sister's arm a gentle squeeze. "C–can you t–tell us about it?"

Lois hiccupped loudly and wiped at her eyes, which only smudged her black mascara, making the tears look like little drops of mud rolling down her cheeks. "It's Mike!" she wailed.

"Is something wrong with Michael?" Grandma asked. "I saw him a little while ago, and he looked fine to me."

"Oh, he's fine all right," Lois ranted. "He's so fine that he's decided to take over the planning of our wedding."

"Isn't that the b–bride's job?" Tabby inquired.

"I thought so, until this evening." Lois blew her nose on a napkin and scowled. She didn't look nearly as beautiful tonight as she had the last time Tabby had seen her. That was the night of Tabby's birthday party. Lois didn't have little rivulets of coal-colored tears streaming down her face then.

"Tell us what happened," Grandma prompted.

Lois looked around the yard anxiously. Her gaze came to rest on her fiancé, sitting with some of his family at another table.

Tabby glanced that way as well. She was surprised when Mike looked over and scowled. At least she thought it was a scowl. Maybe he'd just eaten one of Mom's famous stuffed mushrooms. Tabby didn't know why, but those mushrooms always tasted like they'd been filled with toothpaste instead of cream cheese.

"Mike doesn't want us to get married the first Saturday in October after all," Lois whined, jerking Tabby's thoughts back to the situation at hand.

"He doesn't?" Grandma handed Lois another napkin. "Does he want to call the whole thing off?"

Lois drew in a shuddering breath. "He says not, but I have to wonder. Mike thinks we should have more time to get to know one another before we tie the knot. He wants to postpone the wedding until June, and he waited till tonight to drop the bomb."

"June?" Grandma exclaimed. "Why, that's ten months away!"

"That's not a b–bad idea," Tabby interjected. "I mean, s–sometimes you th–think you know a p–person, and then he g–goes and does something to r–really throw you a c–curve ball."

Grandma and Lois both turned their attention on Tabby. "Are you talking about anyone in particular?" Grandma asked.

Tabby shook her head. "No, n–not r–really." She had no intention of telling them about Seth. They'd never understand the way things were. Besides, they weren't supposed to be talking about her right now. This was Lois's engagement party, and apparently there wasn't going to be a wedding. . .at least not this year. "Do M–Mom and D–Dad know yet?" she asked.

Lois shook her head. "I only found out myself a few minutes ago." She reached for Tabby's hand and gripped it tightly. "What am I going to do?"

Tabby swallowed hard. She could hardly believe that her confident, all-knowing little sister was asking her advice. If only she had the right answers. Thinking back to the devotions she'd done that morning, Tabby quoted the following Scripture: " 'Don't let your hearts be troubled.

Trust in God, and trust also in me.'"

Lois's face was pinched, and her eyes were mere slits. "What on earth are you talking about? Why would I trust in you? What can you do to help my situation?"

Tabby bit back the laughter rising in her throat. Even though she and Lois had both gone to Sunday school when they were children, Lois had never shown much interest in the things of God. In fact, she'd quit going to church when she turned thirteen. "That verse from the book of John is saying you should trust God and not allow your troubles to overtake you. 'Trust in God, and trust also in me.' That was Jesus speaking, and He was telling His followers to trust in Him, as well as in God." Tabby smiled at her sister. "As I'm sure you already know, Jesus and God are one and the same. So, if you put your trust in God, you're trusting Jesus too."

Lois's mouth was hanging wide open, and Grandma was looking at Tabby as though she'd never seen her before.

"What? What's wrong?" Tabby questioned.

"Do you realize you just quoted that Bible verse and gave me a little pep talk without missing a single word? No stuttering, no stammering, nothing," Lois announced. "I think that must be a first, don't you, Grandma?"

Grandma smiled. "I wouldn't say it was a first, because I can remember when Tabby was a little girl and didn't have a problem with stuttering." She reached over and gave Tabby's hand a gentle pat. "I think it's safe to say when Tabby feels convicted about something, she forgets her insecurities, so her words flow uninterrupted."

Tabby wasn't sure how to respond to Grandma's comment, but she never had a chance to, because Lois cut right in. "Well, be that as it may, it doesn't solve my problem with Mike. How am I going to convince him to marry me in two months? I'll just die if I have to wait until next summer."

Grandma's hand made an arc as it left Tabby's and landed on Lois's. "Everything will work out, dear. Just do as Tabby says, and put your trust in the Lord."

Tabby looked over at her grandmother, and her heart swelled with love. If Grandma was beginning to believe, maybe there was some hope for the rest of the family. With more prayer and reliance on God, there might even be some hope for her. Perhaps she just needed to trust the Lord a bit more.

Chapter Eighteen

When rain started falling around eight o'clock, everyone went inside. Tabby decided to head for home, knowing the roads would probably be bad. Besides, she was anxious to be by herself. This had been some evening. First, her parents' little put-downs, then the news that Lois wasn't getting married in October, followed by that special time she, Grandma, and Lois had shared. For a few brief moments, Tabby had felt lifted out of her problems and experienced a sense of joy by offering support to her sister. If only Lois hadn't ended up throwing a temper tantrum right before the party ended. She and Mike had spent most of the evening arguing, and when they weren't quarreling, Lois was crying. Tabby couldn't help but feel sorry for her.

"No matter when the wedding is, you can keep the automatic two-cup coffeemaker I gave you tonight," Tabby told Lois just before she left. She said goodbye to the rest of the family and climbed into her car. It had been a long week, and she'd be so glad to get home and into bed. Maybe some reading in the Psalms would help too. Despite his troubles, David had a way of searching his soul and looking to God for all the answers to his problems and frustrations. Tabby needed that daily reminder as well.

The freeway was still crowded, though it was not quite as bad as it had been earlier. To make matters worse, the rain was coming down so hard Tabby could barely see out her windshield. She gripped the steering wheel with determination and prayed for all she was worth.

By the time Tabby reached the Lakewood exit, she'd had enough. She turned on her right blinker and signaled to get off. Traveling the back roads through Lakewood, Fircrest, then into Tacoma would be easier than trying to navigate the freeway traffic and torrential rains. At least she could travel at a more leisurely pace, and she'd be able to pull off the road if necessary.

Tabby clicked on her car radio as she headed down the old highway. The local Christian station was playing a song by a new female artist. The words played over and over in Tabby's head. *"Jesus is your strength, give to Him your all. . . . Jesus wants your talents, please listen to His call. . . ."*

The lyrical tune soothed Tabby's soul and made her think about Seth again. For weeks he'd been telling her to use her talents for the Lord. "That's because he's trying to change me," she murmured. "Seth's more concerned about finding the perfect woman than he is about me using my talents for God."

Even as she said the words, Tabby wondered if they were true. Maybe Seth really did care about her. It could be that he only wanted her to succeed as a ventriloquist so she could serve the Lord better.

"But I am serving the Lord," Tabby moaned. "I bake cookies for shut-ins, take my turn in the church nursery, teach the day care kids about Jesus, tithe regularly, and pray for the missionaries. Shouldn't that be enough?"

As Tabby mulled all this over, she noticed the car in front of her begin to swerve. Was the driver of the small white vehicle drunk, or was it merely the slick road causing the problem? *Maybe the man or woman is driving too fast for these hazardous conditions,* she reasoned. Tabby eased up on the gas pedal, keeping a safe distance from the car ahead. If the driver decided to slam on his brakes unexpectedly, she wanted plenty of room to stop.

She was on a long stretch of road now, with no houses or places of business nearby. Only giant fir trees and bushy shrubs dotted the edge of the highway. The vehicle ahead was still swerving, and just as it rounded the next corner, the unthinkable happened. The little car lurched, spun around twice, then headed straight for an embankment. Tabby let out a piercing scream as she watched it disappear over the hill.

Tapping her brakes lightly so they wouldn't lock, Tabby pulled to the side of the road. Her heart was thumping so hard she thought it might burst, and her palms were so sweaty she could barely open the car door. Stepping out into the rain, Tabby prayed, "Oh Lord, please let the passengers in that car be okay."

Tabby stood on the edge of the muddy embankment, gazing at the gully below. She could see the white car, flipped upside down. She glanced up at the sky. Tree branches swayed overhead in a crazy green blur, mixed with pelting raindrops. She took a guarded step forward; then with no thought for her own safety, she scrambled down the hill, slipping and sliding with each step. Unmindful of the navy blue flats she wore on her feet or the fact that her long denim skirt was getting splattered with mud, she inched her way toward the overturned vehicle.

When she reached the site of the accident, Tabby noticed the wheels of the car were still spinning, and one tire had the rubber ripped away. Apparently there had been a blowout, which would account for the car's sudden swerving.

Tabby dashed to the driver's side. The window was broken, and she could see a young woman with short brown hair lying on her stomach across the upside-down steering wheel. There was only a few inches between her head and the roof of the car. She could see from the rise and fall of the woman's back that she was breathing, but her eyes were closed, and she didn't respond when Tabby called out to her.

A pathetic whine drew Tabby's attention to the backseat. A young child, also on her stomach, called, "Mommy. . . Mommy, help me!"

Tabby's brain felt fuzzy, and her legs were weak and rubbery. She had no idea how to help the woman or her child. She certainly wouldn't be able to get them out by herself, and even if she could, she knew from the recent CPR training she'd taken, it wasn't a good idea to move an accident victim who might have serious injuries. What this woman and child needed was professional help. She'd have to go back to the car and call 911 on her cell phone. If only she'd thought to grab it before she made her spontaneous descent.

"D–don't be afraid, little g–girl," Tabby called to the child. "I'm g–going to my c–car and c–call for help. I'll b–be right b–back."

The blond-haired girl, who appeared to be about five years old, began to sob. "I don't know you, and you talk funny. Go away!"

A feeling of frustration, mixed with icy fingers of fear, held Tabby in its grip. She hated to leave but knew she had to. "I'll b–be right b–back," she promised.

As she scrambled up the hill, Tabby could still hear the child's panicked screams. They tore at her heart and made her move as quickly as possible. By the time she reached her car, Tabby was panting, and her fears were mounting. What if the car was leaking gas? What if it caught on fire and she couldn't get the passengers out in time? The stark terror that had inched its way into her head was now fully in control. She felt paralyzed of both body and mind.

She offered up another quick prayer and slid into the car, then reached into the glove box for her cell phone. With trembling fingers, she dialed 911. When an operator came on, Tabby stuttered and stammered so badly the woman had to ask her to repeat the information several times. Tabby was finally assured that help was on the way and was instructed to go back to the car and try to keep the occupants calm.

How in the world am I going to do that? she wondered. *The little girl didn't even want to talk to me.*

Suddenly, Tabby remembered Rosie, who was in the backseat. She'd taken the dummy to work that day, in order to put on a short routine for the day care kids. *Maybe the child will feel less threatened talking to Rosie than she would me.*

Tabby reached over the seat and grabbed the dummy. "Well, Rosie, you're really gonna be put to the test this time."

Back down the hill she went, feeling the squish of mud as it seeped inside her soft leather shoes and worked its way down to her toes. Her clothes were drenched, and her soggy hair hung limply on her shoulders. In the process of her descent, Tabby fell twice. The second time, Rosie flipped out of her arms and landed with a thud on an uprooted tree. Tabby picked her up, only to discover that Rosie's face was dirty and scratched, her head had come loose, and the control stick was jammed. Not only would Rosie's slot-jaw mouth no longer move, but the poor dummy looked a mess!

"Now what am I going to do?" Tabby lamented. "Rosie was my only hope of reaching that child."

"I can do everything through Christ, who gives me strength." The scripture verse that popped into Tabby's mind offered some comfort and hope. She closed her eyes briefly and pictured the Lord gathering her into His strong arms. He loved her. He cared about her, as well as the two accident victims

in that car down there. With His help, Tabby would step boldly out of her shell and serve Him in whatever way He showed her. She could do all things, because of His strength.

"Lord, I really do need Your strength right now. Please calm my heart and let me speak without stuttering, so I can help the little girl not be so afraid."

When Tabby hurried to the car, the child was still crying. She knelt next to the open window and turned Rosie upside down, hoping the sight of the small dummy might make the girl feel better. "This is my friend, Rosie. She wants to be your friend too," Tabby said softly. "Can you tell me your name, sweetie?"

The child turned her head slightly, and her lips parted in a faint smile. "It's Katie, and I'm almost six."

Tabby released the breath she'd been holding. Progress. They were making a little bit of progress. "Rosie's been hurt, so she can't talk right now," she said. "Why don't the two of us talk, though? Rosie can just listen."

Katie squinted her blue eyes, but finally nodded. "Okay."

Tabby's confidence was being handed over to her. She could feel it. She hadn't expected such a dramatic answer to her prayer, but the doors of timidity were finally swinging open. *Thank You, Lord.* Tabby tipped her head to one side and leaned closer to the window. Now Rosie's head was poking partway in. "Are you hurting anywhere?" she asked Katie.

"My arm's bleedin', and my head kinda hurts," the child said, her blue eyes filling with fresh tears.

"I used my cell phone to call for help," Tabby explained. "The paramedics should be here soon. Then they'll help you and your mommy get out of the car."

Katie choked on a sob. "Mommy won't wake up. I keep callin' her, but she don't answer."

Tabby wasn't sure how to respond. Even though Katie's mom was breathing, she could still be seriously hurt. She might even die. Katie had good reason to be scared.

"Listen, honey," she said with assurance, "I've been praying for you and your mommy. The Lord is here with us, and help is on the way. Let's talk about other things for now, okay?"

Katie nodded, but tears kept streaming from her eyes. It tore at Tabby's heartstrings, but she was thankful the child was willing to talk to her now. She was also grateful for answered prayer. Since she'd returned to the battered car, she hadn't stuttered even once.

"What's your last name, Katie?"

There was a long pause, then finally Katie smiled and said, "It's Duncan. My name's Katie Duncan."

"What's your mommy's name?"

"Mommy."

In spite of the stressful circumstances, Tabby had to bite back the laughter bubbling in her throat. Children were so precious. That's why she loved working with the kids at the day care. She'd probably never marry and have children of her own, and being around those little ones helped fill a void in her heart.

"I have a dolly too, but she's not half as big as yours," Katie said, looking at Rosie.

Tabby chuckled. "Rosie's a ventriloquist dummy. Do you know what that means?"

Katie shook her head.

"She's kind of like a big puppet. I make her talk by pulling a lever inside her body."

"Can you make her talk right now?"

Tabby sucked in her bottom lip. "Rosie's control stick broke when she fell down the hill."

Katie's chin began to quiver, as a fresh set of tears started to seep from her eyes.

"I suppose I could make her talk," Tabby said quickly. "Her mouth won't move, though. Could you pretend Rosie's mouth is moving?"

"Uh-huh. I like to pretend. Mommy and I do pretend tea parties."

"That's good. I like to play make-believe too." Tabby tipped Rosie's head, so Katie could see her better. Using her childlike ventriloquist voice, she said, "I'm Rosie Right, and I'm always right." *Now what made me say that? That's the line Seth always uses with his dummy, Rudy.*

"Nobody but God is always right. Mommy said so," Katie remarked.

Tabby nodded. "Your mommy's right. Rosie's just a puppet. She can't always be right, and neither can people. Only God has all the answers."

"Do you go to school, Rosie?" Katie asked the dummy.

"Sometimes I go to day care," Rosie answered. "Tabby works there."

The next few minutes were spent in friendly banter between Rosie, Tabby, and Katie. Tabby was glad she could keep the child's mind off the accident and her unconscious mother in the front seat, but when a low moan escaped the woman's lips, Tabby froze. Now she had two people to try to keep calm.

Chapter Nineteen

"Oh! Oh! I can't breathe," Katie's mother moaned. "My seat belt. . .it's too tight."

Tabby pulled Rosie quickly away from the window and placed one hand on the woman's outstretched arm. "Please, try to remain calm."

The woman moaned again. "Who are you?"

"I'm Tabitha Johnson. I was in the car behind you, and I saw your car swerve, then run off the road. You ended up going over the embankment, and now the car's upside down."

"My name is Rachel Duncan, and I need to get this seat belt off. Do you have a knife?"

Tabby shook her head. "That's not a good idea. If we cut the belt loose, your head will hit the roof, and that might cause serious damage if there's a neck injury."

Rachel's eyelids closed, and she groaned. "Katie. . .Where's Katie?"

"Your little girl is still in the backseat," Tabby answered. "We've been visiting while we wait for the paramedics."

"Mommy, Mommy, I'm here!" Katie called.

Rachel's eyes shot open. "I'm so sorry about this, Katie. Mommy doesn't know what happened."

"From the looks of your right front tire, I'd say you had a blowout," Tabby said.

Rachel's swollen lips emitted a shuddering sob. "I told Rick we needed to buy a new set of tires."

"Rick?"

"Rick's my husband. He had to work late tonight, so Katie and I went to a movie in Lakewood. We were on our way home when it started raining really hard." She grimaced. "I hope someone gets us out of here real soon. I don't think I can stand being in this position much longer."

"Are you in pain?" Tabby asked with concern.

"My left leg feels like it might be broken, and my head's pounding something awful."

"Would you mind if I prayed for you?" Tabby didn't know where she'd gotten the courage to ask that question. It wasn't like her to be so bold.

"I'd really appreciate the prayer," Rachel answered. Tears were coursing from her eyes, but she offered Tabby a weak smile. "I'm a Christian, I know how much prayer can help."

Tabby placed Rosie on the ground and leaned in as far as she could. "Heavenly Father," she prayed, "Rachel and Katie are in pain and need medical attention as soon as possible. I'm asking You to bring the paramedics here quickly. Please give them both a sense of peace and awareness that You are right here beside them."

Tabby had just said "amen" when she heard the piercing whine of sirens in the distance. "That must be the rescue vehicles," she told Rachel. "I think I should go back up the hill to be sure they know where we are. Will you be all right for a few minutes?"

"Jesus is with us," Katie squeaked.

"Yes, He's by our side," Rachel agreed.

"All right then, I'll be back as quick as I can." Tabby pulled away from the window and started up the hill as fast as she could, thankful the rain had finally eased up.

A police car, a fire truck, and the paramedics' rig were pulling off the road by her car when she came over the hill. Gasping for breath, she dashed over to one of the firemen. "There's a car down there," she panted, pointing to the ravine. "It's upside down, and there's a woman and a little girl trapped inside."

"Could you tell if they were seriously injured?" one of the paramedics asked as he stepped up beside her.

"Rachel—she's the mother—said her head hurt real bad, and she thinks her leg might be broken. Katie's only five, and she complained of her head hurting too. She also said her arm was bleeding."

He nodded, then turned to his partner. "Let's grab our gear and get down there."

The rescue squad descended the hill much faster than Tabby had, but she figured they'd had a good deal more practice doing this kind of thing.

Tabby followed, keeping a safe distance once they were at the scene of the accident. She did move in to grab Rosie when a fireman stepped on one of the dummy's hands. Poor dirty Rosie had enough injuries to keep her in Seth's shop for at least a month. Right now Tabby's concerns were for Rachel and her precious daughter, though. She kept watching and praying as the rescuers struggled to free the trapped victims.

When they finally had Rachel and Katie loaded into the ambulance, Tabby breathed a sigh of relief. The paramedics said it didn't appear as though either of them had any life-threatening injuries, although there would be tests done at the hospital. Before the ambulance pulled away, Tabby promised Rachel she would call her husband and let him know what happened.

One of the policemen, who identified himself as Officer Jensen, asked Tabby a series of questions about the accident, since she'd been the only witness.

"You are one special young lady," the officer said. "Not only did you call for help, but you stayed to comfort that woman and her daughter." He glanced down at the bedraggled dummy Tabby was holding. "From the looks of your little friend, I'd say you went the extra mile, using your talent in a time of need."

Tabby smiled, although she felt like crying. For the first time in a long while, she'd forgotten her fears and self-consciousness, allowing God to speak through her in a way she never thought possible. Throughout the entire ordeal, she'd never stuttered once. It seemed like a miracle—one she hoped would last forever. Up until now, she believed that unless her family treated her with love and respect, she could never become confident. How wrong she'd been. How grateful to God she felt now.

When Tabby got into her car, she reached for the cell phone and called Rick Duncan at the number Rachel had given her. He was shocked to hear about the accident but thankful Tabby had called. He told her he'd leave work right away and head straight for Tacoma General Hospital. Tabby could finally go home, knowing Rachel, Katie, and Rick were in God's hands.

Tabby awoke the following morning feeling as though she'd run a ten-mile marathon and hadn't been in shape for it. The emotional impact of the night before hit her hard. If she could get through something so frightening, she was sure the Lord would see her through anything—even dealing with her unfeeling parents and self-centered sister. Instead of shying away from family gatherings or letting someone's harsh words cut her to the quick, Tabby's plan was to stand behind the Lord's shield of protection. She could do all things through Him, and as soon as she had some breakfast, she planned to phone Tacoma General Hospital and check on Rachel's and Katie's conditions. Then her next order of business would be to visit Beyers' Ventriloquist Studio.

Seth had dialed Tabby's phone number four times in the last fifteen minutes, and it was always busy. "Who is on the phone, and who could she be talking to?" he muttered. "Maybe I should get in my car and drive on over there."

Seth figured Tabby was still mad at him, and he wondered if she'd even let him into her apartment. Well, he didn't care if she was mad. He'd made up his mind to see her today.

Seth left the red-nosed clown dummy he'd been working on and walked into the main part of his shop just as the bell on the front door jingled. In walked Cheryl Stone.

"Good morning, Seth," she purred. "How are you today?"

Seth's heart sank. The blue-eyed woman staring up at him with a hopeful smile was not the person he most wanted to see. "Hi, Cheryl. What brings you here this morning?"

"Does there have to be a reason?" Cheryl tipped her head to one side and offered him another coquettish smile.

Seth felt the force of her softly spoken words like a blow to the stomach. Cheryl was obviously interested in him. "Most people don't come to my shop without a good reason," he mumbled. "Are you having a problem with Oscar again?"

Cheryl gave the ends of her long red hair a little flick and moved slowly toward Seth. "Actually, I'm not here about either one of my dummies."

Seth swallowed hard and took a few steps back. *Now here's a perfect woman. She's talented, confident, poised, and beautiful. How come I don't go after her?* He groaned inwardly. *I'm in love with Tabby Johnson that's why.* There was no denying it, either. Shy, stuttering Tabitha, with eyes that reminded him of a wounded deer, had stolen his heart, and he'd been powerless to stop it.

With determination, Seth pulled his thoughts away from Tabby and onto the matter at hand. "Why are you here, Cheryl?"

"I've been asked to be part of a talent contest sponsored by Valley Foods. My father works in the corporate office there," Cheryl explained.

"What's that got to do with me?"

"I was hoping you'd be willing to give me a few extra lessons." She giggled. "I know I'm already a good ventriloquist, but I think you're about the best around. Some more helpful tips from you might help me win that contest."

Seth cleared his throat, hoping to stall for time. At least long enough so he could come up with some legitimate excuse for not helping Cheryl. He had an inkling she had a bit more in mind than just ventriloquist lessons.

His suspicions were confirmed when she stepped forward and threw her arms around his neck. The smell of apricot shampoo filled his nostrils, as a wisp of her soft red hair brushed against his cheek.

"Please say you'll do this for me, Seth," Cheryl pleaded. "Pretty please. . . with sugar and spice. . .now don't make me ask twice."

Seth moaned. Cheryl was mere inches from his face now, but all he could think about was Tabby. He opened his mouth to give Cheryl his answer, when the bell on the door jingled. Over the top of Cheryl's head, he saw the door swing wide open.

It was Tabitha Johnson.

Chapter Twenty

Seth expected Tabby to turn around and run out the door once she saw Cheryl in his arms. She didn't, though. Instead, she marched up to the counter and plunked her dummy down. "I'm sorry to interrupt," she said in a voice filled with surprising confidence, "but I need you to take a look at Rosie. Do you think you can spare a few minutes, Seth?"

Seth reached up to pull Cheryl's arms away from his neck. He was guilty of nothing, yet he felt like a kid who'd been caught with his hand inside a candy dish. He could only imagine what Tabby must be thinking, walking in and seeing what looked like a romantic interlude between him and Cheryl.

He studied Tabby for a few seconds. She looked different today—cute and kind of spunky. Her hair was curled too, and it didn't hang in her face the way it usually did. Her blue jeans and yellow T-shirt were neatly pressed, and she stood straighter than normal.

"Do you have time to look at Rosie or not?" Tabby asked again.

Seth nodded, feeling as if he were in a daze. Tabby wasn't even stuttering. What happened to Timid Tabitha with the doe eyes? He glanced down at Cheryl and noticed she was frowning. "Excuse me, but I have to take care of business," he said, hoping she'd get the hint and leave.

Cheryl planted both hands on her slim hips and whirled around to face Tabby. "Can't you see that Seth and I are busy?"

"I'll only keep Seth a few minutes; then he's all yours," Tabby said through tight lips.

A muscle in Seth's jaw twitched. "I'll call you later, Cheryl," he said, turning toward the counter where the dummy lay.

"Yeah, okay," Cheryl mumbled.

When he heard the door close, Seth heaved a sigh of relief. At least one problem had been resolved.

Tabby was trembling inwardly, but outwardly she was holding up quite well—thanks to the Lord and the prayer she'd uttered when she first walked into Seth's shop. Seeing Cheryl Stone in Seth's arms had nearly been her undoing. Only God's grace kept her from retreating into her old shell and allowing her tongue to run wild with a bunch of stuttering and stammering. It still amazed her that ever since the car accident last night she hadn't stuttered once. God really had changed her life.

"What in the world happened to Rosie?" Seth asked, breaking into Tabby's thoughts. "She looks like she got roped into a game of mud wrestling. I'd say she came out on the losing end of things."

Tabby snickered. "It was something like that." Then, feeling the need to talk about what happened last night, she opened up and shared the entire story of the accident she'd witnessed.

Seth listened intently as he examined the dummy. When Tabby finished talking, he looked up from his work and groaned softly. "I'm sure thankful you're okay. You were smart to keep a safe distance from that car when it began to swerve. It could have been your little hatchback rolling down the hill."

Tabby swallowed hard. Was Seth really concerned about her welfare? Was that frown he wore proof of his anxiety?

"Now about Rosie. . . ," Seth said, pulling her back to the immediate need.

"How bad is the damage? Will Rosie ever talk again?"

Seth's green eyes met Tabby's with a gaze that bore straight into her soul. "She will if you want her to."

Tabby blinked. "Of course I do. Why wouldn't I?"

Seth cleared his throat a few times, as though searching for the right words. "After that program at the crusade, you didn't seem any too anxious to continue using your ventriloquistic talents."

She nodded. "You're right about that, but since last night I'm seeing things in a whole new light."

He raised his eyebrows. "You are? In what way?"

"For one thing, God showed me that I don't have to be afraid of people or circumstances which might seem a bit unusual or disturbing," she explained. "I was really scared when that car went over the embankment. When I found Rachel and her daughter trapped inside their overturned vehicle, I nearly panicked." Tabby drew in a deep breath and squeezed her lips together. "Little Katie wouldn't even respond to me at first. I was stuttering so much I scared her. Then I thought about Rosie in the backseat of my car, and I climbed back up the hill to get her."

Seth nodded. "Kids will react to a dummy much quicker than they will an adult." He smiled. "Guess we're a bit too intimidating."

"I dropped Rosie on the way down the hill, and by the time I got to the wreck, I realized her mouth control was broken." Tabby shrugged. "I had to talk on my own, and I asked God to help me do it without stuttering. I wanted Katie to be able to understand every word, so she wouldn't be afraid."

"So poor Rosie took a trip down the muddy incline for nothing?" Seth asked, giving the dummy's head a few taps with his knuckle.

Tabby shook her head. "Not really. After Katie and I talked awhile, I began to gain her confidence. Then I put Rosie up to the window and made her talk, without even moving her lips."

Seth tipped his head back and roared.

"What's so funny?"

"If Rosie's lips weren't moving, then who was the ventriloquist, and who was the dummy?"

Tabby giggled and reached out to poke Seth playfully in the ribs. "Ha! Very funny!" She wiggled her nose. "I'll have you know, Mr. Beyers, my dummy is so talented, she can talk for two without moving her lips!"

Seth grinned, and his eyes sparkled mischievously. "And you, Miss Tabitha Johnson, are speaking quite well on your own today."

Tabby felt herself blush. "I haven't stuttered once since last night." She placed her palms against her burning cheeks. "God gave me confidence I never thought I would have, and I'm so grateful."

"I think it was because you finally put yourself fully in His hands."

Tabby was tempted to ask Seth if he thought she was worthy of his love now. After all, he'd wanted her to change. Instead of voicing her thoughts, she nodded toward Rosie. "Is there any hope for her?"

Seth scratched the back of his head and smiled. "I think with a little help from some of my tools and a new coat of paint, Rosie will be up and around in no time at all."

Tabby smiled gratefully, but then she sobered. "Will the repairs be expensive?"

Seth winked, and she pressed a hand to a heart that was beating much too fast.

"Let's see now. . . The price for parts will be reimbursed with two or three dinners out, and labor. . .well, I'm sure we can work something out for that as well," Seth said, never taking his gaze off her. "Something that will be agreeable to both of us." He moved slowly toward her, with both arms extended.

Tabby had an overwhelming desire to rush into those strong arms and declare her undying love, but she held herself in check, remembering the little scene she'd encountered when she first entered Seth's shop. It was obvious that Seth had more than a business relationship with Cheryl.

Seth kept moving closer, until she could feel his warm breath on her upturned face. She trembled, and her eyelids drifted shut. Tabby knew she shouldn't let Seth kiss her—not when he was seeing someone else. Her heart said something entirely different, though, and it was with her whole heart that Tabby offered her lips willingly to Seth's inviting kiss.

Tabby relished the warmth of Seth's embrace, until the sharp ringing of the telephone pulled them apart.

"Uh, guess I'd better get that," Seth mumbled. He stepped away from Tabby and moved across the room toward the desk where the phone sat.

Tabby looked down at Rosie and muttered, "I think I was just saved by the bell."

∞

As Seth answered the phone, his thoughts were focused on Tabby. He'd wanted to hold her longer and tell her everything that was tumbling around in his mind. He needed to express his feelings about the way he'd treated her in the past and share the scriptures the Lord had shown him. Maybe they'd be able to pick up where they left off when he hung up the phone. Maybe. . .

"Seth Beyers," he said numbly into the receiver. "Huh? Oh, yeah, I'd be happy to take a look at your dummy. I'm about to close shop for the day, but you can bring it by on Monday."

Relieved to be off the phone, Seth returned to Tabby. She was standing over Rosie, looking as though she'd lost her best friend. "She'll be okay, I promise," he said, reaching out to pull Tabby into his arms. He leaned over and placed a kiss on her forehead. Her hair felt feathery soft against his lips, and it smelled like sunshine.

She pulled sharply away, taking him by surprise. She'd seemed willing a few minutes ago. What had happened in the space of a few minutes to make her so cold?

"How long till she's done?" Tabby asked.

"I could probably get her ready to go home in about a week. How's that sound?"

She shrugged. "That'll be fine, I guess." She turned and started for the door.

"Hey, where are you going?" he called after her.

"Home. I left the apartment before Donna got up, and since I came home so late last night, I promised to fill her in on the accident details this morning."

Seth rushed to her side. "Don't tell me I'll be taking the day off for nothing."

She blinked several times. "I don't get it. What's your taking the day off got to do with me?"

"I'd really like to spend the day with you. That is, if you're not tied up."

"I just told you. . ."

"I know. You want to tell Donna about last night." Seth grabbed Tabby's arm and pulled her to his side again. "Can't that wait awhile? We have some important things to discuss, and I thought we could do it at the park."

"Point Defiance?"

He nodded.

Tabby hung her head. He knew she was weakening, because she'd told him before how much she loved going to Point Defiance Park.

"Wouldn't that be kind of like a date?" she murmured.

He laughed. "Not kind of, Tabby. . .it is a date."

"Oh. Well, I guess my answer has to be no."

His forehead creased. "Why, for goodness' sake? Are you still mad at me for coercing you into doing that vent routine?"

She shook her head. "No, I've done what the Bible says and forgiven you. Besides, what happened at the crusade was really my own fault. I could have said no when you asked me to perform. I could have prayed more and allowed God to speak through me, instead of letting myself get all tied up in knots, and ending up making my routine and me look completely ridiculous."

Seth gently touched her arm. "Neither you nor your routine was ridiculous, Tabby." He chewed on his lower lip, praying silently for the right words to express his true feelings. "Tabby, you're not the only one God's been working on lately."

"What do you mean?"

"Through the scriptures, He's showed me that I've been expecting too much. I wanted the perfect woman. . .one who'd fit into my preconceived mold. I thought I needed someone who would radiate with confidence and who'd have the same burning desire I do to share her talents with others by telling them about the Savior."

Tabby nodded. "I was pretty sure you felt that way, and I really couldn't blame you, but it did make me mad. I knew I could never be that perfect woman, so I was angry at you, myself, and even God."

Tears welled up in her dark eyes, and when they ran down her cheeks, Seth reached up to wipe them away with his thumb. "You don't have to be the perfect woman, Tabby. Not for me or anyone else. All God wants is for us to give Him our best." He kneaded the back of his neck, trying to work out the kinks. "I tried to call you last night. I wanted to tell you what God had revealed to me. I was planning to tell you that it didn't matter if you stuttered, had no confidence, or never did ventriloquism again. I just wanted you to know that I love you, and I accept you for the person you are. . .one full of love and compassion."

"Love?" Tabby looked up at him with questioning eyes.

He nodded. "I know we haven't known each other very long, but I really do love you, Tabby."

"But what about Cheryl Stone?"

His brows furrowed. "What about her?"

"After seeing the two of you together, I thought—"

"That we were in love?"

She only nodded in response.

Seth's lips curved into a smile, then he let out a loud whoop.

"What was that for?"

"I don't love Cheryl," Seth said sincerely. He dropped to one knee. "This might seem kind of sudden, and if you need time to think about it, I'll understand." He smiled up at her. "If you wouldn't mind being married to a dummy, I'd sure be honored to make you my wife. After we've had a bit more time to go on a few more dates and get better acquainted," he quickly added.

Tabby trembled slightly. "You—you w–want to marry me?"

Seth reached for her hand and kissed the palm of it. "You're stuttering again. I think maybe I'm a bad influence on you."

She blushed. "I'm just so surprised."

"That I could love you, or that I'd want to marry you?"

"Both." Tabby smiled through her tears. "I love you so much, Seth. I never thought I could be this happy."

"Is that a yes?" he asked hopefully.

She nodded as he stood up again. "Yes! Yes! A thousand times, yes!"

"How about a December wedding? Or is that too soon?"

"December? Why that month?"

"I can't think of a better Christmas present to give myself than you," he said.

She sighed deeply and leaned against his chest. "That only gives us four months to plan a wedding. Do you think we can choose our colors, pick out invitations, order a cake, and get everything else done by then?"

A dimple creased her cheek when he kissed it. "I'm sure we can." There was a long pause, then he whispered, "There is one little thing, though."

"What's that?"

"I don't want our wedding cake to have peanut butter filling."

Tabby pulled back and gave him a curious look.

"My peanut butter phobia, remember?"

She giggled. "Oh, yes. Now how could I forget something so important?"

Seth bent down and kissed her full on the mouth. When the kiss ended, he grinned.

"What?"

"I must be the most blessed man alive."

"Why's that?"

"If a man is lucky, he finds a wife who can communicate her needs to him. Me. . .well, I'll always know what my wife needs, because she can talk for two." He winked at her. "Now that we've had our little talk, do you still want to go to the park?"

She smiled. "Of course I do. I can't think of a better place for us to start making plans for our future."

Epilogue

Tabby had never been more nervous, yet she'd never felt such a sense of peace before. Next to the day she opened her heart to Christ, today was the most important day in her life.

Much to her sister's disappointment, Tabby had beaten her to the marriage altar. Tabby took no pleasure in this fact, but it did feel pretty wonderful to be married to the man she loved. Lois would find the same joy when it was her turn to walk down the aisle. By then, maybe she'd even be a Christian.

Tabby glanced at her younger sister, sitting beside Mike and her parents at a table near the front of the room. Thanks to Tabby's gentle prodding, Lois had recently started going to church. Now if they could just get her fiancé to attend.

The wedding reception was in full swing, and Tabby and Seth were about to do a joint ventriloquist routine. It was the first time she'd ever done ventriloquism in front of her family. Tabby gazed into her groom's sea-green eyes and smiled. If someone had told her a year ago she'd be standing in front of more than a hundred people, married to a terrific guy like Seth, she'd never have believed them. It still amazed her that she no longer stuttered or was hampered by her shyness. God was so good, and she was glad for the opportunity to serve Him with her new talent.

She felt the warmth of Seth's hand as he placed Rosie into her arms. He probably knew she was a bit nervous about this particular performance. He bent down and pulled Rudy from the trunk. With a reassuring smile, he quickly launched into their routine.

"How do you feel about me being a married man?" Seth asked his dummy.

Rudy's head swiveled toward Tabby. "I can see why you married her, but what's she doin' with a guy like you?"

153

Before Seth could respond, Rosie piped up with, "Don't talk about Seth that way, Rudy. I think he's real sweet."

"I think so too," Tabby put in.

Rudy snorted. "He's not nearly as sweet as me." The dummy's head moved closer to Tabby. "How 'bout a little kiss to celebrate your wedding day?"

Tabby wiggled her eyebrows up and down. "Well. . ."

"Now, Rudy, what makes you think my wife would want to kiss a dummy?"

Rudy's wooden head snapped back to face Seth. "She kisses you, doesn't she?"

The audience roared, and Tabby felt herself begin to relax. Even Dad was laughing, and Mom was looking at her as though she was the most special person in the whole world. Maybe she wasn't such a disappointment to them after all. Maybe her newfound confidence could even help win her parents to the Lord.

"You know, Seth," Rudy drawled, "I hear tell that once a man ties the knot, his life is never the same."

"In what way?" Seth asked.

"Yeah, in what way?" Rosie echoed.

Rudy's eyes moved from side to side. "For one thing, some women talk too much. What if Tabby starts speaking for you, now that you're married?"

Tabby leaned over and planted a kiss on Rudy's cheek, then did the same to Seth. "Yep," she quipped, "from now on, I'll definitely be talking for two!"

Clowning Around

To Gordon, Kathy, Dell, and Bev—
special friends who are great at clowning around.

Chapter One

Lois Johnson slid her fingers across the polished surface of her desktop. *I love this job* she told herself with a smile. She had been working as secretary for Bayview Christian Church only a few weeks, but she already felt at ease. She wasn't making as much money now, she reminded herself, but she had a lot less pressure than when she'd worked as a legal secretary in downtown Tacoma.

Lois hoped her job here would be a ministry, so she could do something meaningful while using her secretarial skills. She was a fairly new Christian, having accepted the Lord as her personal Savior during a recent evangelistic crusade. Now she had an opportunity to work in her home church where she felt comfortable.

Her older sister, Tabby, had told her about the position. Tabby worked in the day care center sponsored by Bayview Church and had heard that Mildred Thompson, the secretary then, was moving to California. Tabby had notified Lois right away, knowing she wasn't happy in her old job.

A vision of Tabby and her husband, Seth Beyers, performing their ventriloquist routine flashed into Lois's mind. The young couple worked well together, shared a love for Christ and the church, and were so much in love.

Lois stared at the blank computer screen in front of her then pushed the button to turn it on. *I hope I can find an area of service as Tabby and Seth have.* After attending the church for a year, she had signed up to teach a first-grade Sunday school class. She enjoyed working with children and felt she was helping to mold their young lives in some small way. But she wondered if she could be doing more.

As Lois waited for the computer to boot up, she let her mind wander. She'd come a long way in the last few months. The pain of breaking up with her ex-fiancé had diminished considerably. Since she'd become a

Christian and started reading her Bible every day and spending time in prayer, her attitude toward many things had changed. No longer was she consumed with a desire for wealth and prestige. She knew money in itself wasn't a bad thing, but her yearning for more, simply for personal gain, had been wrong. Instead of being so self-centered and harsh—especially with her sister, who had been shy and had suffered with a problem of stuttering—with God's help, Lois was learning to be more patient and kind.

Thank You, Lord, for helping Tabby overcome her problems and for changing my heart. Show me the best way to serve You. She hesitated. *And if You have a man out there for me, please let me know he's the right one.*

Lois frowned and twirled her finger around a long, blond curl. She'd been wounded deeply when Michael Yehley postponed their wedding. Then he broke things off completely once she started inviting him to go with her to church. He'd made it clear he had no interest in religious things, didn't need them, and could take care of himself.

Lois knew Michael hadn't been right for her. She also knew she could never love another man who wasn't a Christian or whose only goal in life was climbing the ladder of success. *Lord, if You have a man in mind for me, then he'll have to fall into my lap because I'm not planning to look for anyone. The chances of that are slim to none,* Lois told herself.

Joe Richey was exhausted. He'd been on the road six weeks, doing a series of family crusades, Bible schools, and church camp meetings. He'd even managed to squeeze in a couple of kids' birthday parties. As much as he enjoyed clowning, he needed to rest. He'd just finished a five-day Bible school in Aberdeen, Washington, which had ended this morning at eleven o'clock. On his way home, he had stopped at the cemetery to visit his parents' graves. When Joe was eight years old, his father was killed in an accident involving the tour bus he drove around the Pacific Northwest. His mother had passed away last summer from lung cancer.

A knot formed in Joe's stomach when he opened the front door of his modest, two-story home in Olympia. When his mother died, he hadn't shed a single tear, and he wasn't about to cry now. In fact, Joe hadn't cried since his father's death almost seventeen years ago. If today hadn't been the anniversary of his mother's death, he probably wouldn't have stopped at the cemetery. It was a painful reminder of his past.

Carrying his red-and-green-checkered clown costume in one hand and a battered suitcase in the other, Joe trudged up the steps to the second floor. He entered his bedroom and flung open the closet door. "Maybe I should take off for a few days and head to the beach," he said aloud, setting the suitcase on the floor and hanging up his costume. "But right now, I guess I'll settle for a hot bath and a long nap."

He yanked a red rubber clown nose out of his shirt pocket and stuffed it into the drawer where all his clown makeup and props were kept. "I'll be okay. Just need to keep a stiff upper lip and a smile plastered on my face." Joe glanced in the mirror attached to his closet door and forced his mouth to curve upward.

The phone rang sharply. He crossed the room and lifted the receiver from the nightstand by his bed. "Joe Richey here."

He listened to the woman on the other end of the line, nodding occasionally and writing the information she gave him on a notepad. "Uh-huh. Sure. My schedule's been as tight as a jar of pickles all summer, but things are slowing down some now. I'm sure I can work it in. Okay, thanks."

Joe hung up the phone and sank onto the bed with a moan. "One more crusade, and then I'll take a little vacation." He glanced over the notes he'd jotted down. "It's only a forty-five-minute drive from Olympia to Tacoma. It'll be a piece of cake."

After discussing the church bulletin with Richard Smith, the associate pastor, Lois returned to her desk, and the phone rang. She smiled when she heard her sister's voice. "Hi, Tabby, what's up?"

"I was wondering if you could meet me for lunch today."

"Sure—sounds good. Should I come downstairs to the day care, or do you want to come up here?"

"Neither. I'd like to take you out for lunch. You've been cooped up in that office so much since you started working here, even eating lunch at your desk sometimes. Today's Friday, so I think we should celebrate. Let's go to Garrison's Deli."

Lois sighed. She didn't feel much like going out, even though the sun was shining brightly on this pleasant summer day and the fresh air would probably do her some good. She preferred to stay at her desk and eat the bag lunch she'd brought, but she didn't want to disappoint Tabby. She'd done plenty of that in the past. Now that Lois was trying to live her faith, she made every attempt to please rather than tease her sister.

"Sure—what time?" Lois asked.

"Donna's taking her lunch break at noon, so how does one o'clock sound?"

"Great. See you then." Lois hung up the phone and grabbed that day's mail. The first letter contained a flyer announcing a special service at another church in the north end of Tacoma. It listed all the people in the program, including Tabby and Seth. Lois noticed the program was a little over a week away, so she decided to make copies of the flyer and insert one into each bulletin to be handed out on Sunday.

By twelve-thirty, Lois had finished the bulletins and was stuffing the flyers inside each one when Sam Hanson, the senior pastor, stepped into her office. "Have you had lunch yet, Lois?" he asked. Sam and his wife, Norma, were always concerned about her.

She shook her head but kept her eyes focused on the work she was doing. "I'm meeting Tabby at Garrison's Deli in half an hour."

"That's good to hear. I was afraid you planned to work through lunch again."

Lois looked up. "Not today."

The pastor smiled. "I'm glad you're taking your position seriously, Lois, but we don't want you to work too hard."

"I'm grateful for the opportunity to work here." Lois smiled too. "I love my new job, and sometimes it's hard to tear myself away."

"Which is precisely why Norma and I think you should get out more," he said. "A lovely young woman like you needs an active social life."

She shrugged. "I do get out. I drive to Olympia to visit my folks at least twice a month."

"That's not quite what we meant."

"I know, but I'm okay, really."

Pastor Hanson nodded. "Anytime you need to talk, though, I'm a good listener. And so is Norma." He winked. "Since my office is right next door, you won't have far to go."

"Thanks, Pastor. I'll keep that in mind."

Lois found Tabby waiting in a booth at the deli. "Sorry I'm a few minutes late," she said, dropping into the seat across from her sister.

Tabby smiled, her dark eyes gleaming. "No problem. I figured you probably had an important phone call or something. I've only been here a few minutes, but I took the liberty of ordering us each a veggie sandwich on whole wheat bread, with cream cheese and lots of alfalfa sprouts."

Lois chuckled. "We may not look much like sisters, but we sure have the same taste in food." She nodded toward the counter. "What did you order us to drink?"

"Strawberry lemonade for you and an iced tea with a slice of lemon for me."

"Umm. Sounds good. An ice-cold lemonade on a hot day like this should hit the spot."

"It is pretty warm," Tabby agreed. "Kind of unusual weather for Tacoma, even if it is still summer."

"I heard on the news that it might reach ninety by the weekend," Lois commented.

Tabby's dark eyebrows raised. "Guess we'd better find a way to cool off then."

Lois drew in a breath. Last year she'd been invited to use the Yehleys' swimming pool on several occasions. It was heated, so even when the weather was cool, the pool was a great place to exercise or simply relax. Lois wouldn't be swimming in Michael's pool this year, though. She didn't care. She could always go to one of the many fitness centers in town or, if she felt brave, take a dip in the chilly waters of Puget Sound Bay. Michael and his parents had no place in her life anymore, and neither did their pool!

"Lois. Earth to Lois."

Lois's eyelids fluttered. "Oh—you were talking to me, and I was daydreaming?"

Tabby laughed. "Something like that."

"What were you saying?"

"I was telling you about the special service Westside Community Church is having a week from Saturday night."

Lois nodded. "I already know. We received a flyer in the mail today."

Tabby frowned. "Kind of late notice, wouldn't you say?"

"That's what I thought, but I made copies and inserted them in the bulletins for this Sunday."

"Seth and I are doing a ventriloquist routine," Tabby said.

"Yes, I saw your names on the flyer."

They heard their order being announced, and Tabby slid out of the booth. "I'll be right back."

"Want some help?" Lois called after her.

"No, thanks. I can manage."

When Tabby returned a few minutes later, Lois offered up a prayer, and they started eating their sandwiches.

"I was hoping you would come to the service at Westside," Tabby said between bites. "You don't go out much anymore, and I thought—"

Lois held up her hand. "You thought you'd apply a little pressure." She clucked her tongue against the roof of her mouth. "You and the Hansons wouldn't be in cahoots, would you?"

Tabby flicked her shoulder-length, chestnut-colored hair away from her face. "Whatever gave you such a notion?"

Lois lifted her gaze toward the ceiling. "I can't imagine."

"I really would like you to come," Tabby said. "Seth and I will do our routine, they'll have a Gospel clown and an illusionist, and Donna's going to do one of her beautiful chalk art drawings." She leaned across the table and studied Lois intently. "If it weren't for a creative illusionist's testimony, you probably wouldn't be where you are today."

Lois narrowed her eyes. "You mean sitting here at Garrison's, drinking strawberry lemonade, and eating a delicious sandwich?"

Tabby grinned. "I meant that you wouldn't be working for our church. For that matter, if you hadn't committed your life to Christ during a crusade, you probably wouldn't be going to church."

"I know."

"So will you come to the program? I always feel better when I look out into the audience and see your beautiful face smiling back at me."

Lois grinned. How could she say no to the most wonderful sister in the world? "I'll be there—right in the front row."

Chapter Two

Joe stood in the small room near the main platform in the sanctuary of Westside Community Church, waiting his turn. He was dressed in a pair of baggy blue jeans, with a matching jacket, decorated with multicolored patches. He wore a bright orange shirt under his jacket, a polka dot tie, and a bright red rubber nose. Attached to his hair was a red yarn wig, and a floppy blue hat perched on top. Black oversized shoes turning up at the toes completed his clown costume.

Joe peeked through the stage door window and saw Seth and Tabby Beyers on stage with their two dummies. He had watched the young couple perform on other programs and knew audiences loved them. Their unusual ventriloquist routine would be hard to follow.

I'm not doing this merely to entertain, Joe reminded himself. *It isn't important whom the audience likes best. What counts is whether we get across the message of salvation and Christian living.* Entertain, but have a positive impact on people's lives—that's what he'd been taught at the Gospel clowning school where he'd received his training several years ago.

Joe reached inside the pocket of his clown suit, and his fingers curled around a stash of balloons. He knew one of the best things in his routine was the balloons he twisted into various animals. After every performance, a group of excited kids would surround him, wanting to talk to the goofy clown and to get a balloon animal.

Joe heard his name being called and grabbed the multicolored duffel bag that held his props. For some reason he felt edgy tonight. He didn't understand it because he had done hundreds of programs like this one. He figured it must be due to fatigue since he'd been on the road so much lately and needed a vacation.

Then "Slow-Joe the Clown" stepped onto the stage. Opening his bag of tricks, he withdrew a huge plastic hammer with a shackle attached. He held the mallet over his head. "I'm all set now to open my own hamburger chain," he announced.

The audience laughed, and Joe moved to the edge of the platform, holding his props toward the spectators. "If my hamburger chain doesn't work out, I'm thinking about raising rabbits." He pursed his lips. "Of course, I'm gonna have to keep 'em indoors, so they'll be ingrown hares."

Everyone laughed again, and Joe winked, dropped the hammer back into the bag, and pulled out a blue balloon. He blew into it, holding the end and stretching the latex as the balloon inflated. Tying a knot, he twisted two small bubbles in the center of the balloon and locked them together in one quick twist. Then he made five bubbles and formed the body of a baby seal. The lowest part of the balloon was the neck, and Joe added another bubble at the top, so the seal looked as if it were balancing a ball on the end of its nose.

Gripping his floppy hat, Joe tipped his head back and balanced the balloon seal on the end of his rubber nose. The crowd roared as he moved slowly about the stage, waving one hand and trying to keep the seal in place. When the seal toppled off, Joe explained how some people try to balance their lives between church, home, and extracurricular activities but don't always succeed.

Then he twisted more balloons into a blue whale, a humpback camel, and a lion with a mane. After each creation, Joe told a Bible story, including one about Daniel in the lions' den.

Next, Joe grabbed five red balls from his bag, tossing them one at a time into the air and juggling them. As he did so, he faced the audience. "I often get busy with my clowning schedule and have to juggle my time a bit. But I always feel closer to God when I take time out to read the Bible and pray. Just like juggling balls, our lives can get crazy and out of line with God's will."

Joe let one ball drop to the floor. "I took my eyes off the ball and messed up." He caught the other four balls in his hands and bent down to pick up the one he'd dropped. "The nice thing about juggling is, I can always start over again whenever I've made a mistake. The same is true of my spiritual life. God is always there, waiting for me to trust Him and accept His love and forgiveness for me."

Joe concluded his routine by creating a vibrant balloon bouquet that resembled a bunch of tulips. "I'd like to recognize someone special in the audience," he said, shading his eyes with his hand and staring out at the congregation. "Nope. I don't recognize a soul!"

Several people chuckled. Then he asked, "Has anyone recently had a birthday?"

Murmurs drifted through the crowd, but no one spoke up.

"Okay—let's do this another way. Anyone have a birthday today?" Silence greeted him. He waved the bouquet in the air. "How about last week?" Still no response. "Come now, folks—don't be shy. I'm sure at least one person in this group has had a birthday recently."

At last someone's hand went up in the front row. Joe grinned. "Ah-ha—a pretty lady with long blond hair has finally responded."

Lois slid down in her seat. *What in the world possessed me to raise my hand?* She'd celebrated her twenty-second birthday two weeks ago, but she didn't need the whole audience looking at her now, which was exactly what they were doing!

The tall clown moved toward her. He wore a broad smile on his white-painted face, and his hand was outstretched. "A beautiful bouquet for the birthday gal," he said with a deep chuckle.

Lois forced herself to smile in return.

"Do you know what flowers grow between your nose and chin?"

She shook her head.

"Tulips!"

Everyone laughed, and the clown winked at Lois. "Would you like to tell us your name and when you celebrated your birthday?"

"My name is Lois Johnson, and my birthday was two weeks ago."

Slow-Joe shuffled his feet, lifted his floppy hat, then plopped it back down on his head. "Ta-da!" He held out the bouquet to her.

Suddenly, the young girl sitting beside Lois bounced up and down, crying, "I want a balloon! I want a balloon!" She leaped out of her seat and lunged forward, obviously hoping to grab a balloon out of Slow-Joe's hands. Instead she tripped and tumbled against his knees. He wobbled back and forth, and the audience laughed loudly.

Lois wondered if this were part of the act, but suddenly Joe fell forward and landed in her lap. She figured it had to be an accident and the child was just over-excited. Or was it? Hadn't she told God that if He wanted her to have a man, He'd have to drop him into her lap? She swallowed hard and stared into the clown's hazel eyes.

"Sorry," he mumbled. "Don't know how that happened." He handed Lois the balloon bouquet and stood up. He turned back to face the audience and wiggled his dark eyebrows. "Let's sing the birthday song to Lois, shall we?"

Lois felt the heat of embarrassment creep up her neck. *This is what I get for being dumb enough to raise my hand.*

The young girl who had been sitting next to her now stood beside the clown. Before anyone could say anything, she started singing at the top of her lungs: "Happy Birthday to you. . ."

The audience joined in, and Lois stared straight ahead, wishing she could make herself invisible. When the song was over, she leaned toward Slow-Joe and whispered, "Thanks for the flowers."

He nodded, took a bow, and dashed backstage.

Lois sat through the rest of the program feeling as if she were in a daze. Why had the clown singled her out? *Well, after all, I did raise my hand when he asked who'd had a birthday recently,* she reminded herself. *What else could he do?*

When the service was over, Lois made her way to the foyer, where she found Tabby and Seth standing by the front door. She tapped her sister on her shoulder. "You guys were great as usual."

Tabby turned and smiled. "Thanks. Your part of the program wasn't bad either."

"Yeah, we were watching from offstage," Seth said, patting Lois on the back. "Maybe you should leave your secretarial job and become a clown. You had the audience in stitches."

Lois groaned. "It was that goofy clown who made everyone laugh." She shook her head. "It was bad enough that he fell into my lap, but he only embarrassed me more by having everyone sing to me."

"Aw, it was all in fun," Seth said with a chuckle.

"We're heading out for some pie and coffee. Want to join us?" Tabby asked, giving Lois a little nudge.

She shrugged. "Sure—why not? At least there I won't have any reason to hide my face."

Chapter Three

The all-night coffee shop Seth picked was bustling with activity. Lois slipped into a booth by the window, and Tabby and Seth took the other side.

"You ladies feel free to order anything you want," Seth said, offering Lois a wide smile. "This is my treat, so you may as well go overboard and order something really fattening if you feel so inclined."

Tabby snickered. "Does my little sister look as if she ever goes overboard when it comes to eating?" She wagged a finger toward Lois. "What I wouldn't give to have a figure like yours."

Lois shook her head. "My high metabolism and a half hour of aerobics every day might help keep me looking thin, but I have been known to indulge. Especially when chocolate is involved."

"Women and their addiction to chocolate!" Seth grabbed Tabby's hand and gave it a squeeze. "I guess if that's your worst sin, I can consider myself very blessed."

Tabby groaned. "You know I'm far from perfect, Seth."

"What's this about someone being perfect?"

The three young people turned toward the masculine voice. Even without his costume and clown makeup, Lois would have recognized that smile. Slow-Joe the Clown wiggled his eyebrows and gave her a crooked grin.

"Good to see you, Joe. I was just telling my beautiful wife how lucky I am to have her." Seth gestured toward the empty seat next to Lois. "Why don't you take a load off those big clown feet and join us for pie and coffee?"

"Don't mind if I do." Joe dropped down beside Lois. She squirmed uneasily and slid along the bench until her hip bumped the wall. "It's good to see you again, birthday girl." He extended his hand. "I don't think we've been formally introduced. I'm Joe Richey."

"I–I'm Lois Johnson," she said. "Tabby's my sister, and Seth is my brother-in-law."

As they shook hands, Joe's face broke into a broad smile. "Sure hope I didn't embarrass you too much during my performance tonight."

"Well—"

"So tell me, Seth—how'd you meet this perfect wife of yours?" Joe asked, changing the subject abruptly.

Lois felt a sense of irritation, but at the same time she was relieved Joe had interrupted her and taken the conversation in another direction. At least she wasn't the focus of their discussion anymore.

"Tabby took one of my ventriloquist classes, and I was drawn to her like a moth heading straight for a flame." Seth turned his head and gave Tabby a noisy kiss on her cheek.

Joe chuckled. "Since I'm not married, I don't consider myself an expert on the subject, but I recently heard about a man who met his wife at a travel bureau."

"Oh?" Seth said with obvious interest. "And what's so unusual about that?"

Joe grinned and turned to wink at Lois. "She was looking for a vacation, and he was the last resort."

Everyone laughed, and Lois felt herself begin to relax.

"Adam and Eve had the only perfect marriage," Joe continued, his eyes looking suddenly serious.

"What makes you say that?" asked Tabby.

Joe tapped his knuckles on the table. "Think about it. Adam didn't have to hear about all the men Eve could have married, and Eve wasn't forced to listen to a bunch of stories about the way Adam's mother cooked."

Seth howled, and Tabby slapped him playfully on the arm. He tickled her under the chin. "The other day I heard my wife telling our neighbors I was a model husband. I felt pretty good about that until I looked up the word in a dictionary."

"What did it say?" Lois asked, putting her elbows on the table and leaning forward.

"A model is a small imitation of the real thing."

Another gale of laughter went around the table, but the waitress came then to take their order. Lois figured it was time to get serious, so she ordered a cup of herbal tea and a brownie. Tabby settled for coffee and a maple bar. Both men asked for coffee and hot apple pie, topped with vanilla ice cream. While they waited for their orders, the joke telling continued.

"I've heard that marriage is comparable to twirling a baton, turning hand springs, or eating with chopsticks," Joe said with a sly grin on his face. "It looks really easy till you try it."

"I wouldn't know. I'm an old maid of twenty-two," Lois interjected.

Joe bobbed his head up and down and chuckled. "Wow, that is pretty old."

Tabby wrinkled her nose. "Not to be outdone—when Seth and I got married, it was for better or worse. I couldn't do better, and he couldn't do worse."

Remembering the days of her sister's low self-esteem, Lois quickly jumped in. "That's not true, Tabby, and you know it."

Tabby raised her eyebrows and looked at Lois. "I was only kidding."

Joe nudged Lois gently in the ribs with his elbow. "Did you know this is National Clown Month?"

She shook her head.

"Yes, and as a clown I feel it's my duty to make as many people laugh as possible." Joe then tapped Lois on the shoulder. "Do you like to laugh?"

"Sure."

"And do you enjoy making other people laugh?"

She shrugged. "I suppose so."

"Then maybe you've got what it takes to be a clown." Joe grinned. "Don't mind me—I'm always trying to recruit others to become clowns."

Lois wasn't sure what to say in response, so she merely turned her head away and stared out the window. The idea of her becoming a clown seemed ridiculous. She studied her little green car sitting under the street light next to Seth's black Bronco. If she could only come up with a legitimate excuse, she'd forget about her chocolate treat and head straight for home. Joe Richey was cute and funny, but at the moment he was making her feel rather uncomfortable.

Joe clenched his teeth and squished the napkin in his lap into a tight ball. *I think I've blown it with this woman. I had her laughing one minute, and the next minute she's giving me the silent treatment. What'd I say or do that turned her off?*

"When will your next performance be, Joe?" Seth asked.

"Tonight was my last one for a while."

"How come?" Tabby questioned. "I'd think a funny guy like you would be in high demand."

"I guess I am, because I've been doing back-to-back programs all summer," Joe said. "I'm in need of a break, though. Thought I might head for the beach or go up to Mt. Rainier to relax."

Seth nodded. "Makes sense to me. All work and no play—well, you know the rest of that saying. Even Jesus needed to get away from the crowds once in a while. If you don't take time for yourself, you'll burn out like a candle in the wind."

"How long have you been clowning?" Lois asked.

At least she's speaking to me again. Joe turned his head and offered her his best smile. "Ever since I was a kid, but professionally for about two years."

As Joe leaned even closer to Lois, his senses were assaulted by the subtle fragrance of peaches. *It must be her shampoo.* He wondered if her hair was as soft as it looked, and he fought the urge to reach out and touch the long, golden tresses. "Do you live around here, Lois?" he asked.

"Tabby and I grew up in Olympia, and our folks still live there." Lois smiled. "We both settled in Tacoma when we found jobs here."

Joe tapped the edge of his water glass with one finger. "I'm from Olympia too."

"Really? What part of town?" Lois asked.

"The north side."

"Lois drives to Olympia a couple of times a month," Tabby said, smiling at Joe. "Maybe you two should get together sometime."

Lois nearly choked on the sip of water she'd just taken. She had the distinct feeling she was being set up. Maybe her well-meaning sister had planned it so Joe would meet them at the coffee shop. It might be that the little schemer was trying to play matchmaker. *Who knows? Tabby could have been behind that whole scenario at the church tonight. She may have asked Joe to single me out with the balloon bouquet and birthday song.*

Lois resolved to have a little heart-to-heart talk with her sister. If she ever had another man in her life, she needed to do the picking. Tabby might have her best interests at heart, but she wasn't Lois's keeper. Besides, Lois wasn't looking for a man now.

She gave Joe a sidelong glance, and he smiled, a slow, lazy grin that set her heart racing. *He sure is cute. And he did fall into my lap.* The waitress brought their desserts, which helped Lois force her thoughts off the man who was sitting much too close. She concentrated on the piece of chocolate decadence on her plate. A little sugar for her sweet tooth and some herbal tea to soothe her nerves, and she would be right as rain.

Chapter Four

"Don't keep me in suspense. Did he call or what?"

Lois glanced over her shoulder. Tabby had just entered the church office and was looking at her like an expectant child waiting to open her birthday presents.

"Did who call?"

"Joe Richey."

"No, he didn't call," Lois answered as she shut down her computer for the day.

"You did give him your phone number, didn't you? I thought I saw you hand him a slip of paper the other night when we were at the coffee shop."

Lois slid her chair away from the desk and stood up. "Tabby Beyers, get a life!"

Tabby folded her arms across her chest and wrinkled her nose. "I have a life. I'm a wife, a day care worker, and a ventriloquist."

Lois puckered her lips. "Then that ought to keep you busy enough so you can manage to mind your own business and not mine."

Tabby stuck out her tongue. "For your information, I'm only interested in your welfare."

"I appreciate that." Lois smiled, her irritation lessening. "If you don't mind, though, I think I can worry about my own welfare."

Tabby shrugged. "Whatever you say. Starting next month I won't be around much to meddle in your life, anyway."

Lois drew her brows together. "What's that supposed to mean? You and Seth aren't planning to move, I hope."

Tabby shook her head. "We'd never intentionally move from Tacoma. We like it here too much." She fluttered her lashes. "It's all that liquid sunshine, you know."

Lois laughed and reached for her purse, hanging on the coat tree by

174

the door. "If you're not moving, then why won't you be around much?"

"We're going on an evangelistic tour with several other Christian workers," Tabby explained. "We'll be traveling around the state of Washington and to a few places in Oregon and Idaho. Probably be gone at least a month. Maybe longer if we get a good response."

"Is Slow-Joe the Clown going with you?" Lois asked. She didn't know why, but she hoped he wasn't. They'd only met a few nights ago, so she hardly knew the man. She'd never admit it to Tabby, but Joe had promised to call. She looked forward to it, because there was something about the goofy guy that stirred her interest, even if she had felt uncomfortable in his presence. She wasn't sure if it were his silly antics and wisecracks, his hazel eyes with the gold flecks, or his mop of curly brown hair that made him so appealing.

"Lois, are you listening to me?"

Lois whirled around to face her sister. "Huh?"

"You asked if Joe Richey was going on tour with us, and I said no. But you're standing there staring at your purse as if you're in a world of your own." Tabby wrinkled her nose. "I'm sure you didn't hear a word I said."

Lois laughed self-consciously. "I guess I was kind of in my own world."

Tabby's eyes narrowed. "Thinking about Joe, I'll bet."

Lois couldn't deny it, so she asked another question. "If you're going on tour for a month or longer, how will Donna manage the day care?"

Tabby waved her hand. "She already has that covered. Corrie, our helper, has a friend who has been taking some child development classes. Donna thought she'd give her a try." She shrugged. "Who knows? Maybe I'll quit the day care. Then Corrie can take my place."

"Quit the day care?" Lois could hardly believe it. "But you love working with the kids. I can't imagine your doing anything else."

Tabby started for the door. "How about becoming a full-time mother?"

Lois's mouth dropped open. "You're pregnant?"

"Not yet, but I'm hopeful. Seth and I have been married two years, you know. We both think it's time to start a family."

Sudden envy surged through Lois, and she blinked several times to hold back tears that threatened to spill over. She loved children. That was why she was teaching a Sunday school class. How ironic. *Tabby used to be jealous of me, and now I feel the same way toward her. Help me in this area, Lord.*

Joe searched through his closet for the right clothes to take to the beach. It could be windy, cold, rainy, or sunny along the Washington coast, even during the month of August. He'd probably need to take a couple of sweatshirts, some shorts, one or two pairs of jeans and, of course, his most comfortable pair of sneakers.

His favorite thing to do at the ocean was beachcomb. The flower beds in his backyard gave evidence of that. Pieces of driftwood adorned nearly every bed, and scattered throughout the plants were shells of all sizes and shapes. Stationed beside his front door were two buoys he'd discovered after a winter storm one year, and a fishbowl full of beach agates was displayed on his fireplace mantel.

Joe wondered why he didn't sell the old house he'd grown up in and buy a small cabin near the beach. He knew it would be more peaceful there. But then he'd be farther from the cities where he found most of his work.

As he packed his clothes into his suitcase, Joe noticed one of his clown suits lying on the floor. He'd forgotten to put it in the hamper.

"Joseph Andrew Richey, you're a slob! You need to learn to pick up after yourself." Joe could hear his mother's sharp words, as if she were standing right there in his room.

She had always been a neat freak, unless she was in one of her down moods. Then she didn't care what she or the house looked like. Joe could never understand how his mother could yell at her children one day to pick up their things and the next day sink into such despair that she'd need a bulldozer to clear the clutter off the kitchen table.

"No wonder Brian left home the day he turned eighteen," Joe mumbled. He bent down to pick up the clown suit and shook his head. "I wouldn't be surprised if my little brother isn't still running from job to job, trying to dodge his problems."

His brother had a hot temper and had been fired from several positions because he couldn't work well with others and didn't want to take orders from his boss. Joe prayed for Brian regularly, but he'd given up trying to talk to him; their last discussion had ended in a horrible argument, and Joe figured he might never hear from his brother again.

Pushing thoughts of his brother aside, Joe dropped the clown suit into the hamper. Without warning, another one of his mother's accusations pounded in his head.

"You're not going to wash that without checking the pockets, I hope."

Joe chuckled. "No, Mom. I wouldn't dream of it."

He stuffed his hand inside one deep pocket and withdrew three red pencil balloons and one green apple balloon. "Whew! Wouldn't want to put these babies in the washing machine."

Joe plunged his hand into the other pocket and pulled out a slip of paper. "Hmm—what's this? Somebody's phone number?" He sank to the edge of his bed and stared at the paper. Who'd recently given him a number, and why hadn't he been smart enough to jot down a name to go with it?

Joe grimaced. He'd probably forget his own name if it weren't on his driver's license.

"Think hard, Joe. Whose number is on this piece of paper?"

Lord, if this phone number is important, help me remember.

Still nothing.

Joe stretched out across the bed, and within a matter of minutes he was asleep. Several hours later he awoke, feeling more refreshed than he had all day.

Sitting up, he noticed the slip of paper lying on the bed. He looked intently at the phone number, and a wide grin spread across his face. "Lois Johnson! Tabby's sister gave me her number when we met at the coffee shop the other night."

Feeling as if he'd been handed an Oscar, Joe grabbed the telephone off the small table by his bed. He punched in the numbers and waited for Lois to pick up, but only a recorded message answered. He hated talking to machines so he didn't leave a message.

"Guess there's no hurry," he assured himself. "I'll call her after I get back from the beach."

Chapter Five

Joe set his suitcase inside the front door, plodded to the living room, and sank wearily to the couch. Two weeks at the beach should have revived him. But they hadn't. His body felt rested, but he had a sense of unrest deep within his soul. Maybe he would feel better once he started working again. That's what he needed—a few more crusades or a couple of birthday parties to get him back on his feet.

Joe forced himself off the couch and headed for the kitchen. He hoped to find at least one job opportunity waiting for him on his answering machine. He didn't want to start hunting for programs. He had never been good at promoting himself, and so far he hadn't needed to. Word of mouth had served him well.

Among the messages, he heard five requests for his clown routine. Two were for church rallies, and the other three involved birthday parties. Even though the parties were mainly for entertainment, he still felt as if he were doing something worthwhile by providing children with good, clean fun. He usually gave some kind of moral lesson with his balloon animals, so at least the children were being exposed to admirable virtues and not merely being entertained.

Feeling a surge of energy, Joe returned the calls, lined up each program, and wrote the dates and times on his appointment calendar. The business end of Joe's clowning was important, and he tried to stay organized with his programs, even if he weren't always structured at home. It wouldn't do to forget or arrive late for an engagement. In fact, it could cost him jobs if he did it too often.

He was heading upstairs to unpack his suitcase when he spotted the slip of paper with Lois Johnson's number on it. He dialed but reached her answering machine, as he had two weeks ago.

"Isn't that woman ever at home?" Joe muttered. He hung up the phone without leaving a message. "I'll try again after I unpack and see if there's anything in the refrigerator to eat."

Pastor Hanson had insisted Lois take off early from work today so she decided to explore some of the new stores at the Tacoma Mall. She didn't have a lot of money to spend, but she knew how to shop for bargains. If a store were having a good deal on something, she'd be sure to find it. Besides, Tabby and Seth had left the day before, and she was feeling lonely. A little shopping would help take her mind off her troubles. At least it would be a temporary diversion.

Lois parked her car in the lot on the north side of the mall then slipped off her navy blue pumps and replaced them with a pair of comfortable walking shoes. It might not look fashionable to shop in an ankle-length navy blue dress and a pair of black sneakers, but she didn't care. It wasn't likely she'd see anyone she knew at the mall.

Lois grabbed her purse, hopped out of the car, and jogged to the mall's closest entrance. Her first stop was a women's clothing store where she found two blouses for under ten dollars and a pair of shorts that had been marked down to five dollars because summer was nearly over.

Next she entered a bed and bath store in hopes of finding a new shower curtain. Her old one had water stains and was beginning to tear. The clerk showed her several, but they cost too much. Lois was about to give up when she noticed a man heading her way. She stood frozen in her tracks, her body trembling.

Lois glanced around for something to hide behind, but it was too late. Michael Yehley was striding toward her, an arrogant smile on his face. Feelings of the old hurt and humiliation knifed through her, and she fought to keep from dashing out of the store.

"Well, well, if it isn't my beautiful ex-fiancée," Michael drawled. He was dressed in a dark brown business suit, white shirt, and olive green tie with tan pinstripes. He had never projected a flashy image, but he did carry about him an air of superiority. His dark hair, parted on the side, his aristocratic nose, and his metal-framed glasses gave him a distinguished appearance Lois had once found attractive.

She took a step back as he reached for her hand. "H–hello, Michael. I'm surprised to see you here."

"My mother's birthday is coming up, and I thought I'd get something for her newly redecorated bath." He grinned at her. "She's going with an oriental theme this time."

This time? How many other times has your mother redecorated her bathroom? Lois feigned a smile. "I'm sure she'll like whatever you choose. You always did have impeccable taste."

Michael looked directly at her. "I thought so when I chose you." He wrinkled his nose, as though some foul odor had suddenly permeated the room. "Of course, that was before you flipped out and went religious on me."

Lois swallowed hard. Michael first postponed their wedding because he thought she was too young and they hadn't known each other long enough. But later, after she became a Christian, he had forced her to choose between him and God. When she told him she wouldn't give up her relationship with Christ, he'd said some choice words and stormed out of her apartment. He had called a few weeks later, informing Lois she was acting like a confused little girl and that she should call if she ever came to her senses. That had been two years ago, but even now it hurt. Especially with Michael looking at her as if she'd been crazy for choosing God over him. She certainly didn't want the man back in her life. She had tried hard enough after her conversion to get him to attend church, but it always caused an argument. Michael had been adamant about not needing any kind of religious crutch, and he'd told her he wasn't going to church, no matter how many times she asked.

"How about joining me for a cup of coffee?" Michael asked. "We can try out that new place on the other side of the mall."

Lois opened her mouth, but he cut her off. "It'll be like old times, and you can fill me in on what you've been up to lately." He gave her a charming smile. "Besides, you look kind of down. Hot coffee and some time with me will surely cheer you up."

Lois shook her head. "You know I don't like coffee, Michael."

"You can have tea, soda, whatever you want." He took hold of Lois's arm and steered her toward the door.

"What about the gift you were planning to buy your mother?" she asked.

"It can wait."

Why was she letting him escort her along the mall corridor? Was she so lonely she'd allow him to lead her away like a sheep being led to slaughter?

When they reached the café, Michael found a table. He ordered a mocha-flavored coffee, and Lois asked for a glass of iced tea.

As they waited for their beverages, Michael leaned across the table and studied Lois intently. "Tell me why you quit working for Thorn and Thorn."

Her eyes narrowed. "News sure travels fast. When did you hear I'd quit?"

His lips curved into a smile. "I'm a lawyer, remember, sweetie? Ray Thorn and I had some business dealings a few weeks ago, and he filled me in."

"I'm working as a secretary for Bayview Christian Church."

He grimaced. "That must mean you're still on your religious soapbox."

Lois glanced down at her hands, folded in her lap. Her knuckles were white, and she was trembling again. Did Michael think it would help if he brought up her faith?

"I'm not on a religious soapbox," she said with clenched teeth. "I love the Lord, I'm enjoying my new job, and—"

He held up one hand. "And you obviously care more about all that than you do me."

She sucked in her bottom lip. "What we once had is over, Michael. You made it perfectly clear you weren't interested in marrying a religious fanatic. And from a scriptural point of view, I knew it would be wrong for us to get married if you weren't a Christian."

Michael's face grew red, and a vein on the side of his neck began to pulsate. "Are you saying I'm not good enough for you?"

"It's not that. With our religious views being so opposite, it wouldn't have worked out. We would always be arguing."

"As we are now?"

She nodded.

The waitress arrived then, and Lois and Michael sat in silence for a while, sipping their drinks. Lois wished she hadn't come here with him. Nothing good was resulting from this little meeting.

"I'm sorry things didn't work out for us, Michael," she murmured, "but, as I said before, I could never have married someone who didn't share my belief in God."

The waitress brought the bill and placed it next to Michael's cup. He gulped down the rest of his coffee and stood, knocking the receipt to the floor. "Some things never change, and you're obviously one of them!"

He bent down to pick up the bill. "Nice shoes," he said in a mocking tone, as he pointed to Lois's sneakers. "Real stylish."

Lois blinked back the burning tears threatening to spill over. So much for her afternoon shopping spree making her feel better. Michael had a knack for getting under her skin; he'd made her cry on more than one occasion, even when they were dating and supposed to be in love. Lois still found him physically attractive, but now she was even more convinced that he was not her type.

Michael stalked off, but a few seconds later he returned to the table with a grim expression on his face. "I just want you to know—I harbor no ill feelings toward you. I'm getting on with my life, and apparently you are too."

Lois only nodded. Her throat was too clogged with tears, and she was afraid if she tried to speak she would break down. She didn't love Michael anymore, but seeing him again and hearing the way he talked about her faith made her know for certain she'd done the right thing. Her unshed tears were for the time she'd wasted in a relationship that had gone nowhere. She also ached for Michael, that he would discover the same joy she had in a personal relationship with God. Only then had she found freedom from the pursuit of wealth and power, and she wished the same for him. She thought of the people lost in their sin, refusing to acknowledge they'd done anything wrong and turning their backs on God and the salvation He offered through the shed blood of Christ. She sincerely hoped Michael would choose to receive this gift.

Suddenly Michael leaned close to her ear and whispered, "If you should ever come to your senses, give me a call." With that, he kissed her abruptly on the cheek, turned, and was gone.

Lois was too stunned to move. She could scarcely catch her breath.

A half hour later Lois unlocked the door to her apartment and heard the phone ringing. She raced to grab it before the answering machine picked up. "Hello."

"Lois, is that you?"

"Yes. Who's this?"

"Joe Richey—the goofy Gospel clown who fell into your lap a few weeks ago."

Lois's heart pounded, and she drew in a breath to steady her nerves. Since he hadn't called, she'd given up hope that he might.

"You still there, Lois?"

His mellow voice stopped her thoughts. "Yes, I'm here—just a little surprised to hear from you."

"I said I'd call, and you did give me your phone number," Joe reminded her.

"I know, but it's been over two weeks, and—"

"And you gave up on me."

"I–I guess I did."

"I've been to Ocean Shores, taking a much-needed vacation."

"Did you have a good time?"

"It was okay. I did a lot of walking on the beach and slept late every morning." Joe chuckled. "Something I hardly ever do when I'm at home."

Lois twirled the phone cord around her finger, wondering what to say next.

"Listen—the reason I'm calling is, I was wondering if you'd like to go bowling this Friday night."

Lois paused as she tried to absorb what Joe had said.

"You do know how to bowl, don't you?"

"Yes, but not very well."

"Maybe I can give you a few pointers. I've been bowling since I was a kid and have a pretty good hook with my ball."

Lois giggled. In her mind's eye she could picture Joe lining up his ball with the pins, snapping his wrist to the left, then acing a strike on the very first ball.

"So what do you say? Would you like to go bowling?"

"Sure—I'd love to."

Chapter Six

Lois paced between the living room window and the fireplace. Joe should have been here fifteen minutes ago. Had he encountered a lot of traffic on the freeway between Olympia and Tacoma? Had he forgotten the time he'd agreed to come? Maybe he'd stood her up. No, that wasn't likely. Joe seemed too nice of a guy to do something so mean. He did appear to be a bit irresponsible, though. He'd said he would call her after they met at the coffee shop, but he'd gone on vacation and hadn't phoned until two weeks later.

"Sure hope I'm doing the right thing by going out with Joe," Lois murmured. "He's funny and cute, but not really my type." What exactly was her type? She'd once thought Michael fit the criteria—charming, good-looking, smart, and financially well off. Weren't those the qualities she was looking for in a man?

"That was then, and this is now," Lois said as she checked her appearance in the hall mirror. She had a different set of ideals concerning men now. The most important thing was whether he were a Christian or not, and next came compatibility.

The doorbell rang, and Lois jumped. She peered through the peephole in her apartment door and saw one big hazel-colored eye staring back at her.

"Sorry I'm late," Joe apologized when she opened the door. "You gave me your address the other night, but I forgot where I laid it and spent fifteen minutes trying to locate it." Before she could reply, he pulled a bouquet of pink carnations from behind his back and handed them to her. Their hands touched briefly, and Lois was caught off guard by the feelings that stirred deep within.

"I hope these will make up for my forgetfulness," Joe said with a big smile.

Lois smiled too and inhaled the subtle fragrance of the bouquet. "Thanks for these. Carnations are my favorite. Come inside while I put them in water."

Joe followed her into the kitchen, and after she'd filled a vase with water and inserted the flowers, she turned to him and smiled. He was dressed in a black knit polo shirt and a pair of blue jeans. Nothing fancy, yet she thought he looked adorable. *It must be that crooked grin. Or maybe it's his curly brown hair. I wonder what it would feel like to run my fingers through those curls.* Lois halted her thoughts. She barely knew Joe, and after being hurt by Michael she hoped she was smart enough not to rush into another relationship.

"You look great tonight," Joe said. "In fact, we resemble a pair of matching bookends."

Lois glanced down at her black tank top and blue jeans. "Let's hope we match as well at the bowling alley."

"No big deal if we don't." Joe's eyebrows wiggled up and down. "That'll make it more interesting."

Joe sat on the bench, with his arms crossed and a big smile on his face, watching Lois line up her ball with the pins. Her golden hair, held back with two small barrettes, glistened under the bowling alley lights and made him wish he could touch it and feel its softness. He had no plans of becoming emotionally involved with anyone right now, but something about Lois drew him in a way he'd never experienced with other women. Was it merely her good looks, or did Lois have the kind of sweet spirit he desired in a wife? *Wife? Now where did that thought come from?*

Lois squealed with delight when she knocked down half the pins on her first throw, forcing Joe's thoughts back to the game. "Good job!" he exclaimed, pointing both thumbs up in the air.

She pivoted and smiled at him, revealing two dimples he hadn't noticed before. "Not too bad for an amateur, huh?" She grabbed her ball when it returned to the rack and positioned herself in front of the alley. This time her aim was a bit off, and the ball made it halfway down before it veered to the right and rolled into the gutter.

Lois returned to her seat, looking as if she'd lost her best friend. "That little boy a couple of lanes over bowls better than I do."

Joe patted her on the shoulder. "It's only a game, and you're doing your best."

She shrugged. "My best doesn't seem to be good enough."

"You know what they say about practice."

"I don't bowl often enough to get in much practice."

"Guess we'll have to remedy that."

She tipped her head to one side, and her blue eyes sparkled in the light. "Is that your way of asking me out again?"

He grinned. "Sure—if you're interested in dating a goofy guy like me."

Lois giggled and poked him on the arm. "You did look pretty silly awhile ago when you were trying to bowl with your back to the alley."

He tweaked her nose. "Don't slam the technique. I knocked four pins down that time."

"Next I suppose you'll try to juggle three bowling balls at the same time."

"I think they might be a bit heavy," he answered with a smile. "I could see about juggling three or four pins though."

She jabbed his arm again. "You would, wouldn't you?"

Joe stood up, retrieved his ball from the return rack then turned back to face Lois. "Hang around me long enough, and you'll be surprised at what I can do."

After bowling three games, they walked over to the snack bar for hamburgers and french fries. Joe ordered a cherry soda and Lois a glass of lemonade before finding an empty booth.

Lois eyed Joe curiously as he poured ketchup on his fries. He looked like a little boy in a man's body, with eyes that twinkled like stars, a mouth turned up, and freckles spattered across the bridge of his nose.

He glanced up then. "A nickel for your thoughts," he said, smiling.

She could feel her cheeks grow warm. "Oh, uh, well, I was just wondering about something."

"What is it?"

"Well, I realized I don't know much about you. I know you're a Gospel clown and you live in Olympia, but that's about all."

Joe shrugged. "There's not much to tell."

"What about your family?"

"What about them?"

"Do you have any brothers or sisters?"

"Just a brother who's a few years younger than I am."

"Where do your folks live?" she asked.

Joe stared at the table. "They're both dead."

"Oh, I'm sorry. What happened?"

"I'd rather not talk about it right now, if that's okay," he said, looking down at the table.

"Sure," Lois said, suddenly uncomfortable with the direction their conversation had taken. She hesitated before speaking, hoping she could find a better topic to discuss. "Do you work at any other job besides clowning?"

"I went to trade school right out of high school and learned how to be a mechanic," he answered. "I worked at a garage not far from home for a while, but after I started clowning, the job turned to part-time; finally I quit altogether."

"You mean you make enough money clowning to support yourself?"

He nodded. "Yes, but I'll never be rich. Besides crusades, Bible camps, and other church-related functions, I do birthday parties for kids of all ages. I've also entertained at some senior centers and have even landed a couple of summer jobs at the Enchanted Village near Seattle."

She nodded. "I know where that is. My dad used to take me there when I was a kid."

"What about your sister? Didn't she go too?"

Lois swallowed hard. How could she tell Joe about her childhood and Tabby's without making him think she was a spoiled brat? The truth was that until she trusted the Lord with her life, she'd been exactly that. "Let's just say Tabby was afraid of most of the rides there, and our dad had no patience with her fears."

Joe shook his head slowly. "She sure doesn't seem afraid of much now. In fact, I've seen her do some routines that would rival anything the big-time ventriloquists have done. And she didn't act one bit nervous either."

"Tabby has come a long way in the past few years. All she needed was to gain some confidence, and now she's using her talents to tell others about the Lord." Lois paused. "In the past we weren't very close. I was often critical of her. Things are much better between us now, and I can honestly say I love my sister to pieces. I owe that to the Lord."

Joe leaned across the table and took Lois's hand. A jolt of electricity shot up her arm. "I'm not trying to change the subject, but I've tried calling you a couple of times during the day, and I always get your answering machine. Do you work or go to school someplace in Tacoma?"

"For the past couple of weeks I've been working as the secretary at Bayview Christian Church in the north end of Tacoma," she said.

"And before that?"

"I was a lawyer's secretary."

Joe whistled and released her hand. "Wow! You must have been making some big bucks! What prompted you to give up such a job and take on a church secretary's position, which I'm sure doesn't pay half as much?"

Lois paused. Should she tell Joe about Michael and their broken engagement? It was part of the reason she'd decided to leave her job. The junior partner at the firm was a friend of Michael's, and Lois knew he kept her ex-fiancé updated on her comings and goings. Michael had said as much when they'd run into each other at the mall the other day.

"You're right," she replied. "My job at the church isn't very lucrative, but it does pay the bills, and I consider it to be a ministry of sorts."

His eyebrows lifted. "How so?"

"Many folks call or drop by the church, needing help with food, clothing, or spiritual matters. I'm not a trained counselor so I always send people with serious problems to one of the pastors, but I do pray for those who have a need."

"How long have you been a Christian?" he asked.

"Almost two years. Tabby and I went to church when we were kids, but I never took it seriously until shortly after she and Seth got married. I think seeing how my sister changed when she started using her talents to tell others about the Lord helped me see the emptiness in my own life." Lois lowered her gaze. "I wasn't a very nice person before I became a Christian. The truth is I was spoiled and self-centered and mean to my sister most of the time."

"But, as you said earlier, you and Tabby get along now, right?"

She nodded. "We're as close as any two siblings could be."

A strange look crossed Joe's face, and Lois wondered what he was thinking. Before she could voice the question, Joe said, "When I was eight years old, I went to Bible school. That's where I realized I had sinned and asked God to forgive me." He smiled. "Ever since then I've wanted to serve Him through some form of special ministry."

"Do you enjoy clowning?"

He chuckled. "Yep. I guess it's in my nature to make people laugh. I feel happier when I'm clowning around."

Lois was about to respond when Joe grabbed two straws from the plastic container sitting on their table and stuck one in each ear. "You think I could patent this?" he said in a teasing voice. "Hearing aids with no need for batteries." He shook his head from side to side, and the straws bounced up and down.

Lois stifled a giggle behind her hand. With his eyes crossed and two blue straws dangling from each ear, Joe looked hilarious. She was glad for those few minutes of finding out a little more about him. But she wondered if he ever stayed serious for long, and if so, would she find that side of him more appealing?

Joe tilted his head to one side and mentally replayed the questions she'd asked. She was not only beautiful but smart, and she'd laughed at his corny jokes and goofy antics. The only uncomfortable moment had come when she questioned him about his family.

He watched Lois drinking her lemonade. Her lips were pursed around the tip of the straw, and she drank in slow, delicate sips. *Wonder what it would feel like to kiss those rosy lips.* He gave his ear a sharp pull, hoping the gesture would get him thinking straight again. This was only their first date. He shouldn't be thinking about kissing Lois.

"You're staring at me."

He blinked then smiled. "Yeah, I guess I am."

"Do I have ketchup on my chin or something?"

"Nope. I was just thinking I'd like to get to know you better."

Lois nodded. "I'd like to know you better too."

"How about coming to one of my programs?" Joe asked. "I'll be part of a revival service at one of the largest churches in Puyallup next Friday night. We'll have performers from all over the Pacific Northwest." He smiled at her. "After the program, maybe we can go out for pie and coffee."

"Sounds like fun."

"So will you come?"

"I'd love to."

Joe smiled again, feeling as if he'd been handed a birthday present when it wasn't even his birthday.

Chapter Seven

Lois sat spellbound as the Gospel illusionist on stage at Puyallup Christian Church performed a disappearing dove trick. "After the flood, Noah sent out first a raven, then a dove, in search of dry land," he told everyone. He placed a live dove inside a silver pan, covered it with a lid, and opened it again. The bird was gone. A few minutes later, it reappeared inside the illusionist's coat.

Lois applauded with the rest of the audience.

After that, she watched two clowns perform using mime. Neither of them held her interest the way Joe did, though. They were more sophisticated in their approach, and throughout their routine they never uttered a word, as was the custom with mimes.

A group of puppeteers followed the clowns, and an artist did a beautiful chalk drawing of the resurrection of Christ. Lois thought of Tabby's friend, Donna, who also did chalk art. She knew Donna hadn't gone on tour with Tabby and Seth, since she had the day care to run, but she'd expected to see her here tonight. She thought Donna's drawings were every bit as good as the one being done now.

When she heard Slow-Joe the Clown being announced, Lois smiled. He was the main reason she'd come tonight.

Joe was comfortable in the costume he'd chosen—a cowboy clown suit, complete with ten-gallon hat, chaps, and bright red leather boots. His red-and-white-striped shirt offset his baggy white pants with red fringe sewn to the pockets and side seams. He wore his usual white face paint and red rubber nose, but he'd added a fake mustache to give him a rugged, cowboy look.

As Joe stepped onto the stage, he swung a rope over his head and hollered, "Yahoo! Ride 'em, cowboy!" Everyone cheered and clapped.

Joe threw the rope into the air, spun around as it fell to the ground, and shouted, "Now wait a minute! Where did that silly rope go? I had it in my hands a minute ago, and now it's disappeared."

When the laughter died down, Joe pivoted on his heels and tripped over the rope, which was lying a few inches in front of him. Next, he grabbed two folding chairs, draped the rope across the back of each one, then tied both ends in a knot. "Before I came out here, someone dared me to do this, so now I'm gonna walk the tightrope."

"Don't do it!" a child's voice shouted.

"Would you like to do it instead?" Joe called back.

"No, it's not safe!"

Joe eyed the rope. Then, slowly, deliberately, he lifted one foot, paused, and set his foot back down. "Anyone have an umbrella? I might need it for balance," he said to the audience.

"It's not safe!" the child yelled again.

Joe looked at the rope, tipped his head slightly, then bent to examine it more closely. "The rope looks strong, but the chairs might not hold my weight. Maybe I should do this the cautious way." With that, Joe quickly undid the rope, snapped it over his head, did a few fancy twirls, then flopped the rope onto the floor in a straight line. "Now it's safe!"

With exaggerated movements he stepped onto the rope, placing one boot in front of the other, and walked the tightrope. When he came to the end, he turned to the audience and bowed. He heard several snickers, but nobody clapped. Frowning, he tugged gently on his mustache. "You didn't think that trick was impressive?" he asked the audience, turning his hands palm up. A few more snickers filtered through the room.

"I'll tell you what's impressive," Joe continued. "Doing what you know is right, even when others try to get you to do something that could be bad for you. Someone dared me to walk this tightrope while it was connected to two chairs. If I'd taken that dare, it would have been pretty stupid.

"God gave each of us the ability to discern what's right and wrong," Joe continued. "Even if you want to be liked and think taking a dare is cool, you need to use your brain and decide what's best for you in any situation." He pointed to the rope at his feet. "I don't have an umbrella for balance, the folding chairs aren't very sturdy, and I've never walked a tightrope in my life, so I decided to do the sensible thing." He turned and went back across the rope. "I walked a tightrope that was lying safely on the ground."

Everyone clapped, and Joe reached into his pocket to retrieve a balloon. "I'm going to create my favorite balloon critter now—Buzzy the Bee."

He inflated the balloon to make the insect's body, twisted one-third of it off for the head, then withdrew and blew up a second balloon. After he'd tied a knot, he formed a circle with the balloon. He twisted it in half to make two smaller circles, which would become the bee's wings. These were attached to the body with another twist. Using a black marking pen, Joe drew a face on the bee and rings around its middle.

"Whenever I see a bee, I'm reminded that God wants me to bee a good witness, bee kind to others, and bee faithful about going to church," he said, holding up the balloon. Joe stepped off the stage and handed the bee to the child who had warned him about the unsafe tightrope.

He ended his routine by spinning the rope over his head and telling the audience each of them had talents they could use to serve the Lord in some way.

Later that evening, at the restaurant where she and Joe had gone for dessert, Lois found herself once again enthralled with Slow-Joe the Clown's wit and goofy smile. "I could tell you were having fun during your performance tonight," she said.

"I always have fun when I'm on stage." Joe leaned across the table. "Speaking of fun, and changing the subject, I was at the mall the other day and stopped in to use the men's room."

Lois covered her ears with her hands. "Is this something I need to hear?"

Joe grinned. "When I was in the men's room, I noticed a sign on the wall, above a padded shelf. It read: 'Baby Changing Station.'" Joe shook his head slowly. "Can you imagine anyone wanting to leave their kid there, hoping it'll be changed when it comes out?" He chuckled and gave her a quick wink.

Lois groaned. "Don't you ever get tired of cracking jokes?"

"Nope." Joe reached for his cup of coffee. "So what do you do when you're not working?" he asked, changing the subject again.

She shrugged her shoulders. "I teach a first-grade Sunday school class, drive to Olympia to visit my folks a couple times a month, and read a lot."

"Nothing just for fun?"

"Reading a good book can be fun." Lois stared into her cup of tea for a moment, then glanced up and saw Joe dangling his spoon with two fingers, directly in front of her face.

"Very funny," she murmured.

Joe dropped the spoon and reached for her hand, and at once Lois felt her face flame. Was Joe flirting with her? The way he kidded around all the time she couldn't be sure if he was serious or teasing.

"The Puyallup Fair starts next weekend," Joe said. "Would you be interested in tagging along with me, maybe sometime Saturday afternoon?"

Lois nodded and smiled. They could find lots of fun things to do at the fair, and it would give her another opportunity to get to know Joe better.

"Great! I have to warn you, though—I get a little carried away when I ride the roller coaster, especially after I've inhaled a couple of cotton candies."

She gulped. The roller coaster? Surely Joe didn't expect her to ride that horrible contraption!

Chapter Eight

As Lois and Joe headed to the Puyallup Fair in his blue pickup truck, a surge of excitement coursed through her.

"Here we are," Joe announced when they pulled into the parking lot near the fairgrounds.

Lois focused on her surroundings. She saw people everywhere, which was nothing unusual for a fair this size. Today it seemed worse than any other time she could remember, though. Maybe it was because of the unseasonably warm weather they'd been having in the Pacific Northwest. Sunshine brought people out by the droves, and something as entertaining as the fair had a lot of appeal.

Joe turned and grinned at Lois after he'd placed his parking stub on the dash. "Ready for an awesome day?"

She smiled in return. "Ready as I'll ever be."

Hand in hand, they made their way to the entrance gates. Joe bought two admission tickets, and they pushed through the revolving gate.

"Where would you like to start?" Joe asked as he grabbed a map of the fairgrounds from a nearby stand.

Lois shrugged. The crisp aroma of early fall mingled with cotton candy, corn dogs, and curly fries, teasing her senses. "I don't know—there's so much to see."

"And do," Joe added. "Why don't we start with the rides? That way we won't be tilting, whirling, and somersaulting on full stomachs or with our arms loaded with stuffed animals."

"Stuffed animals?"

He chucked her under the chin and wiggled his eyebrows, a habit she was coming to enjoy. "Yeah, I'm pretty good at knocking down pins at my favorite arcade game. Last time I came here, I went home with two giraffes, a sheep, and a huge pink bear."

Lois giggled as she tried to envision Joe carrying that many stuffed animals back to his truck. Of course, she reminded herself, he might have been with a date. Why else would he have tried to win so many prizes?

"You don't think I'm capable of winning anything?" Joe said, inclining his head and presenting Lois with a look that reminded her of a puppy begging for a treat.

"It's not that. I just can't imagine how you ever carried them all out of here."

"I admit I did have a little help. I gave one giraffe and the bear to some kids who'd spent all their money trying to win a prize and had come up empty-handed. The other giraffe and the sheep went home with me, and now they occupy a special place in one corner of my bedroom."

"So you have a circus theme in your room?"

"More like Noah's ark," he said, grabbing her hand again and pulling her through the crowd. "Which ride is your favorite?"

"Well—"

"Please don't tell me you like them all," he said in a teasing voice. "I don't think we have time or money enough to go on every one."

"Actually, the only rides I enjoy are the gondola, the Ferris wheel, and the merry-go-round."

Joe shook his finger at her and clicked his tongue. "All baby rides. If we're going to remember this day so we can tell our grandchildren about it, we need to do something really fun and exciting."

"Like what?" Lois asked, a knot forming in her throat.

"The roller coaster, of course!"

As they approached the midway, Lois grew more apprehensive. She hadn't ridden on the roller coaster since she was sixteen, and then she'd embarrassed herself in front of her friends. She could feel her fears mounting as she watched the cars climb the track, knowing they would zoom down and up again, and around the bend made her stomach lurch just thinking about it.

"You okay?" Joe asked with a note of concern. "You look a little green around the gills."

Lois swallowed hard, fighting down a wave of nausea. "I, uh, had a bad experience on the roller coaster one time."

197

"How long ago was that?"

"I was sixteen and had come here with a bunch of kids from my high school."

Joe nudged her in the ribs. "You're all grown up now, so riding the curvy monster should be easy as pie."

"Why don't you go on it alone, and I'll find a bench and watch from the ground below, where I'll be safe?" She nodded toward a mother and her two children who were walking by. "I'd much rather people watch, if that's okay."

"You can watch people from up there." Joe pointed to the climbing coaster, and Lois swallowed back another wave of nausea. "You'll be safe with me—I promise."

Before Lois could respond, Joe grabbed her around the waist and propelled her toward the ticket booth. "Two for the roller coaster," he announced to the woman behind the counter. Tickets in hand, he led Lois to the line where people stood waiting for the ride.

Lois wasn't sure what to do. She didn't want to make a scene in front of all these people, but if she rode on what Joe referred to as "the curvy monster," she was certain she would.

"Don't be nervous," Joe whispered in her ear. "Just hold my hand real tight, and when we're riding the wooden waves, scream like crazy. It wouldn't hurt to pray a little either," he added with a chuckle.

Standing in line, Lois's fears abated some. Being with Joe made her feel carefree, and his jovial spirit and playful attitude kept her laughing. But when they were ushered to the first seat of the coaster, her throat tightened again. What if she got sick as she had when she was a teenager? Or, worse yet, what if she threw up on Joe's white polo shirt? She decided to turn her head away from him, just in case.

"Smile—you're on Candid Camera," Joe said, reaching for her trembling hand.

She moaned. "I hope not. I'd be mortified if the whole world saw me right now."

Joe nuzzled her ear with his nose. "You've never looked more beautiful."

"Yeah, right."

"I'm serious," he asserted. "I love your silky yellow hair, and those bonny blue eyes of yours dazzle my heart."

Lois's heart began to pound, and it wasn't just because the roller coaster had started up the incline. Did Joe think she was beautiful, and had she dazzled his heart? With his clowning around so much, she couldn't always tell if he were serious or not. She didn't have long to ponder the question, for they'd reached the top and were about to cascade down the first part of the track.

"Yowzie! Zowzie!" Joe hollered as they began their descent. "This is way cool!"

Lois braced herself against the seat and held on tight. She screamed— and screamed—and screamed some more, until they reached the bottom and began to climb the next hill.

"That wasn't so bad, was it?" Joe asked.

Lois shook her head quickly, too afraid to speak. The truth was that it hadn't been as awful as she'd remembered. At least this time she'd managed to keep her breakfast down—so far.

"Here we go again," Joe roared in her ear. "Hang on tight and yell like crazy!"

Lois complied. It felt good to holler and howl as the up-and-down motion of the coaster caught her off guard and threw her stomach into a frenzy. It was actually fun, and she was having the time of her life.

At the end of the ride Lois felt exhilarated, instead of weak and shaky as she'd expected. "Let's go again!" she shouted.

Joe chuckled. "Maybe later. Right now I'm ready to ride the Ferris wheel."

Lois sighed. After their wild ride on the roller coaster, the Ferris wheel would seem like a piece of cake. It would be mellow and relaxing, though, and that was probably a good thing. It had been a long time since Lois had been this keyed up, and she was a bit concerned that she might make a mistake and blurt out to Joe how much she liked him. *I don't want to scare him away. He's too good to be true, and I need to go slowly.* If she and Joe were going to have a relationship, she knew it was better not to push or reveal her feelings too soon.

The day sped by like a whirlwind. They moved from one ride to the next and even stopped to eat barbecued ribs, coleslaw, and a huge order of curly fries, with lemonade and, later, soft chocolate ice cream cones. Joe won Lois a fuzzy, brown teddy bear and a huge spiral vase filled with gaudy pink feathered flowers. She loved it. The truth was that she would have been happy with a jar of old marbles if Joe had won them for her. Today had been like a fairy tale, and she wished it would never end. But it was getting late, and they both needed to be at church in the morning. She had a Sunday school class to teach, and Joe had told her he was scheduled to do a program at his home church in Olympia.

It was a little past ten when Joe walked Lois to her apartment door. She started to fidget. Would he kiss her good night? This was their third date, and so far he'd only held her hand, slipped his arm around her waist, and nuzzled her neck a few times. She didn't want him to see how nervous she was so she decided to ask him more questions about himself.

"You seem so naturally funny, Joe. I'm curious—did you get your humor from your dad or your mom?"

Joe stood there and stared at her while she waited for him to answer her question. She hoped he would tell her more about his family. Instead, he bent his head toward her and puckered his lips.

Lois held her breath then and closed her eyes. He was going to kiss her, and she was more than ready.

"Thanks for a great day." Joe gave her a quick peck on the cheek. "You were a good sport to ride that roller coaster with me." He squeezed her arm gently then turned to go. "See you, Lois."

Disappointment flooded Lois's soul as she watched him walk away. "So much for a perfect day," she muttered. Had she said or done something to turn him off? Maybe Joe didn't like her as much as she liked him. Would he call her again?

Chapter Nine

Lois had given Joe her work phone number, hoping he might call during the day if he was busy doing programs at night. Four days had passed since their date to the fair, but still no word from him. The weekend would be here soon, and Lois was beginning to think she would have to spend it alone. Of course, she could make plans to visit her folks. They lived in Olympia, and so did Joe. Would that be a good enough excuse for her to drop by his house and say hello? Should she call first or stop by unannounced? What if that peck on the cheek and Joe's "See you, Lois" had been his way of letting her know he wouldn't be calling again? Even though he'd acted as if he enjoyed their day at the fair, he had made no promises to call.

She didn't want to scare him off. But if she didn't let him know she was interested in a relationship, he could slip through her fingers. She saw it as a no-win situation, and she felt frustrated.

As she prepared to leave the church after work on Friday afternoon, the pastor and his wife stopped her in the hallway. "Hi, Lois. How are things going?" Pastor Hanson asked.

"Good. Is there something I can do for you before I go?"

"No, but Norma just mentioned how you seemed a little down this week. We were wondering if you wanted to talk about anything before you head out for the weekend."

"Oh, well, I hate to bother you. You've both had a busy week."

"We're not in a hurry, Lois," the pastor's wife assured her. "We don't have any plans for the evening."

Lois studied the floral pattern in the carpet. Should she tell them why she was feeling so uptight? She felt sure they would hold in confidence whatever she told them. Besides, she knew they'd counseled several couples recently, some married and some about to be. No doubt they had good insights on men and dating and how to know God's will for finding that special person. Maybe she should get their opinions about Joe.

Lois looked up and smiled. "Actually, you might be able to help."

"Let's go to the study then," Pastor Hanson suggested.

Once they were in the office, Lois took a seat across from the Hansons. "I've recently met a clown," she began.

The pastor chuckled. "You've just met a guy and already labeled him as a clown?"

Lois smiled. "No, he really is a clown." She leaned forward in the chair. "Joe Richey is a Gospel clown, and I met him at a crusade at Westside Community Church a few weeks ago. He sort of fell into my lap."

The pastor's eyebrows shot up. "Oh?"

"You see—I told God that if He wanted me to find a man, He'd have to drop him into my lap." She paused then related the rest of the story, including the part about the little girl rolling into Joe and knocking him over.

The pastor and his wife laughed.

"That must have been quite a sight," Norma Hanson said.

"It was pretty embarrassing. Especially when Joe landed in my lap."

"I can imagine," she agreed kindly.

"After the program, Tabby and Seth invited me to join them for dessert at a nearby restaurant, and Joe showed up. I was wondering if Tabby planned the whole thing, but she said no when I asked her a few days later."

Pastor Hanson leaned forward on his desk. "Changing the subject for a minute—and we'll get back to it—I was wondering if you've heard anything from Tabby and Seth since they went on tour."

"Only once. Tabby called to say their group was in Baker City, Oregon, and they were having successful revival services. She said they might stay on the road a few more weeks."

"That's good news. I hope the rest of their trip goes as well," Pastor Hanson said.

"So do I."

"Now back to your clown. What's troubling you about him?" he asked.

Lois drew in a breath and let it out quickly. "Joe and I have gone out a few times since we met, and even though I don't know him well yet, I really like him."

"Well, that's good, Lois. You know we were hoping you would get out more. I'm sure you're talking with the Lord about this."

She nodded. "Oh, yes. I've done nothing but pray. The trouble is that I haven't received any answers, and I'm not sure whether Joe returns my feelings."

"What makes you think that?" Mrs. Hanson asked.

"He dropped me off after our date last Saturday and, after a quick kiss on the cheek, said, 'See you, Lois.'" She swallowed against the lump lodged in her throat. "He hasn't called all week, and I'm worried he won't."

"Because he didn't say he'd call, or you're just not sure he will?"

"A little of both," she admitted. "Anyway, I'm planning to drive to Olympia tomorrow, and since Joe lives in Olympia—"

"You thought you'd try to see him," the pastor said, finishing Lois's sentence.

She nodded.

"I'm not sure I believe it's always the man's place to pursue a relationship, though that's what worked best for Norma and me. And since I don't know Joe personally, I can't say how he would respond to your visiting him." He looked at her. "Did you plan to call first?"

"I don't have his phone number or address, so I'll need to get them from the Olympia phone book once I'm in town." Lois shrugged. "I'm not sure I should drop by without calling first." She looked down at her hands. "Besides, he may not want to see me anyway."

"Why do you think that, Lois?" Mrs. Hanson asked. "Didn't he enjoy your dates?"

"He seemed to, but then Joe always appears to be having a good time. He's a goofy guy who likes to laugh and make wisecracks and do silly things." Lois blinked against the burning at the back of her eyes. She didn't want to break down in front of the pastor and his wife. "Joe makes me laugh and feel carefree. It's something I've never felt with any other guy."

"Would you like our opinion, or do you feel better after talking about it?" the pastor asked.

"I'd like your opinion, if you wouldn't mind sharing it," Lois said.

"If it were me, I'd probably get Joe's phone number and call him. Tell him you're in town, and if he invites you to stop by, you'll know he wants to see you again."

"And I agree with Sam, Lois," Mrs. Hanson said. "I think that's a good idea."

Lois sighed with relief. That's what she had thought too, but it helped hearing it from them. Calling first would be much better than barging in unannounced. If Joe didn't want to see her, at least she would be spared the humiliation of looking him in the face when he told her so.

Lois stood up, a smile on her face. "Thanks for taking the time to listen."

Pastor Hanson smiled. "We'll be praying for you, Lois."

His wife gave her a hug. "Everything will work out fine. You can be sure of that."

Joe felt tired and out-of-sorts, although he never would have admitted it. On Monday he'd put on an hour-long program at a senior center, plus two kids' birthday parties the following day. This morning he had another party to do.

"Well, I'm glad people want me for my clowning and the balloon animals, especially for parties," he said aloud. "But I don't feel nearly as fulfilled as when I can present the Gospel too. Oh well, it does help pay the bills," he reminded himself.

He zipped up his rainbow-colored clown suit, recalling the squeals of delight from the younger children when he'd worn it to a party. He put on a fuzzy wig with different shades of blue and a cone-shaped hat streaked with lots of colors. Joe had contrived many of his costumes, most of them from rummaging through thrift stores. A professional seamstress at his church had made the other ones, including the one he wore now.

Joe remembered asking his mother to make his first costume. He knew she could sew and thought she might enjoy taking part in his ministry, but she'd refused and then scolded him for expecting her to work her "fingers to the bones" and get nothing in return.

"Did your love always have to be conditional, Mom?" Joe murmured as he studied his reflection in the mirror on the back of his closet door. "Couldn't you have supported me and offered your love freely?"

Joe stuck out his tongue at the clown he saw staring back at him. At least he could hide behind the makeup, which had taken him nearly an hour to apply. His nonsensical costume took only five minutes to don, but it made him appear to be someone else. From the minute he dipped his finger into the jar of grease paint and slapped some of the goop onto his face, Joe was in character. Even though he knew deep inside that he would always be little Joey Richey, who could never please his mother, everyone seemed to love him when he was a clown.

"Forget about Mom and how she made you feel," Joe said, as if he were speaking to someone else. "She's gone now, and it's best for you to put on a happy face." He smiled at the image in the mirror then turned to leave when he heard the phone ring.

"Joe Richey here," he said.

"Hi, Joe. It's Lois."

Joe felt his heart slam into his chest at the sound of Lois's voice. He'd wanted to call her all week, but somehow he hadn't found the time. "Hey, Lois. What's up?"

"I'm in Olympia. I came to see my folks and thought if you weren't busy maybe we could get together while I'm here."

Joe frowned. He'd like nothing better than to be with Lois. If he'd had his way, they would find something fun to do and spend the whole day together. But he couldn't. He had a birthday party to do, and afterward he was supposed to meet with someone at the hospital about doing a special program for some of the staff next week.

"I'm busy today, Lois," Joe said. Did she know how much it pained him to turn her down?

"Oh, I see. Well, I thought it was worth a try. Guess I'll let you go then. 'Bye, Joe."

"No, don't hang—" It was too late. The phone went dead. Lois hadn't given him a chance to explain. She probably thought he didn't want to see her.

"Oh, no! I can't call her back—I don't know where she was calling from." Joe snapped off his bedroom light. "I'll have to wait until next week when I can drive to Tacoma and try to straighten things out." He hurried out of the door, still wishing he could have explained.

Lois left the phone booth and climbed back into her car. Feeling the weight of Joe's rejection, she let her head drop against the steering wheel. Each breath stung as she struggled to keep from dissolving into tears. It was exactly as she feared. Joe didn't want to see her anymore, and he was too polite to come right out and say so. If only he'd been more direct the other night when he'd taken her home from the Puyallup Fair, she wouldn't have called him at his home. He probably thought she was chasing after him.

She'd been foolish to let Joe steal her heart so soon. The happy clown's warm smile and carefree manner had captured her senses, but Lois knew she would have to be more careful from now on. She needed to guard her heart and her feelings.

Chapter Ten

It was Monday morning, and Lois had been staring at her computer screen for the last five minutes, unable to type a single word. She needed to finish Pastor Hanson's sermon, since he'd given her his notes when she first arrived at work. She also had a stack of mail to go through, but Lois wasn't in the mood to do any of it. She was still feeling the pain of Joe's rejection. If only they could have met for a few minutes on Saturday, to talk and maybe share a meal. Would it have made any difference if they had? Tossing the question around in her mind brought no relief from Lois's frustrations. With sheer determination, she forced her thoughts off Joe and onto the work she needed to do.

By noon Lois had managed to catch up, and she decided to go out to lunch, hoping it would brighten her day. The deli was close to the church, and she could order her favorite veggie sandwich. She'd be glad when Tabby came back so she wouldn't have to eat alone.

Joe hurried up the front steps of Bayview Christian Church. He hoped he wasn't too late. It was noon, and Lois might have already left for lunch. He drew in a breath as he opened the door, suddenly colliding with someone.

"Joe!"

"Lois!"

"What are you doing here?"

"I came to see you."

She took a step backward. "You did?"

He nodded. "I needed to explain about Saturday. You hung up before I had the chance to tell you why we couldn't get together." He looked at her. "Are you all right? I didn't mean to bump into you like that. I guess I was rushing too much."

"I'm okay. I'm on my way to lunch now," she said, turning away.

He touched her arm. "Mind if I join you?"

She shrugged. "I–I suppose we could talk at the deli down the street. That's where I was planning to eat."

Joe's stomach growled at the mention of lunch. He hadn't eaten a decent breakfast that morning because he'd been in such a hurry to get to Tacoma and see Lois. "That sounds good to me."

Lois led the way, and soon they were seated in a booth at the deli. Joe ordered a hamburger, fries, and a cola, while Lois asked for her favorite sandwich and a glass of iced tea.

They ate in silence for the first few minutes, and Joe used the time to study the young woman sitting across from him. A few pale freckles dappled her cute, upturned nose. Funny, he'd never noticed them before. *Maybe I should pay more attention to details.*

Joe knew he couldn't stall forever. It was time for him to explain about Saturday. If he didn't, they might spend the rest of their lunch without talking. He had a feeling Lois was pretty miffed at him. "I was on my way out to do a kid's birthday party when you called the other day. Later I had to see one of the men on the hospital board about doing a program at their staff meeting next week. That's why I didn't have time to get together with you when you were in Olympia." He winked and offered Lois what he hoped was his best smile. "Am I forgiven for not explaining then and for not calling after our last date? I was really bogged down all week."

Was that a look of relief he saw on Lois's face? She'd seemed so tense only a moment ago, but now she was smiling.

"Thanks for explaining, Joe. I thought maybe you didn't want to see me anymore or that you'd rather I not come to your house." Her gaze dropped to the table. "I figured you might be afraid for me to meet your family."

He reached across the table and took her hand. "I live alone. I have ever since my mother died from lung cancer a year ago."

"I'm sorry about your mother. I should have remembered you said both of your parents were gone."

"Would you like to go out with me this Saturday?" he asked, abruptly changing the subject.

"What did you have in mind?" Her forehead wrinkled. "I hope you weren't planning to take me for another roller coaster ride."

He shook his head. "Not in the real sense of the word. Besides, I think our relationship has already had a few ups and downs."

He saw her throat constrict as she swallowed. "Does that mean we have a relationship?"

"I hope so." He grinned and wagged his finger. "About our Saturday date—"

"Yes?"

"It's a surprise, so you'll have to wait and see where I'm taking you."

"At least tell me how I'm supposed to dress."

"Wear something casual. Maybe a pair of blue jeans and a sweatshirt." He nodded toward the window. "As you can see by the falling leaves, autumn is here, so there's a good chance the weather will be chilly and rainy."

"What time will you pick me up?"

"How does eleven o'clock in the morning sound?"

"I'll be ready."

An hour later, Lois was seated in front of her desk, feeling satisfied. Not only had she eaten a terrific lunch, but things were okay with her and Joe, and they were going out again. So much for her plan to guard her heart.

Lois tried to rein in her thoughts and concentrate on a list of names she needed to contact regarding church business, but an image of Joe's smiling face kept bobbing in front of her. She realized they had little in common, with his being a clown and her being Miss Serious. But he made her laugh, and she thought he could probably charm the birds right out of the trees.

Lois could feel the knots forming in her shoulders. She wondered if she'd be able to discard her fears and trust Joe not to hurt her. She hoped she could because she was beginning to care for him.

The telephone rang, halting Lois's thoughts. She needed to stay focused on her job. "Bayview Christian Church," she answered.

"Lois, is that you?"

"Tabby?"

"The one and only," her sister answered. "How are you doing?"

"Fine. How about you and Seth? Will you be coming back to Tacoma soon?"

"That's the reason I'm calling. We've decided to stay on tour awhile longer. I checked in with Donna earlier, and she says everything's fine at the day care."

"I've heard that too."

"Seth's a little worried about his ventriloquist shop, but he was caught up on all repairs before we left, so I think it will be okay if he's gone another few weeks."

"I'm sure it will be fine," Lois agreed.

"What's new with you?" Tabby asked, changing the subject. "Did that cute, funny clown ever call?"

"Yes, and we've gone on a couple of dates. In fact, he's taking me out again this Saturday."

"That's great. Where are you going?"

"Joe said it was a surprise." Lois drew in a breath then released it in a contented sigh. "I don't see how he could top our last date."

"Where'd you go?"

"To the Puyallup Fair, and Joe talked me into riding the roller coaster."

Tabby's sharp intake of breath indicated her reaction. "And you lived to tell about it?"

"It turned out to be a lot of fun," Lois admitted. "I think I've finally overcome my fear of the crazy ride."

"That's wonderful. I'm glad you and Joe are getting along so well. You two should be good for each other."

"What's that supposed to mean?"

"You tend to be a bit solemn sometimes, and Joe's playfulness will help you see the humorous side of life. Joe's a big kidder, so your serious side should give him some new perspectives."

Lois nodded, not even caring that Tabby couldn't see her reaction. Her sister was right. Lois definitely could use more joy in her life, but Joe more serious? Was that even possible?

Chapter Eleven

As Joe prepared for his date with Lois, he began to have second thoughts. He enjoyed her company. More than he had any other woman he'd ever dated, in fact. He knew she was a Christian, and he was physically attracted to her, but something was holding him back. Was it the serious side of Lois that bothered him, or the personal questions she'd asked him? Joe never talked to anyone about his mother's emotional problems, his brother's leaving home, or even the details of his parents dying. It was too painful, and he'd found his own way of dealing with it, so why dredge up the past? Yet several times, when he and Lois had gone out, she'd brought up his family. So far, he'd managed to distract her or change the subject, but how long could he put her curiosity on hold?

Joe hopped into his truck and slammed the door. "Guess I'll have to keep her too busy laughing to ask any serious questions today."

Lois grabbed her sweater and an umbrella from the stand. She'd looked out her living room window and saw Joe pull up to the curb in front of the apartment complex. It was fifteen minutes after he'd said he would be there, so she hurried out the door, glad her apartment was on the ground floor and within easy reach of the street.

"I would have come to the door to get you," Joe said when she opened his truck door and slid into the passenger's seat.

"I was ready and figured it would save time."

"Looks like you came prepared." He nodded toward her umbrella.

Lois glanced out the window at the cloudy sky. "Even though it's not raining at the moment, it could be later on."

"You're probably right," he agreed.

"So where are we heading?"

"Remember? It's a surprise."

Lois glanced at her blue jeans and peach-colored knit top. Joe had told her to wear something casual for their date, so she hoped she looked okay. He was dressed in a pair of jeans and a pale blue sweatshirt, which probably meant they weren't going anywhere fancy. Relieved, she leaned against the headrest and decided to enjoy the ride. She had a habit of worrying over little things, but being around Joe was helping her relax.

By the time they turned onto the freeway and headed north, Lois's curiosity was piqued. Were they going to Seattle? Whidbey Island? Vancouver? She was about to ask, but Joe posed a question just then.

"Heard anything from your sister and brother-in-law lately?"

She nodded. "Tabby called me the other day. She said their evangelistic tour has been quite successful, so they've decided to keep on going for a couple of more weeks."

Joe tapped the steering wheel with both thumbs. "That's great. Maybe I should have gone with them. It's always rewarding to put on a Gospel program and see folks turn their lives over to the Lord."

"I've heard Tabby say that many times," Lois agreed. "Sometimes I feel jealous when she tells me how many people accept Christ after one of their performances."

"Why would you feel jealous?"

She sighed deeply. "My sister is using her talents for the Lord and helping people find a personal relationship with Him. That's part of what she and Seth do. I, on the other hand, have no talents to share."

"You're a secretary for the church, right?"

"Yes," she said, nodding, "but it doesn't seem like much."

"Not everyone has the ability to type, file, organize, and keep an office running smoothly. I'd say that's a talent in itself."

"You may be right, but it's not the same thing as what you and Tabby and Seth are involved in." Lois paused a moment. "Sometimes I think I should pursue some kind of Christian ministry that could be part of a Gospel presentation."

Joe reached across the seat for her hand. "How about becoming a Gospel clown? There's always room for one more."

She giggled. "Me?"

"Yes, you."

"I don't know the first thing about clowning."

"You don't have to. There are plenty of classes you can take. In fact, I'll be teaching one at a seminar in Bremerton next month." He winked at her. "It might be fun to have someone enrolled in my class who likes to ride roller coasters and eat cotton candy."

She swatted his arm playfully. "You're the one who likes to do those things, silly. I was coerced into riding the roller coaster, and one bite of cotton candy was enough to last me all day."

"I stand corrected," he said with a chuckle. "Think about what I said, Lois. Even if you decide clowning isn't for you, I promise it'll be a fun class."

"I'll consider it. Thanks for telling me about it."

Half an hour later, Joe exited the freeway and headed toward the Seattle Center. He was glad their conversation had been kept light and upbeat. Lois hadn't once mentioned his past. Of course, he'd kept her busy listening to his stories about the birthday parties he'd recently done, and then he'd told her several corny jokes.

"Ah-ha! So you're taking me to the Seattle Center!" Lois exclaimed.

"Yep. Sound like fun?" He glanced over to gauge her reaction.

She offered him a pleasant smile. "More carnival rides?"

"Nope—the Space Needle!"

Her mouth dropped open like a broken hinge. "You're kidding, right?"

He shook his head. "I thought we'd eat lunch in the restaurant up there. We can enjoy the magnificent view of Puget Sound."

Lois's face paled. "Uh, I really would rather eat at the food court, with my feet on solid ground."

Joe laughed. "Don't tell me you're afraid to go up in the Space Needle."

"Okay, I won't tell you that."

"Scared we might have an earthquake while we're in the elevator heading to the top?" he teased.

"I hadn't even thought about that prospect." Lois gripped the edge of the seat. "How about if I wait on the ground while you check out the beautiful sights?"

He shook his head. "No way! I planned to do something special for this date, and I aim to see it through to the finish."

When Lois didn't reply, he glanced her way again. She was leaning against the headrest with her eyes closed. "Lois, are you asleep?"

Her eyes snapped open, and she shot him a pleading look. "I don't want to go to the Space Needle for lunch. I'm not up to it today."

Not up to it? What exactly was Lois saying? "Want to explain?" he asked.

"I'm afraid of heights, Joe. I have been ever since I was a little girl and my dad took me to the top of the Space Needle."

"But you're all grown up now," he argued. "And I won't let anything happen to you—I promise. Besides, you went on the roller coaster at the Puyallup Fair, and that's pretty high off the ground."

She shot him an exasperated look. "That wasn't half as high as the Space Needle, and it was moving at such rapid speeds. I didn't have time to think about how high I was."

"How about this—we'll go up and see the sights then come right back down and have lunch at the food court. Does that sound okay?"

"Lunch at the food court would be great, but I'm still not sure about going up in that needle."

"It'll be a breeze."

"Anything like riding the roller coaster?"

"You said you had fun."

"I did, after I got over my initial fear," she admitted.

"This won't be any different. Once you take in the beautiful scenery below, you'll be begging me to bring you back for another ride to the top of the world."

"Okay. I'm not thrilled about it, but I'll give it a try," Lois said with a deep sigh.

They pulled into a parking lot near the Seattle Center, and Joe found a spot before she could change her mind. He felt confident that once they were on the observation deck she would relax and enjoy her surroundings.

∞

Lois fidgeted and pulled nervously on the straps of her purse as they stood inside the enclosed area, waiting for the next elevator to take them to the top. *"The top of the world."* Wasn't that what Joe had called it? *I only hope I don't do something stupid up there. What if I get dizzy when I look down? What if I don't look down and still feel faint? What if—?*

Joe slipped his arm around Lois and tickled her ribs. "It's going to be okay. Trust me."

She squirmed, giggled, and tickled him back. The distraction was helping her relax. Each time Lois was with Joe, she liked him more. He could make her laugh, and he'd convinced her to ride the roller coaster. Now she was standing at the foot of the Space Needle. Was there no end to this man's persuasions?

The elevator door zipped open, and the attendant ushered them in. Lois felt herself being crowded to the back of the elevator, as the elevator filled with people. Joe's arm tightened around her waist, and she leaned into him and whispered, "I hope I don't live to regret this."

He chucked her under the chin. "You'll be fine."

"I sure hope so."

Without warning, Joe bent his head and kissed Lois's lips, snatching her breath away and causing her arms to go limp at her sides. Before she had time to regain her bearings, they were at the top, and Joe had pulled away.

"Here we are," he announced.

Lois gulped and took a tentative step forward. Mount Rainier and everything in the distance radiated beauty beyond compare, but the things directly below resembled ants, toy cars, and tiny buildings that looked like children's blocks. A wave of dizziness hit her, and she inhaled deeply, hoping to squelch the dizzy feeling before she toppled over.

"You doing okay?" Joe asked as he pulled Lois closer to his side.

"I–I feel kind of strange."

"It's the gorgeous view. It takes your breath away, doesn't it?"

She pressed her lips together and stood there like a statue.

"Come on! Let's go to the railing and see what we can see."

Before Lois could respond, Joe grabbed her hand and pulled her away from the wall where she'd been hovering. A few seconds later they were standing on the edge of the world. At least that's how it felt to Lois. Joe was right. The roller coaster at the fair had been child's play compared to this. Even though the rails were enclosed, Lois felt as if she might tumble over the edge to her death. No way could she stay up here long enough to eat lunch in the revolving restaurant!

"Can we go back down now?"

Joe didn't seem to hear what Lois was saying, as he whistled some silly tune and studied the panorama below.

Lois stood slightly behind him, leaning into his back, and praying she wouldn't pass out. She closed her eyes, hoping it would make her feel better, but the knowledge of where she stood was enough to make her head spin.

After what seemed like an eternity, Joe turned to face her. "Have you seen enough?"

Lois had seen more than she cared to see. She headed toward the nearest elevator and was thankful they didn't have to wait as long as they had when they went up. She breathed a sigh of relief when the elevator door opened.

"That was awesome!" Joe announced as they stepped inside. "We were up so high I think I saw some of the passengers' faces looking out of the window in a jet that whizzed by."

Lois moaned. How could Joe make a joke at a time like this? Didn't he realize she'd nearly died of fright up there?

"Hey, you know what I think?"

She glared at him. "I can't imagine."

"Maybe we should go up in a plane for our next date."

"You have to be kidding!"

"I love being in the air. The only thing I don't like about plane travel is the waiting and, of course, having some airline personnel go through my belongings." Joe chuckled. "Airport security has been really tight lately. In fact, the last time I boarded a plane, they confiscated my most important possession."

"Really—what was that?" Lois asked, feeling a little better now that they were heading for solid ground again.

Joe's lips curved into a dopey little smile. "My sharp wit!"

Chapter Twelve

The rest of the day in Seattle passed swiftly. Joe bought Lois a souvenir replica of the Space Needle, to remind her she'd actually gone up in it, and they ate lunch at the food court, sharing a Mexican dish large enough for two. After walking around the entire Seattle Center and enjoying the sights and sounds, Joe suggested they go to the waterfront.

Lois loved the salty smell of the bay and eagerly agreed. The next several hours were spent browsing the various gift shops, touring the aquarium, and finally having fish-and-chips at Ivar's Fish Bar. Now they were on their way home, and Lois dreaded having to tell Joe goodbye. She enjoyed being with him and wondered if she could love him. It amazed her sometimes that he could see the humor in almost any situation.

Leaning her head against the window, Lois closed her eyes and relived the memory of Joe mimicking the seals they'd seen at the aquarium. He'd done everything but stand on his head to get them to bark and slap their fins against the wooden deck when they begged for food.

"What's that little smile about?" Joe asked, breaking into Lois's thoughts.

She opened her eyes and glanced over at him. "I was thinking about how much fun I had today."

Joe grinned like a Cheshire cat. "You mean you're not mad at me for dragging you into the Space Needle?"

Her lower lip protruded. "Well, maybe a little. . . ."

"But I kept you well entertained the rest of the day, and you've decided to forgive me, right?"

She nodded and smiled.

"Maybe we can go to Snoqualmie Falls for our next date," he suggested. "We'd better do it soon, though, 'cause it's almost October, and the weather will be turning cold and damp soon."

Lois's heartbeat quickened. Joe wanted to see her again, and he was already talking about where they might go. "I haven't been up to the falls in ages. It's beautiful there, and we could take a picnic lunch."

His forehead wrinkled. "Since the weather is turning colder, and rain is a likely possibility, I'm not sure the picnic idea would fly, unless we eat in my truck."

She agreed. "A picnic lunch inside your truck sounds like a great idea."

"When would you like to go?" Joe asked.

"I'm pretty flexible. It's your hectic schedule we'll need to plan around. When will you have another free Saturday?"

He shrugged. "I'd better check my appointment book after I get home. I'll give you a call as soon as I know which day will work best."

"Sounds good to me," she said.

Joe was glad they'd made it through the day without Lois's asking too many personal questions. Maybe she had given up on the idea of digging into his past and decided they could simply have a good time whenever they were together. That was all he wanted, wasn't it—just to enjoy Lois's company? No strings attached and no in-depth conversations about confidential things. It was too painful to talk about the past. Joe had managed fine all these years by clowning around, and he wasn't about to let his guard down now.

"Would you like to come in for a cup of coffee before you head back on the road?" Lois asked as they stopped in front of her apartment complex.

He smiled. "Sure, that would be great." Joe hopped out of the truck and sprinted around to the other side to help Lois down.

As they strolled up the front sidewalk, Joe noticed a broken beer bottle lying in the grass. "Looks like folks choose to litter no matter where they live," he muttered.

"I know," Lois said. "My apartment manager does his best to keep the yard free of debris, but it's almost a full-time job."

Joe bent down to pick up the shattered glass. "I'll carry this in and drop it in your garbage can, if that's all right."

"Sure. It will be one less thing for poor Mr. Richards to face in the morning."

In Joe's hurry to retrieve what was left of the bottle, he didn't notice the jagged edge and cut his hand. "Ouch!" He cringed and dropped the piece of glass as a sharp pain shot through his hand then continued up his arm. "Guess I should be more careful when I'm playing with glass."

Lois frowned. "Here—let me take a look at that." She reached for Joe's hand, and a stream of dark blood oozed between his fingers and landed on her palm. "Oh, my! That looks like a nasty cut. I think you may need stitches."

Joe shrugged it off as though it were no more than a pinprick. "Naw, it'll be fine once we get inside and I can wash my hand and slap on a bandage."

She gave him a dubious look, then handed over a clean handkerchief she'd taken from her purse. "Wrap this around the wound until we get indoors."

"What about the broken glass?"

"You'd better leave it for now. At the moment we have more pressing things to worry about."

Joe followed Lois to her apartment door. She unlocked the door and opened it for him to enter.

"I have antiseptic and bandages in the bathroom." Lois motioned to the kitchen table. "Have a seat and I'll get my first-aid kit."

"I can manage," Joe mumbled. "Just point the way to the bathroom."

"Are you sure you don't want my help? It's going to be difficult to work with only one hand."

He shook his head, although his hand was throbbing like crazy.

"The bathroom's the first door on the left," she said, nodding in that direction.

A few seconds later, Joe stepped into the bathroom, held his hand under the faucet, and turned on the cold water. A river of red poured from the wound. The room seemed to spin around him, and a wave of nausea rushed through his stomach. He leaned against the sink and moaned. "Guess I might need a couple of stitches after all."

"What was that?" Lois called from the other room.

"Could you come here a minute?"

She was at his side in a flash, concern etched on her face. "You look terrible,

Joe. Maybe you should put your head between your legs, before you pass out."

"I can't stop the bleeding. I think you were right about my needing stitches." He smiled, but it took effort. "Guess we'll have to postpone our plans to go up to Snoqualmie Falls for a while."

She looked at his hand and shuddered. "It's bleeding badly. I'd better get a towel." Lois opened a small cabinet and withdrew a bath towel. She wrapped it tightly around his hand and led him toward the door. "I'm driving you to the hospital, and you'd better not argue."

"I wouldn't dream of it," he mumbled. Funny, he'd never felt this woozy when he'd seen blood before. Maybe he was getting soft in the head.

Lois slipped one arm around Joe's waist, and they headed outside. "Mind if we take your truck?" she asked. "My car's in the parking garage, and I don't want to take the time to get it."

"Sure—that's fine. The keys are in my left pocket," he said as she helped him into the passenger's seat.

Lois pulled out the keys, hooked Joe's seat belt in place, closed the door, and ran around to the driver's side.

"St. Joseph's Hospital is only a few miles from here," she told him.

"That's good." Joe leaned his head back and tried to conjure up some pleasant thoughts so he wouldn't have to think about the throbbing in his hand or the blood already soaking through the towel.

When Lois parked the truck in front of the emergency room, Joe breathed a sigh of relief. At last he would get some help.

After they checked in at the emergency room desk and filled out forms, Joe and Lois took seats and waited. Apparently, an accident involving three vehicles had occurred across town, and those people were receiving treatment now. The woman at the desk had told Joe he would be examined as soon as possible.

Lois recognized one of the nurses on duty as her neighbor Bonnie McKenzie. She knew from the few conversations she'd had with Bonnie that she worked at St. Joseph's, was single, and dated often. Lois had seen more than a few men come to the apartment building to take out the vibrant redhead.

In a short time, Bonnie called Joe's name.

"I'll wait here, Joe," Lois told him. "You go on back."

"Oh Lois—won't you come too?" Joe asked. "I'd really like it if you would."

Before she knew it, Lois was sitting beside the table on which Joe was lying, wishing she could be anywhere else but there. Hospitals made her nervous. They smelled funny, and most of the people who came to the ER were in pain—including Joe. She could see by the pinched expression on his face that he was hurting, although he kept telling jokes while the nurse administered a local anesthetic and cleaned the wound.

"I still can't get over the fact that Tacoma would name one of their hospitals after me," Joe said with a wink.

"What do you mean?" asked Bonnie.

"St. Joseph." Joe chuckled. "You know, if hospitals are places to get well, then tell me this—why do they serve such awful food?"

Before the nurse could respond, a tall man with gray hair entered the room and introduced himself as Dr. Bradshaw. Lois could see by the stern expression on his face that he was strictly business.

The doctor examined Joe's hand and gave the nurse some instructions. "Now lie back and relax, Mr. Richey. This won't hurt."

Joe's head fell back onto the small pillow. "That's because Nurse Bonnie has numbed my hand."

Dr. Bradshaw made no reply but quickly set to work.

Lois turned her head away and studied the wall. She had no desire to watch the doctor put stitches in Joe's hand, even if she was fairly sure he wouldn't feel any pain.

"This is like an operation, isn't it, Nurse Bonnie?" Joe asked.

"I suppose it could be categorized as such," she replied with a chuckle.

"From what I hear, the definition of a minor operation is one that someone else has, so I guess mine falls into the major operation category," Joe said with a loud guffaw.

Why is he doing this? Can't the man be serious about anything? Lois peeked at Joe, who was grinning from ear to ear. Nurse Bonnie was also smiling, but the doctor's face was a mask of austerity. *At least someone besides me sees the seriousness of all this.*

"We're nearly finished," the doctor said at last.

Lois breathed a sigh of relief, but Joe told another joke. "Does anyone here know what a specialist is?"

"Certainly," the nurse replied. "It's a doctor who devotes himself to some special branch of medicine."

"Not even close," Joe said. "A specialist is a doctor who has all his patients trained so they only get sick during his regular office hours."

Dr. Bradshaw groaned and shook his head, Bonnie chuckled, and Lois just sat there. *Maybe I'm too serious for my own good,* she thought, feeling her cheeks grow warm. *Bonnie obviously thinks Joe's funny, and maybe he's clowning around because it's the only way he knows how to deal with the pain. He could dislike hospitals as much as I do, but he sure does show it in a different way.*

The doctor cleared his throat. "Bandage this fellow's hand then give him a tetanus shot, Miss McKenzie. When I looked at Mr. Richey's chart, I noticed he's overdue for one." He turned and strode out of the room.

Lois noticed that Joe's face had turned white. He pressed his lips into a tight line as the nurse stuck the needle in his arm. Afterward, he plastered another silly grin on his face. "Say, did you hear about the guy who was always getting sick with a cold or the flu?"

Bonnie shrugged her shoulders. "That could be just about anyone."

He nodded. "True, but this guy was shot so full of antibiotics that every time he sneezed he cured half a dozen people."

Bonnie laughed and gave Joe's good hand a little pat. "Be sure to keep that wound clean and watch for infection. If you see anything suspicious, get right back in here."

Joe hopped down from the table. "Sure thing, but I live in Olympia. So if I have any problems the hospital there will probably get my business." He glanced over at Lois and winked. It was the first time he'd looked her way since they'd come into the examining room.

"Ready to go?" Lois asked.

"Ready as I'll ever be. Sure am glad you're driving, though. My left hand feels like it's ten sizes too big with this huge roll of bandage Nurse Bonnie has slapped on me."

"It's for your own good, Mr. Richey," the nurse said as she led them out of the room. "Take care now, and, Lois, I'll probably see you around our apartment complex."

Lois waved to Bonnie and hurried out the door. She was anxious to get outside and breathe some fresh air.

A short time later Lois drove away from the hospital and headed for the freeway. "Hey—where are we going?" Joe asked. "Your place is that way." He pointed with his right hand.

"I'm taking you to Olympia."

His eyebrows shot up. "You're driving my truck—remember?"

"I know that."

"How will you get back to Tacoma? And where will you stay tonight?"

"My dad can pick me up at your house, as soon as I make sure you're okay, and then drive me back tomorrow. I'll stay at their house tonight."

"Why didn't I think of that?" Joe laughed.

Lois smiled. "You just had stitches—remember?"

Chapter Thirteen

Lois woke up feeling groggy and disoriented. It took her a few minutes to realize she was in her old bedroom at her parents' home in Olympia. She yawned, sat up, and glanced at the clock on the table by her bed. It was almost eight o'clock. There was no way she and Dad could drive to Tacoma for her to shower, change, and still make it in time for Sunday school. She would have to call the superintendent and ask him to find a substitute for her class. If she left right away, she might make it for the morning worship service.

Maybe I should call Joe and see if he'd like me to go with him to his church this morning. Then Lois remembered she didn't have a change of clothes since she hadn't planned to stay all night at her parents' home. *The least I can do is give him a call and see how he's doing this morning.*

Lois reached for the telephone and dialed Joe's number.

"Joe Richey here." Joe's deep voice sounded sleepy, and Lois figured she had probably awakened him.

"Hi, it's Lois. I was wondering how your hand is this morning."

"It's still pretty sore, though I think I'll live." He laughed, but it sounded forced. "Thanks for coming to my rescue last night."

"You'd have done the same for me."

"You have that right."

There was a long pause. "Well, I should let you go. I need to spend a few minutes with my parents then hurry back to Tacoma if I'm going to make it in time for church."

"I'd invite you to visit my church with me, but I think it might be best if I lie low today. The doctor said I should ice my hand if there's swelling and try to rest it for the next twenty-four hours."

"That makes sense to me," Lois said. "Is there anything I can do for you before I head home?"

"No, I think I can manage. Thanks for offering though."

"Guess I'll be seeing you then."

"Have a safe trip back to Tacoma."

"Thanks. Take care now."

"You too. Bye, Lois."

Lois hung up the phone and went down to the kitchen, where she found her parents sitting at the table, drinking coffee.

"There's more in the pot." Dad lifted his mug as she entered the room. Even with his paunchy stomach and thinning blond hair, she still thought her father was attractive.

She smiled and shook her head. "Thanks, Dad. I'd rather have tea."

"There's some in the cupboard above the refrigerator," her mother said. "What would you like me to fix for breakfast?"

"I'll just grab a piece of fruit," Lois replied. "Dad, can you drive me to Tacoma right away?"

His eyebrows lifted. "So soon? What's the rush?"

She took a seat at the table. "I've already missed Sunday school, and I'd like to at least get there in time for church."

Her mother sighed. "Church—church—church. Is that all my two daughters ever think about anymore?"

Lois held back a retort. Instead she smiled and said, "Have you heard from Tabby recently?"

"She sent us a postcard from Moscow, Idaho, a few weeks ago," her mother answered. "Her note said she and Seth were extending their time on the road."

"I'm glad Tabby finally got over her shyness," her dad interjected, "but I don't see why she has to run around the countryside preaching hellfire and damnation."

Lois felt her face flame. Not too many years ago she'd have felt the same way about her sister. But now that she was a Christian, she understood why Tabby wanted to share the Good News. "Tabby and Seth don't preach hellfire and damnation, Dad. They share God's love and how people can know Him personally through His Son, Jesus Christ."

Her dad shrugged and rubbed a hand across his chin. "Whatever."

Lois grabbed a banana from the fruit bowl and stood up. "Will you drive me back to Tacoma?"

He nodded curtly. "If that's what you want. You know me—always aim to please."

It was harder to do things with one hand than Joe had expected. *Maybe I should've asked Lois to come by this morning and fix me a decent breakfast.* He shook his head as he struggled to butter a piece of toast. He hadn't realized until now how dependent he was on using both hands to do simple, basic things. "Guess it wouldn't have been fair to expect her to give up going to church and play nursemaid to me."

Joe dropped into a chair and stared blankly at the Sunday morning newspaper. He'd come to care for Lois. But did he have anything to offer a woman like her? She was sophisticated and beautiful and blessed with a sweet, Christian spirit. She didn't seem prone to mood swings, which probably meant she was nothing like his mother. Still, Joe was holding back from any kind of commitment. What bothered him most was that he had no secure job, never knowing from week to week, month to month, where, when, or even *if* he would be called to do another program. What kind of future did he have to offer a wife?

"A wife?" Joe moaned. "Why am I even thinking about marriage?" After his mother died, he'd told himself he would never marry. Even though he'd been concerned about finding a woman whose emotions were stable, he was even more worried about his inability to support a family. Like Jesus' disciples, Joe lived from month to month on what others gave in payment for the services he rendered as a clown.

He glanced at his Bible, lying beside the newspaper. "I don't need to waste my time on these negative thoughts," he muttered. "I can look in my Bible for verses that remind me to have a merry heart."

Lois slipped into the pew, realizing she was ten minutes late, but glad she'd made it to church at all. Her dad hadn't been happy about driving her home before he'd read the Sunday newspaper. But at least they'd enjoyed a good visit in the car, though Lois was careful to keep the conversation light and away from religious things. It troubled her the way her parents were so opposed to church and faith in God and even talking about spiritual matters. She wanted them to see their need for Christ's forgiveness of their sins.

If Tabby and I keep praying and showing Mom and Dad we love them, maybe someday it will happen.

Lois opened her hymnbook and joined the congregation in singing "Love Lifted Me." After a few lines, she felt her burdens become lighter as she thought about how much God loved her. Enough to send His Son to die in her place.

When the service was over, Lois spotted Tabby's friend Donna talking to the senior pastor and his wife. Lois waited patiently until they were finished, then she stepped up to Donna and gave her a little nudge. "How's everything with you?"

Donna shrugged. "Okay, but I'll sure be glad when Tabby's back. Things aren't the same without her, and the day care kids miss her something awful."

Lois was about to comment, but Donna cut her off. "Tabby really has a way with children. I think she'll make a good mother someday, don't you?"

Lois nodded. "I agree."

Donna motioned for Lois to move away from the crowd, and the two of them found a spot in one corner of the room. "So what's new in your life?"

"Well, I—"

"Hey, Lois, I'm glad to see you made it to church."

Lois turned and smiled at Dan Gleason, the Sunday school superintendent.

"I asked one of our older teens to take your class, and she said everything went fine," he told her.

"That's great. Thanks for taking care of things on such short notice," Lois responded.

"No problem." Dan grinned and reached up to scratch his head. "Say, I was wondering if you'd be interested in having Carla Sweeney help you every week. She'll graduate from high school in June and wants to find some kind of ministry within the church."

Lois smiled. She would love to have some help with her class.

Sometimes she felt she had more kids than she could handle. An extra pair of hands would be helpful when it came to craft time as well. "Sure! Tell Carla I'd be happy to have her as my assistant."

Dan nodded, said goodbye, and walked off. Lois turned back to Donna, but she was gone.

Lois shrugged and headed for the nearest exit. It would be good to get home where she could relax for the rest of the day.

Chapter Fourteen

Lois was sitting in front of her computer at work on Monday morning when she felt someone's hand touch her shoulder. She whirled around and was surprised to see her sister standing there.

"Tabby! When did you get back? Why didn't you call?"

Tabby held up one hand. "Whoa! One question at a time, please."

Lois stood and gave her sister a hug. "It's so good to see you."

"It's great to see you too. Seth and I got in late last night, which is why I didn't call. I decided to surprise you instead."

"You did that all right." Lois nodded toward the chair next to her desk. "Have a seat and tell me about your trip."

Tabby dropped into the chair and smiled. "It was awesome, Lois. Everywhere we went there were spiritual conversions. I feel so energized—I think I could hike up Mt. Rainier and not even feel winded."

Lois chuckled and gave her sister's arm a gentle squeeze. "Now that I'd like to see."

"Seriously, though, I wish you could have been there to see people asking Jesus into their hearts." Tabby's eyes misted.

"I wish that too," Lois murmured.

Tabby grinned. "What's new in your life? Are you still seeing Joe Richey?"

Lois nodded. "Up until last Saturday I was. I'm not sure about the future though."

Tabby's eyebrows furrowed. "Why not?"

"I'm worried that Joe and I might not be suited for one another. He probably needs someone more carefree and fun loving than I am. Maybe I should bow out, before one of us gets hurt."

"Bow out? You have to be kidding! I can see how much you care about Joe. It's written all over your face."

Lois hated to admit it, but Tabby was right. In spite of Joe's refusal to see the serious side of things, she was falling headlong into the tunnel of love.

"Did something happen between you and Joe to make you question your relationship?" Tabby asked.

"Sort of."

"Want to talk about it?'

"I–I guess so." Lois nodded toward her computer screen. "I really should get back to work right now. And you're probably expected in the day care center. Why don't we meet at our favorite spot for lunch, and I'll tell you about it then?"

Tabby stood up. "Sounds good to me." She smiled. "I'll meet you at Garrison's at noon."

Lois watched as Tabby left the room. Her sister walked with a bounce to her step and an assurance she'd never had before she started using her talents to serve the Lord. *Talents.* There was that word again. Lois couldn't help but envy others like Tabby and Seth who were both ventriloquists, Donna and her beautiful chalk-art drawings, and Joe with his Gospel clown routines. What could Lois do that would have an impact on people's lives? Were being the church secretary and teaching a Sunday school class enough for her?

You could take the clowning class Joe is scheduled to teach next month, a little voice reminded her. *You won't know if you'd enjoy clowning until you give it a try.*

Lois grabbed her desk calendar and studied the month of October. She didn't have anything pencilled in, except a dental appointment, and the church harvest party. "I have the time," she murmured. "The question is, do I have the talent?"

Garrison's Deli was crowded, but Lois and Tabby found a small table in the corner. They both ordered veggie sandwiches and ate as they chatted.

"Tell me what the problem is with you and Joe," Tabby prompted her. "I thought you'd decided it didn't matter whether you and he were equally matched."

Lois shrugged. "I did think that for a while, but the other night Joe cut his hand, and—"

"What happened? Was he hurt bad?"

"He was dropping me off at my apartment, and a bottle was lying in the front yard. When he picked it up, he cut his hand."

Tabby grimaced. "That's terrible. Did he need stitches?"

"Yes, and all during the process he kept cracking jokes." Lois wrinkled her forehead. "I could see by the look on his face that he was pretty stressed out; yet he kept making small talk and telling one joke after another." She sighed. "I guess he was trying to cover up his real feelings, but it made me wonder if he even knows how to be serious."

"Have you ever thought maybe Joe is so used to clowning he doesn't know when to quit? It could be that once you know him better, you'll see another side of the man."

"You think I should keep seeing him?"

"Of course. In the months since you and Michael Yehley broke up, I haven't seen you look so content." Tabby patted Lois's hand. "Instead of hoping Joe will become more serious, why not try to be more lighthearted yourself?"

Lois contemplated her sister's last statement. "You could be right. Maybe I'll take one of Joe's clowning classes and find out how much humor I have inside of me."

It had been a little over a week since Joe had cut his hand. The pain had subsided, and he was finally able to use it again. He'd had only one program in the last week, so that gave him time to allow the injury to heal—and the opportunity to think about his friendship with Lois.

Joe stared at his morning cup of coffee. Was their relationship going anywhere? He thought they'd had a great time at the Seattle Center last Saturday, but after he'd cut his hand and she'd taken him to the hospital, Lois seemed kind of distant. He hoped she wasn't prone to mood swings after all.

An uninvited image flashed onto the screen of Joe's mind, and a hard knot formed in his stomach. He could see himself and his little brother, Brian, sitting on the steps of their front porch. They were blowing bubbles and having a great time. Mom was seated in a wicker chair nearby, doing some kind of needlework. One minute she was laughing and sharing in the joy Joe felt as each bubble formed. But the next minute she was shouting at him. "Do you plan to sit there all day blowing bubbles, Joe, or are you going to weed those flower beds?"

Joe's throat constricted as the vision of his mother became clearer. She was wearing a pair of men's faded blue overalls, and her long, dark hair hung in a braid down her back. Her brown eyes flashed with anger as she jumped up from her seat, marched across the porch, and grabbed hold of Joe's ear. "Do you hear me, boy? Why are you wasting the day with those stupid bubbles?"

Tears stung the back of young Joe's eyes as he rose to his feet. "I–I didn't even know you wanted the flower beds weeded."

"Speak up! I can't understand when you mumble!"

"I didn't know you wanted me to do any weeding today," Joe said, much louder this time.

"Of course you knew. I told you that yesterday."

Joe handed his bottle of bubbles to Brian. "You might as well have some fun, even if I have to work all afternoon."

Brian's expression was one of pity, but he took the bubbles and looked away. Joe sauntered down the steps, as though nothing unusual had happened. In fact, by the time he reached the shed where the gardening tools were kept, Joe was whistling a tune.

The sharp ringing of the telephone jolted him back to the present. He was glad for the interruption. It always hurt when he thought about the past. It was difficult to deal with his pain over the way Mom used to be, but at least she'd committed her life to the Lord the night before she died. That was comforting, even though it hadn't erased the agony of the past.

The phone kept on ringing, and Joe finally grabbed the receiver. "Joe Richey here."

"Hi, Joe. It's Lois."

Joe's lips twitched, as he tried to gather his whirling thoughts into some kind of order. "What's up, Lois?"

"I called to see how your hand is doing."

"Much better, thanks," he said, flexing the fingers of the hand that had been cut.

"I'm glad to hear it." There was a long pause. "I also wanted to tell you, Joe, that I've made a decision."

A feeling of apprehension crept up Joe's spine. Was she going to say she didn't want to see him anymore? "What decision is that?"

"It's about that clowning class you'll be teaching in Bremerton next month."

Joe expelled the breath he'd been holding. "What about it?"

"I've decided to take you up on your offer. I want to learn how to be a clown."

Chapter Fifteen

L ois sat in the front row of a classroom with about fifty other people. She held a pen and notebook in her hands and was ready for Slow-Joe the Clown to begin his presentation.

Joe swaggered into the room, dressed in a green-and-white checkered clown costume and wearing white face paint with a red nose. "Good mornin', folks! Glad you could be here today." He spotted Lois, waved, and gave her a quick wink.

She smiled at him but wished he hadn't singled her out.

"The first thing you should know about clowning is that clowns aren't just silly comedians who dress up in goofy costumes to entertain kids." Joe shook his head. "No, clowns are performing artists, and to be a successful clown you need to possess certain skills."

Lois stared down at her hands, now folded in her lap across the notebook. What skills did she have, other than being able to type eighty words a minute, answer the phone with a pleasant voice, and keep the church office running as smoothly as possible? She couldn't juggle balls, twist balloons into cute little animals, or think of anything funny to say. Did she have any business taking this class?

"The first recorded reference to clowning dates back to about 2270 BC," Joe stated. "A nine-year-old reportedly said, 'A jester came to rejoice and delight the heart!' Until the mid-1800s, most clowns wore very little makeup. Many clowns today do wear makeup, and each type of face paint can have some kind of meaning." Joe pointed to his cheek. "Take the white-faced look I'm wearing. Clowns who wear this type of makeup are usually the reserved, refined kind of clown." He offered the audience a lopsided grin. "Of course, there are exceptions to every rule."

Lois's hope began to soar. *Maybe I'm an exception. Maybe I can pretend to be sappy and happy.*

Joe moved over to the board and picked up a piece of chalk. He wrote in bold letters, *"What Is a Clown Character?"*

Lois smiled to herself. *You. You're a clown character, Joe Richey.*

"Each clown must somehow be different from all the other clowns," Joe said with a note of conviction. "Your unique personality is what will make you stand out from the rest. The makeup and clothes you choose to wear will enhance this creation. Your clown's appearance, way of moving, actions, and reactions are all influenced by your character's personality."

Joe seemed so confident and in his element talking about clowning. Lois picked up her notebook and pen again to take some serious notes.

"Next," Joe said, writing on the board, "ask yourself this question: What do I need to be a great clown? You could add some balloon animals to your routine. Or how about a bright orange vest? A few tricks? Juggling? A pet bird?" He shook his head. "While those are all good props and fun additions to your routines, the things you'll probably need more than anything else are improvisational skills, character development and, most important, a knowledge of the elements of humor."

Lois sighed and placed her notebook back in her lap. *Elements of humor. Sure hope I learn some of those today.*

"Have you ever noticed how we often make assumptions about people based on what they are wearing?" Joe asked. "For instance, picture a man dressed in a pair of faded blue jeans with holes in the knees and a sweatshirt with a college logo on the front. He's wearing paint-stained tennis shoes and a wedding ring on his left hand, and he's holding a cup of coffee in one hand. What do we know about this person?"

"The guy's married and has a college degree, but he's too poor to buy new clothes," a young man in the audience called out.

"Could be," Joe said with a nod. "Anybody else have an idea?"

"The gentleman could be an educated, hard worker who likes to putter around the house," the older woman sitting beside Lois suggested.

Joe smiled. "You may be right. The point is, we can't always judge someone by the clothes he wears. His actions play a major role in defining who he is." Joe turned to the board and wrote, *"Your character's appearance and personality must be consistent to seem real."* He pivoted back to the audience. "If you dress in black, the audience will expect you to be an elegant or somber character, because clothing conveys a meaning. If you wear a baggy, torn costume, people will get the idea you're a hobo clown." He winked at the audience. "Since most clowns don't make a lot of money, this particular costume would be kind of appropriate."

Lois laughed along with everyone else. The concept of clowning was more complicated than she'd imagined it to be. If she was going to become a Gospel clown, she'd have to come up with the kind of character she wanted to be. Next, she would need to find or make a suitable costume—one that would affirm the personality of her clown character. And that was only the beginning. She would still need to find a gimmick like balloon twisting or juggling—and be humorous.

Lois turned and glanced at the clock on the back wall. In fifteen minutes the class would be dismissed for a break. She wondered if she should head back to Tacoma or force herself to sit through the rest of Joe's class, hoping she might find some sense of direction.

"The more outrageous your personality, the more outlandish your costume should be," Joe said. "Contrary to popular belief, a good clown outfit is not a mixture of mismatched, odd-sized clothes. A costume you design, using your own choice of colors and prints, becomes your trademark."

Joe moved to the front of the room. "Here's an example of what I mean." He withdrew several balloons from his pocket, quickly blew up each one, and twisted them until he'd made something that resembled a hat. He then proceeded to add several curled balloons, sticking them straight up. He placed the hat on his head. The audience laughed, and Joe looked at the end of his nose so his eyes were crossed. "I'm so thankful I'm not bald anymore. Now I can change my name from Joe to Harry."

Joe Richey was not only a clown by profession, but he was also the funniest man Lois had ever known. Not that she knew him all that well, she reminded herself. In the short time they'd been dating, he'd told her very little about himself. She wondered why.

When the class was dismissed at the break, several people surrounded Joe, pelting him with questions. Lois knew this was her chance to escape. Joe wouldn't know she was gone until the next session began. She left the room, headed for the front door of the church then stopped. Did she want to leave? How would she know if she had the ability to become a clown if she didn't stay and learn more?

She turned and headed for the snack bar. She would grab a cup of tea and a cookie and march back into that classroom and soak up all the information she could.

The class was over at five o'clock, and Lois was tempted to linger. She wanted to spend a few minutes alone with Joe, but he was busy answering more questions and demonstrating some of his balloon techniques. She decided to head for home, knowing it would take almost an hour to get back to Tacoma. Tomorrow was Sunday, and she still had a little preparing to do for her Sunday school class craft. She would have to talk to Joe some other time.

Joe thought Lois would wait after class, but when he finished talking to the last student he discovered she was gone. Had she been in such a hurry to get back to Tacoma that she couldn't even say goodbye?

He shrugged and grabbed up his notes. *Maybe it's my fault. I should have told her earlier that I wanted to take her to dinner.*

Joe was fairly certain Lois had enjoyed his class; he'd caught her laughing whenever he looked her way. He'd also seen her taking notes. Was she interested in pursuing a career in Gospel clowning, or had she taken the class only out of curiosity?

Maybe she did it for a lark. Could be Lois has no more interest in clowning than she does me. Joe slapped the side of his hand with his palm. "Oh, man! You shouldn't have made any reference to clowns being poor. That's probably what turned her off."

Joe pulled himself to his full height and plastered a smile on his face. *Get a grip. It's not like Lois said she doesn't want to see you anymore. Besides, I'm supposed to be happy, not sad. Isn't that what clowns do best?*

Chapter Sixteen

For the next two weeks, Lois studied her notes from Joe's clowning class, in hopes of doing a short skit for her Sunday school class. Joe had called her a few times, but he hadn't asked her out; he said he was swamped with Gospel programs and kids' birthday parties.

Lois missed not seeing him, but she kept busy practicing her clowning routine and had even made a simple costume to wear. The outfit consisted of a pair of baggy overalls, a straw hat with a torn edge, a bright red blouse, and a pair of black rubber boots, all of which gave her a hillbilly look.

Finally, Sunday, morning arrived, and Lois stood in the first-grade classroom, dressed in her costume, waiting for the children and her helper to arrive. She'd worn her hair in two ponytails with red ribbons tied at the ends, and had pencilled in a cluster of dark freckles on her cheeks and nose. In an attempt to make her mouth appear larger, she had taken bright red lipstick and filled in her lips then gone an inch outside with color. She also wore a red rubber clown nose.

Lois's main concern was the skit she'd prepared. Had she memorized it well enough? Could she ad lib if necessary? Would the kids think it was funny, yet still grasp the Gospel message?

Feeling a trickle of sweat roll down her forehead, she reached into her back pocket and withdrew a man-sized handkerchief. She wiped the perspiration away and was stuffing the cloth into her pocket when the children started pouring into the room. "Look! Miss Lois is dressed like a clown!" one girl squealed.

"Yeah! A clown is here!" another child called out.

"Are you gonna make us a balloon animal?"

"Can you juggle any balls?"

"How about some tricks?"

The questions came faster than Lois could answer. She held up her hand to silence the group, looking around frantically for Carla Sweeney, the teenager who had promised to help. "If you'll all take a seat, I'll answer each of your questions one at a time."

The children clambered to the tables, and as soon as they were seated, their little hands shot up. Lois answered each child, letting them know she couldn't juggle, didn't know how to make balloon animals, and had no tricks up her sleeve. She did, however, have a skit to present. Relief flooded her when Carla slipped into the room, and before the children could fire more questions at her, Lois launched into her routine.

Using an artificial flower and a child's doctor kit, she did a pantomime, showing how the flower was sick and needed healing. She then explained out loud how the idea was compared to people who have things in their lives that make them sin-sick. "Jesus is the Great Physician," she said. "He will take away our sins if we ask Him to forgive us."

The children seemed to grasp the message, but they weren't spellbound, as the audience was when she'd seen Joe perform.

After class Lois washed her face, changed out of her costume, and slipped into a dress to wear to church. *Maybe I need to take another clowning class. I could learn how to juggle or maybe do some tricks. . .anything to leave a better impression.*

After church, Lois went with Tabby and Seth to dinner at a restaurant along the waterfront. As soon as they were seated, Seth informed Lois that this was the place he and Tabby had eaten after returning from their first date in Seattle.

Sitting at the table overlooking the beautiful bay, Lois couldn't help but feel a little jealous of her sister. She was married to her soul mate and glowed like a sunbeam. Lois knew she was still young and had plenty of time to find the right guy, but she didn't want to wait. She'd met a Christian man—one who made her laugh and feel accepted and who didn't seem to care about wealth, power, or prestige. She saw only one problem: Joe kidded around so much that she didn't think he'd ever take their relationship seriously.

"Lois, did you hear what I said?"

Tabby's pleasant voice halted Lois's disconcerting thoughts. She turned away from the window and offered her sister a half-hearted smile. "Sorry. I guess I was deep in thought."

"Tabby and I have an announcement to make," Seth declared.

Lois lifted her eyebrows. "I hope you're not leaving on another trip. I really missed you guys while you were gone."

Tabby shook her head. "I think we'll be sticking close to home for the next several months."

"Yeah—seven to be exact," Seth put in. He slipped his arm around Tabby and drew her close.

Lois narrowed her eyes. "I don't get it. Why will you be staying close to home for the next seven months?"

Before Tabby could reply, the light suddenly dawned. "Are you expecting a baby?"

Her sister nodded, and tears welled up in her eyes. "The baby's due in the spring."

With mixed emotions, Lois reached across the table and grasped Tabby's hand. "Congratulations!" She glanced over at Seth. "I'm happy for both of you."

Lois was delighted to hear her sister's good news. It meant she would soon be an aunt, and Tabby deserved the opportunity to be a mother. But somewhere inside was her own desire to be married and have a family. She only hoped it would happen someday. "You'll both make good parents," she said sincerely.

"Sure hope so, 'cause we're really excited about this," Tabby said.

The waitress came to take their order, interrupting the conversation.

"I put on a little clowning skit for my Sunday school class this morning," Lois said, after the waitress left the table.

Tabby's eyebrows shot up. "Really? What prompted that?"

"I took one of Joe's clowning classes a few weeks ago."

"You never said a word about it," Tabby said, shaking her finger at her sister.

"I wanted to see if I could do it before saying anything."

"So how'd it go?" Seth asked.

Lois shrugged. "Okay, I guess. The kids seemed to get the message, but

I think they were disappointed because I didn't do anything exciting, like balloon twisting, juggling, or some kind of trick."

"If you think clowning is something you want to pursue, maybe you should take another class or two," Tabby suggested.

"I hear there's going to be a workshop in Portland next weekend," Seth said. "A clown from Salem will be teaching the class. He has a bubble-blowing specialty he's added to his routines. Should be interesting."

Lois leaned forward, smiling. "I might look into that one. I think blowing bubbles would be a whole lot easier than creating balloon animals."

Tabby snickered. "As I recall, you always did enjoy waving your wand around the backyard and seeing how many bubbles you could make at one time."

Lois laughed. "And you liked to see how many you could pop!"

Joe hung up the phone and sank to the couch. Still no answer at Lois's place. She should have been home from church by now.

Just then the phone rang, causing Joe to jump. He grabbed the receiver. "Joe Richey here."

"Hey, big brother! Long time no talk to."

Joe's mouth fell open. He hadn't heard from Brian in nearly a year. Not since he'd called asking to borrow money to pay his overdue rent.

"Joe. You still there, buddy?"

Joe inhaled sharply and reached up to rub the back of his neck. He could almost see his brother's baby face, long scraggly blond hair and pale blue eyes. "Yeah, I'm here, Brian. What have you been up to?"

"Keepin' busy. And you?"

"Oh, about six feet two." Joe chuckled at his own wisecrack, but Brian's silence proved he wasn't impressed. "You still living in Boise?"

"Not anymore. I needed a new start."

Joe shook his head. *A new start, or are you leaving another string of bad debts?* He could only imagine how much his kid brother had probably messed up this time.

"I call Seattle my home these days, so we're practically neighbors."

"Seattle? How long have you been living there?"

"A couple of months." Brian cleared his throat. "I'm driving a taxi cab."

Joe wrinkled his brows. "You're a taxi driver? What happened to the sporting goods store you were managing in Boise?"

"I, uh, got tired of it."

Joe flexed his fingers. He thought his brother's voice sounded strained. No doubt Brian's previous employer had asked him to leave. It had happened before, and unless Brian learned to control his tongue it would no doubt happen again.

"If you've been in Seattle for a while, why is this the first time I've heard from you? I was in that neck of the woods a couple of weeks ago and could have looked you up."

"Well, I've—"

"Been busy?"

"Yeah. Seattle's a jungle, you know."

"I can't argue with that." Joe's thoughts took him back to the date he'd had with Lois at the Seattle Center. He'd seen more cars on the road that day than he had for a long time, and people milled about the center like cattle in a pen. He didn't envy Brian's having to weave his way in and out of traffic all day, transporting irate customers to their destinations.

"Listen, Joe. The reason I'm calling is, well, I was wanting to—"

"I don't have any extra money, Brian," Joe interrupted. "I can barely manage to pay my own bills these days."

"What bills?" Brian shouted. "Mom left you the house and the money from her insurance policy, so I would think you'd be pretty well set."

Joe felt a trail of heat creep up the back of his neck. If Brian hadn't run off to do his own thing, leaving Joe to deal with their mother's emotional problems, maybe he would have inherited more from the will. As it was, Mom was crushed when her youngest son left home and seldom called or visited them.

Forcing his ragged breathing to return to normal, Joe plastered a smile on his face. He didn't know why, since his brother couldn't see him through the phone. Whenever Joe was riled, putting on a happy face seemed to help. It was the only way he knew how to handle stress. Besides, he wasn't about to let Brian push his buttons. One emotional son in the family was enough. Joe would keep his cool no matter how hard his brother tried to goad him. "Let's change the subject, shall we, Brian?"

"Did you ever stop to think I might have called for some other reason than to ask for money?" Brian's tone had a definite edge.

Joe snorted. "You never have before."

"You know what they say—there's a first time for everything."

Joe's patience was waning, and he knew if he didn't end this conversation soon, he might lose control. He couldn't let that happen. It would be a sign of weakness. He drew in a breath and let it out slowly. "Why did you call, Brian?"

"To wish you a happy birthday."

Joe leaned his head against the sofa cushion and chuckled. "My birthday's almost two weeks away, little brother. It's next Friday, to be exact."

"Next Friday, huh? Guess I forgot."

"It's no big deal." *Mom used to make a big deal out of her birthday* Joe thought ruefully. *But she usually ignored Brian's and my birthdays.*

"Doin' anything special to celebrate?"

"Well, I'm hoping Lois and I might—"

"Lois? Who's she?"

"A friend." *A very special friend. But I'm not about to tell you that.*

"Where's the party going to be? Maybe I'll drive down to Olympia and join you."

"I'm not planning any big wing-ding to celebrate my twenty-fifth birthday. If I do anything at all, it'll just be a quiet dinner someplace nice."

"Okay. I get the picture. You don't want your loud-mouthed, hot-tempered little brother crashing your party. I can live with that. After all, it's nothing new for you to give me the brush off."

Joe opened his mouth to refute his brother's last statement, but he heard a click, and the phone went dead. "Now what I have done?" he moaned.

With a firm resolve not to dwell on the unpleasant encounter he'd had with Brian, Joe dialed Lois's number again. Her answering machine came on, and this time he left a message.

"Lois, this is Joe. I'm still pretty busy this week. I have two more birthday parties to do, not to mention a visit to a nursing home and a spot on a local kids' TV show. Things are looking better for the following week, though, and next Friday is my twenty-fifth birthday." He paused. "I, uh, was hoping you might be free to help me celebrate. Please give me a call when you get in—okay? Talk to you soon. Bye."

Chapter Seventeen

It was close to six o'clock when Lois returned to her apartment Sunday evening. After dinner with Tabby and Seth, she had driven through Point Defiance Park, then stayed for a little while at Owen's Beach.

Dropping her purse on the coffee table, she noticed her answering machine was blinking. She clicked the button then smiled when she heard Joe's message asking her to help him celebrate his birthday. "I wonder what I can do to make it special," she murmured.

She reached for the phone and dialed Joe's number. She was relieved when he answered on the second ring. "Hi, Joe. It's Lois."

"Hey, it's good to hear your voice. Did you get my message?"

"Yes, I did. I just got in."

"What do you think about next Friday night?"

"So you need someone to help you celebrate your birthday?"

"Yeah, and I can't think of anyone I'd rather spend it with than you."

Lois grinned. Joe sounded sincere, and she was beginning to think he really did care for her.

He cleared his throat. "We'll get back to my birthday plans in a minute, but I've been meaning to ask you something, Lois."

"What's that?"

"I was wondering why you hightailed it out of my clowning class two weeks ago."

"I could see you were busy, and I didn't want to cut in on your time with the people who stayed to ask questions."

"I thought you might not have enjoyed the class," he said. "I was planning to ask you to dinner, but when I realized you'd left I figured the worst."

"The worst?"

"Yeah. I thought maybe you hated my class and didn't have the heart to say so."

Lois's heartbeat quickened. Joe had wanted to ask her out, and he thought she didn't like the class? She felt terrible about leaving him with the wrong impression. "I did enjoy your clowning presentation."

"Is it about the money then?"

"What? What money?"

"The fact that most Gospel clowns aren't rich."

"Money's not an issue with me, Joe," Lois said, smiling. "It used to be, but not anymore. I realized it wasn't so important when I broke up with a man who had money but wasn't a Christian."

She heard Joe release his breath. "I'm glad we settled that." He groaned softly then followed it with a chuckle. "I've had enough unpleasantness for one day."

"What happened today that was unpleasant?"

"I had a phone call from my kid brother, Brian," he replied. "It seems he's left his job in Boise, Idaho, and lives in Seattle now."

Lois held her breath. Was Joe finally going to open up and talk about his family?

"He called under the guise of wishing me a happy birthday, but I think he really wanted money," Joe continued.

"Is Brian unemployed?"

"He said he's driving a cab, but from past experience. . ." Joe's voice trailed off, and he was silent for a moment. "Let's not talk about my renegade brother—okay? I'd much rather discuss our dinner plans for next Friday."

Lois smiled. "I'd love to help celebrate your birthday, Joe. How about letting me pick the place? I'll even drive to Olympia to get you."

"You're going to be my chauffeur?"

"Yes."

"Oh, boy! Does a white stretch limo come with the deal?"

She giggled. "I'm afraid you'll have to settle for my little, green clunker."

He moaned. "Well, if I must."

"I'll be by to pick you up at six o'clock sharp, so you'd better be ready and waiting."

"Yes, ma'am."

Lois hung up the phone, feeling happier than she had all day. Joe wanted her to help celebrate his birthday, and now she could plan to do something special.

On the drive to Portland Saturday morning, Lois was a ball of nerves. What if she took the second clowning class and still had no audience appeal? What if she lacked the courage to do a program in front of anyone besides her Sunday school kids? She knew she was probably expecting too much. After all, this would only be her second course in clowning, and Rome wasn't built in a day. She didn't have much time, though. Joe's birthday was a week away, and she was determined to give him a surprise he'd never forget.

When Lois pulled into the parking lot of First Christian Church, she was amazed at all the cars. "There must be a lot of people interested in clowning," she murmured, turning off the engine.

Stepping inside the foyer of the large brick building, she realized why so many cars were parked outside. She saw that not only were classes in clowning being offered, but also ones in puppetry, ventriloquism, illusions, and chalk art. It reminded her of the story Tabby had told of her first encounter with ventriloquism and meeting Seth Beyers.

Lois stopped in front of the table marked CLOWNING BY BENNY THE BUBBLE MAN and registered for the class. A young woman dressed as a Raggedy Ann type of clown handed Lois a small notebook and a name tag.

A short time later, Lois was seated at the front of the class. *Joe would sure be surprised if he knew I was taking another clowning class. I'm glad he's not teaching at this seminar, or else he would have discovered my little secret by now.*

She forced her thoughts off Joe and onto Benny the Bubble Man, who with the help of his assistant, Raggedy Ruth, was demonstrating the art of making bubbles in different sizes and shapes. The pair expertly used a variety of wands and even a straw.

Lois thought it looked pretty simple until everyone in the class was given a jar of soapy liquid and instructed to make a bubble chain. She'd always prided herself on being adept at blowing bubbles, but her childhood tricks had involved making only one, two, or maybe three effervescent balls at one time. Making a string of six to eight bubbles was difficult, if not impossible. Even with Raggedy Ruth's help, Lois fumbled her way through the procedure. Something as tedious as this would take weeks, maybe months of practice, and she had only until next Friday.

"Maybe I should have taken one of the other clowning classes," she muttered.

"You're doing fine. Just keep practicing," Ruth assured her.

Lois was the last student to leave the classroom; she was determined to learn at least one bubble maneuver that might impress Joe and show him she could act as goofy as he did. If she could learn to be a clown, maybe Joe would start to show his serious side. It seemed like a fair trade to Lois.

Chapter Eighteen

Lois leaned back in her office chair and yawned. How could she ever stay awake the rest of the day? For the last four nights she'd been up late, practicing her clown routine and blowing bubbles until her lips turned numb. She'd finally managed to make a chain of eight small bubbles and a bubble within a bubble, but she didn't think either trick was too exciting. Neither was her hillbilly clown costume.

Maybe I should forget the whole idea and take Joe to dinner as he's expecting. At least then I won't be as likely to embarrass myself.

Lois grabbed the stack of bulletins in front of her and started folding them. On the front cover was a picture of a nurse taking a child's temperature. Suddenly, an idea popped into her head. A new outfit—that's what she needed. A costume and some props. A small shop on the other side of town sold tricks, costumes, and other clowning aids. She would go there as soon as she got off work.

Joe stared out his living room window. It was raining, which was nothing unusual for fall weather in the Pacific Northwest. He wasn't going to let it dampen his spirits, though. Today was his birthday, and he was going to dinner with Lois. *Sure hope she drives carefully on the freeway. It's bound to be slick with all this liquid sunshine. She should have let me drive to Tacoma and pick her up.* He glanced at the clock on the wall. *Five minutes to six. She should be here any minute.*

Joe sat on the couch to wait and turned his thoughts in another direction. He'd been presenting a program at a nearby nursing home the previous week when the son of one of the patients offered him a job. The man owned a hotel and needed several full-time entertainers. The position paid well and had some fringe benefits, but it involved secular clowning and would leave little time to minister as a Gospel clown. He pulled out the man's business card and studied it for a minute. He'd told him he would think about it, but Joe knew he couldn't accept the position no matter how well it paid. He always seemed to need money, but his primary goal as a clown was to see people's lives changed through faith in Christ. If he spent most of his time entertaining, simply to amuse others, he'd lose precious opportunities to witness about God.

I'll call him in the morning and let him know I've decided not to take the job.

The doorbell rang then. He grinned. It must be Lois.

Lois smiled when Joe opened the door. He looked so nice, dressed in a tan shirt, dark brown blazer, and matching slacks. He'd worn a tie too—a silly cartoon character standing on its head. "Happy birthday, Joe. You ready to go?" she said, reaching up and kissing him on the cheek.

Joe nodded enthusiastically. "Yes! I've been waiting all day for this." He drew her into his arms and kissed her upturned mouth.

"Are you having your dessert first?" she asked, tipping her head to one side.

He nodded and gave her a playful wink. "Absolutely! I may have more dessert after dinner, though."

Lois felt her cheeks grow warm. She hoped the rest of the evening went as well as these first few minutes.

"Where are we off to?" Joe asked as he followed Lois to her car. "Are we finally going to Snoqualmie Falls for that picnic?"

"Not tonight." Lois opened the door on the passenger's side and motioned for Joe to get in. "Don't ask me any more questions. My lips are sealed."

"You're going to chauffeur me, aren't you?"

"Yes, and you'd better get in before the rain turns us into a couple of drowned rats."

"It seems like ages since we last saw each other," Joe said as they started for the freeway. "I've missed you, Lois."

She glanced at him out of the corner of her eye. "Ditto."

"Anything new in your life since we last talked?"

"Nothing much. How's your busy schedule? Anything exciting happening in the life of Slow-Joe the Clown?"

"I was offered a job last week," he answered. "It pays really well, but I'm going to call the guy tomorrow and turn it down."

"Why?"

"It's a secular position that would take a lot of my time. I wouldn't be able to do nearly as many Gospel presentations."

"I'm sure you've prayed about it," Lois said.

"I have." He reached for her hand. "Do you think I'm dumb for giving up the money?"

She shook her head. "Not at all."

Joe squeezed her fingers. "I'm glad you feel that way."

They drove in silence for a while, listening to the Christian radio station Lois had turned on. When they left the freeway, Lois headed across town to the north end. Soon she pulled up in front of a quaint, three-story house with gray siding.

Joe gave her a strange look. "Where are we? This doesn't look like a restaurant to me."

She smiled and turned off the engine. "It's not. This is where Tabby and Seth live."

"He has his ventriloquist shop in the basement, right?"

Lois nodded. "Have you ever been here?"

"No, but Seth told me about it. He said the place used to belong to his grandparents."

"Right again," she said as she unbuckled her seat belt.

"So what are we doing here? Are Seth and Tabby joining us for dinner?"

"Yes, they are." Lois turned in her seat to face Joe. "I hope you don't mind."

He shrugged and smiled. "Sure—whatever."

"Let's go inside and see if they're ready."

"Why don't I wait here and you get them?"

Lois knew her surprise wouldn't work if Joe didn't go inside the house. "Their place is really neat. I'd like you to see it," she insisted.

Joe was quiet.

"They have lots of antiques," Lois added, "and Seth has an old ventriloquist dummy he's dressed as a clown."

Joe undid his seat belt and opened the car door. "Okay, you win. Let's go inside."

They walked up to the Beyers' front porch, and Lois was about to turn the knob on the door. "Wait, Lois," Joe said, reaching for her hand. "There aren't any lights in the windows. Maybe they're not home."

"They're probably at the back of the house." Lois grasped the knob and opened the door. It was dark inside, and she grabbed Joe's hand then led him along the hallway, feeling her way as she went.

"Are you sure they're home?" Joe asked. "I don't hear a sound."

"Just hush and stay close to me."

They stepped into the living room, and in the next moment the lights snapped on. "Surprise!" a chorus of voices shouted. "Happy birthday, Joe!"

At once Joe painted on a happy face and backed away from the exuberant people who had greeted him. This was a surprise party, and it didn't take a genius to realize Lois was behind the whole thing. Besides Seth and Tabby, he recognized several other people with whom he'd done Gospel presentations. His biggest surprise was seeing his brother. Joe didn't know how it was possible, since none of his friends knew Brian. Other than Lois, he'd never mentioned him to his associates.

Joe leaned close to Lois and whispered, "How did my brother get here?"

She opened her mouth to reply, but Brian cut her off. "I'm here because she called around until she located the cab company I work for. I guess she thought you'd be happy to see me."

Joe swallowed hard and forced his smile to remain in place. "Of course I'm glad to see you. I'm just surprised." He gave Brian a quick hug, then turned to face Lois. "I thought we were going out to dinner."

Her face turned pink, and she squeezed his hand. "I wanted to do something different for your birthday."

Seth stepped forward and grasped Joe's shoulder. "You're lucky to have someone as special as my wife's sister looking out for you. Lois has worked hard planning this shindig in your honor."

Joe felt like a heel. He should be grateful Lois cared so much about him. He couldn't let her know how disappointed he was at not spending the evening alone with her. He reached over and hugged her. "Thanks for the surprise."

"There's more to come!" Lois said excitedly. "Besides the pizza, cake, and other goodies, I've planned a special program in your honor."

Joe raised his eyebrows. "A program? Now that does sound interesting."

Lois breathed a sigh of relief when she realized Joe seemed okay with her change of plans. She hoped he would enjoy the festivities, especially since he always seemed to be the life of the party. She led him across the room and pointed to the recliner. "You sit here and visit with your friends while I go change into my party clothes."

He wrinkled his forehead. "I think you look fine in what you're wearing."

Lois glanced down at her beige slacks and rose-colored knit top. "I won't be long, and I hope you won't be disappointed." She leaned over and gave him a light kiss on the cheek then hurried out of the room. Tabby was behind her, and they both giggled as they started up the stairs leading to the bedrooms.

"I can't believe you're going through with this," Tabby said as she pulled Lois into her room.

Lois nodded soberly. "I hope I'm not making a mistake."

Tabby shook her head. "I don't think so. In fact, it might be just the thing that will bring Joe Richey to his knees."

"I don't get it."

"Knees. . .marriage. . .proposal. . . ."

Lois waved her hand. "Get real, Tabby. Joe and I have been dating only since August. We barely know each other."

"But you're a couple of lovesick puppies," Tabby asserted. "I can see it all over your faces."

Lois shrugged. "Let's get my costume on and forget about love, shall we?"

A half hour later, the sisters emerged from the bedroom. Tabby went down the steps first, and Lois followed, wearing a nurse's uniform and carrying a satchel full of props.

She stood in the hallway, while Tabby stepped into the living room. "Ladies and gentlemen, it's my privilege to introduce our special guest tonight—the lovely nurse, Lois Johnson!"

Lois skipped into the room. "Is there a patient in the house? Somebody please provide me with a sick patient!"

On cue, Seth jumped up from his seat and grabbed hold of Joe's hand. "Here's your patient, Nurse Lois, and he's one sick fellow!"

Lois placed a chair in the middle of the room and asked Joe to sit down. Then she opened her satchel, drew out an oversized pair of fake glasses, and put them on. Next she removed a rubber chicken and threw it into the air. "Oops! No dead birds around here!" she exclaimed. "It's my job to make people well."

She pulled a can of peanuts out of the bag and grinned at Joe. "I hear you've been feeling under the weather lately." Before he could respond, she tossed him the can. "Remove the lid, please."

Joe lifted the top, and a paper snake sailed into the air, almost hitting him in the nose. He stared at Lois for a second then burst into gales of laughter.

Lois dipped her hand into the satchel again and retrieved an oversized toothbrush. "Open real wide," she said, tipping Joe's head back. He opened his mouth, and she pretended to brush his teeth while she blew on the end of the toothbrush. A stream of bubbles drifted toward the ceiling. Joe laughed so hard his face turned cherry red. He thought she was funny, and apparently so did everyone else, for they were all laughing, clapping, and shouting for more.

"Now, sick patient, I'd like you to lie on the floor," Lois instructed. As Joe complied, she turned to face Tabby. "May I have the sheet, please?"

Tabby reached into a basket that was sitting on the floor and pulled out a white sheet. Lois threw the sheet over Joe, leaving only his head and feet exposed.

"I understand you're having some trouble with your left arm these days," Lois said, as she grabbed Joe's arm and raised it a few inches off the floor. Suddenly Joe's left leg came up, and everyone howled. She couldn't believe it; Joe was playing along with her routine.

Lois pushed on his leg, and up came the right arm. She shoved that down, and Joe's other arm shot up. They continued the game a few more minutes, until Lois announced, "I think this patient is well enough for some pizza. But before that I'd like to present him with a beautiful flower."

Lois drew a fake flower from her bag. Joe sat up, and she handed it to him. "Take a whiff and tell me what you smell."

Joe held the flower up to his nose and inhaled deeply. Lois squeezed the stem, and a stream of water shot out and hit Joe in the face. He yelped, then jumped up and began chasing Lois around the room. "I've always wondered what it would be like to catch a nurse!" he cried.

By the time Joe caught Lois, they were both laughing so hard tears were running down their cheeks. Lois had planned a few other things for her routine, but she knew she couldn't go on with the rest of the show. She didn't think she needed to anyway, since she had shown Joe what she'd learned about clowning and helped to make his birthday one to remember.

Joe couldn't believe how much he was enjoying the party. Lois was very funny when she decided to let her hair down.

"I didn't realize you'd learned so much about clowning during my short class," Joe said to Lois. They were all sitting around the table eating chocolate cake and strawberry ice cream.

She gave him a sheepish grin. "I took another class last Saturday in Portland."

"Ah-ha! I wondered where you were when I tried to call that afternoon." Joe needled her in the ribs. "Now the two of us can team up and do all sorts of routines at church functions."

"Speaking of church—have you found a church home in Seattle yet, Brian?" Seth asked, turning to Joe's brother.

Brian scrunched up his nose. "I'm religious enough. I don't need an hour of boring church every Sunday to make me a better person."

"Since when did you get religious?" Joe asked his brother.

"It's like this—when I drive my cab around the city, people pray a lot!"

"Yeah, I'm sure your passengers do pray," Joe said, forcing a smile. "As I recall, you always had a lead foot."

Brian frowned. "To be a cabby, you have to know how to move in and out of traffic."

"If you want my opinion—"

"I respect your opinion," Brian interrupted, "but I'd respect it even more if you kept it to yourself."

Joe opened his mouth to offer a comeback, but he felt Lois's hand touch his under the table. He wondered if she was trying to signal him to change the subject, so he squeezed her fingers in response. "This cake is delicious. Did you make it, Lois?"

She shook her head. "Tabby did the honors. I was too busy trying to come up with some kind of goofy clown skit."

"That nurse routine you did was pretty impressive," Seth interjected. "You and Joe work well together."

Joe draped his arm across Lois's shoulder and whispered in her ear, "We do, don't we?"

Chapter Nineteen

Over the next few weeks Joe and Lois saw each other often. They visited Snoqualmie Falls and had a picnic in Joe's truck, drove up to Mount Rainier for a day of skiing, and got together at Lois's place to practice some joint clowning routines. On the night of Joe's birthday, he'd convinced Lois she had talent and suggested she use it to help him evangelize. Lois thought that after more practice she might be able to do some kind of routine with him.

She was still concerned about his inability to be serious, as well as his refusal to talk about his brother or other family members. She had noticed the way Joe and Brian related at the party and knew a problem existed between them. She kept hoping and praying he would open up to her as they drew closer to one another, but so far he'd remained the jokester. Her own clowning around didn't deter him either. If anything, Joe seemed to be even goofier. She worried that he might have something to hide, some family skeletons buried beneath his lighthearted exterior. She was concerned that those things, whatever they were, might put a wedge between them, either now or in the future.

Today was Thanksgiving, and Lois had invited Joe, Brian, Seth, and Tabby for dinner. Her sister had volunteered to bring the pies, but Lois insisted on doing the rest. She was eager for Joe to sample her cooking, and she hoped Brian's presence would help him relax and talk about his family.

By one o'clock, the turkey was almost cooked. Lois boiled the potatoes, then finished setting the table in her small dining room with her best china. The guests would be here any minute, and she was looking forward to the day ahead.

Seth and Tabby arrived first, bringing two pumpkin pies and one apple, along with a carton of whipping cream. "It looks like you've outdone yourself," Tabby said as she studied the table.

Lois smiled and took one of the pies from her sister. "It's my first attempt at holiday entertaining, and I wanted everything to be perfect."

Seth whistled. "If the smell of that bird is any indication of what dinner's going to taste like, then I'd say everything will be more than perfect."

Lois winked at her brother-in-law and motioned toward the couch. "Have a seat, and when Joe and his brother arrive you can keep them entertained." She nodded at Tabby. "The two of us have some work to do in the other room."

Tabby set her pies on the countertop and grabbed one of Lois's aprons from a drawer. "What would you like me to do first?"

"How about mashing the potatoes while I make some gravy?"

"I think I can manage that."

Lois noticed that Tabby's stomach was protruding slightly, and a pang of jealousy stabbed her heart. What if she never married or had any children? Could she learn to be content with being an aunt? *I don't need to think about this now*, she chided herself. *There's too much to do.* She focused her thoughts on stirring the gravy.

By the time Lois and Tabby were ready to serve dinner, Joe and Brian arrived. They hadn't come together, but Lois figured that was because Joe had been driving from Olympia and his brother from Seattle, which was in the opposite direction.

Joe greeted Lois with a kiss on the cheek, and soon everyone was seated at the table. Lois asked Seth to say the blessing then excused herself to bring in the turkey. Moments later she placed the platter in front of Joe amidst everyone's oohs and ahhs and asked if he would carve the bird.

"You picked the right guy for the job," he said with a grin. "When Brian and I were growing up, carving the bird was always my responsibility."

"Did your dad teach you how?" Tabby inquired.

"He was killed in an accident involving the tour bus Dad drove. Joe and I were both kids," Brian answered before his brother could open his mouth. "I hardly remember our father."

"My folks died when I was pretty young too," Seth said. "Grandma and Grandpa Beyers raised me after Mom and Dad were killed. Then later, when they decided to move to a retirement center, they gave me their home."

"After Dad's death, our mother raised us." Brian frowned. "At least that's what she thought she was doing."

Lois's interest was piqued. What did Brian mean by saying his mother *thought* she was raising them? She turned to him. "It must have been hard for your mother to raise two boys without a father. I'm sure she did the best she could."

Brian snorted and reached for a biscuit from the basket in the center of the table. "If Mom had done the best she could, she would have admitted she was sick and taken the medicine the doctor prescribed. Now she's dead, and we're left with only each other and a lot of bad memories."

Lois glanced at Joe, sitting on the other side of her, and hoped he would add something to Brian's comment.

Joe was silent. With a silly grin plastered on his face, he reached for the tray of fresh vegetables, grabbed a cherry tomato, poked a hole in one end, then stuck the whole thing on the tip of his nose. "How's this for a new clown face?" he asked with a chuckle. He reached into the tray again and withdrew two cucumber slices. He cut a hole in each one then placed them over his ears. Next he grabbed a carrot and stuck that in his mouth. "What'd ya think ub this?" he mumbled.

Everyone but Brian laughed at Joe's silly antics. "If you don't want to discuss our mother's problems, that's fine—but let's not make these folks think you're ready for the loony bin as well," Brian said.

The carrot dropped to his plate as Joe opened his mouth. "I don't think we should be having this discussion right now. Today's Thanksgiving, and we ought to be concentrating on having a good time and being thankful for all we have, instead of talking about someone who made her peace with God and isn't here to defend herself."

Joe's face was as red as the tomato still dangling from his nose, and Lois wondered what she could do to help ease the tension. She offered up a quick prayer then reached over and took his hand. "Maybe after dinner you can do one of your juggling routines. In the meantime, how about slicing that turkey before we all starve?"

Joe snatched both cucumbers off his ears and the tomato from his nose and placed them on the edge of his plate. Without another word, he grabbed the knife and stuck it into the bird.

Joe's insides were churning like a blender running on full speed. How dare his brother air their family's dirty laundry in front of Lois and her relatives! If he hadn't been trying so hard to keep his emotions in check, he might have shouted at Brian to shut up and eat, rather than make himself look foolish by putting on a vegetable clown face. Lois probably thought he was the one with a mental problem. Keeping control of his emotions was important to Joe. If he acted on his feelings, he might flip out, the way Mom had on more than one occasion.

Joe found himself beginning to care more and more for Lois, and he didn't want to turn her off by losing his cool—or by revealing too much about his family. Making a joke out of things was the only way he knew how to cope with the unpleasant things in life. It was better than turning to drugs or alcohol, as Brian had when he was a teenager. Joe hoped his brother had given up those bad habits, but after today it was obvious he still hadn't learned to control his tongue.

Many times when they were growing up Brian had blurted out something to someone about their mother and her mood swings. Joe had tried then to talk to him about keeping their family affairs quiet, but his little brother seemed to take pleasure in letting everyone know their mother had a serious problem. When Brian finally graduated from high school and left home, Joe hated to admit he was relieved. At least his brother could no longer talk about their personal lives. Joe felt a sense of duty to Mom and had continued to live with her until she died. In all that time, he'd never told anyone about her problem with extreme mood swings or discussed the way it had made him feel.

"When's your next performance, Joe?"

Seth's question drew Joe out of his reflections, and he smiled and passed him the plate of turkey. "I'm scheduled to do one tomorrow at the Tacoma Mall. It's part of the pre-Christmas festivities, and I'll be making some balloon animals to give out to the children who visit Santa."

"Sounds pretty corny if you ask me," Brian muttered. "If I had a choice, I'd choose driving in and out of traffic all day rather than spend five minutes with a bunch of runny-nosed, rowdy kids."

All eyes were focused on Brian. Joe knew Tabby and Seth were expecting a baby in the spring and that Lois loved kids. He could only imagine what Lois and her family must think of his self-centered brother.

"Kids and laughter are what makes the world go around," Joe said. "I love working with the little tykes because they spread happiness, peanut butter, and chicken pox."

Brian frowned. *"Humph!* And that coming from someone who's a big kid himself! You were always Mom's funny little boy, full of jokes and wisecracks, and never wanting to rock the boat or make any waves."

Joe inhaled sharply. He thought about telling Brian he'd made up a new beatitude: *Blessed are they who have nothing to say and can't be persuaded to say it.*

Just then Seth spoke up.

"The turkey is great, Lois. You really outdid yourself."

"Yes, everything tastes wonderful," Tabby agreed.

Lois smiled, and her face turned pink. "Thanks."

Joe patted his stomach. "They're right; the meal was terrific. In fact, tomorrow I'll probably have to go on a diet." He winked at Lois. "Whenever I have to start applying my clown makeup with a paint roller, I know it's time to lose weight."

Everyone, except Brian, laughed at Joe's joke. He was eating mashed potatoes at lightning speed. *That's okay,* Joe mused. Brian never did appreciate a good pun. Maybe I should try another one and see if that gets any response.

"You look kind of stressed out, Brian. Must be ready for those tasty desserts Tabby brought, huh?"

His brother's forehead wrinkled, but he remained silent.

Joe chuckled. "Stressed spelled backwards is desserts."

Again, everyone but Brian laughed. Instead he narrowed his eyes at Joe. "You're really sick, you know that? I don't see how anyone as beautiful and intelligent as Lois could put up with you clowning around all the time."

Brian's words pierced Joe. He wondered if Lois felt the same way about his silliness. If she did, she'd never said anything. In fact, she was learning to be a clown herself, so that must mean she liked his goofy ways and wanted to be more like him—didn't it?

261

Chapter Twenty

As Lois put away the last of the clean dishes from their Thanksgiving meal, her mind wandered. Joe's brother had revealed some important things about their past, including that their mother had suffered with a mental illness. Could that be why Joe was reluctant to talk about his family? Maybe it was also why Joe showed only his silly side. Lois had a hunch Joe had a lot of pain bottled up inside and for some reason was afraid to let it out. She wondered what it would take to break down the walls he'd built up. She wished he'd stayed around after the others left, but he was the first person to say he needed to leave.

Lois had no idea why Joe needed to go home, since today was a holiday and he had no clowning engagements scheduled. She'd tried to talk to him for a few minutes in front of her apartment building, but he'd hurried away, mumbling something about the ocean calling to him.

She sank into a chair at the kitchen table and closed her eyes. She could still picture Joe sitting at her dining room table during dinner, leaning slightly forward. His pinched face and forced smile betrayed the tension he must have felt when Brian began talking about their mother's condition.

"Dear Lord," Lois prayed, "I think Joe is deeply troubled and needs Your help. Please show me if there's something I can do."

Joe had intended to go home after he left Lois's, but he couldn't face his empty house tonight. Not when he had Mom on his mind. He drove past the Olympia exit and headed toward the coast. Maybe he would feel better after some time at the beach. A blast of salt sea air and the cold sand sifting into his sneakers would get him thinking straight again. So what if he only had the clothes on his back and no toothbrush? If he stayed more than a day he could buy what he needed.

"Lord, I've blown it with Lois," Joe prayed. "I could see by the look on her face during dinner that she's fed up with me. Did hearing about Mom's problems turn her off, or was she irritated because I wouldn't hang around and talk?"

Joe's stomach ached from holding back his feelings. He wanted to pull his truck to the side of the road, drop his head onto the steering wheel, and let the tears that had built up through the years spill over like water released from a dam. He couldn't, though. He had to keep driving until the Pacific Ocean came into view. He needed to drown out the past. Joe didn't care that by leaving town he'd have to cancel the performance he was scheduled to give at the Tacoma Mall the next afternoon. So what if they never asked him to do another clowning routine? Right now he didn't care if he ever worked again.

Lois hadn't heard anything from Joe since Thanksgiving, and now it was Friday of the following week. She'd been tempted to call several times but decided she should give him more time to make the first move.

She turned off her computer and was about to call it a day when the pastor's wife entered her office.

"How are things going, Lois?" she asked. "Do you and your clown friend have big plans for the weekend?"

"It's going okay here at work." Lois swallowed against the knot in her throat. "I haven't heard from Joe all week, and frankly I wonder if he will ever call again."

Norma Hanson slipped into the chair beside Lois's desk. "Would you like to talk about it?"

Lois hesitated then took a deep breath. "I found out Thanksgiving that his mother had severe mood swings, and he acted strange after his brother blurted out the information." She sighed. "I think Joe's past might have something to do with the way he makes light of everything."

The pastor's wife handed Lois a tissue from the box on her desk. "Does Joe's humor bother you?"

Lois smiled through her tears. "Actually, I think he's been good for me, and his joking has helped me learn to relax and have a good time." She paused. "I just wish he could show his serious side too. If he even has one, that is."

The older woman nodded. "I'm sure he does. Maybe he needs more time. Perhaps as your friendship grows, he'll open up to you more."

"I hope so, Mrs. Hanson." Lois reached for her purse. "Well, I mustn't take up any more of your time."

"I'm glad to listen anytime and even offer an opinion if you ask," she said, smiling. "Before you go, though, let's have a word of prayer."

A whole week at the beach, and Joe still felt as if his world were tilting precariously. He couldn't afford to spend any more nights in a hotel, and it wasn't warm enough to pitch a tent on the sand. Besides, he was expected to perform at his home church on Sunday morning. It was bad enough he'd missed the mall program right after Thanksgiving. He certainly wouldn't feel right about leaving Pastor Cummings in the lurch. Especially when his clowning skit was supposed to be the children's sermon for the day and coincide with the pastor's message.

With his mood matching that of the overcast sky, Joe climbed into his pickup on Saturday morning and headed home.

On Sunday morning, he was still struggling with feelings he kept pushing down. He was determined to put on a happy face and act as if nothing were wrong.

Checking to see that his chaps were in place and donning his floppy red cowboy hat, he entered the sanctuary through a side door near the pulpit.

"Howdy, pardners!" Joe shouted as he sprinted onto the platform, twirling a rope over his head. "Anyone know what the rope said to the knot?"

When no one responded, Joe said, "You're naughty!"

Several children in the front row giggled, and Joe winked at them. "Today we'll be talking about witnessing and inviting our friends to church," he announced. "I'll need a helper, though. Any volunteers?"

A few hands shot up, and Joe pointed to a young boy. "What's your name?"

"Billy," the boy told him.

"Well, come on up, Billy, and stand right over there." Joe pointed to the spot where he wanted Billy to stand then took several steps backward. "Now let's think of some ways we can witness to our friends about Jesus." In one quick motion, Joe twirled his rope, flung it over the boy's head, and cinched it around his waist. "There! I've roped you real good, and now you've gotta listen to the pastor's message."

Billy looked at Joe as if he'd taken leave of his senses. "Guess ropin' your friends isn't the best way to invite them to church." He undid the rope. "Hmm. . .what else could I do to get someone to come to church?"

Joe tipped his head to one side, pressed his lips together, then snapped his fingers. "I know! I'll handcuff this young man and force him to come to church." Joe reached into his back pocket and pulled out a pair of plastic handcuffs. He dangled them above Billy's head, and several children laughed. "You don't think that's a good idea?"

"That wouldn't be nice!" a little girl shouted.

Joe nodded. "You're right. It wouldn't be." He tapped the toe of his cowboy boot against the floor. "Let's see now." Joe bent down so he was on the same level with the boy. "If you're not willing to go to Sunday school with me, I won't be your friend anymore."

Billy raised his eyebrows. Joe chuckled then ruffled the child's hair. "Guess that's not the way to witness either."

Joe began to pace the length of the platform. "What's the best way to witness? What's the best way to witness?" He stopped suddenly, nearly running into the boy. "Hey! You still here?"

Billy nodded. "Do you want me to sit down?"

Joe shook his head. "No way! We still haven't shown these kids the best way to witness."

Billy tapped Joe on the arm, and Joe bent down so the boy could whisper something in his ear. When he lifted his head again, Joe was smiling. He turned to face the audience. "This young man thinks I should offer him something so he'll agree to come to Sunday school with me." He winked. "And I think I have the perfect gift."

Joe reached into another pocket of his baggy jeans and grabbed a couple of pencil balloons. The first one he inflated flew across the room, and everyone howled. When he blew up the next one, he twisted it quickly into an animal. "Here you go, son—your very own pony." He handed Billy the balloon creation then told him he could return to his seat.

Next Joe pulled a small New Testament from his shirt pocket. He opened it and turned a few pages. "In Mark, chapter 16, verse 15, Jesus commanded His disciples to go into the world and preach the Good News to all creation." He held up the book. "That means we should do the same. We need to tell others about Jesus, and one of the ways we can do that is by inviting our friends and relatives to Sunday school and church where they can hear Bible stories about Him."

Joe moved to the end of the platform and held up the rope and hand-cuffs. "Forcing them to come isn't the answer." He drew a fake flower from his vest pocket and showed the audience. "If you use some form of bribery, it might get them here—but will it keep them?" He shook his head. "I doubt it, and I don't think that's the way Jesus meant for us to preach the Good News. We need to live the Christian life so others will see Jesus shining through us. Then, when we invite our friends and family to church, they'll want to come and see what's it all about." He shook his head slowly. "Shame on me for trying to make you think otherwise."

Joe held the flower in front of his own face and squeezed the attached bulb. A stream of water squirted on his nose, and the audience clapped heartily. Joe took a bow and dashed out of the room.

Joe didn't wish to disturb the church service, so he stayed in the small room outside the sanctuary, listening to the pastor's message from his seat near the door. After the congregation was dismissed, Joe stepped over to the pastor. "If you're not too busy, may I speak with you for a few minutes?"

"Sure, Joe. I have time to talk now."

Joe followed Pastor Cummings down the hall to his office where they sat down in easy chairs.

The pastor leaned forward. "You're an excellent clown, Joe. God's given you a special talent, and it's good to see you using it for Him."

Joe folded his arms. "If I can bring a smile to someone's heart, it's a ministry worth doing."

Pastor Cummings nodded. "Most people seem to open up to a clown.

I've noticed that the barriers seem to come down the minute you step into a room."

"You're right, but I've seen a few exceptions," Joe said. "I remember being in a restaurant one time to do a kid's birthday party, and an older man was sitting at a nearby table. He seemed nervous by my presence and stayed hidden behind his newspaper until I left."

"Guess he forgot what it was like to be a child."

Joe shrugged. "Could be."

Pastor Cummings wrinkled his forehead. "Maybe the man was afraid to laugh. Some people have a hard time getting in touch with their emotions—especially if they've been hindered during their growing-up years."

Joe shifted uneasily in his chair. Could the pastor see inside his heart and know how discouraged he'd been as a child? Did he know how hard it was for him to get in touch with his feelings?

"What did you wish to speak with me about, Joe?"

Joe's nerves were as taut as a rubber band. This was going to be harder than he thought. "I'm. . .dating a woman now who is. . .well, Lois tends to be kind of serious."

"Does that bother you?" the pastor asked.

"Not really, because she's recently taken a couple of clowning classes and is learning to relax and joke around."

"Then what's the problem?"

"I think I'm the problem," Joe said.

"How so?"

"Lois wants to know about my family and what went on in my past."

"And I take it you'd rather not talk about that part of your life?"

Joe nodded. "The truth is, I don't even want to think about the past, much less discuss it."

He took a few deep breaths and tried to relax. The only sound was the soft ticking of the clock on the wall behind the pastor's desk.

Suddenly an image of Joe's mother popped into his mind. He could see her shaking her finger at him. He could hear her shouting, *"You're a slob, Joseph Andrew Richey! Why can't you do anything right?"* She slapped his face, then ran from his room, sobbing and shouting obscenities.

"Why was she always so critical?" Joe mumbled to himself. "Why was everything I did never good enough?" His voice lowered even more. "Why couldn't she at least say something positive about me?"

"Who was critical of you, Joe?"

Joe raised his head. Pastor Cummings was staring at him. "Oh. I guess I was sort of daydreaming. All of a sudden I could see my mother and hear her shouting at me."

"Both of your parents are dead, as I recall from what you told me when you first started coming here. Is that right?" the pastor asked.

Joe nodded.

"Were you and your mother close?"

"I–I guess so. I did everything she asked, even when she wouldn't take her medicine and sort of flipped out."

"Was your mother ill?"

Joe swallowed past the lump wedged in his throat. How could he explain about Mom? Would Pastor Cummings understand, or would he be judgmental, the way Joe's childhood friends had been when they'd seen his mother in one of her moods?

"Being able to talk about your feelings will help you get in touch with them," the pastor prompted.

"My mother was mentally ill," Joe blurted out. "She was diagnosed with manic depression, but she never acknowledged it or took the medicine the doctor prescribed."

"I see. And how did her illness affect you, Joe?"

Joe stood suddenly. "I've spent the last week alone, wrestling with my past, and I thought I was ready to talk about it—but now I don't think I am."

The older man nodded. "It's okay. We can talk more when you're ready."

Joe was almost to the door when he felt the pastor's hand touch his shoulder.

"I want you to know, Joe, that I'm here for you. Anytime you need to talk, I'm available," Pastor Cummings said in a sincere tone.

Joe nodded and forced a smile on his face. "Thanks. I'll remember that."

Chapter Twenty-One

Lois stared at the telephone, praying it would ring. If only she would hear from Joe. It had been two weeks, and she was getting more worried. She was reaching for the phone when it rang.

Startled, she grabbed the receiver. "Hello."

"Hi, Lois. It's Joe."

Lois felt as though the air had been squeezed from her lungs. She hadn't talked to Joe since Thanksgiving and had almost given up hope of ever hearing from him again.

"Are you still there, Lois?"

"Yes, I'm here."

"How have you been?"

"Fine. And you?" Lois knew they were making small talk, but she didn't know what else to say. Things seemed strained between them.

"Well, the reason I'm calling is, I was wondering if you're still mad at me."

"I was never mad, Joe."

"Okay. Irritated then."

"Not even that. I was a bit disappointed because you left so abruptly on Thanksgiving and wouldn't tell me what was bothering you."

"I'm sorry, but my brother had me pretty upset," Joe said. "I took off for Ocean Shores and stayed a whole week."

"An impromptu vacation?" Lois asked.

"I needed time to think. I've been doing a lot of that lately."

"What have you been thinking about?"

"You. Me. My past."

"Want to talk about it?"

"I'd like to talk about you and how you make me feel," he replied.

"Oh. How's that?"

Joe paused. Then in a high voice he sang, "Some might think I'm a clown who laughs and doesn't like to frown. But I'm really a lovesick fellow who's too scared to say so 'cause he's yellow."

Lois laughed, in spite of her confused feelings. "Did you make up that little ditty?"

"Guilty as charged."

Lois wondered if Joe really did love her. In a roundabout way he'd said he did, if his silly tune proved how he felt. She chuckled as she played the words of Joe's song over in her head.

"You're laughing at my love tune?" Joe asked.

"Not really. It's just—"

"I'll be the first to admit I can't carry a tune in a bucket."

Before she could reply, he asked another question. "Are you doing anything special for Christmas?"

Lois hesitated. Was he hinting at spending the holiday together, or was he trying to change the subject? "I'll be spending Christmas Eve with Tabby and Seth and his grandparents, at their retirement home. On Christmas Day we'll be in Olympia with Mom, Dad, and my grandmother."

"If you're coming to Olympia, why don't you stop by my house for a while? You could make it either before or after your visit with your folks."

Lois considered Joe's offer then asked, "Don't you have any plans for Christmas?"

"Brian said he might stop by sometime on Christmas Eve, but other than that I'm on my own."

Lois's heart sank at the thought of Joe spending the holiday by himself. It wasn't right for anyone to be alone on Christmas Day. "Why don't you come over to my parents' place for Christmas dinner? They aren't Christians, but they're very hospitable, and I'm sure they'd enjoy meeting you."

"Will Seth and Tabby be there?"

"As far as I know."

Joe was silent for a moment, and then he chuckled.

"What's so funny?"

"Nothing. I'd like to join you for dinner. Just give me your parents' address, tell me what to bring, and I'll be there with my Christmas bells on."

Lois groped for her slippers and padded to the bedroom window. She had been hoping for a white Christmas, but the brilliant blue sky that greeted her on Christmas morning was filled with sunshine and fluffy white clouds. She studied the thermometer stuck to the outside of the glass. Ten degrees above freezing, so there was no snow on the horizon. At least it wasn't raining. Lois would be driving the freeway from Tacoma to Olympia on bare, dry roads, and for that she was thankful.

She had spent Christmas Eve in pleasant company with Tabby and Seth and his dear Christian grandparents. Today would be a sharp contrast. Although her grandmother had recently become a Christian, her parents still refused to see their need for the Lord. Lois hoped her light would shine so they could see how God had changed her life for the better. Tabby and Seth felt the same way. And with Joe there for Christmas dinner, her parents would be surrounded by Christians. She hoped it would make a difference in their attitude toward spiritual things.

Whistling "Jingle Bells," Joe sauntered up the sidewalk toward the Johnsons' brick home. He was in better spirits this Christmas than he had been in many years. Brian had come by his home the night before and told him he'd found a tract someone had left in his cab. He'd been civil and even said he was thinking about going to church. That was an answer to prayer, and if Brian did start attending church, maybe he would finally see his need for Christ. Joe had witnessed to his brother several times over the years, but Brian always refused to talk about it. Now Joe felt as if there might be hope. He would continue to pray for his younger brother and with God's help try to understand him and work toward a better relationship.

Joe glanced down at the Christmas present he'd brought for Lois. He was also carrying a box of cream-filled chocolates he planned to give her folks. He was eager to meet them and hoped they liked candy.

He hesitated a second then rang the bell. Almost at once Lois opened the front door, and the sight of her took his breath away. She was wearing a blue velvet dress that matched her eyes and almost reached to her ankles.

Her hair hung down her back, held away from her face with two pearl combs. He thought she looked like an angel.

"Come in," Lois said, warming Joe's heart with her smile. The sparkle in her eyes told him she was glad to see him.

He handed her the wrapped package, along with the chocolates. "The gift's for you, and the candy is for your folks."

"That's so sweet. I have something under the tree for you too."

Joe followed Lois down the hall and into a cozy living room, where Seth and Tabby sat on the couch beside a middle-aged woman he assumed was Lois and Tabby's mother. She had brown hair and eyes like Tabby's, and her smile reminded him of Lois. Across the room sat an older woman with short, silver-gray hair and pale blue eyes. Lois's grandmother, he guessed. A man with thinning blond hair, a paunchy stomach and eyes the same color as Lois's was relaxing in a recliner near the fireplace. He stood when Joe entered the room. To complete the picture, a fir tree decorated with gold balls and white twinkle lights took up one corner of the room. Joe inhaled the woodsy scent and smiled. It was a pleasant scene, and he was glad he'd come.

"Mom, Dad, Grandma," Lois said with a sweep of her hand, "I'd like you to meet Joe Richey." She turned to Joe and smiled, then nodded toward the woman sitting beside Tabby. "This is my mother, Marsha Johnson."

Mrs. Johnson offered Joe a tentative smile. "Welcome, and Merry Christmas."

Lois gestured toward the older woman sitting in the rocking chair. "I'd like you to meet my grandma, Dottie Haskins."

Grandma Haskins winked at Joe. "It's so nice we're finally able to meet. We've heard a lot about you, young man."

Joe grinned when he noticed Lois was blushing. Apparently she'd been talking about him to her family. "Thanks. It's great to be here."

Lois's father came forward, his hand extended. "And I'm Earl Johnson." He scrutinized Joe a few seconds, then his face broke into a broad smile. "I understand you're a clown."

Joe nodded, reaching for his hand.

"I remember seeing some hilarious clown routines when I was a kid and went to the circus. Have you ever worked in a circus?"

"No, I'm a Gospel clown, but I also do kids' birthday parties and some other events."

"Well, I'm pleased to meet you, Joe."

"Likewise, Mr. Johnson."

"Earl. Please call me Earl."

Joe pumped his hand. He liked Lois's dad. The man had a firm handshake, and he seemed taken with the idea that Joe was a clown.

"Look what Joe brought," Lois said, handing the box of chocolates to her mother.

Mrs. Johnson looked at Joe and smiled warmly. "Thank you. I'll pass the candy around after dinner so everyone can have some."

"Unless Tabby gets one of her pregnancy cravings and can't resist the temptation to dive into the box before then," Seth said with a deep chuckle. He winked at Joe and nudged his wife gently in the ribs.

"How would you like to sleep on the couch tonight?" Tabby asked, wrinkling her nose at Seth.

He held up one hand. "Not on Christmas Day. It wouldn't be right to kick a man out of his warm bed on Christmas."

Everyone laughed, and Joe took a seat on the floor in front of the fireplace. It felt good to be here with Lois and her family. It had been a year since he'd spent Christmas with anyone, and that had been just Mom and him.

Lois placed the gift Joe had given her under the tree and dropped down beside him, settling against a couple of throw pillows. "Dinner should be ready soon, but if you're hungry we put some cut-up veggies and dip on the coffee table."

Joe glanced at the tray on the table, and his stomach rumbled. He was hungry, but he thought he'd better not fill up on munchies, since the real thing would be served soon.

Everyone engaged in small talk for a while, then Mrs. Johnson stood up. "I'd better check on the turkey."

"Would you like some help, Mom?" Tabby asked.

"That's okay, honey. You look kind of tired today, so stay put and rest."

Mrs. Johnson's gaze swung to her younger daughter, and immediately Lois stood to her feet. She looked down at Joe. "Keep the fire warm. I'll be back soon."

∞

Lois helped take the turkey out of the oven, then mashed the potatoes while her mom made gravy. She hoped everything was going okay in the living room. Joe appeared to be well received by her family and at ease with everyone.

"Dad seems to have taken a liking to your clown friend," her mother said.

Lois smiled. "Joe's an easy guy to like."

"Like or love?"

Lois's head came up at her mother's direct question. "Who said anything about love?" She searched for words that wouldn't be a lie. "Joe and I are good friends, and even though I care deeply for him, we do have a few problems."

Her mother stirred the gravy. "What kind of problems?"

"Joe's very reserved when it comes to talking about his past, and he doesn't show any emotion but laughter."

"But don't you think being around someone who looks at the bright side of life would be better than having a friend who's full of doom and gloom?"

Lois nodded. "Yes, you're right about that. But too much laughter and clowning around could get to be annoying at times. It seems as if it would be better to have something in between, more of a balance, for a relationship to work."

"You have a point, dear, but keep an open mind. A man can have much worse traits than being a funny guy."

"I know, Mom, and I'm trying to stay open-minded."

Her mother moved away from the stove and went to the sink. "This gravy is still a bit too thick. I'd better add more water to the flour mixture."

"I imagine you're looking forward to becoming a grandmother in the spring," Lois said then.

Her mother groaned softly. "I'll say, but it's kind of scary to think about being a grandma. It's been a long time since I held a baby, much less changed diapers or tried my hand at burping."

Lois dropped butter into the potatoes. "It will come back to you." She chuckled. "It's probably like riding a bike. Once you learn, no matter how long it's been between rides, you still remember how to hold onto the handle bars and steer the silly thing."

"I hope you're right. I don't want to mess up my role of grandma as badly as I did mothering."

Lois whirled around to face her mother. "What are you talking about? You were a good mother. You always saw that our needs were met."

Her mother's eyes filled with tears. "I did my best to see to your material needs, but I'm afraid I failed miserably at meeting your emotional needs." She blinked several times. "Especially Tabby's. I should never have let your father make fun of her the way he did."

Lois wiped her hands on a dish towel and hurried to her mother's side. She put her arms around her shoulders and hugged her. "I'm afraid Dad wasn't the only one guilty of tormenting Tabby. I did plenty of that myself."

"Another area where I failed," the older woman said tearfully. "I should have prevented it from happening. Instead, I watched you and your father become close while Tabby stood on the sidelines feeling insecure and ugly." She gave Lois's arm a gentle pat. "I'm glad the two of you have mended your fences. Even Dad and Tabby are getting along better these days." She stepped back then looked at Lois. "I. . .went to church with your grandmother last week. Did she tell you?"

Lois's mouth dropped open. "She never said a word, but I'm glad to hear it."

"We asked Dad to join us, but he wouldn't budge out of that recliner of his. He said a game was playing on TV, and he wasn't about to miss it."

Lois smiled to herself. She was so grateful her grandmother had made a commitment to the Lord, and now her mom had attended church. Hope for her dad, for both of her parents, welled up inside her.

Joe sat at the Johnsons' dining room table, enjoying each bite of food he ate. Lois's mother was a good cook, and she also seemed quiet and steady. *Nothing like my mom,* he thought. Being around Lois's father was a pleasure for him too. Since his own dad died when he was young, he'd grown up without a father. *Maybe if Dad hadn't been killed, Mom would have been*

easier to live with. At least she'd have had a husband to lean on, and Dad might have persuaded her to take the medicine the doctor prescribed. Maybe if she'd become a Christian sooner—

"Lois mentioned you use balloon animals and some juggling in your clown routines."

Grandma Haskins's pleasant voice pulled Joe abruptly from his thoughts.

"Oh—yes, I do," he said, blinking.

"Maybe you could give us a demonstration after we've finished dinner and opened our gifts," Lois's mother suggested.

Joe looked at her and smiled. "I suppose I could put on a little skit."

"When I was a boy I used to dream about running away from home and joining the circus," Lois's dad put in. "I either wanted to be a clown or a lion tamer." His stomach jiggled when he laughed.

Joe chuckled. "Now that's quite a contrast, Mr. Johnson—I mean, Earl. Did Lois tell you she's learned some clowning tricks?"

He felt an elbow connect to his ribs and knew Lois wasn't thrilled with his question.

"She's never mentioned it," her mother said, raising her eyebrows. "Lois, maybe you and Joe could perform a routine together, the way Tabby and Seth do."

"That would be fun to watch," Tabby agreed.

Joe glanced at Lois and saw her frown. He knew she wasn't happy about doing a clown routine with him. He reached for her hand under the table. "Lois has taken only a couple of clowning classes, and she's still practicing. Maybe it would be best if I went solo this time."

Lois let out her breath. "Joe's right—he will do much better without me."

Chapter Twenty-Two

During the rest of dinner, Joe remained quiet, answering questions only when they were directed to him. He was reviewing in his mind the clown routine he planned to do, as well as thinking about what he wanted to say to Lois before he went home.

After they finished eating and the table was cleared, everyone moved to the living room to open Christmas presents. Joe felt out of place, as each member of Lois's family exchanged gifts. Besides the candy, he'd brought only one gift, and that was for Lois. Joe had hoped to give it to her in private, but it didn't look as if that would happen.

"Only two presents are left," Tabby said, as she stacked the items she'd received onto the coffee table.

"One's mine to give Joe, and the other he brought for me," Lois said. She went to the tree and picked up Joe's gift. Joe followed, and they handed each other their presents.

"Should we open them at the same time or take turns?" Joe asked.

Lois shrugged. "Whatever you'd like to do is fine with me."

"Let's open them together," he suggested. "On the count of three. One—two—three!" Joe reached into the green gift bag and pulled out a necktie with a painting of Noah's ark and a rainbow on the front.

"Thanks, Lois. This is great," he said with sincerity.

"You're welcome." Lois tore the wrapping off her gift and peered inside. Then she looked at Joe.

"What is it?" Tabby asked, craning her neck to see around Seth, who sat beside her on the couch.

Lois held up a bright orange construction worker's hat with a bunch of gizmos attached. Even to Joe it looked weird.

"What in the world is that?" Lois's father asked from his chair across the room.

"It looks like something from outer space," Seth said, laughing. "Why don't you model it for us, Lois?"

Lois stared numbly at the so-called "hat" Joe had given her. Two empty cans of soda pop were attached to either side, each connected to a giant plastic straw that trailed over the top of the hat. A third straw came up the back then down over the bill. Hooked to one corner of the helmet was a microphone cord, which was attached to a small metal box with a red lever on the side. Lois had no idea what Joe expected her to do with it.

"I–I thought it would be a nice addition to your clown outfit," Joe said, his face flushed. "Why don't you try it on and show us what it can do?"

Lois stood there, her gaze shifting from Joe to the gruesome hat and back again. She would never wear such a hideous thing! What had possessed the man to give her this ridiculous Christmas present? She handed the hat to Joe. "Here—you wear it."

He shrugged and set it on top of his head. "I might as well show you how it works while I do my clown routine."

Lois sat down on the couch beside Tabby, folded her arms across her chest, and watched.

Joe flicked the red button on the small box attached to the microphone, and suddenly a high-pitched noise pierced the air.

Lois cupped both hands over her ears and grimaced. She noticed Mom and Grandma had done the same. Tabby, Seth, and Dad were all smiling as if Joe had done something great.

Joe switched the red lever to the right this time, and bells started ringing. He jumped up and down. "Are those Christmas bells, or is the fire alarm going off?" he shouted.

Before anyone could respond, he bent down and grabbed an orange and two apples from the glass bowl sitting on the coffee table. One at a time he tossed the pieces of fruit into the air, and he soon had them going up and down simultaneously.

Lois had to admit that Joe was good at juggling—and all other phases of clowning for that matter. In minutes he could captivate an audience, as he apparently had her family.

"What goes up must come down!" Joe shouted into the makeshift microphone. "Anyone thirsty?" He continued to juggle the fruit as he pretended to drink from the straw connected to the cans. As if that weren't enough of a show, Joe did it while he hopped on one foot.

Everyone cheered, and Lois noticed her father was laughing so hard tears were streaming down his cheeks. Joe's goofy antics had sure made an impression on him. *If Slow-Joe the Clown comes around more often, Dad's interest in spiritual things might even be sparked.*

As he juggled the fruit, Joe talked about Christianity and how people often juggle their routines to squeeze in time for God. When he was finished, he dropped the fruit back in the bowl, then bowed. Everyone clapped, including Lois. Joe had done a good job of presenting the Good News, and he'd made her family laugh. Not only was Slow-Joe a great entertainer, but he was a lot of fun. Was that enough? she wondered.

As the day wore on, Joe began to feel nervous. He liked Lois's family, and he had finally admitted to himself that he was in love with Lois. During the first part of the day she'd been warm and friendly, but since he'd given her that dumb hat and done his impromptu routine, she'd been aloof. He wondered if she were sorry she'd invited him today. It might be his first and last meal at the Johnsons' home, and in his book that would be a real shame.

When Lois excused herself to clear away the dessert dishes, Joe jumped up and followed. "Need some help?" he asked, stepping into the kitchen behind her.

Lois placed the pie plates in the sink. "You rinse, and I'll put the dishes in the dishwasher."

"I think I can handle that." Joe went to the sink and turned on the faucet. He waited for Lois to say something, but she remained quiet as he rinsed the plates and handed them to her.

When the last dish was in place and the dishwasher turned on, Joe reached for Lois's hand. "I had a good time today. Thanks for inviting me to share your Christmas."

She nodded. "You're welcome."

Joe leaned forward, cupped Lois's chin with his hand, and bent to kiss her. She pulled away abruptly. "We should get back to the others."

"I blew it with that dumb gift I gave you, didn't I?"

She looked at Joe, tears gathering in her blue eyes. "You made a hit with my dad."

"But not you?"

She pressed her lips together.

The tears in Lois's eyes were almost Joe's undoing, and he was tempted to pull her into his arms and say something funny so she would laugh. He hated tears. They were for weak people who couldn't control their emotions.

"I'm in love with you, Lois," he whispered.

Lois stared at him, her eyes wide.

"Aren't you going to say something?" he asked, tipping her chin.

"I–I'm speechless."

Joe chuckled and kissed her forehead. When she didn't resist, his lips traveled down her nose and across her cheek then found her lips.

She wrapped her arms around his neck and returned his kiss. Finally, Lois pulled back and sighed, leaning her head against Joe's chest. "I love you too, but I think you might need a woman who's more like you."

Joe took a step backward. "What's that supposed to mean?"

She shook her head slowly. "You're a clown, Joe. You clown through the day and into the night."

"That's my job, and I hope I'm good at what I do."

"You are," she assured him.

"Is it because I don't make a lot of money clowning? Is that the problem?"

Lois shook her head. "I've told you before that I'm not hung up on money. But the thing is, all you ever do is clown around. You make jokes when other people would be saying something serious. You don't show any other emotion besides happiness. I suspect you do it to avoid revealing your true feelings." She paused. "After that scene with your brother on Thanksgiving, I think there's a lot you haven't wanted to share with me. I respect your privacy, Joe. But if we're going to continue our relationship, don't you think you need to trust me by sharing what happened in your past that has upset you so much?"

Joe looked at his feet. Lois was right; he needed to be up-front with her and stop hiding behind his clown mask to keep from facing his true feelings. But he wasn't sure he could do either yet. Maybe he needed a few more sessions with Pastor Cummings.

"I'm not ready to discuss my family's problems at the moment," he said, offering her what he hoped was a reassuring smile. "But if you'll be patient with me, I hope maybe someday. . ."

She squeezed his hand. "Let's both be praying about this, okay?"

He nodded and brought Lois's fingers to his lips. "I'd better be going. It's been a great day, and no matter what happens down the road, always remember I love you."

Chapter Twenty-Three

Joe sat in the chair across from Pastor Cummings's desk, his left leg propped on top of his right knee. Today was his fourth counseling session, and each time he entered this office he became more uncomfortable. The pastor had a way of probing into Joe's subconscious, and some of the things he'd found there scared Joe.

"Tell me more about your mother," the older man said.

Joe released his breath and with it a deep moan. "Well, I've told you she was very depressed one minute and happy the next, and she only got worse after Dad was killed. Her moods were so unpredictable and her expectations ridiculous." He dug his fingers into the sides of the chair and fought against the urge to express his anger. "It was because of Mom's actions that Brian left home shortly after high school. She made our lives miserable when she was alive, but I still loved her."

"Of course you did, Joe." Pastor Cummings leaned forward, resting his elbows on the desk. "What did you do about your mother's actions?"

Joe shrugged his shoulders. "To avoid her anger, I gave in and let her have her way on things—even stuff I felt was wrong." He looked at the pastor. "It was easier than fighting back and suffering the consequences of her frequent outbursts."

"If I've been hearing you right, you felt as though your mother wanted something you weren't able to give."

Joe moved in the chair, putting both feet on the floor. "That's correct. Sometimes I just wanted to shout, 'Go away, Mom, and leave me alone!'"

"But you thought by your mother's actions that your feelings didn't matter?"

Joe nodded again.

"The truth is, they do matter. Because you didn't want to be like your mother, you've chosen to stuff your feelings down deep inside." Pastor

Cummings picked up his Bible. "Part of the healing process is being able to accept the pain. God made our feelings, and He uses them to help guide us."

Joe only shrugged.

"Do you let yourself cry when you're hurting, Joe?"

Joe shook his head. "Tears are a sign of weakness. Mom was weak, and she cried a lot. Brian was weak, and he ran away from home." Joe pointed to himself. "I chose to stay and take care of Mom, even though she never showed any appreciation." He frowned. "When she was nice, I felt myself being drawn into her world, like a vacuum sucks lint from the carpet. When she was hateful, though, I wanted to hide my head in the sand and cry until no more tears would come. But I didn't."

"It's not a weakness to cry or hurt, son. Tears can be a key element to strength."

Joe blinked. He'd never thought of tears being related to strength.

Pastor Cummings held the Bible out to Joe. "Here—open to Ecclesiastes, chapter three. Then read verses one to four."

It took a few seconds for Joe to locate Ecclesiastes. He read the passage aloud:

" 'To every thing there is a season, and a time to every purpose under the heaven. . . . A time to weep, and a time to laugh; a time to mourn, and a time to dance.' " He paused and looked at the pastor. "I guess I've never read those verses before, or if I have they never hit home."

"The Lord reveals the meaning of His Word when the need arises. Perhaps you weren't ready to accept the truth before today."

Joe swallowed hard. Pastor Cummings was right; he hadn't been ready. Even now, when he'd been hit with the truth, he was having a difficult time dealing with it. He'd spent so many years hiding behind his clown mask, refusing to show any emotion other than laughter, and even that was forced at times. He felt like a phony, realizing how often he'd clowned around or cracked jokes when deep inside he felt like weeping. Part of him wanted to give in to his tears. Another part was afraid if he did he might never stop crying.

"Mom asked the Lord to forgive her and committed her life to Him shortly before she died," Joe said. "Even though I knew God had forgiven her for treating me so badly, I guess I never forgave her." Joe lowered his head. "I've always felt guilty about it, so maybe that's part of the reason I've been hiding behind humor."

"You've discovered a lot in our last few sessions," the pastor said softly. "It will take time for you to put it into the proper perspective. For now, though, pat yourself on the back and rest in the Lord. He will show you how and when to cry if you need to."

Joe nodded, feeling as if his burden was much lighter than when he'd entered the pastor's study. Maybe someday he would even be ready to discuss his feelings with Lois.

The month of January and the first days of February drifted by like a feather floating in the breeze. Lois kept busy with her secretarial duties at the church during the week, and she spent most weekends helping Tabby redecorate their guest room, turning it into a nursery for the soon-coming baby. It kept her hands busy and her mind off Joe Richey. Since they'd said goodbye on Christmas Day, she'd heard from him only twice. Once he'd called to tell her how much he liked the cute tie she'd given him, and today she'd received a Valentine's card from him in the mail.

"Hey, sis. You look as if you're a thousand miles away."

Tabby's sweet voice pulled Lois out of her musings, and she swivelled her chair around to face her sister.

"You're good at sneaking up on me," Lois said with a grin.

Tabby ambled across the room and lowered herself into the chair beside Lois's desk. She patted her stomach. "I'm practicing for motherhood. Aren't moms supposed to be good at sneaking up on their children and catching them red-handed?"

Lois chuckled. "You're right, but I was only typing a memo for Pastor Hanson. So you didn't catch me with any red color on my hands," she added, smiling.

"It looked more like you were daydreaming to me," Tabby said in a teasing tone. "Unless you've learned how to make that computer keyboard work without touching the keys."

"I guess I *was* caught red-handed," Lois admitted with a sigh.

"What, or shall I say whom, were you thinking about?"

Lois handed the Valentine to her sister. "This came in today's mail."

Tabby's eyes opened wide as she read the verse inside the card. "Sounds like the guy's got it bad, and it's a far cry from the funny clown hat he gave you for Christmas."

Lois lifted her gaze to the ceiling. "Sure—that's why he never calls or comes around anymore."

"Maybe he's been busy with performances. Entertaining is what he does for a living, you know." With her finger, Tabby traced the outline of the red heart on the card. "This Valentine could be a foreshadow of something to come, you know."

Lois was silent then finally said, "Yes, it could be."

Tabby stepped over to Lois's chair. "There are only two ways to handle a man." She laughed. "Since nobody knows what either of them is, I suggest you give the guy a call and thank him for the beautiful card."

"I'll think about it," Lois murmured. "But I've called him a lot over the last few months, and I don't want to seem pushy."

Tabby hugged her sister. "There's nothing pushy about a thank-you."

"True." Lois smiled. "Okay, I'll call him tonight."

"Good for you." Tabby started toward the door. "I need to get back to the day care. I've taken a longer break than I'd planned." She stopped suddenly and sniffed the air. "Say! Do you smell something?"

Lois drew in a breath. "Smoke. It smells like there's a fire somewhere in the building!"

Chapter Twenty-Four

Joe had battled the desire to see Lois for several weeks. But today was Valentine's Day, and he'd decided to take action. She would no doubt have received his card by now, so he hoped the sentimental verse might pave the way.

As he headed toward Tacoma on the freeway, all he could think about was the need to make things right with Lois. Through counseling with Pastor Cummings and studying the scriptures, he'd finally forgiven his mother and come to grips with his past. Now he wanted to share everything with Lois. He hoped she would be receptive.

A short while later, Joe drove down the street toward Lois's church. His heart lurched when he saw two fire trucks parked in front of the building. As he pulled his pickup to the curb, he could see firemen scurrying about with hoses and other pieces of equipment. Billows of acrid smoke poured from the church.

Joe sprinted from his truck across the lawn, only to be stopped by a fireman. "You can't go in there, sir. A fire started in the janitor's closet, and it's spread throughout most of the building."

"My girlfriend—she works here," Joe said between breaths. He would do anything to find Lois. "I have to get inside!"

The fireman put his hand on Joe's arm. "It's not safe. We're doing everything possible to put the fire out, so please stay out of the way."

Joe dashed to the back of the church, thinking he could slip in that door unnoticed. He had to find Lois and see if she was all right. Others might also be trapped in the church.

He had almost reached the door when two firemen stepped between him and the building. "Where do you think you're going?" one of the men asked.

"I need to get inside. My girlfriend—"

"Oh, no you don't!" the other fireman shouted. "There's been a lot of damage to the structure. Most of the fire is out, but it's not safe in there."

Joe looked around helplessly, wondering if he could get inside another way. "What about the people inside?" he asked, feeling his sense of panic taking control.

He filled his lungs with air and prayed. *Dear Lord, please let Lois and everyone else be okay.*

Joe felt someone touch his arm. "I thought I saw your truck parked out front. What are you doing here?"

He spun around at the sound of Lois's voice, and the sight of her caused tears to flood Joe's eyes. His stomach knotted as he fought to hold back the tide of emotions threatening to wash over him. He didn't want to cry, but the tears came anyway. He was so relieved to see that Lois wasn't inside the church and appeared to be okay. "Thank God you're not hurt!" he exclaimed.

She smiled at him and reached up to wipe away the tears that had fallen onto his cheeks. "Joe, you're crying."

He nodded and grinned at her. "Yeah, I guess I am." He grabbed Lois around the waist and lifted her up, whirling them both around. "Thank You, Lord!" he shouted. "Thank You a thousand times over!"

"Put me down, you silly man! I'm getting dizzy," Lois said breathlessly.

Joe set her on the ground then placed both hands on her shoulders and stared into the depths of her indigo eyes. "Are you really all right, and did they get everyone out in time?"

She nodded, and her eyes pooled with tears. "Everyone is fine, but the building isn't. I'm afraid what's left of it may have to be torn down."

"The church can be rebuilt," Joe said, "but human life is not replaceable."

"You're so right," Lois agreed. "When the fire broke out, Tabby and I were in my office. Our first thought was about the day care kids who were in the basement."

Joe felt immediate concern. "Were they hurt?"

She shook her head. "Not a single child. Almost everyone was out of the building before the fire trucks even arrived."

"When I got here and saw all the commotion, then looked around and didn't see you, I was afraid you were trapped inside the church," Joe said, feeling as if he might cry again.

Lois smiled up at him. "It's nice to know you care so much."

Joe clasped her hand and gave it a gentle squeeze. "Thanks to my pastor's wise counsel and God's Word, I'm learning to put the past behind and show my emotions. That's why I drove over here, Lois. I wanted to tell you about it." He pulled a bunch of balloons from his jacket pocket and held them up. "I also wanted to give you these."

She tipped her head to one side. "Some deflated balloons?"

He chuckled and wiped his sweaty palms on the side of his blue jeans. "Well, I'd planned to show up at your office with a bouquet of balloon flowers—like the ones I made you the night we first met." Joe cleared his throat. "I, well, I came here to ask you a question."

"What question?"

Joe felt jittery all of a sudden. If he weren't careful, he would slip into the old Joe—the clown who didn't know how to show his real feelings.

He stuffed all but one balloon back in his pocket then blew up that one and twisted it into a wiener dog. He handed the pooch to Lois, bowed low at the waist and said, "Lois Johnson, will you be my housewife—I mean, maid—I mean—"

Lois stepped away, a puzzled look on her face. "You're such a big kidder, Joe."

Joe watched Lois walk next door to the senior pastor's house. She'd thought he was clowning around when he tried to propose, and now she was probably mad at him.

Tears welled up in his eyes at the thought of losing her. He had meant for the proposal to be sweet and tender, and he'd botched it up but good, giving her a balloon dog then asking her to be his housewife. "What a jerk she must think I am," Joe mumbled, staring down at his feet. "What can I do now?"

"Go after her," he heard a voice whisper behind him. He turned to find Tabby standing near him. "Tell her you weren't kidding but just got nervous and messed up your presentation."

"Yeah, I guess you're right. I hope she'll believe me."

Tabby patted Joe on the back and started across the lawn toward the parsonage.

Joe sucked in a breath and offered up a quick prayer. Tabby was right; he did need to do something—quickly.

Lois couldn't believe Joe was crying one minute, telling her he'd been in counseling and was learning to express his feelings, and the next minute he was joking about something as solemn as marriage. In light of the seriousness of the church fire, he was probably just trying to get her to chuckle. She shouldn't have been so sensitive. She wished she hadn't walked away so abruptly without letting him explain.

Tabby had entered the parsonage a few minutes earlier and gone inside with the others. Rather than talking about the fire with everyone, Lois was sitting on the front porch, trying to sort things out. She closed her eyes and was about to pray when she heard a familiar voice.

"Lois, I need to talk to you."

She opened her eyes as Joe took a seat beside her. He was smiling, but she saw the tension in his jaw. His smile seemed fake, like the one he painted on when he dressed as a clown.

He leaned closer, his face inches from hers, and Lois let out a sigh.

"I'm sorry about the dumb proposal and balloon dog," he murmured. "Would you take a walk with me so we can talk?"

She hesitated for a moment, uncertain what to say.

Joe grabbed Lois's hand and pulled her gently to a standing position.

She looked up at him. "What's going on?"

"I'm taking you someplace special."

Lois was tempted to resist. She couldn't explain the funny feeling she got every time she saw Joe. At some moments, like now, she had to fight the urge to throw herself into his arms.

They left the pastor's yard and walked in silence, until the small chapel behind the church came into view. It was used for intimate weddings, baptisms, and foot washing. "At least this building didn't catch on fire," Lois said as Joe opened the door and led her inside.

Joe nodded and motioned for her to take a seat on the front pew. Then he knelt on one knee in front of her.

She squirmed uneasily and held her breath. What was he up to now?

"I love you, Lois," he whispered. "I know I'm not the ideal catch, and I'll probably never make a lot of money, but if you'll have me as your husband, I promise to love you for the rest of my life. Will you please marry me?"

Lois's vision clouded with tears as she smiled at Joe. "Yes. A thousand times, yes!"

His face broke into a huge grin. "Can I take that as a yes?"

She chuckled and winked at him. "It's a definite yes."

Joe stood and helped Lois to her feet then pulled her into his arms. "From now on we can clown around together, but I promise to get serious sometimes too."

She laid her head against his chest and sighed contentedly. "I'd like that, Joe. I want to spend the rest of my life telling others about God's love, and I want to be the kind of wife who loves you no matter how much you clown around."

The Neighborly Thing

Chapter One

"The perfect home," Sinda Shull murmured as she stood on the sagging front porch of her new house. "Perfect for my needs, but oh, what a dump!"

Her friend, Carol Riggins, drew Sinda close for a hug. "Seattle's loss is Elmwood's gain, and now the town won't be the same." She snickered, then her expression sobered. "I'm really glad you decided to leave the past behind and move here for a fresh start."

Sinda's thoughts fluttered toward the past, then quickly shut down. That was part of her life better left uninvited. She pulled away from her friend, choosing not to comment on her reasons for moving from Seattle. "Sure hope I can figure out some way to turn this monstrosity into a real home."

"I thought you bought the place to use for your business."

"I did, but I have to live here too."

Carol nodded. "True, and fixing it up should help get your mind off the past."

Pushing back a strand of hair that had escaped her ponytail, Sinda frowned. Carol might think she knew all about Sinda's past, but the truth was, her friend knew very little about what had transpired in the Shull home over the years. When the Rigginses moved into their north Seattle neighborhood, Sinda and Carol were both twelve. By then Sinda and her father had already been living alone for two years. Dad didn't like her to have friends over, so Sinda usually played at Carol's house. It was probably better that way. . .less chance of Carol finding out her secrets.

Sinda heard footsteps and glanced to the left. A tall man wearing a mail carrier's uniform was walking up the sidewalk leading to the house next door. The sight of him pulled Sinda's mind back to the present, and she slapped at the dirt on her blue jeans. "Let's not spoil our day by talking about the past, okay?"

Carol pulled her fingers through her short blond curls and nodded. "We've managed to get you pretty well moved in with no problems, so I'd better get going before I ruin everything by dredging up old memories." She patted Sinda's arm. "I can't imagine what it must feel like to lose a parent, let alone both of them."

The image of her father and his recent death from a heart attack burned deep into Sinda's soul. In order to force the painful memories into submission, Sinda had to swallow hard and refocus her thoughts. "I—I appreciate all you've done today, Carol."

"What are friends for?" Carol gave Sinda another hug, then she turned to go. "Give a holler if you need my help with anything else," she called over her shoulder.

Sinda grimaced. "With the way this place looks, you can probably count on it."

Glen Olsen poured himself a tall glass of milk, then another one for his ten-year-old daughter, Tara. It had been a long day, and he was bone tired. He'd encountered two new dogs on his route, been chewed out by an irate woman whose disability check hadn't arrived on time, and he had a blister the size of a silver dollar on his left foot. All Glen wanted to do was sit down, kick off his boots, and try to unwind before he had to fix supper.

He handed Tara her glass of milk and placed a jar of ginger cookies they'd baked the day before in the center of the kitchen table. "Have a seat and let's have a snack."

"Dad, have you met our new next-door neighbors yet?" Tara reached into the container and grabbed two cookies, which she promptly stuffed into her mouth.

Glen followed suit and washed his cookies down with a gulp of milk. "Nope, but when I got home this afternoon, I saw two women standing on the front porch."

Tara's brown eyes brightened. "Really? What were they doing?"

Glen dropped into the chair across from her and bent over to unlace his boots. "They were talking, Nosey Rosey."

"Dad!" Tara wrinkled her freckled nose and looked at him as though he'd lost his mind. "Did you see any kids my age?"

He gingerly slipped his left foot free and wiggled his toes. "Like I said. . .just the two women. I saw one of them drive off in a red sports car, and the other lady probably went inside."

Tara tapped her fingernails along the checkered tablecloth. "That doesn't tell me much. When it comes to detective work, you're definitely not one of the top ten."

Glen chuckled. "What do you mean? I told you all I know. Just because I'm not as good at neighborhood snooping as some people I know. . ."

"I'm not a snoop! The correct word for my career is 'detective'!"

"Detective—snoop—what's the difference?" Glen wagged his finger. "You need to mind your own business, young lady. People don't like it when you spy on them."

"What makes you think I've been spying on the neighbors?"

"Elementary, my dear daughter. Elementary." Glen gulped down the rest of his milk and grabbed a napkin out of the wicker basket on the table. "May I remind you that you've done it before? I'm surprised you don't have the full history on our new neighbors by now."

Tara's mahogany eyes, so like her mother's, seemed to be challenging him, but surprisingly, she took their conversation in another direction. "These cookies are great, Dad. You're probably the best cook in the entire world!"

Glen raised his eyebrows. "I might be the best cook in our neighborhood, or maybe even the whole town of Elmwood, but certainly not the entire world. Besides, you usually help me with the cooking." He reached across the table and gave Tara's hand a gentle squeeze.

She smiled in response, revealing a pair of perfectly matched dimples. "Say, I've got a terrific idea!"

"Oh, no!" Glen slapped one hand against the side of his head. "Should I call out the Coast Guard, or does that come later?"

"Quit teasing, Dad."

"Okay, okay. What's your terrific idea, kiddo?"

Tara's eyes lit up like a sunbeam as a slow smile swept across her face. "I think we should take some of these yummy cookies over there." Tara marched over to the cupboard and brought a heavy paper plate to the table, then piled it high with cookies.

Glen reached down to rub his sore foot and asked absently, "Over where?"

She smacked her hand against the table, and a couple cookies flew off the plate. "Over to our new neighbor's house. You're always lecturing me about being kind to our neighbors, so I thought it would be the neighborly thing to do."

"Let me get this straight," Glen said, reaching for one of the cookies that had fallen to the table. "You want to take some of our delicious, best-in-the-whole-neighborhood cookies, and go over to meet our new neighbors. Is that right?"

Tara jumped to her feet. "Exactly! That way we can find out if they have any kids my age." She tipped her head to one side. "Of course, if you're too scared—"

"Me? Scared? Now what would I have to be scared of?"

"That big old house is pretty creepy looking."

"For you, maybe," Glen said with a hearty laugh. "As for me—I'm not only a great cook, but I'm also a fearless warrior."

"Can we go now, Dad?"

Glen studied his daughter intently. It was obvious from the determined tilt of her chin that she was completely serious about this. Whenever Tara came up with one of her bright ideas, he knew she wasn't about to let it drop until he either agreed or laid down the law. In this case he thought her plan had merit. "I suppose your idea does beat spying over the garden fence," he said, sucking in his bottom lip in order to hold back the laughter that threatened to bubble over.

"I don't spy," she retorted as her hands went to her hips.

"I've heard through the grapevine that you're always spying on someone with those binoculars I made the mistake of buying you last Christmas. If you had your way, you'd probably be going over every square inch of our new neighbor's house with a fine-tooth comb." Glen waved his hand for emphasis.

"I would not!" Tara went back to the cupboard, took out some plastic wrap, and covered the plate of cookies. "Ready?"

Glen stood up. "I'm game if you are." He grabbed a light jacket from the coat tree near the back door, stepped into his slippers, and threw Tara her sweater. "Come on. I'll show you how brave I can be."

Glen glanced over his shoulder and saw that Tara was following his lead out the back door. As they stepped off the porch, he felt her jab him in the ribs. "Just in case you do get scared, remember that I'll be with you, Dad."

A catchy comeback flitted through Glen's mind, but he decided against saying anything more.

They moved across the grass, and Glen opened the high gate that separated their backyard from the neighbor's. The dilapidated, three-story home was in sharp contrast to the rest of the houses in their neighborhood. Dark, ragged-looking curtains hung at the windows, peeling green paint made the siding resemble alligator skin, and a sagging back porch indicated the whole house was desperately in need of an overhaul. The yard was equally run-down; the flower beds were filled with choking weeds, and the grass was so tall it looked like it hadn't been mowed for at least a year.

"This place gives me the creeps," Tara whispered as she knocked on the wooden edge of the rickety screen door. "I don't know why anyone would buy such a dump."

Glen shrugged. "It's not so bad, really. Nothing a few coats of paint and a little elbow grease wouldn't cure."

"Yeah, right," Tara muttered.

When the back door opened, a woman who appeared to be in her thirties stood before them holding a small vinyl doll in one hand. She was dressed in a pair of faded blue jeans and a bright orange sweatshirt smudged with dirt. Her long auburn hair was in a ponytail, and iridescent green eyes, peeking out of long eyelashes, revealed her obvious surprise. "May I help you?" she asked, quickly placing the doll on one end of the kitchen counter.

With a casualness he didn't feel, Glen leaned against the porch railing and offered the woman what he hoped was a pleasant smile. He cleared his throat a few times, wondering why it suddenly felt so dry. "My name's Glen Olsen, and this is my daughter, Tara. We're your next-door neighbors. We dropped by to welcome you to the neighborhood."

Tara held out the paper plate. "And to give you these."

The woman smiled slightly and took the offered cookies. "I'd invite you in, but the place is a mess right now." She fidgeted, and her gaze kept darting back and forth between Glen and Tara, making him wonder if she felt as nervous about meeting them as he did her.

"That's all right, Mrs.—"

"My name's Sinda Shull, and I'm not married," she said with a definite edge to her voice.

"I guess that means you don't have any kids," Tara interjected.

Glen gave his daughter a warning nudge, but before she could say anything more, the woman answered, "I have no children."

"But what about the—"

"We'd better get going," Glen said, cutting Tara off in midsentence. "Miss Shull is probably trying to get unpacked and settled in." His fingers twitched as he struggled with an unexplained urge to reach out and brush a wayward strand of tawny hair away from Sinda's face. Shifting his weight from one foot to the other, he quickly rubbed his sweaty palm against his jacket pocket and extended his hand. "It was nice meeting you."

As they shook, Glen noticed how small her hand was compared to his. And it was ice cold. *She really must be nervous.* He moistened his lips, then smiled. "If you need anything, please let me know."

She let go and took a step backward. "Thanks, but I'm sure I won't need anything."

Glen felt a tug on his jacket sleeve. "Come on, Dad. Let's go home."

"Sure. Okay." He nodded at Sinda Shull. "Good night, then."

Sinda didn't usually allow self-pity to take control of her thoughts, but tonight she couldn't seem to help herself. She'd only been living in Elmwood one day, and already she missed home—and yes, even Dad. In spite of her father's possessive, controlling, and sometimes harsh ways, until his death he'd been her whole world. He'd taken her to church, supplied food for the table, and put clothes on their backs. He had taught Sinda respect, obedience, and. . .

Sinda moved away from the kitchen table, placing her supper dishes in the sink. She was doing it again. . .thinking about the past. Dad was dead now, and for the first time in her life she was on her own. For the last year she'd learned to become independent, so what difference did her past make now? She blinked back tears and clenched her teeth. "I won't dwell on the things I can't change."

As she turned toward the cupboard, Sinda spotted the plate of cookies lying next to the doll she'd put there earlier. "Why was I so rude to the neighbors?" she moaned. "I don't think I even thanked them for the goodies."

She squeezed her eyes shut as a mental picture of her father flashed onto the screen of her mind. *How would Dad have reacted if he'd witnessed me being rude?* She took a deep breath, holding her sides for several seconds and willing the pain to go away. There was no point wasting time on these reflections, and there was no time for neighborly things. She had a house that would take a lot of work to make it livable, much less serve as a place of business. So what if she'd been rude to Glen Olsen and his little girl? They'd be living their lives, and she'd be living hers. If they never spoke again, what would it matter?

Sinda ran warm water into the sink and added some liquid detergent, staring at the tiny bubbles as they floated toward the plaster ceiling. "I came here to get away from the past, and I've got a job to do. So that's that!"

"Our new neighbor seems kind of weird, doesn't she, Dad?" Tara asked as the two of them were finishing their supper of macaroni and cheese.

Glen had other thoughts on his mind, and even though he'd heard her question, he chose not to answer.

"Dad!"

He looked up from his half-eaten plate of food. "Yes, Tara?"

"Don't you think Sinda Shull is weird? Did you see the way she was dressed?"

Glen lifted his fork but didn't take a bite. "What's wrong with the way she was dressed? She just moved in, and those were obviously her working clothes."

Tara gazed at the ceiling. "She looked like a pumpkin in that goofy orange sweatshirt, and—"

"Do I need to remind you what the Bible says about loving our neighbors and judging others?" he interrupted. "The woman seemed nice enough to me, and it's not our place to pass judgment, even if she should turn out to be not so nice."

Tara groaned. "You would say that. You always try to look for the good in others."

"That's exactly what God wants us to do." Glen shoveled some macaroni into his mouth, then washed it down with a gulp of water.

She frowned at him. "What if the person you think is good turns out to be rotten to the core?"

"I hardly think Sinda Shull is rotten to the core." Glen shook his head. "Besides, only God knows what's in someone's heart."

Tara wrinkled her nose. "You can believe whatever you like, but I've got a bad feeling about that woman. I'm trusting my instincts on this one."

"I say your instincts are way off!" He scowled. "And don't go getting any ridiculous notions about spying on Miss Shull. It's not the—"

"I know, I know," she interrupted. "It's not the neighborly thing to do." He nodded.

Tara tapped a fingernail against her chin. "Can I ask you a question?"

"I suppose."

"Why would a woman who isn't married and has no kids be holding a doll when she answered the door?"

Glen shrugged. "Maybe she has relatives or friends with children."

Tara remained silent for several seconds, as though she were in deep thought. "She acted kind of nervous, didn't you think? And did you see those green eyes of hers?"

Glen smiled. Oh, he'd seen them all right. Even for the few minutes they'd been standing on Sinda's back porch, it had been hard to keep from staring into those pools of liquid emerald. *Get a grip,* he scolded himself. *You can't let some new neighbor woman make you start acting like a high school kid—especially not in front of your impressionable young daughter.*

"Sinda's eyes remind me of Jake," Tara said, jolting Glen out of his musings.

"Jake? What are you talking about, Tara?"

"She's got cat's eyes. She could probably hypnotize someone with those weird eyes."

Glen leaned on the table, casting a frown at his daughter. "I think you, little Miss Detective, have an overactive imagination. You watch way too much TV, and I plan to speak to Mrs. Mayer about it. While I'm at work, she needs to watch you a bit more closely."

Tara's lower lip protruded. "I don't watch too much TV. I just have a sixth sense about people. Right now my senses are telling me that Sinda Shull is one weird lady, and she needs to be watched!"

Chapter Two

Sinda pulled her white minivan into the driveway and stopped in front of the basement door. She had more than enough work to do today. There were boxes to unload, stacks of paperwork to go through, and numerous phone calls to make. The list seemed endless, and there was no telling how long it might take to get everything accomplished.

With mustered enthusiasm, Sinda climbed out of the van and went around to open the tailgate. There were five large boxes in back. Knowing they wouldn't unload themselves, she pulled the first one toward her and began to carefully lift it.

"Hi, there!"

Sinda jumped at the sound of a child's voice. The same little girl who had brought her cookies the other night was crouched in the picture-perfect flower bed next door. She had a shovel in one of her gloved hands and appeared to be weeding.

"Were you speaking to me?" Sinda asked from across the small white picket fence.

"I said 'hi.'" The child stood up and brushed a clump of dirt from the knees of her dark blue overalls.

"Hello. It's Tara, right?"

The young girl wore her cinnamon brown hair in a ponytail, and it bounced with each step she took toward Sinda. "Yeah, my name's Tara." She pressed her body against the fence, and her dark eyes looked at Sinda with such intensity it made her feel like she was on trial.

Sinda glanced down at her blue cutoffs and yellow T-shirt, gave her ponytail a self-conscious flip with one hand, then lifted the box. "I guess we're both doing chores today, Tara."

Tara pushed a loose strand of hair away from her face. "Would you like me to see if Dad can come over and carry some of those boxes into the house? The one you're holding looks kind of heavy."

Sinda clutched the box tightly to her chest. She hated to admit it, but it was a bit weighty. Accepting help from a neighbor she hardly knew was not her style, though. It hadn't been Dad's style, either. In fact, if he'd had his way, she wouldn't have associated with any of their Seattle neighbors during her adolescence. It was lucky for Sinda that she and Carol had gone to school together. That's when they'd become good friends, and Sinda had decided to play at Carol's house as often as she could. Of course, it was usually after school, when Dad was still at work, or on a Saturday, when he was busy running errands.

"You look really tired. Should I call Dad or what?"

Tara's persistence jolted Sinda out of her musings. "No, I'm fine. Don't trouble your father."

"I'm sure it wouldn't be any trouble. Dad likes to help people in need."

Sinda grunted. "What makes you think I'm in need?"

Tara moved quickly away from the fence, looking as though she'd been stung by a wasp. "Okay, whatever."

"I'm sorry I snapped," Sinda called as she started up the driveway toward her basement entrance. "Thanks for the offer of help."

Tara went back to her weeding, but Sinda had an inkling she hadn't seen or heard the last of the extroverted child.

A short time later, when she'd finished unloading the back of the van, Sinda went around front and opened the passenger door. She blew the dust off her watch and checked the time, then withdrew a large wicker basket and carried it into the house. "How I wish this was the last load," she muttered, "but I'll probably be hauling boxes from my storage unit for weeks."

"Just what do you think you're doing, young lady?" Glen barked when he entered Tara's bedroom and found her gazing out the window with binoculars pointing at the front yard of their new neighbor's house.

Tara jumped, nearly dropping the binoculars. "Dad! Don't scare me like that!"

"Sorry, but I did knock first. You obviously didn't hear me, because you were too busy spying."

"I was watching Sinda Shull." Tara turned away from the window. "I don't trust her. I think she's up to something."

Glen planted both hands on his hips. "Up to something? What do you think the woman's up to?"

Tara dropped the binoculars onto the bed and moved closer to Glen. She spoke in a hushed tone, as though they might be overheard. "I don't think I have quite enough evidence yet, but with a little more time, maybe I can get something incriminating on her."

He raised his eyebrows. *Where does this kid learn such big words?* "Honestly, Tara. What kind of incriminating evidence could you possibly have on someone as nice as Sinda Shull?"

Tara flopped onto the bed with a groan. "Nice? How do you know she's nice? You don't even know her."

Glen reached up to rub the back of his neck. He was beginning to feel a headache coming on, and he sure didn't need an argument with his mischievous daughter right now. "Sinda seemed nice enough to me."

"You've only met her once," Tara argued. "If you knew her better, you'd soon see that my intuition is right."

Glen's lips curved into a smile. "You know, kiddo, you might be right about that."

"You think she's up to something?"

He shook his head. "No, but I think we should get to know her better."

"Oh. I guess that would help."

"In fact, I believe I'll invite her over here for dinner. Tomorrow afternoon sounds good to me."

Tara's expression turned to sheer panic. "You're kidding, right?"

"I'm totally serious. What better way to get acquainted than over a nice candlelit dinner?"

"Candlelit?" Tara came straight off the bed. "Don't you think that might be carrying neighborliness a bit too far?" She sniffed deeply. "Besides, Sunday is our day to be together. We don't want to spoil it by having some stranger around, do we?"

Glen bent down, so his eyes were level with Tara's. "You said you thought it would help if we got better acquainted with the neighbor."

"I know, but—"

"Then don't throw cold water on my plans. I think I should go over there right now and ask her. If Sinda agrees to join us for dinner, I'll fix fried chicken, and maybe some of those flaky buttermilk biscuits you like so well." He clasped his hands together and flexed his fingers until several of them popped. "Let's see. . .what shall we have for dessert?"

Tara grabbed his arm and gave it a firm shake. "Dad, get a grip! It's just one little dinner, so we can find out more about the weirdo neighbor. You don't have to make such a big deal out of it."

"No more 'weird neighbor' comments. In the book of Luke we are told to love our neighbors as ourselves, and Romans 13:10 reminds us that love does no harm to its neighbor. That includes not making unkind comments about our neighbors." He started for the door, but hesitated. "I'm going over to Sinda's, and when I get back, you should be doing something constructive. And put those binoculars away."

"Can I borrow the camcorder for a while?"

"No."

"But, Dad, I—"

"You've done enough spying for one day."

The back door of Sinda's house hung wide open, with only the rickety old screen door to offer protection from the cool spring breeze whistling under the porch eaves. Glen's feet brought him to the door as his thoughts wandered. *Is this really a good idea? Will Sinda be receptive to my dinner invitation?* With a resolve to go through with the plan, he looked around for a doorbell but found none. He rapped lightly on the side of the screen door, and when there was no response, he called out, "Hello! Anybody home?" Still nothing. He leaned forward and peered through a hole in the screen, listening for any sounds that might be coming from within. "Hello!"

There were no lights on in the kitchen, and he couldn't see much past the table and chairs sitting near the door. The thought crossed his mind to see if the screen was unlocked, and if it wasn't, maybe he'd poke his head inside. *That would be categorized as snooping,* he reminded himself. *I'm getting as bad as that would-be detective daughter of mine.*

Glen had about decided to give up when another thought popped into his mind. Maybe Sinda's out front. That's where Tara was spying on her.

He stepped off the back porch, nearly tripping on one of the loose boards, then started around the side of the house. He had just rounded the corner when he ran straight into Sinda. She held a bulky cardboard box in her arms and appeared to be heading for the front door.

"Excuse me!" the two said in unison, each taking a step backward.

"That box looks kind of heavy. Would you like me to carry it for you?" Glen offered.

She shook her head. "It's not that heavy. Besides, I've already made several trips to my storage unit today, and I can manage fine on my own."

Glen eyed her speculatively. Tara was right about one thing. Sinda's green eyes did look sort of catlike. It was difficult not to stare at them. He drew from his inner reserve and lowered his gaze. *Get yourself under control. You didn't come over here to ask for a date or anything. It's just a simple home-cooked meal, done purely as a neighborly gesture.*

Glen cleared his throat a few times, and Sinda gave him a questioning look. "Is there something I can do for you, Mr. Olsen?"

"Glen. Please call me Glen." Now that he'd found his voice again, he decided to plunge ahead. "I was wondering—that is, my daughter and I would like to invite you over for dinner tomorrow afternoon." He rushed on. "I make some pretty tasty fried chicken, and there's always plenty. Please say you'll come."

Sinda shifted the box in her arms. He could tell it was much too heavy for her, but if she didn't want his help, what could he do about it?

"I wouldn't want to put you or your wife out any," Sinda stated as she moved toward the house.

Glen followed. "My wife?"

She nodded but kept on walking.

"Oh, I'm not married. I mean, I was married, but my wife died of leukemia when Tara was a year old."

Sinda stopped in her tracks and turned to face him. Her green eyes had darkened, and if he wasn't mistaken, a few tears were gathering in the corners of those gorgeous orbs.

"I'm so sorry, Mr. Olsen. . .I mean, Glen. I'm sure it must be difficult for you to be raising a daughter all alone."

"It can be challenging at times," he admitted.

"I'm surprised you haven't remarried," Sinda remarked. "A child really does need a mother, you know."

An odd statement coming from a single lady, and her tone sounded almost reprimanding. Glen shrugged. "Guess I've never found a woman who could put up with me." *Or my daughter,* he added mentally. The truth was, he had dated a few women over the years, but Tara always managed to scare them off. She was more than a little possessive of him and had made his dates feel uncomfortable with her unfriendly attitude and constant interrogations. Most of them backed away before he could deal with Tara's jealousy.

"How 'bout it?" Glen asked, returning to the question at hand. "Will you come for dinner? It'll give us a chance to get better acquainted."

"Fried chicken does sound rather tasty." Sinda paused and flicked her tongue across her lower lip. "Okay, I'll come."

Glen could hardly believe she had accepted his invitation. The other night Sinda seemed rather standoffish. Maybe she'd just been tired. "How does one o'clock sound?" he asked.

"That'll be fine. Can I bring anything?"

"Just a hearty appetite." He turned toward his own yard. "See you tomorrow, Sinda."

Chapter Three

"I still don't see why we've gotta have that woman over for dinner," Tara whined as Glen drove them home from church Sunday afternoon.

"You're the one who gave me the idea of getting to know her better." He smiled. "Who knows, you might even find you'll actually enjoy yourself."

"I doubt it," Tara mumbled.

"Just try," he said through clenched teeth. "Oh, and Tara?"

"Yeah, Dad?"

"Be on your best behavior today. No prying into Sinda's private life. If she volunteers any information about herself, that's one thing, but I don't want you bombarding her with a bunch of silly questions. Is that clear?" He glanced at her out of the corner of his eye.

She shrugged. "How are we gonna find out what she's up to in that creepy old house if we don't ask a few questions?"

Glen's patience was waning, and he scowled at Tara. "Sinda is not up to anything."

"I saw her carrying a wicker basket into her house the other day," she persisted. "And you know what I heard?"

"There's nothing unusual about a wicker basket."

"But I know I heard a—"

"Tara Mae Olsen!" Glen usually had more patience with his daughter, but today she was pushing too far. "I don't want to hear another word. Sinda Shull is our neighbor, and we're going to enjoy dinner while we try to get to know her better."

Tara sniffed deeply. "I'm just glad you didn't ask her to go to church with us."

A pair of amazing green eyes flashed into Glen's mind, and he smiled. "I should have thought of that. Maybe next time I will ask her. If she hasn't already found a church home, that is."

Sinda glanced at her reflection in the bay window as she stood on the front porch of the neighbor's split-level rambler. She'd decided to wear a pair of khaki slacks and an off-white knit top for dinner at the Olsens'. She'd chosen a pair of amber-colored tortoise shell combs to hold her hair away from her face, and even though she might look presentable, she felt like a fish out of water. *Probably as out of place as my archaic house looks next to this modern one,* she mused. *What on earth possessed me to accept Glen's dinner invitation?* It wasn't like her to be sociable with people she barely knew. Dad had taught her to be wary of strangers and not to let anyone know much about their personal business.

With that thought in mind, Sinda was on the verge of turning for home, but the front door unexpectedly swung open. "You're ten minutes late," Tara grumbled as she motioned Sinda inside.

Sinda studied the child a few seconds. A thick mane of brown hair fell freely down Tara's back, and she was dressed in a red jumper with a white blouse. The freckles dotting the girl's nose made her look like a cute little pixie, even if she did seem to have a chip on both shoulders. *Such a rude young lady. Why, if I'd talked to someone like that when I was a child. . .*

With determination, Sinda refocused her thoughts. "I'm sorry about being late. I hope I haven't ruined dinner."

"It would take more than ten minutes to wreck one of Dad's great meals. He's the best cook in the whole state of Washington."

"Then I guess I'm in for a treat," Sinda responded with a forced smile.

"Dad's out in the kitchen getting everything served up. He said for us to go into the dining room."

Sinda followed Tara down the hall and into a cozy but formal eating area. It was tastefully decorated, with a large oak table and six matching chairs occupying the center of the room. The walls were painted off-white, with a border of pale pink roses running along the top. A small pot of purple pansies sat in the middle of the table with two pink taper candles on either side. The atmosphere was soft and subtle. Hardly something most men would have a hand in, Sinda noted. She offered Tara another guarded smile. "The flowers are lovely."

"They're from my mother's garden. She planted lots of flowers the year before I was born. Dad takes good care of them, so they keep coming back every year. He says as long as the flowers are alive, we'll have a part of Mom with us." Tara lifted her chin and stared at Sinda with a look of defiance. "Dad loved her a lot."

"I'm sure he did." Sinda swallowed against the constriction she felt tightening her throat. She had to blink several times to keep unwanted tears from spilling over. *What's wrong with me today? I should be able to get through a simple thing like dinner at the neighbor's without turning into a basket case.*

"Have a seat," Tara said. "I'll go tell Dad you're here."

The young girl sashayed out of the room, and Sinda pulled out a chair and sat down. Tara returned a few minutes later, carrying a glass pitcher full of ice water. She filled the three glasses, placed the pitcher on the table, then flopped into the seat directly across from Sinda.

"Something smells good," Sinda murmured, for lack of anything better to say. Why was Tara staring at her like that? It made her feel like a bug under a microscope.

"That would be Dad's fried chicken. He wanted me to tell you that he'll be right in." Tara plunked her elbows on the table, rested her chin in her palms, and continued to stare.

"Is there something I can do to help?" Sinda asked hopefully.

"Nope. Dad's got everything under control."

"What grade are you in?" Sinda was hoping a change in subject might ease some of the tension.

Tara began playing with the napkin beside her plate. She folded it in several different directions, opened it, and then refolded it. "I'm in the fourth grade," she finally answered without looking up from her strange-looking work of art.

"Do you like school?"

"It's okay, but I can't wait for summer break in June. Dad and I always do lots of fun stuff in the summertime. We usually spend all our Sundays together too." Tara looked pointedly at Sinda.

Refusing to let the child intimidate her, Sinda asked, "Who looks out for you when your father's at work?"

"Mrs. Mayer. She's been my babysitter ever since I can remember."

"Is your dad a mailman?" Sinda asked, taking the conversation in another direction. "I've seen him dressed in a uniform, and it looked like the kind mail carriers usually wear."

Tara nodded. "Yep, he's a mailman all right. Dad has a walking route on the other side of town."

No wonder he looks so physically fit. Sinda had noticed a whole lot more about Glen Olsen than the uniform he wore, but she'd never have admitted it—especially not to his daughter.

"Now that you know everything about us, tell me something about you," Tara blurted out.

Sinda felt her face flush. She wasn't about to disclose anything from her past. Her life was not a book, left open for anyone to read. "There—isn't much to tell."

"Why did you buy that creepy old house?"

Sinda gave Tara a blank stare. Where were the child's manners, anyway?

"I heard that all the property on this block belonged to the first owner of your house. They built new homes all around it." Tara wrinkled her nose, as though a putrid smell had suddenly invaded the room. "Your house looks really weird sitting on the same block with a bunch of nice homes."

How could Sinda argue with that? Especially when she'd thought the same thing herself. "You're probably right," she agreed. "However, I got the house for a reasonable price, and it's perfect for my needs."

Tara's eyes brightened as she leaned forward on her elbows. "What exactly are those needs?"

Sinda blinked rapidly. *Why is she asking so many questions?*

"What do you do in that big old house?"

"Do?"

"Yeah. What I really want to know is why you—"

Tara's words were cut off when her father stepped through the swinging door separating the kitchen from the dining room. "Sorry to keep you lovely ladies waiting. It took some time to get everything dished up." Glen looked over at Sinda and offered her a friendly grin. "I hope you'll soon see—or rather taste that the wait was worth it." He placed a huge platter of fried chicken on the table. "I'm glad you could join us today, Sinda."

"It was nice of you to invite me, Glen."

Glen took a seat at the head of the table. "Tara, would you please run out to the kitchen and bring in the salad and potatoes?"

"Can't you do it?"

Sinda sucked in her breath, waiting to see how Glen would respond to his daughter's sassy remark.

"I'll be lighting the candles," he said patiently.

Sinda could hardly believe how soft-spoken he was. She'd expected him to shout at Tara and tell her she was being insolent.

"Dad, you're really not going to turn this into a fancy dinner, are you?" Tara asked, casting her father a pleading glance.

Glen turned toward Sinda and gave her a quick wink. "It isn't every day that the Olsens get to entertain someone so charming."

Sinda felt the heat of embarrassment creep up the back of her neck. There was no denying it—Glen was quite a handsome man. His wavy, dark hair and sparkling blue eyes were enough to turn any woman's head. She averted her gaze and pretended to study the floral pattern on the dinner plate in front of her.

"Tara, I asked you to bring in the salad and potatoes."

"Okay, okay. . .I'm going."

Tara left the room, and Glen pulled a book of matches from the front pocket of his pale blue dress shirt. He proceeded to light the candles and had just finished when Tara returned, carrying a bowl of mashed potatoes.

"Don't forget the salad," he reminded.

The child gave him a disgruntled look, then she stomped off toward the kitchen. A few minutes later she was back with a tossed green salad.

"Thank you, Tara. Great, we're all set now," Glen said, offering Sinda another warm smile. She was beginning to wonder if he ever quit smiling. Even when his daughter was acting like a brat, he kept a pleasant look on his face. It was a little disconcerting.

Tara reached for a piece of chicken, but Glen stopped her. "We haven't prayed yet."

"Sorry. I forgot."

When Glen and Tara bowed their heads, Sinda did the same. It had been awhile since she'd prayed—even for a meal. She knew why she'd given up praying; she just wasn't sure exactly when it had happened. Somehow it felt right to pray today, though. Glen seemed so earnest in his praises to God. Of course. . .

"Amen."

When she realized the blessing was over, Sinda opened her eyes and helped herself to a drumstick. "Everything looks and smells wonderful." She bit into the succulent meat and wasn't disappointed.

Tara sniffed the air. "Speaking of smells—I think something's burning."

Glen jumped up, nearly knocking over his glass of water. "My buttermilk biscuits!" He raced from the room, leaving Sinda alone with his daughter one more time.

Sinda spooned some mashed potatoes onto her plate and added a pat of butter from the butter dish sitting near her. She was about to take a bite, when the next question came.

"Do you know who Mrs. Higgins was?"

"My Realtor said she was the previous owner of my house."

"Yep, and she was really weird too."

Sinda wasn't sure if Tara had emphasized the word *she* on purpose or not, but with a slight shrug, she decided to ignore the remark.

"Mrs. Higgins hardly ever left that creepy old house, and sometimes you could hear strange noises coming from over there." Tara's forehead wrinkled. "Some of the neighborhood kids think your house is haunted."

"What do you believe, Tara?"

"Dad says the noises were probably her old blind dog, howlin' at the moon. He thinks I shouldn't believe what other kids say—especially stuff like that." The child tore a piece of dark meat from the chicken leg she'd speared with her fork. "You couldn't pay me enough money to live in that creepy old place." She tapped the tines of her fork against the edge of her plate.

Glen stepped back into the dining room, interrupting Tara a second time. "That was close! My biscuits were just seconds from being ruined." He set the basket of rolls and a jar of strawberry jam on the table, then took his seat. "I believe I can finally join you in eating this meal."

"The fried chicken is wonderful," Sinda said, licking her lips. "I think

Tara's right. You are the best cook in Washington."

Glen transmitted a smile that could have melted the ice cubes in Sinda's glass of water. "You'll have to try some of my famous barbecued chicken this summer."

"Oh, great," Tara muttered.

Glen shot his daughter a look that Sinda construed as a warning, and she swallowed so hard she nearly choked. Maybe Tara's dad wasn't quite as pleasant or patient as he first let on. "What did you say, Tara?" Glen's voice had raised at least an octave.

"I said, 'That sounds great.'"

Glen nodded at Tara, then Sinda. "I think so too."

Sinda dipped her head, unsure of what to think or how to respond.

"So, how about it, Sinda? Would you be interested in trying some of my barbecued chicken sometime this summer?"

Without even thinking, she replied, "I always enjoy a good barbecue." *Now, what made me say that?*

"Great!" Glen declared with another winning smile. "The first time I do barbecued chicken, I'll be sure to let you know."

Chapter Four

Glen couldn't believe his eyes! Tara was peering through the cracks in the tall fence that separated their backyard from Sinda's. He'd just paid Mrs. Mayer her monthly check for watching Tara and seen her to her car. Now he had to deal with this? Slowly, he snuck up behind Tara and dropped one hand to her shoulder. "At it again, Miss Olsen?"

She spun around. "Dad! You've gotta quit sneakin' up on me like that. I'm too young to die of a heart attack."

"Maybe so, but you're not too young to be turned over my knee," he said, biting back a smile. While Glen did believe in discipline, he'd never had to resort to spanking Tara. Ever since she was old enough to sit in front of the TV, and he'd discovered how much she enjoyed it, he had used restrictions from television whenever she got out of line. It had always been fairly effective too.

With hands planted firmly on her small hips, Tara stared up at him. "Dad, I was only—"

"Don't say anything more," he interrupted. "I'm not interested in your excuses." He glanced down at the ground. "Look where you're standing! You're going to ruin your mother's flowers if you're not careful."

Tara hopped out of the flower bed, just missing the toe of his boot. "Sorry," she mumbled. "I'll try to be more careful when I'm doing my investigating."

"I think you should leave the detective work to the Elmwood Police Department and try acting your age, Tara—keeping in mind that you're only ten years old and should be playing, not spying." Glen pointed toward the house. "Why don't you go play with your dolls for a while?"

Tara's forehead wrinkled. "I can't waste my time playing, Dad. I'm on a case right now. Besides, dolls are dumb. I put mine away in the hall closet ages ago."

He drew in a deep breath, reached for Tara's hand, and led her to the picnic table on the other side of the yard. "Why don't we have some cookies and lemonade? After we've filled our stomachs with something sweet, maybe we can talk about this some more." He guided her to one of the wooden benches.

Tara's eyes brightened. "That's a great idea, Dad. Mrs. Mayer made fresh lemonade when I got home from school. I think there's still a few ginger cookies left too." She smiled up at him. "Of course, you're gonna have to make more pretty soon. Can't have an empty cookie jar, now can we?"

"No, that would never do," Glen said with a chuckle. "Maybe one evening this week I'll do some more baking, but that's only if you can stay out of trouble."

She offered him a sheepish grin. "I think I can manage."

"Good girl." Glen gave one of her braids a light tug. "Don't move from this spot. I'll be right back with cookies and lemonade."

When he returned a few minutes later, Glen was relieved to see that Tara was still sitting at the picnic table, and Jake was lying in her lap, purring like a motorboat.

"That cat sure has it easy," Glen said as he placed a tray loaded with cookies, napkins, a pitcher of lemonade, and two glasses in the center of the table. "All he ever does is laze around."

Tara stroked the gray-and-white cat behind its ears. "Yeah, he's got life made most of the time. Of course, he does work pretty hard when he chases down mice or poor, defenseless birds."

Glen took a seat on the bench across from her and studied the cat. "His green eyes sure are pretty."

Tara reached for a cookie. "Speaking of green eyes—I need to tell you something about our green-eyed neighbor lady."

Glen snapped to attention. "Sinda?" Against his will, and probably better judgment, he'd been thinking about Sinda ever since she'd come to dinner.

"Uh-huh."

"What about her?"

Tara leaned as far across the table as she could and whispered, "I saw her carrying more boxes into the house today."

"Sinda only moved in a few weeks ago, Tara. She told me the other day that she still has some things in storage and is bringing them home a little at a time."

"You don't understand," Tara asserted. "There was something really strange about one of those boxes."

Glen raised his eyebrows. "Strange? In what way?"

"Well, there was a—"

Tara's words were halted when Jake screeched, leaped off her lap, sailed across the yard, then scampered up the maple tree. Tara jumped up. "Ow! Stupid cat! He dug his claws into my legs!"

"I wonder what's gotten into him?" Glen shook his head. "It's not like Jake to carry on like that for no reason."

"That's why," Tara said, pointing to the gate that separated their back-yard from Sinda's. It was open slightly, and a puny black dog poked its head through the opening. "Oh, great! You know how much Jake hates dogs."

A smile lifted the corners of Glen's mouth. "Yeah, and that little dog looks so ferocious."

Before Tara could respond, the dog took off like a streak of lightning, heading into the Olsens' yard, straight for the maple tree. Sinda was right behind him, calling, "Bad dog! Sparky, come back here right now!"

Glen's smile grew wider as he watched Sinda chase the small dog around his yard. He left the picnic table and moved toward her. "Is that your dog?"

"Yes," Sinda answered breathlessly. "He's a bundle of fury too! He won't come when I call him, and I've already discovered that he likes to sneak out of the yard. No wonder he was advertised as 'free to good home.'"

Sparky was now poised under the maple tree, barking furiously and looking as though he could devour a mountain lion.

"He's after Jake!" Tara screamed, running toward the dog. "Dad, do something, quick!"

Sinda gave Glen a questioning look. "Jake?"

"Jake is Tara's cat. He ran up the tree when your pooch poked his head into our yard."

"I'm sorry," Sinda apologized. She moved in on Sparky, bent down, and scooped the yapping terrier into her arms.

"I didn't even know you owned a dog," Glen remarked. "We haven't seen or heard anything of him until a few minutes ago."

"Actually, I don't. I mean, I didn't have a dog before today." Sinda had to yell in order to be heard above the dog's frantic barking.

"He's kind of cute. Probably good company for you," Glen said in an equally loud voice.

"I did get him for companionship, but I also wanted a watchdog." Sinda held on tightly to the squirming, yapping terrier.

"He sure does bark loud. That should be enough to scare anyone off," Tara put in.

"Maybe he'll calm down if we move away from the tree." Glen took Sinda's arm and guided her toward the picnic table. "Would you like to join us for some cookies and lemonade? I'll go inside and get another glass."

Sinda looked down at the bundle of fur in her arms. "Thanks, but I'd better get this little rascal back home." She started moving toward the gate.

"Why do you need a watchdog?" Tara asked, stepping in front of Sinda. "Is there something weird going on in that creepy old house of yours?"

"Tara!"

"No, no. I mean, everything's fine," Sinda stammered.

Glen couldn't help but notice how flustered she was. Her face was red as a tomato, her hair was in complete disarray, and she looked like she was on the verge of tears. "Tara, move out of Sinda's way so she can take the dog back to her yard."

Tara stepped aside, but Glen could see by the stubborn set of her jaw that she was none too happy about it.

Sinda offered Glen the briefest of smiles, then she disappeared into her yard.

"What's that scowl you're wearing about?" Glen asked as Tara slumped onto the picnic table bench.

"Don't you see it, Dad?"

"See what?"

Tara squinted her eyes at him. "Can't you see how weird Sinda is?"

"I don't think she's weird." Glen snorted. "You, on the other hand, are apparently getting some weird ideas from watching too much TV. I'm going to speak to Mrs. Mayer about putting a limit on how much television you can watch after school."

"But, Dad, I—"

"A girl your age should be playing with her friends, not sitting in front of the TV all afternoon." Glen made an arch with his hand. "Instead, you're trying to dig up something on the neighbors!" He glanced across the yard searching for inspiration. "The flower beds could use some investigating. As soon as you finish your snack, you can get busy tending the garden."

Tara stuck out her lower lip and folded her arms across her chest. "I didn't do anything wrong."

Glen held up one finger. "You were spying." A second finger joined the first. "You were rude to Sinda." A third finger came up. "Then you said she's weird." He frowned deeply. "We keep discussing these same manners problems over and over, Tara. I'm going inside to start supper. You need to have that weeding finished before it's ready."

By the time Sinda clipped a leash to Sparky's collar and secured him to a long chain hooked to the end of her clothesline, she was all done in. "Maybe getting a dog was a bad idea," she mumbled as she gave the furry creature a gentle pat. "So far, you've been nothing but trouble."

The little dog tipped his head and looked up at her as though he was truly sorry. Sinda couldn't help but smile. "I'll bring you inside after a while." She turned and headed for the house. Sparky let out a pathetic whine, and she almost changed her mind about bringing him in before she fixed supper. When she was growing up, Sinda had always wanted a dog, but her father would never allow it. He used to say that pets were nothing but trouble, and after today Sinda thought he might have been right. Still, dogs were supposed to be companions and loyal friends. At least the mutts she'd seen on TV had been devoted to their masters.

When Sinda reached the back porch, she stopped beside the outside faucet and turned on the spigot. They hadn't had much rain yet this spring, and she figured the yard, though overgrown, could use a good drink. As the sprinkler came on, a spray of water shot into the air, and a miniature rainbow glistened through the mist.

She swallowed against the nodule that had formed in her throat.

Rainbows always made Sinda think of her mother and, like it was only yesterday, she could hear Mother saying, *"Rainbows are a reminder of God's promises. Whenever you see one, remember how much He loves you."*

"Do You love me, God?" Sinda whispered as she looked up at the cloudless sky. "Has anyone ever truly loved me?"

The telephone was ringing when Sinda entered the kitchen a few minutes later. She grabbed the receiver with one hand while she reached for a towel with the other. In the process of turning on the hose, she'd managed to get her hand and both sneakers wet. Of course, when a faucet leaked like a sieve, what else could she expect?

"Hello," she said breathlessly into the cordless phone.

"Hi, Sinda, it's me."

Sinda dropped into a chair at the kitchen table. "Hey, Carol, how are you?"

"I was going to ask you the same question. I haven't heard from you in a while, and I was worried you might have worked yourself to death."

"Not quite, but from the looks of things, I'll be forever trying to get the rest of my things unpacked, not to mention getting this old place fixed up so it's livable."

"Know what I think you need?"

"What?"

"A break from all that work."

Sinda couldn't argue with that. She'd been working around the clock ever since she moved into the monstrosity she was dumb enough to call home.

"How about meeting me for lunch at Elmwood City Park tomorrow afternoon? If you don't take a little break, you'll end up cranky as a bear who's lost all his hair."

"I guess I could spare an hour or so."

"Great! See you at one, and be ready for fun!"

Sinda grinned. Carol had always thought she was a poet. Over the years, her friend's goofy rhymes and lighthearted banter had gotten Sinda through more than one pity party. *At least Carol taught me how to laugh.* Sinda wondered what her life would have been like if she'd been raised in a normal home with two loving parents. Instead, her childhood had been filled with loneliness, disappointment, countless rules, and sometimes hostility. But it was all Mother's fault. Dad went through so much because of her.

"Sinda, are you still there?"

Carol's question drove Sinda's thoughts back to the present, and she felt grateful. She was tired of living in the past. Tired of dwelling on the negative. She'd come to Elmwood to begin a new life, and she was determined to at least make her business venture successful.

"I'm here, Carol," she murmured. "I'll see you tomorrow at one."

Chapter Five

"I'm glad you suggested this little outing," Sinda told Carol as they settled onto a park bench. She leaned back with a contented sigh. "It's such a beautiful spring day, and everything is so lush and green."

"It's that time of year, my dear." Carol poked Sinda in the ribs. "We usually get lots of liquid sunshine in the spring, but this year we're falling short of our average rainfall, so it won't stay green long if we don't get some rain soon."

Sinda made no comment, and Carol took their conversation in another direction. "You know, I was beginning to worry about you."

"How come?"

"Ever since you moved here, all you've done is work. It's been nearly a month, so I thought it was time you got out of that stuffy old house and did something fun."

Sinda opened her lunch sack and withdrew the ham sandwich she'd thrown together for their Saturday afternoon picnic. "For your information, I have gotten out of the house a few times."

"Really? Where did you go, Miss Social Butterfly?" Carol laughed and gave Sinda's arm a little squeeze.

"I've been shopping a few times, made several trips to my storage unit, stopped at the department of licensing, and I had dinner at the neighbor's one Sunday afternoon."

Carol raised her eyebrows. "Which neighbor was that?"

"The one next door. I'm sure I told you about Glen and his daughter bringing me some cookies the day I moved in."

"Yes, you did, but you didn't say anything about having dinner with them." Carol puckered her lips. "I'm surprised to hear you're seeing a man. You've never been much for dating."

"I'm not seeing anyone," Sinda said, choosing to ignore her friend's reminder about her lack of a social life. "It was just a friendly, get-to-know-your-neighbor dinner. Don't read any more into it than that."

Carol shook her head slowly. "I'm glad to have you living closer, but I'd be even happier if I knew you were truly at peace. You've had moods of melancholy as long as I've known you, and any time I've asked what's wrong, you've always avoided the subject."

"I appreciate your concern—always have, in fact. I've just never wanted to talk about my problems." Sinda stared off into space. "Besides, talking doesn't change anything."

"Maybe not, but it's good for the soul, which in turn brings happier thoughts," Carol responded.

Sinda glanced back at her friend. "My work keeps me plenty busy. And I have a good friend who meets me at the park for lunch whenever she thinks I'm working too much." She paused and winked at Carol. "That's all the happiness I need. Besides, you should concern yourself with your own love life and quit worrying about me."

Carol smiled and crossed her fingers. "I think I may have found my man."

"Is it the guy you told me about who works at the bank?"

"Gary Tarrol is our new loan officer." Carol elbowed Sinda in the ribs. "I don't know what I'll do if we should start dating and things get serious."

For a minute Sinda wondered if her friend was as leery of marriage as she was, but then she remembered how boy crazy Carol had been when they were teenagers. In fact, Sinda was amazed that Carol wasn't already married and raising a family.

"My motto is: Find the right guy and let your heart fly!" Carol continued. She batted her eyelashes dramatically. "Can you imagine me living the rest of my life with a name like Carol Tarrol?"

Sinda giggled. "It might be kind of cute. Especially since you like rhyming so well."

Her friend grimaced and opened her can of soda. "Not that well. Maybe I should look for someone with a better last name." She took a drink, then wiped her mouth on a napkin. "Now tell me—how's business?"

Sinda frowned. "I haven't done much advertising yet, so things are still kind of slow. There are lots of kids in this world, though, and just as many eager adults. I'm sure I'll do okay once the word gets out. In fact, I'll probably do as well here in Oregon as I did in Seattle."

"I have a friend who might need your services," Carol said. "She has a four-year-old daughter."

"Tell her to give me a call. I'm sure we can work something out." Sinda tossed her empty sandwich wrapper in the garbage and stood up. "Let's take a quick hike around the lake, then I need to get back home." As they started to walk away, she glanced over her shoulder. There were two young girls crouched in the bushes, not far from the bench where she and Carol had been sitting. One of the children wore her brown hair in pigtails. *That's Tara Olsen. Now, why would she be hiding in the bushes?*

Sinda stood in front of her open kitchen window, talking on the phone. "Yes, they're quite safe in my basement. I'd be happy to take her off your hands," she said into the receiver. "We can discuss the price further once I've taken a good look at her." Sinda jotted a few notes on a tablet she kept near the phone, said goodbye, and hung up. Mrs. Kramer would be by soon with her delivery, then Sinda could grab a quick bite of dinner and try to get a few bills paid.

"Oh, to be wealthy and carefree," she murmured. "Even carefree would be nice."

Sinda could feel a cord of tension grip her body, like a confining belt after a heavy meal. Her mouth compressed into a tight line as her mind dragged her unwillingly back to the past. Dad had always stressed the importance of good stewardship. In his words that meant *"Pay every bill on time, give God His ten percent, and never spend money foolishly."* Sinda tried to be prompt about bill paying, but now that Dad was gone, she no longer worried about giving God any money. Why should she? God hadn't done much for her. First she'd lost Mother, and now Dad was dead. Didn't God see her pain? Didn't He care at all? Must the misery in her life keep on growing like yeast rising in bread?

She glanced around the kitchen, noting the faded yellow paint on the walls. The cream-colored linoleum was coming up in several places, and all the appliances were outdated. *Was I wrong to buy this place? If Dad were still alive, would he lecture me for spending my inheritance foolishly?*

The sound of a car door slamming shut drew Sinda's contemplations to a halt. It was probably Mrs. Kramer, since she only lived a mile away. *I'll worry about my ill-chosen spending some other time. Right now I've got business to tend to.*

Glen stepped inside the back door, his arms full of groceries. He'd no more than set the bags on the table when Tara burst into the room. "Am I ever glad to see you!"

"Why, thank you, Miss Olsen. I'm happy to see you too." Glen rubbed his hands briskly together. "It's been a long Saturday, and after work I had to run some errands and grocery shop. Scoot on into the living room and tell Mrs. Mayer I'm home now. I'll put away the groceries, then we'll see what we can pull together for supper. What appeals to you, honey? Tacos? Pizza?"

Tara tugged on his shirtsleeve. "I need to talk to you."

"In a minute," he said as he opened the first sack and withdrew a bag of apples. "Now do as I said."

Tara turned on her heels and was about to exit the room when Mrs. Mayer poked her head through the doorway. A radiant smile filled her broad face, and her pale blue eyes twinkled. Glen often thanked God for providing this pleasant, Christian woman to watch Tara every afternoon and on the Saturdays he was scheduled to work. "Do you need me to do anything else before I head for home?" the older woman asked.

Glen shook his head and placed the apples into the fruit bowl. "Can't think of a thing, Mrs. Mayer, thanks. Tara and I will see you at church tomorrow morning."

"Sure enough. Enjoy the rest of your evening." Mrs. Mayer waved her hand and exited through the back door.

Tara inched closer to her father. "Now can we talk?"

Glen put the perishable items in the refrigerator, then withdrew a carton of milk. "Are there any donuts left from the picnic you'd planned this afternoon with Penny, or did the two of you eat them all?" he asked, ignoring his daughter's perturbed look.

Tara shook her head. "We left a few, but Dad, we need to talk!"

325

Glen knew that Tara tended to be overly dramatic about most things. For some time now he had been trying to teach her to be patient and give him a chance to settle in so they could chat over a snack. Whatever she had to say could wait at least that long. "You get the donuts, and I'll pour us each a glass of milk. We'll sit at the table, and you can tell me what's on your mind. Then I've got to finish putting away the groceries and get busy making supper."

He started toward the table, but Tara halted his steps by positioning herself directly in front of him. "I think you should call the police."

Glen's eyebrows furrowed. "The police? What are you talking about?"

"Our neighbor. I'm talking about our new neighbor."

"Sinda?"

Tara's nose twitched as she pursed her lips. "She's the only new neighbor we have, isn't she?"

Glen frowned. "What's Sinda got to do with the police? Did she ask you to have me call them? Is she having some kind of problem?" Even though he didn't know Sinda very well, his heart squeezed at the thought of her being in some kind of trouble. "I'd better go over there and check on her." He placed the carton of milk on the table and started for the back door.

"No, don't!" Tara's tone was pleading, and she grabbed his hand. "Let the police handle this, Dad."

"Handle what?"

Tara pointed at the table. "Sit down, and I'll tell you all about it."

As soon as they were both seated, Tara leaned forward with her elbows on the table, and in her most serious voice she announced, "There's a little kid in Sinda's house."

Glen drew in a deep breath and mentally counted to ten. "So there's a kid visiting Sinda. I see. And we should call the police because. . . ?"

"Sinda is buying and selling children!" Tara exclaimed. "That's against the law, and she's gotta be stopped."

Glen massaged the bridge of his nose. "Could we talk about this after dinner?"

"I'm telling you the truth!" Tara shouted. "Now, are you going to call the police or not?"

"What should I tell them?"

"Sinda is committing a crime. When people commit crimes, you're supposed to call the police."

He looked at her pointedly. "What crime has Sinda supposedly committed?"

"I just told you. She's buying and selling kids! I know of at least one who's locked in her basement right now."

Glen was tempted to laugh at the absurd accusation. "What were you watching on TV today?"

Tara gave him an icy stare. "I know what you're thinking, but I'm not making this up. That woman is a criminal."

"What sort of proof do you have?"

"I saw a lady bring a kid over to Sinda's house a little while ago. When the woman left, the kid wasn't with her."

Glen slowly shook his head. This story was getting better and better. "So tell me again, what is it that's illegal about babysitting someone's child?"

"Sinda drove off in her minivan a few minutes after the lady left, but the kid wasn't with her. She left it all alone in that creepy old house."

"Maybe you just didn't see the child leave with her."

"There's more, Dad."

"More?"

"I've been watching Sinda for several weeks now, and—"

"You mean spying, don't you?" Before Tara could respond, Glen rushed on. "I've warned you repeatedly about that—"

"But I've gathered some incriminating evidence," Tara interrupted.

Glen clicked his tongue. "Incriminating—such a big word for a little girl."

"Would you quit teasing and listen to me?"

"Okay, okay," he conceded. "What incriminating evidence do you have on our new neighbor?"

"I've seen her bring other kids into that house." Tara frowned deeply. "Once she even brought in a baby who was in a wicker basket. I heard it crying." She paused a moment and swallowed hard. "Remember when Sinda first moved in and we went over to meet her and took her a plate of cookies?"

Glen nodded. "I remember."

"She was holding a doll when she opened the door, and she put it down really quick after she saw us. I thought maybe she had kids of her own, but then she told us she wasn't even married."

"So you naturally concluded that Sinda is up to no good." Glen shook his head. "What else haven't you told me?"

"I think that doll belonged to one of the kids she bought and sold. Today Penny and I saw Sinda and some lady with curly blond hair at the park. Sinda was telling the woman about her business, and she said she thought she was going to do okay because there are lots of kids in the world."

"Come on, kiddo. You don't seriously think—"

"That's not all," Tara asserted. "Sinda keeps the children in her basement. I was checking her place out earlier, and I heard her talking on the phone. She was telling one of her customers that's where she puts them." Tara sucked in her breath. "Who knows how many innocent children are being held in that house, only to be sold on the black market?"

Glen leaned his head back and laughed. "Black market? You don't really expect me to believe that a nice woman like Sinda Shull is involved in something like that!"

"Yes, I do." Tara's eyes filled with tears.

Glen sat there for several seconds, trying to decide how best to handle the situation. His daughter had always been prone to exaggerate, but this story was a bit too much. Perhaps Tara's increasingly wild stories were just her way of getting his attention.

"Well, young lady," he finally said, "there seems to be only one way to settle the matter."

Her eyes brightened. "You're gonna call the cops?"

He shook his head. "No, I'm not. We are heading over to Sinda's. We're going to get to the bottom of this once and for all!"

Chapter Six

A knock at the front door, followed by the sound of Sparky's frantic barking, drew Sinda out of the kitchen. She bent down and scooped the little dog into her arms and opened the door. She was surprised to discover Glen and Tara standing on her front porch. "What can I do for you?" she asked hesitantly.

Glen cleared his throat a couple of times and shuffled his feet. "There's a little matter I'd like to get cleared up. I'm sure it's just a silly misunderstanding, though."

"A misunderstanding?" Sinda repeated.

He nodded. "Tara, uh, thinks she's seen something going on over here."

Sinda shifted her weight from one foot to the other as she studied the fading rays of the evening sun dancing across Glen's jet-black hair. Her gaze roamed over his face next. He looked so nervous she almost felt sorry for him. "What do you think is going on?" she asked, shifting her gaze from Glen to his daughter.

"I want to know why you're buying and selling kids!" the child blurted out.

Sinda's mouth dropped open, and she blinked several times. "What?"

Tara narrowed her eyes in an icy stare. It was obvious by the tilt of her head and her crossed arms that the girl was not going to leave without some answers. "Don't try to deny it," Tara huffed. "I've been watching you. I know exactly what you're up to, and we're gonna call the police."

Glen backed away slightly, jamming his hands into the pockets of his blue jeans and staring down at the porch. "My detective daughter thinks you're involved with the black market."

Sinda could see that Glen was embarrassed, yet if there was even a chance that he thought... She forced her attention back to Tara. "I imagine you've seen a few people come and go from my house with small children."

329

Tara's eyes widened and she nodded. "That's right, and you can't get away with a thing like that! See, Dad? She admits it!"

"You're an excellent detective," Sinda admitted.

Tara looked up at her father with a satisfied smile. "I told you. Now can we call the police?"

Glen groaned and slapped his palm against his forehead.

Sinda gently touched Tara's arm, but the child pulled away as though she'd been slapped. "I think you both should come inside and follow me."

"Follow you where?" Glen asked, lifting his dark eyebrows.

The intensity of his gaze sent shivers of apprehension up Sinda's spine. Was he angry? Should she be inviting them inside? Her mouth compressed into a tight line as she considered her options. Did she really want the police coming to her house? Police officers had made her feel uncomfortable ever since. . .

"Where do you want us to follow you to?"

Glen's deep voice invaded Sinda's thoughts, and she jerked her attention back to the situation at hand. "To my basement." She stepped onto the porch and set Sparky down. "Did you close the gate between our yards when you came over?"

Glen nodded, and Sinda motioned them inside. She led the way downstairs, and when they reached the bottom step she snapped on the overhead light.

Tara gasped and grabbed her dad's hand as the beam of light brought into view several small babies and two toddlers lying on a table in the center of the room.

"What in the world?" Glen's open mouth told Sinda how surprised he was by the unusual sight.

"I know this might appear a bit strange, but it's really quite simple." Sinda gestured toward the array of bodies. "You see, I'm a doll doctor, and these are my patients."

Tara's face turned ashen. "But, I–I thought—"

"The children you thought were coming and going from my house were dolls, Tara," Sinda explained. "I don't have my business sign nailed up on the house yet, but I do have a business license and a permit from the city to operate a doll hospital here."

Tara hung her head. "I—I guess I sort of got things mixed up."

"I would say so." Glen gave his daughter a nudge. "Don't you think you owe Sinda an apology?"

"It's all right. There was no harm done," Sinda said quickly. Despite Tara's accusation, she couldn't help but feel sorry for the child. Sinda had made her share of blunders when she was growing up, and Dad had never treated it lightly.

"Tara," Glen stated with a scowl on his face, "you owe Sinda an apology. We'll discuss the consequences of your behavior at home."

Tara continued to stare at the concrete floor. "I'm sorry, Sinda."

Sinda took a few steps toward the child. She wanted to give Tara a hug but didn't think it would be appreciated. Instead, she merely patted the child on top of her head. "It was an honest mistake. Any intelligent little girl could have gotten the wrong impression by what you saw."

Tara's head shot up. "I am not a little girl!"

"Good, then you won't mind doing some honest work to make up for your error," Glen asserted.

Tara's gaze darted to her dad. "What kind of work?"

Glen motioned toward Sinda. "I'm sure the doll doctor can find something for you to do right here in her workshop."

Sinda sucked in her lower lip. "I might be able to use some help." Although she wasn't sure she wanted the help to come in the form of a child's punishment.

"Dad, you know I don't play with dolls anymore," Tara said with a moan.

"You wouldn't be playing, Tara," Sinda insisted. "You'd be helping me with some necessary repairs."

Tara's eyes filled with sudden tears. "It's not fair. This old house is creepy, and I hate dolls!"

Glen bent down so he was making direct eye contact with his daughter. "This case is closed, Tara."

⮾

Glen stood in front of the dresser in his bedroom, studying Tara's most recent school picture. *She's such a cute kid, even though she can be a little stinker at times.* He drew in a deep breath as he reflected on the happenings of the evening. He should never have listened to Tara's crazy idea about Sinda selling kids on the black market, much less gone over there and made a complete fool of himself. He and Tara had been on their own for nine years, and it was hard not to indulge her. He knew he'd let her get too carried away, and tonight's fiasco made him realize how necessary it was to gain control. After they'd come home from Sinda's, he'd fixed dinner, seen to it that Tara did her weekend homework, then sent her to bed without any dessert. All her pouting, pleading, and crying over the idea of going to Sinda's to help repair dolls had nearly been his undoing, but Glen remained strong.

As he moved toward the window and stared at the house next door, Glen's thoughts shifted to Sinda. He hadn't dated much since his wife's death, but of the few women he had gone out with, none had captured his interest the way Sinda had in the short time since they'd met. Some unseen pull made him want to seek out ways to spend more time with her. He wasn't sure if it was the need he sensed in her or merely physical attraction. The vulnerable side of Sinda drew him, but he would need to be cautious. She was like a jigsaw puzzle. So many pieces looked the same, but each time he tried to make them match, the pieces didn't fit. Sinda could be friendly one minute and downright rude the next. He had a hunch she was hiding something, only it was far beyond anything Tara had conjured up in her imagination. Glen's sixth sense told him that Sinda Shull had been hurt and might even be running from someone or something.

The fact that Sinda was a doll doctor had been a real surprise, but even more astonishing was that she'd given no evidence of her unusual occupation until Tara made her ridiculous accusations. Except for having dinner with them that one Sunday afternoon, Sinda had kept pretty much to herself.

"Sure wish I could get to know her better," Glen mumbled as he leaned against the windowpane. *Is Sinda a Christian?* He hoped so, because it would be wrong to begin a relationship with her if she wasn't. He raked a hand through his hair as confusion clouded his thinking. "I'd better pray about this before I approach Sinda with any questions about her faith."

∞

Sinda sat at the long metal table in her basement workshop, watching Tara sand an old doll leg. She couldn't help but notice the forlorn expression on the child's face, and without warning, vague memories from the past bobbed to the surface of her mind. She'd been sad most of her childhood... at least after her mother had gone. She'd tried hard to be the best daughter she could, but she'd apparently fallen short since she was never able to please her father.

I won't think about that now, she scolded herself. *I have work to do.* Quickly reaching for the doll head that went with the leg Tara was sanding, Sinda asked, "Do you recognize this doll?"

The girl's only response was a shake of her head.

"It's one of the original Shirley Temple dolls. It's a true collectable and quite valuable."

Tara squinted her dark eyes at Sinda. "You mean it's like an antique or something?"

Sinda nodded. "Right. See the cracks in her composition body?"

A glimmer of interest flashed across the young girl's face. "What's composition?"

"It's compressed sawdust and wood filler that's been poured into a mold. It has the look and feel of wood, but each part is actually hollow," Sinda explained. She ran her fingers gently along the antique doll's face, relishing the notion that she had the power to transform an old relic into a work of art. "When composition ages, it often cracks or peels. Then it needs to be sanded, patched, and repainted."

"Who's Shirley Temple?" Tara asked as she continued to sand the doll leg.

"She was a child star who used to act in a lot of movies. When she became famous, the Ideal Toy Company created a line of dolls to look like her. Today Shirley Temple dolls are worth a lot of money."

Tara shrugged, as though she'd become bored with the topic. "Say, where are you from, anyway?" she asked suddenly.

"I grew up in Seattle."

"Did you run a doll hospital there?"

Sinda nodded, then picked up a new wig for the doll and applied a thin layer of white glue to the bald head. "I took a home study course and started working on dolls when I was a teenager."

"Did you make lots of money? Enough to buy this creepy old house?"

Sinda clenched her teeth so hard her jaw ached. Tara's inquisition was beginning to get on her nerves. "I've never made enough money repairing dolls to entirely support myself, but after my dad died, I started buying and selling old dolls and a few other antiques."

"So, that's how you could afford this place?"

"My father left me his entire estate, and I used the money from the sale of our house in Seattle to purchase my new home and a minivan."

Tara's freckled nose crinkled, and Sinda was pretty sure more questions were forthcoming. "How come your dad didn't leave everything to your mother? Isn't that how it's supposed to be when a husband dies?"

Sinda's mouth fell open. She hadn't expected such a direct question, not even from her nosey little neighbor. "Uh—well—my mother's gone too." She secured the doll wig in place, fastened a rubber band around the head to keep it from slipping while it dried, then grabbed the other composition leg and gave it a few swipes with a piece of sandpaper.

"When did your mother die?" Tara prompted.

"She's been gone since I was ten."

"I was only a year old when my mother died, so I don't even remember her." Tara shrugged her slim shoulders. "If you have to lose someone, I guess that's the best way—when you're too young to remember."

Sinda's eyes filled with unexpected tears, and unable to stop the thoughts, her mind drifted back in time. Painful memories. So many painful memories. . .

Sinda had been small at the time. . .maybe five or six years old, but she remembered hearing a resonating cry waft through the house, followed by muffled sobs. She closed her eyes and saw herself halt on the stairs. There it was again. Her skin tingled, and her heart began to beat rapidly. A man and a woman were arguing. She held her breath. The woman's pleading escalated, then it abruptly stopped.

Silence.

Sinda's muscles tensed.

The woman screamed.

"What's wrong with Mama?" young Sinda had murmured. "Did she fall?" She hurried up the stairs. . . .

Sinda felt a tug on the sleeve of her sweatshirt. She blinked several times, and the vision drifted slowly away. "What's wrong? I asked you a question, and you spaced off on me," Tara said, giving Sinda a curious stare.

"I–I must have been in deep thought."

"Yeah, I'll say."

"What was your question?"

"I was asking if your doll hospital did so well in Seattle, how come you moved?"

Sinda frowned deeply. How many more questions was Tara going to fire at her? "I thought Elmwood would be a good place to start over," she answered through tight lips.

Tara leaned forward with her elbows on the table. "Why would you need to start over?"

Before Sinda could think of a reply, the telephone rang upstairs. She jumped to her feet, a sense of relief washing over her. "Keep working on that doll. I'll be right back," Sinda said, then she scurried up the steps.

Chapter Seven

Several minutes later, Sinda hung up the phone. She smiled to herself. There was no telling when she might get another offer as good as the one she'd just had. The owner of a local antique shop wanted her to restore five old dolls. Two of them were bisque, and the other three were made of composition. The work was extensive and would bring in a fairly large sum of money. It looked as though Sinda's Doll Hospital was finally on its way.

Too bad Tara hates being here, she thought ruefully. *With all this extra work, I could probably use her help even after she's worked off her debt for spying on me. I wonder if she might be willing to extend the time if I offer some payment.*

Sinda crossed to the other side of the kitchen and opened a cupboard door. Tara might enjoy a treat, and it would certainly keep her too busy to ask any more personal questions.

She piled a few peanut butter cookies onto a plate, then filled a glass with cold milk. She placed the snack on a tray, picked up the cordless phone she'd left in the kitchen, and headed downstairs. She'd only descended two steps when she ran into Tara, nearly knocking the tray out of her hand.

"I–I heard a noise," the child squeaked.

Sinda's eyebrows furrowed. "What kind of noise?"

"A rustling sound. It was coming from one of the boxes over there." Tara pointed toward the wall lined with long shelves, but she never moved from her spot on the stairs.

"It's probably a mouse," Sinda said with a small laugh. "Should we go investigate?"

Tara's eyes grew wide. "No way!"

Sinda tipped her head to one side and listened. "Sparky's barking. Someone may be at the front door." She handed the tray to Tara. "Why don't you go back to the worktable and eat this snack? I'll be right down, then we'll check on that noise." She disappeared before Tara could argue the point.

When Sinda opened the front door, she discovered Glen standing on the porch. He held a loaf of gingerbread covered in plastic wrap. "This is for you," he said as Sparky darted between his legs and ran into the yard.

Little crinkles formed at the corners of his eyes when he smiled, and Sinda swallowed hard while she brushed a layer of sandpaper dust from the front of her overalls. *I wish he wouldn't look at me like that.* "Thanks, I love gingerbread," she murmured, taking the offered gift.

"Has anyone ever told you what gorgeous eyes you have?"

"What?" Sinda's heartbeat quickened.

"You have beautiful eyes."

She felt herself blush and knew it wasn't a delicate flush, but a searing red, covering her entire face. She quickly averted his gaze. "Shall I call Tara?"

Glen shook his head. "I didn't come over to get Tara."

"You—you didn't?" She glanced back up at him, feeling small and shy, like when she was a child. She wished he would quit staring at her. It filled her with a strange mixture of longing and fear.

"I came to bring you the bread, but I also wanted to ask you something."

"What did you want to ask?"

"Do you like Chinese?"

She stood there looking at him for several seconds, then realized he was waiting for her answer. "As in Chinese food?"

He nodded.

"I love Oriental cuisine."

He shuffled his feet a few times, bringing him a few inches closer. "I was wondering if you'd like to go out to dinner with me this Friday night."

Sinda could see the longing in Glen's eyes, and it frightened her. The scent of his aftershave stirred something deep inside her as well. "Just the two of us?" she rasped.

"Yep. I have other plans for my detective daughter."

Warning bells went off in Sinda's head. *Say no. Don't go out with Glen. Do not encourage him in any way!* When she opened her mouth to respond, the words that came out were quite different from those in her head, however. "I'd love to go."

Glen smacked his hands together, and she jumped. "Great! I'll pick you up around six-thirty." He bounded off the porch, calling, "Send Tara home when she's done for the day."

Sinda stood in the doorway, basking in the tingly sensation that danced through her veins. A question popped into her mind. *Would Dad approve of me going out with Glen Olsen?* She shook her head. *I shouldn't be thinking about Dad again.* Sinda was so innocent when it came to dealing with men, but she wanted to find out what Glen was really like. He appeared to be nice enough, but appearances could be deceiving. To the world her father had been a wonderful man, faithful in attending church, and attentive to Sinda's needs. But if Dad had truly loved God, wouldn't his actions at home have revealed it? Wasn't Christianity meant to be practiced in one's personal life, not just at church? As a child Sinda had practically worshiped her dad, but about the time she started into puberty she'd begun to question his motives. Driving the disturbing thoughts to the back of her mind, Sinda focused on the gingerbread Glen had given her. It needed to be put away.

When she returned to the basement, Sinda found Tara sitting on the third step from the bottom. She'd eaten all the cookies and was just finishing her milk. "What are you doing on the steps? I thought you would take the tray over to the table."

"I wasn't going near that box with the weird noise," Tara said, lifting her chin in defiance.

Sinda stepped around the child. "Let's go check it out."

Tara remained seated, arms folded across her chest as though daring Sinda to make her move. "You check it out. I'll wait here."

Sinda shrugged and started across the room. "And I thought you were a detective."

"I am!"

"Then come help."

Sinda glanced over her shoulder and was pleased to see Tara following her. However, it was obvious by the child's hunched shoulders and the scowl on her face that she was anything but thrilled about the prospect of trying to determine the nature of the strange noise.

When they came to the box in question, Tara stepped back as Sinda searched through the contents. "If it is a mouse, aren't you afraid it'll jump out and bite you?"

Sinda glanced over at Tara, who was cowering near the table. "I don't like mice, but I'm not afraid of them. I can't have a bunch of rodents chewing up my valuable doll parts."

"Why not set some traps?" Tara suggested. "That's what we used to do before we got Jake."

"Jake's your cat, right?"

"Yep, and he can get really feisty when there's a mouse around. I'd offer to lend him to you, but he wouldn't get along with your dog."

"You're probably right," Sinda agreed. She rummaged quickly through the rest of the doll parts, then set the box back on the shelf. "There's no sign of any mice. If there was one, it's gone now." She turned to face Tara. "That phone call I had earlier was an antique dealer. She has several old dolls for me to restore."

"Business is picking up, huh?"

Sinda nodded. "It would seem so, and I was wondering if you'd be interested in helping me here two or three afternoons a week."

"I thought I was helping."

"You are. I had a more permanent arrangement in mind," Sinda said. "Of course, I would pay you."

Tara frowned. "I don't like working with dolls. I'd much rather be watching TV or doin' some detective work."

"I really could use your help."

The child shook her head. "Not interested."

It was obvious that little Miss Olsen was not going to budge.

"You're taking Sinda Shull where?" Tara shouted from across the room.

Glen was standing at the stove, stirring a pot of savory stew, but he turned to face his daughter. "I'm taking Sinda out to dinner, and I've arranged for you to stay overnight at Penny's."

Tara scowled at him. "This was Sinda's idea, wasn't it?"

"No, it was not her idea. I asked Sinda out when I took a loaf of gingerbread over there earlier today."

"What time was that?"

"Around four-thirty."

Tara tapped her toe against the linoleum. "I was over there then, and she never told me you stopped by. She didn't say she was going on a date with you, either."

Glen turned back to the stove and started humming his favorite hymn, "Amazing Grace."

"Dad, why are you doing this?"

He kept on humming and stirring the stew.

Tara marched across the room and stopped next to the stove. "Why are you doing this?"

He winked at her. "Doing what?"

She grabbed his hand and gave it a shake. "Dad!"

He pushed her hand away. "Watch out, Tara. You're gonna fool around and get burned."

Tara took a step back, and she stared up at him accusingly. "Why did you invite Sinda to dinner?"

He smiled. "Because, it was the neighborly—"

"Thing to do," she said, finishing his sentence. "It's those green eyes of hers, isn't it?"

"What are you talking about?"

"I'll bet she's got you hypnotized. I saw it happen on a TV show once." Waving her hand in a crisscross motion, Tara said, "She zapped you senseless and put you under some kind of a spell."

Glen looked upward. "Oh Lord, please give me the wisdom of Solomon." He wondered if he should lecture Tara about watching too much TV again, or would it be better to give her a Bible verse to memorize? After a few seconds' deliberation, he chose a different approach. "You're absolutely right, kiddo. Sinda hypnotized me this afternoon. In fact, she put me so far under that I actually thought I was a dog."

"Dad, be serious! Sinda may not be buying and selling kids, but I don't trust her. I still think she's up to something."

"I would advise you to avoid detective work, Miss Olsen," he threatened. "Your last mistake got you thirty days of no TV and apprentice work in Sinda's Doll Hospital, remember?"

Tara's forehead wrinkled. "I'm too old to play with dolls, and Sinda's house is creepy and full of weird noises." She stomped her foot. "There's no way I'd keep working for her after my thirty days are up."

"She asked you to? What'd you tell her?" Glen asked with interest. If Tara kept working for their new neighbor, he might get to see Sinda more often. Besides, it would be a good way for Tara to learn about responsibility.

"I said no." Tara shrugged. "She offered to pay me, but I'm not going to spend my free time sanding and painting a bunch of old dolls!" She scrunched up her nose. "I'm going to discover Sinda's secrets, then we'll see who has the last laugh."

Glen chuckled. "We sure will, and it will probably be me."

Chapter Eight

"Tara, it's time to go!" Glen called from the hallway outside his daughter's open bedroom door.

Tara slammed her suitcase lid shut when Glen stepped into the room. "Would you like me to walk you over to Penny's?"

Tara shook her head. "I'm not a baby, Dad. You can just watch me walk across the street to Penny's if it makes you feel better."

Glen ran his fingers through his freshly combed hair. He thought the offer to walk with her might ease some of the tension between them. Ever since he'd told Tara about his date with Sinda, she'd been irritable. He straightened his tie and smoothed the lapel on his gray sport coat. "Do I look okay? I'm not overdressed, am I?"

"I guess it all depends on where you're goin'," Tara answered curtly. She sauntered out of the room, leaving her suitcase sitting on the floor.

Glen frowned but picked up the suitcase and followed. "I made reservations at the Silver Moon," he called after her.

Tara made no comment until she reached the bottom step. Then she turned and glared up at him. "I don't think you should go to the Silver Moon."

"Why not?"

"That place is too expensive!"

He smiled in response. "I'm sure I can scrape together enough money to pay for two dinners."

"How do you even know Sinda likes Chinese food?"

"She said so. What's this sudden concern about restaurant prices?" Glen exhaled a puff of frustration. He was not in the mood for this conversation.

She shrugged.

Glen bent down and planted a kiss on her forehead. "I'll watch you cross the street." He paused a moment. "Oh, and Tara?"

"Yeah, Dad?"

"You'd better behave yourself tonight."

She pursed her lips. "Don't I always?"

Glen knew it was time to get tough. He couldn't let Tara continue behaving like a spoiled, sassy brat. No matter how much he loved her or how sorry he was that she'd grown up without her mother, he had to remain firm. "I'm serious. You're already on restrictions, and if you pull anything funny at Penny's, I'll add another thirty days to your punishment."

Tara picked up her suitcase and marched out the front door. "Be careful tonight," she called. "Whatever you do, don't look directly into Sinda's weird green eyes!"

Sinda paced between the fireplace and the grandfather clock. Glen wasn't late yet, but she almost hoped he would be. It would give her a few more minutes to compose herself. It had been almost three years since her last date, and that one had ended badly. She could still see the look on Todd Abernathy's face when her father gave him the third degree before they left for the theater. Even worse was when Todd brought her home and was about to kiss her good night. They'd been standing on the front porch, but the light wasn't on, so Sinda figured her father had gone to bed. She found out otherwise when he snapped on the porch light, jerked open the front door, and hollered, "You're late! I can't trust you on anything, can I?" His face was a mask of anger. "You're just like your mother, you know that?" It was the last time Todd ever came around.

Swallowing the pain, Sinda drove the unpleasant memories to the back of her mind and peered into the hallway mirror. Dad wouldn't be waiting for her tonight. If she embarrassed herself in front of Glen Olsen, it would be her own doing.

"I hope I look all right," she murmured as she studied her reflection. She'd chosen a rust-colored, full-length dress to wear and left her hair hanging long, pulled away from her face with a large beaded barrette at the nape of her neck. She didn't know what had possessed her to agree to this date, but she had, so there was no backing out now. When a knock at the front door sounded, her heart fluttered like a frightened baby bird.

She drew in a deep breath as she moved to the hallway and reached for the doorknob.

Glen stood on the porch, dressed in a pair of black slacks, a white shirt with black pinstripes, and a gray jacket. He was smiling from ear to ear and holding a bouquet of pink and white carnations.

Sinda tried to smile but failed. Except for the corsage Dad had given her when she graduated from high school, no one had ever given her flowers before.

A crease formed between his brows. "You're not allergic to flowers, I hope."

"No, no, they're lovely. Let me put them in some water, then I'll be ready to go." Her voice was strained as his gaze probed hers. How could this man's presence affect her so?

Sinda left Glen waiting in the living room while she went to the kitchen to get a vase. When she returned a few minutes later, she found him with his hands stuffed inside his jacket pockets, strolling around the room. He seemed to be studying every nook and cranny. Sinda knew the wallpaper was peeling badly, the dark painted woodwork was chipped in several places, and the plastered ceiling needed to be patched and repainted. And this was just one room! The rest of the house was equally in need of repairs.

"The place is a mess," she said, placing the bouquet on a small antique table near her colonial-style couch.

Glen nodded and blew out his breath. "I'll bet nothing has been done to this old house in years."

Sinda shrugged. She didn't want to spoil the evening by talking about her albatross. "I'm ready to go if you are."

The Silver Moon restaurant was bustling with activity, but since Glen had made reservations, they were immediately ushered to a table. Like a true gentleman, Glen pulled out a chair for Sinda, then took the seat directly across from her.

She shifted uneasily, unsure of what to say, but was relieved when their waiter came and handed them each a menu. At least it gave her something to do with her hands.

"I think we'll have a plate of barbecued pork as an appetizer," Glen told the young man. He gestured toward Sinda. "Does that appeal to you?"

She licked her lips and struggled with words that wouldn't be a lie. At the moment, nothing appealed. *I probably shouldn't have accepted Glen's dinner invitation,* she silently berated herself. She was attracted to the man, and that worried her a lot. "Barbecued pork will be fine," she said with a nod.

When the waiter left, Glen leaned forward and smiled. "You look beautiful tonight."

Heat crept up Sinda's neck and flooded her face. "Thanks. You look nice too."

"Tell me, Doctor Shull, how's that daughter of mine doing in your doll hospital? Is Tara any help at all, or does she get in the way?"

Sinda smiled, and the tension in her neck muscles eased as she began to relax. "I don't think she likes the work, but she has been a big help. I even offered to pay her if she'd keep working for me a few afternoons a week."

Glen's blue eyes sparkled in the candlelight. "Tara told me."

Sinda laughed dryly. "She hated the idea and turned me down flat."

The waiter returned with a plate of barbecued pork surrounded by sesame seeds and a small dish of hot mustard.

Glen placed their dinner order, and as soon as the waiter left, he prayed his thanks for the food. Reaching for his glass of water, he said, "I have a proposition for you, Sinda."

"Oh?" She placed one hand against her stomach, hoping to calm the butterflies that seemed determined to tap dance the night away, and forced her ragged breathing to return to normal.

"It's a business proposition," he said in a serious tone.

A business proposition. Now that might be something to consider. "What kind of business proposition?"

"It's about doll repairing."

"You want to become a doll doctor?"

Glen had just popped a piece of pork into his mouth. He swallowed, coughed, and grabbed for his water again. "Too much mustard," he sputtered.

Sinda bit back a smile. "That's why I prefer ketchup."

"I'm afraid I wouldn't make much of a doll doctor," Glen said after his fit of coughing subsided.

"Why not? I've read about some men who repair dolls in one of my doll magazines."

He nodded. "I'm sure that's true, but it isn't what I had in mind."

"What then?"

"Tara's mother had an old doll that belonged to her grandmother. The doll's been in a box under my bed for years. Tara doesn't even know about it."

"It could be quite valuable."

"I don't know about that, but it does need fixing. When Tara was born, Connie was so excited about having a little girl. She was sure she'd be able to pass the old doll down to our daughter someday." Glen's face was pinched with obvious pain. "Of course that never happened. Connie died a year later."

"It's not too late. You can still give Tara the doll her mother wanted her to have," Sinda said softly.

"I never gave it to her before because I didn't know where to take it for repairs."

"And now you do," she said with a smile. "So, what's the proposition you had in mind?"

Glen took a sip of his hot tea before answering. "The doll's a mess, and I'm sure it'll be expensive to fix." He massaged the bridge of his nose and grimaced. "I'm not even sure it's worth fixing—especially since my daughter isn't too thrilled about dolls these days."

"I'm certain that once Tara finds out it was her mother's, she'll be glad to have it."

"I was thinking maybe we could trade services in payment."

Her eyebrows shot up. "What service might you have to offer me?"

He grinned. "Your place could use a few repairs and some fresh paint. I'm pretty handy with a paintbrush. My carpentry skills aren't half bad, either."

It only took Sinda a few seconds to think about his offer. Except for some new kitchen curtains Carol had helped her make, she hadn't done much in the way of fixing up the old place. "I do need some work done."

She drew in a deep breath and expelled it quickly. "Without seeing the doll and assessing an estimate to restore it, I can't be sure our trade would be a fair one."

"I'm sure you can find enough work for me to do, should the cost be too high."

Sinda suppressed a giggle. "I didn't mean the price of the doll repairs would be too high. I meant the amount of work I need to have done far exceeds anything I could ever do for one antique doll."

Glen eyed her curiously. "I'm not concerned about balancing it out. If I come up short on the deal, maybe you can even things out a bit by agreeing to cook me dinner sometime."

Sinda reached for a piece of pork. What was there about Glen that made her feel so comfortable? Did she dare allow herself to begin a relationship with him—even a working one? She popped the meat into her mouth, wiped her fingers on her napkin, and extended her hand across the table. "You've got yourself a deal."

He looked pleased. At least she thought it was a look of pleasure she saw on his face. Maybe he had indigestion and was merely trying to be polite.

Chapter Nine

"Thanks for the nice evening, Glen. I ate so much I probably won't need to eat again all weekend." Sinda leaned her head against the vinyl headrest in the front seat of Glen's station wagon and sighed deeply.

"It doesn't have to end yet," he said, a promising gleam in his eyes. "We could take a drive out to Elmwood Lake. It's beautiful there in the spring."

With only a slight hesitation, she gave her consent. *What am I doing?* an inner voice warned. *I should really go home.*

Glen turned on the radio and slipped a cassette into place. The rich, melodious strains of a Christian Gospel singer poured from the speakers. "This song, about our soul finding rest, is one of my favorites," he commented.

Sinda closed her eyes and let the music wash over her like a gentle waterfall. It had been so long since she'd listened to any kind of Christian music, and the tape had such a calming effect. "Umm. . .I do enjoy this type of music."

By the time the song ended, Glen had pulled into the parking lot. "We still have a hint of daylight. Want to take a walk around the lake?"

"That sounds nice. I need to work off some of my dinner," Sinda said with a nervous laugh. *I really should be home in bed. . .or working on a doll. . . any place but here.*

"It's getting kind of chilly," Glen remarked. "Want to wear my jacket?"

She shook her head. "No thanks, I'm fine."

They walked along quietly for a while, then Glen broke the silence. "I was wondering if you'd like to go to church on Sunday with me and Tara."

Sinda's shoulders sagged, and she shook her head. "Thanks for asking, but I'd better not."

"Have you already found a church home?"

She stopped walking and turned to face him. "What makes you think I'm a churchgoer?"

He studied her intently for a few seconds. "I—uh—saw an old Bible on your coffee table, so I just assumed—"

"Looks can be deceiving."

He drew back, as though she'd offended him, and she started walking again, a little faster this time.

"You're upset about something, aren't you?" Glen asked when he caught up to her.

A curt nod was all she could manage.

"What is it? What's wrong?"

Unexpected tears spilled over, and she blinked several times trying to dispel them.

Suddenly Sinda's steps were halted as Glen drew her into his arms. "Are you angry with me?"

"No," she muttered against his jacket. She couldn't tell him what was really bothering her.

He pulled slightly away and lifted her chin with his thumb. "It might help to talk about it."

She sniffed deeply and took a step back. "I'd rather not."

"Maybe some other time."

She shrugged. "Maybe."

Then, as if the topic of church had never been mentioned, Glen changed the subject. "So, when would you like to begin?"

She blinked. "Begin?"

"On your house repairs?"

"Oh. I guess you can start whenever it's convenient. When can I take a look at the doll?"

"Whenever it's convenient," he said with a deep chuckle. "How about tonight? Tara's staying over at her friend Penny's, so it would be the perfect time to show you."

Sinda shivered and rubbed her hands briskly over her bare arms. "I suppose that would be all right."

"You are cold." Glen draped one arm across her shoulders, and she shivered again, only this time she knew it wasn't from the cold.

"Tara mentioned that you moved here from Seattle," Glen remarked. "She said you used to run a doll hospital there too."

Sinda nodded. *I wonder what else Tara told her dad.*

"I understand your father passed away, and your mother died when you were Tara's age?"

Sinda skidded to a stop. The camaraderie they'd begun to share had been blown away like a puff of smoke. "We've certainly done our homework, haven't we? I guess your daughter isn't the only detective in the family."

"She is the only one. At least, she thinks she is." Glen chuckled, apparently unaware of her annoyance.

"If you wanted a rundown on my past, why not ask me yourself?" she snapped. "Wouldn't it have been better than getting secondhand information from a child?"

"I did not ask my daughter to get the lowdown on you. She volunteered it—plain and simple."

Glen's tone had cooled some, and Sinda suddenly felt like an idiot. Maybe she was making a big deal out of his questions. Perhaps Dad had taught her too well about keeping to herself. "I guess I jumped to conclusions," Sinda said apologetically. "I think that's enough about me for one night, anyway. Why don't you tell me something about yourself?"

"Let's see now. . .I'm thirty-four years old. I've been a Christian since I was twelve. My parents are missionaries in New Guinea. I have one brother, who is two years younger than me. I'm a mailman who loves his job but hates the blisters he gets when he wears new boots. I love to look for bargains at yard sales and thrift stores. I've been a widower for nine years. My daughter is the official neighborhood snoop, and I'm the best cook in Elmwood." He wiggled his eyebrows. "Anything else you'd like to know?"

Sinda couldn't help but smile. She and Glen Olsen had more in common than she would have guessed. At least she liked yard sales and thrift shops, and they did enjoy the same kind of music and eating Chinese food. Glen was like a breath of fresh air—able to make her smile and even temporarily forget the pain from her past. "How come a good-looking, great cook like you has never remarried?" she asked.

"I have dated a few women since my wife's death," he acknowledged. "I was in too much pain the first few years to even think about another woman, but when I did finally start dating, Tara didn't like it." He reached for Sinda's hand and gave it a gentle squeeze. "To be perfectly honest, until recently I've never met a woman besides my wife, Connie, who could hold my interest."

Until recently? Did he mean her? Dare she ask? She was about to, but he threw a question at her instead.

"How about you? Have there been many men in your life?"

She shook her head, hoping, almost praying, he wouldn't pursue the subject. "It's getting dark. Maybe we should go. You did say you wanted me to take a look at that doll, right?"

Glen nodded, and they turned back toward his car.

Sinda waited in the living room while Glen went upstairs to get the doll. When he returned a short time later, she was standing in front of the fireplace, looking at a photograph on the mantel.

"That was the last picture ever taken of Connie," he said, stepping up beside Sinda. "It was about a year before she died."

She placed the photograph back on the mantel. "She was lovely."

A few tears shimmered in Glen's sapphire-blue eyes as he replied, "Her sweet attitude and Christian faith never wavered—not even when the end came near."

Sinda swallowed hard, trying not to feel his pain, yet in spite of her resolve, her heart went out to Glen. What would it be like to raise a child alone? Her father knew, but she'd never asked him. She hadn't dared to ask any personal questions, especially about her mother.

Yanking her attention away from the captivating, dark-eyed brunette in the picture, Sinda leaned over the coffee table to examine the old doll Glen had placed there.

The bisque-head, ball-jointed doll lay in pieces, and the blond mohair wig was nearly threadbare. Several fingers and toes were missing as well. Sinda held the head gently, turning it over to see if it had any special markings that might indicate who had made it. "Ah...a German doll," she murmured. "She's quite old and a real treasure."

"You mean the doll could be worth something?" he asked, lifting his eyebrows in obvious surprise.

"Several hundred dollars, I'd say."

Glen frowned. "It needs a lot of work, though."

She shrugged her shoulders. "Nothing I haven't done before."

"How long do you think it would take?"

"Probably a month or two."

He nodded and gave her another one of his heart-melting smiles. "Then for the next month you'll have my handyman services." They shook on it to make it official, and Sinda said she should be getting home.

As Glen walked her next door, Sinda could hear Sparky barking from inside the house.

"Be quiet, you dumb dog. You'll alert the whole neighborhood," a child's shrill voice hissed.

"Alert them to what?" Glen bellowed.

Tara, who was crouched in one corner of Sinda's front porch, jumped in obvious surprise, and so did Sinda. "Dad! What are you doing here?"

"I think the question should be 'What are you doing here, Miss Olsen?' Aren't you supposed to be at Penny's?"

Tara rocked back and forth on her heels, clasping her hands tightly together. "I–I—that is—"

Sinda's gaze swung from Tara, to Glen, to a strange-looking object on her front porch. She leaned over for a closer look. "Where did this old trunk come from?" she asked, glancing back at Tara.

The child rubbed the palms of her hands over her blue jeans and licked her lips before she replied. "I—uh—was upstairs in Penny's room, and I happened to glance out the window, when—"

"I'll bet you just happened to," Glen interrupted.

"Go on, Tara," Sinda prompted.

At her father's nod, Tara touched the trunk with the toe of her sneaker and continued. "I saw a dark-colored van pull into your driveway. A man got out, and he took this big thing out of the back. He carried it up the walk and set it on your front porch. Then he knocked on the door, but when nobody answered, he left it and drove away."

"Did you get a good look at the man? Did you see any markings on the van or anything that might give us some clue?" Glen questioned.

Tara shook her head. "No, but I decided to come over here and see if he left a note or anything."

Sinda dropped to her knees beside the trunk. She thought she recognized it, but under the dim porch light she couldn't be sure. "There's a shipping tag attached to the side. It has my name and address on it." She glanced up at Tara. "The man you saw was probably from the freight company who sent the trunk."

"Who's it from, and what's inside?" Tara asked excitedly.

"That is none of our business, young lady." Glen offered Sinda his hand, and she stood up again. "That thing looks kind of heavy. Want me to carry it into the house for you?"

"I'd appreciate it," she replied.

Glen pointed at Tara. "Get on back to Penny's. We're going to have a little talk about this in the morning."

Tara bounded off the porch, but she turned back when she reached the sidewalk. "Say, Dad, what's in that cardboard box you're holding?"

Glen nodded in the direction of Penny's house. "Go!"

Sinda waited until Tara was safely across the street and had entered her friend's house before she opened the front door. Glen handed Sinda the box with the antique doll in it, then he hoisted the trunk to his broad shoulders and followed her inside.

At her suggestion, Glen set the trunk in the hallway, then moved toward the door, hesitating slightly. To her surprise, he lifted his hand and gently touched the side of her face, sending shivers of delight up her spine. She breathed in the musky scent of his aftershave and held her breath as he bent his head toward her. Their lips touched briefly in a warm kiss as delicate as butterfly wings.

"I guess I should apologize for that," Glen whispered when he pulled away. "I'm not usually so forward."

Sinda's cheeks flamed as she realized how much she'd enjoyed the brief kiss. "Good night, Glen," was all she managed to say.

With hands in his pockets and shoulders slightly slumped, Glen ambled out the front door. Did he think she was angry? Should she have said something more?

Sinda shut the door, shuffled to the living room, and slumped to the couch with a groan. She sat there, staring vacantly at the unlit fireplace, then reached up to touch her mouth, still feeling the warmth of Glen's lips. As extraordinary as the kiss felt, she could never let it happen again!

She closed her eyes momentarily, and when she opened them, her gaze rested on the massive trunk sitting in the hallway. Who sent it and why? Should she open it now or wait until morning?

Sinda forced herself to get up from the couch, and she moved slowly across the room. *"Why put off until tomorrow what you can do today?"* She could hear her father's words as if he were standing right beside her. How many times had he reprimanded her for procrastinating? How many times had he screamed at her for forgetting things? Why was it so important to do things right away? Worse yet, why was she still doing things his way? He was dead. Shouldn't she be able to make her own decisions and do things her way?

"I guess old habits die hard," Sinda said as she knelt beside the trunk. With trembling fingers she grasped the handle and pulled. It didn't budge. That's when she noticed the hasp was held securely in place by a padlock. The key! Where was the key?

It had been many years since Sinda had seen the trunk, though she'd never viewed any of its contents. She was certain it was her mother's trunk, which she'd seen in her closet on several occasions. She'd always figured Dad had thrown it out after Mother left. Seeing it now was a painful reminder that her mother was gone forever. It made her feel as if she were ten years old again. . .sad, betrayed, and confused by everything that had happened.

Driving the troubling thoughts to the back of her mind, Sinda directed her focus to the old trunk. On closer examination, she discovered a business card attached to the handle. A light finally dawned. Alex Masters, their family lawyer, must have had access to the trunk, for it was his name and address inscribed on the card.

Without a key Sinda had no way of getting into the trunk tonight. She may as well go up to bed. In the morning she'd give Alex a call and see if he had the key. She was in no hurry to open up old wounds, anyway. There were too many hurts from her past, and after such a lovely evening with Glen, she would rather not think about them.

Chapter Ten

It was Saturday morning, and Tara, recently home from Penny's, had been sent outside to do more weeding in the flower beds. Glen watched her wipe the dampness from her forehead and heard her mutter, "If my mother was still alive, she'd be out here in the garden with me. Dad wouldn't be acting so goofy around our weird neighbor, either."

"Who are you talking to?" Glen tapped his daughter on the shoulder, and she whirled around to face him.

"Myself." She glanced at the toolbox in his hand. "What's that for?"

"Starting today I'll be helping Sinda do some repairs on her house during my free time, so if you need me just give a holler."

Tara's mouth dropped open like a broken hinge. "I thought you and I were goin' shopping today. Summer will be here soon, and I need new clothes."

Glen shrugged. "I had planned to take you to Fuller's Mall, but since you snuck out of Penny's house last night, you'll be spending the entire day doing chores. I've also decided that when your time is up at Sinda's, you can do another thirty days of doll repairs." Tara's eyes widened, and he drew in a deep breath, wondering if he was being too hard on her. He knew he was lenient at times, but there were other times, like right now, when he snapped like a turtle. *I have good reason to be stern with her,* he reasoned. *Tara disobeyed me, in spite of my warnings.*

Tara looked up at him as though she might burst into tears, and he chastised himself for feeling guilty. He leveled her with a look he hoped was admonishing. "If Sinda and I ever go out again, you'll be staying with Mrs. Mayer or at Uncle Phil's."

Tara thrust out her chin. "Aw, Dad, Uncle Phil lives in a dinky little apartment. He has no kids, and there's never anything fun to do there."

Glen couldn't argue with that. His younger, unmarried brother had his own successful business and was hardly ever home, so Phil didn't need a large place to live.

Tara's lower lip protruded. "And I don't see why I have to do more work for that weir—"

"Don't even say it," Glen interrupted. He motioned toward the flower beds. "When you're done weeding here, you can start out front."

"But I did those a few weeks ago," she argued.

"Then do them again!" Glen disappeared, forcing all thoughts of his disobedient daughter to the back of his mind. Right now all he wanted to do was get over to Sinda's and start working.

He opened the gate and trudged through her overgrown yard. *I should offer to mow this mess.* Glen set the toolbox on Sinda's porch and knocked on her back door. She opened it right away, but he was disappointed when she didn't return his smile. She was wearing a pair of dark green overalls and a pale green T-shirt that deepened the color of her eyes, and her hair was pulled up into a ponytail. A strange sensation spread through Glen's chest. Despite her casual attire and sullen expression, he thought she looked beautiful.

"Good morning, Glen," Sinda said with downcast eyes. What was wrong? Why wouldn't she look at him?

"Morning," he responded cheerfully. He hoped his positive mood might rub off on her. "You have my services for most of the day, so where would you like me to begin?"

"You sound rather anxious to work up a sweat on such a warm spring day."

"Just keeping true to my word." He gave her a quick wink, but there was no response. Not even a smile. *It might be that she's upset because Tara was snooping around on her front porch last night. Or maybe it was that unplanned kiss. Should I ask?*

"I haven't started on your wife's old doll yet," Sinda said, breaking into Glen's contemplations.

He shrugged. "I just gave it to you last night."

"Before you tackle any of my house repairs, would you mind moving that old trunk upstairs?" she asked, changing the subject.

"No problem." He stepped inside, hoisted the trunk to his shoulders, and followed Sinda up the stairs.

When they came to the first room, she moved aside. "This room is full of boxes and things I haven't had time to find a place for yet, so let's put it here." She frowned deeply. "I don't even have a key that will open the trunk."

Glen raised his eyebrows. "No key came with it?"

She shook her head. "I have several old keys with some of my antiques, but nothing fits. I found my lawyer's business card on the handle last night, so I'll contact him to see if he has the key."

"Would you like me to break it open? I don't think it would be too difficult."

At first Sinda looked as though she might be considering the offer, but to his surprise she replied, "I'll wait and see what my lawyer has to say. There's no sense ruining a perfectly good padlock if it's not necessary."

Glen turned toward the door. "Where would you like me to begin? Should I start by mowing the lawn?"

"I think I can handle that myself," she said. "Why don't you try to do something about the front porch? It's even more dilapidated than the back porch, and since my customers come to the front door, I'd rather not have someone trip on a loose board and sue me for everything I don't own."

The expression on her face softened, and it made Glen's heart race. He grinned and started back down the stairs with Sinda following on his heels. He was glad the tension he'd felt when he first arrived seemed to be abating. "By the time you finish your breakfast, I should have a fairly good start on the project."

Her forehead wrinkled. "How'd you know I was about to eat breakfast?"

They were at the bottom of the stairs now, and Glen turned to face her. "My daughter's always telling me that I'm the best cook in the world. What kind of cook would I be if I couldn't smell scrambled eggs and sausage?"

Sinda grimaced and covered her face with her hands. "Guess I'm caught. If you haven't eaten yet, you're welcome to join me."

Glen held his stomach and gave her what he hoped was his best grin. He'd eaten a bowl of cereal and a piece of toast around seven, and it was a little after nine now. He could probably eat again.

"Please, Dad, not another Sunday dinner with Sinda!"

Glen was putting away the leftovers from their Saturday evening supper of pizza and salad, while Tara cleared the table.

"Tara Mae Olsen, what is wrong with you? It seems like all you do anymore is whine and complain. What is your problem?"

"It's actually your problem, Dad, not mine," she answered sullenly.

"What is that supposed to mean?"

"Sinda's the problem, not me." Now Tara looked like she was going to cry, and she flopped into a chair and lowered her head to the table.

Glen took the seat across from her and reached out to take her hand, suddenly feeling like a big heel. He hadn't meant to make her cry. "What kind of problem do you see attached to Sinda Shull?"

Tara's head shot up, and tears rolled down her cheeks. "Can't you see it, Dad? She's out to get you."

His mouth dropped open. "You actually think Sinda is out to get me?"

The pathetic look on Tara's face told him that was exactly what she thought.

"I saw her kiss you last night."

Glen's ears were burning. He didn't see how Tara could have known they were kissing. He'd seen her go into Penny's house. Furthermore, he and Sinda had kissed when they were standing in the hallway, in front of the door. Maybe she was only guessing. She was pretty good at that.

Tara stared at the table, her lower lip quivering like a leaf in the wind. "Just how did you manage to see us kissing?"

She sniffed deeply. "I was looking out Penny's bedroom window."

"It was dark when you went back to the Spauldings'," Glen reminded. "And Sinda and I were. . ." He paused and reached up to scratch the back of his head. "You were using those binoculars again, weren't you?"

Tara's face turned pink.

"How many times have I told you to stop spying on people?"

"I wasn't exactly spying," she defended. "I was looking outside. The binoculars just picked you up through that little window in Sinda's front door."

"First, you need to give those binoculars to me until you show yourself trustworthy and ready to respect others' privacy. Second, for the record, Sinda did not kiss me. It was the other way around."

Tara jumped out of her seat, nearly knocking the chair over. "Dad, how could you do such a thing? You hardly even know her!"

"I know her well enough to realize I enjoy her company." He shrugged. "Besides, it's no big deal. It was just an innocent good night kiss." *One that shouldn't have happened,* his conscience reminded. *Sinda refused your invitation to church, and you still don't know if she's ever had a personal relationship with Christ.*

"She's got you hypnotized!"

"Don't start that again, Tara. I'm in perfect control of my faculties." But even as he spoke the words Glen wondered if they were true. Not that he believed he'd actually been hypnotized by Sinda's green eyes. But there was something about the woman that held him captive. Whenever he was with Sinda he had a strange sense of some kind of mystery awaiting him. It was exciting and troubling at the same time.

"The Bible tells us to love our neighbors as ourselves, and I've invited Sinda to come for Sunday dinner again," he said with authority. "She's graciously accepted, and you will be courteous to our dinner guest. Is that clear?"

Tara hung her head. "Yeah, I understand. I wish you did."

Sinda sat at her kitchen table, toying with the piece of salmon on her plate. She loved fish, especially salmon. Tonight she had no appetite, though. She hadn't been able to reach Alex Masters by phone today, and she had mixed feelings about it. Since this was Saturday, her lawyer obviously wasn't in his office, but she'd also gotten his answering machine at home. Even though she wasn't thrilled about the prospect of opening the trunk, there was a part of her that wanted to see what was inside. If it was her mother's trunk, maybe there was something within the contents that could help heal some of her pain.

Resigned to the fact that she'd have to wait until next week to call Alex again, Sinda let her thoughts carry her in another direction. Against her better judgment she had accepted another dinner invitation from Glen. She felt apprehensive about going—especially since she knew better than to allow herself to get close to a man.

Sinda thought about how Glen had spent most of the day working on her house. He'd replaced rotten boards on the front porch steps, repaired a broken railing, and helped her strip the torn wallpaper in the dining room. Then, shortly before he left, he had extended the dinner invitation. Sinda had been so appreciative of all this work that she'd accepted without even thinking.

What kind of power does that man hold over me? she fumed. *I should know better than to let my guard down because Glen seems kind and is easy to talk to. By his actions he appears to be nice, but is he all he claims to be?*

Sirens in the distance drove Sinda's thoughts unwillingly back to the past. Whenever she heard that shrill whine she remembered the frightening night when the police showed up at their door, demanding to know if someone had been injured. Sinda had heard one of the police officers say they'd had a report from a neighbor about hearing loud voices coming from the Shulls' home. Dad was able to convince the officer that everything was fine, and the shouting the neighbor heard was probably just the TV turned up too loud. Sinda remembered hearing her parents hollering at each other that night. Of course, that had been a regular occurrence, even though her mother always assured her there was nothing to worry about.

As the sound of the sirens diminished, so did Sinda's thoughts from the past. She jabbed at the fish on her plate and exclaimed, "I'll go to dinner tomorrow because I promised, but after that I won't accept any more social invitations from Glen!"

Chapter Eleven

A s Sinda rang the Olsens' doorbell the following day, she noticed that she felt a bit more relaxed than she had the previous time she'd come to dinner. Not only did she know Glen and Tara better, but she had a sense of peace about her decision last night. She would try to be a good neighbor, but nothing more.

When Tara opened the front door, the distinctive aroma of oregano assaulted Sinda's senses, and she sniffed the air. "Something smells good."

"Dad's fixing spaghetti."

"I love most any kind of pasta dish." Sinda stepped inside, even though she hadn't been invited.

Tara gave her an icy stare, but she led the way to the kitchen without another word. When Glen turned from the stove and offered her a warm smile, Sinda squeezed her lips together to keep her mouth from falling open. How could any man look so good or so masculine when he was wearing an oversized apron and holding a wooden spoon in one hand?

"You're right on time. Dinner's almost ready, and I thought we'd eat in here." Glen nodded toward the kitchen table, which had already been set.

"Is there anything I can do to help?" Sinda asked hopefully. Anything would be better than standing here like a ninny, gawking at Glen and wishing. . . What was she wishing for anyway?

Using his spoon, Glen motioned toward the table. "Have a seat, and we can talk while I finish dishing things up." He glanced at Tara, who was leaning against the cupboard with her arms folded across her chest. "Honey, would you please fill the glasses with water?"

The child did as he requested, but Sinda could tell by Tara's deep sigh and slow movements that she was not happy about it.

"Your kitchen looks so clean and orderly." Sinda laughed self-consciously. "I love to cook, but you should see my kitchen clutter after

I'm done with a meal. It looks like a tornado blew in from the east."

Glen chuckled. "I wasn't always this efficient. I've had lots of practice, and lots of help from Tara, which is probably why I appear so capable."

Sinda toyed with the fork lying beside her plate. "I've been cooking since I was a young girl, and I still make messes. I guess some people tend to be neater than others."

Tara came to Sinda's water glass, and Sinda quickly moved to one side, barely in time to avoid being caught in the dribbles that weren't quite making it into her glass. "Sorry about that," the child mumbled.

"Tara, why don't you go out to the living room until dinner is served?"

"There's nothing to do out there," the child moaned. "I can't watch TV, and—"

"Read a book or play with Jake. Sinda and I want to visit."

Tara stomped out of the room, and Glen turned to face Sinda. "Returning to our discussion about your cooking abilities—I thought the breakfast you fixed yesterday tasted great, and I never even looked at your kitchen clutter."

Sinda grimaced. "That meal wasn't much to write home about."

"Maybe you'd like the chance to cook a real meal for me. Then I can judge for myself how well you cook." Glen winked at her. "And I promise not to critique your cleaning skills."

Sinda felt her face flame as she sat there silently watching his nimble fingers drop angel-hair pasta into the pot of boiling water on the stove. When he finished, he looked her way again. "Guess a guy shouldn't go around inviting himself to dinner, huh?"

"It's not that," Sinda was quick to say. "It's just—I've been thinking maybe we might be seeing too much of each other."

"I enjoy your company, and I kind of hoped you liked being with me. After all, we both like to cook, love to go to yard sales and thrift stores, and even enjoy the same kind of relaxing music." A deep, crescent-shaped dimple sprang out on the right side of Glen's mouth as he smiled. Funny, she'd never noticed it before.

Sinda's face grew even warmer. "I do enjoy being with you, Glen, but—"

"Then let's get better acquainted."

Sinda could feel her resolve fly right out the window, and she swallowed hard. Glen was right; they did have a few things in common. "Maybe we can try dinner at my house next Sunday. Tara's invited too, of course," she added quickly.

"Sounds great, and the invitation to attend church with us is still open if you're interested."

Sinda's heart began to race, and she wasn't sure if it was Glen's smile or the mention of church. "I think it would be best to stick with dinner," she said, feeling as though she couldn't quite get her breath.

"I was hoping you might have changed your mind about going to church."

Sinda reached for her glass and took a sip of water before she answered. "I went to church every Sunday with my dad."

"Did you ever commit your life to Christ?"

She nodded slowly. "When I was ten years old and went to Bible school, I accepted Jesus as my Savior." Was that a look of relief she saw on Glen's face?

"That's great, and it gives us one more thing in common." He frowned slightly. "So, if you're a Christian, how come you're not interested in finding a church home?"

Sinda licked her lips, searching for the right words. How could she tell Glen, a man she was just getting to know, what had happened to her faith in God? "I—uh—could we please change the subject?"

Glen nodded and began to drain the spaghetti into the strainer he'd placed in the sink. "Is there anything you'd like me to bring to dinner next Sunday. . .maybe some dessert?"

You are dessert, Glen Olsen. It's just too bad I'm on a diet, Sinda thought as she shrugged her shoulders. "Some dessert would be nice."

The following week, Sinda became even more fretful than usual. It wasn't until Thursday when she finally heard from her lawyer. Then it was only to say that he'd been on vacation when she'd called. When Sinda questioned him about the trunk, he informed her that it had been in storage for several years. Though not mentioned in the will, it was her father's verbal request that she should have it after he died. Alex had forgotten all about the trunk until a bill arrived from the storage company a few weeks ago. When she asked him about the key, he said he hadn't been given one.

Wondering if she should break the lock or keep looking for a key that might fit, Sinda decided to do nothing for the time being. She wasn't even sure she wanted to see the contents of the trunk, so maybe more time was what she needed.

Another reason for Sinda's stress was Tara Olsen. The child's most recent act of disobedience had extended her time working in Sinda's doll hospital to another four weeks. While Sinda did appreciate the extra help, having Tara around seemed to add to her problems. She had to be extra careful not to let the girl see the antique doll Glen had asked her to repair. She'd have to do those restorations whenever Tara wasn't around. The sullen child was also sneaking around, nosing into places that were none of her business. Sinda had no idea what the would-be detective was looking for, but it irritated her, nonetheless.

Today was Saturday, and Tara was in the basement, cleaning the body of an ink-stained vinyl doll. Glen was up on the second floor, working in the bathroom, and Sinda was in the kitchen, making a pitcher of iced tea. She could hear him moving around overhead—a thump here—the piercing whine of a drill there. She could only imagine how he must look right now, bent over the sink, tools in hand, trying to make it usable.

Sinda placed the tea in the refrigerator and opened the basement door. She had to check on Tara and quit thinking about Glen Olsen!

When she entered the doll hospital a few minutes later, Sinda found Tara scrubbing the stomach of the vinyl doll with diluted bleach and a toothbrush, an effective treatment for ink stains.

"How's it going?" Sinda asked, peering over the child's shoulder.

Tara shrugged. "Okay, I guess."

"Have you heard any more strange noises down here?"

"Not today, but I still think this old house is creepy. Aren't you afraid to live here alone?"

Sinda shook her head. Even if she were a bit apprehensive at times, she'd never admit it to Tara. She sat down in the chair on the other side of the table. "I have Sparky for protection, so there's no reason to be afraid."

Tara lifted her gaze to the ceiling. "You'd never catch me living in a place like this."

"Maybe when your dad's finished with the critical repairs it will look less creepy."

Tara's head lurched forward as she let out a reverberating sneeze.

Sinda felt immediate concern. "Is that bleach smell getting to you?"

Tara sneezed again. "I think it is."

"Why don't you set it aside and work on something else?" Sinda placed the doll on a shelf and handed Tara another one. "This little lady needs her hair washed and combed." She gave the child a bottle of dry shampoo, used expressly for wigs. "You can work on it while I run upstairs and tend to a few things. I'll call you in about fifteen minutes, then we can have a snack. How's that sound?"

"Whatever," Tara mumbled.

Glen leaned over the antiquated bathroom sink, wondering if he'd be able to fix the continual drip, drop, drip. From the looks of the nasty green stain, it had been leaking for quite a while. In a house this old, where little or no repairs had been done, Glen figured he'd be helping out for a good many weeks. He smiled to himself. It would mean more time spent with Sinda. Maybe he'd be able to find out what was bothering her, and why, if she was a Christian, she had no interest in church.

"Dad! Dad!" Tara rounded the corner of the bathroom and skidded to a stop next to him.

Glen knew right away that something was wrong—Tara's eyes were huge, and he felt her tremble as she clung to him. "What's wrong, honey? You scared me half to death, screaming like that."

"You're scared?" she sobbed. "Go to that spooky basement by yourself, then you'll be scared!"

Glen pulled away slightly so he could get a better look at her face. "What are you talking about?"

"Strange noises! Moving doll parts! I'm telling you, Dad, this house has to be haunted!"

Glen gave Tara's shoulders a gentle shake. "Take a deep breath and calm down."

"I heard a noise! A doll leg jumped out of a box! This place is creepy, and I want to go home." Tara's voice was pleading, and she squeezed Glen around the waist with a strength that surprised him. He wasn't sure how to deal with her hysteria and wondered if she might even be making the story up just to get him away from Sinda. He gritted his teeth. *If this is a ploy, she's not going to get away with it.*

◯◯

Sinda entered the bathroom, but stopped short when she saw Tara clinging to her father. "I thought you were in the basement, Tara."

"She heard a noise." Glen shrugged his shoulders and looked at Sinda with a helpless expression. "She thinks your house is haunted."

Tara seemed close to tears, and Sinda felt sorry for her. She was about to ask for an explanation, when Tara blurted, "A doll leg jumped right out of a box! I saw it with my own eyes."

Glen held up his hands. "What can I say?"

"I think I can take care of this little problem." Sinda started for the door.

"You're not going down there, are you?" Tara cried.

"Yes, I am. Me and Panther."

"Panther?" Glen and Tara said in unison.

"Panther's my new cat," Sinda explained as she started down the stairs.

Glen and Tara were right behind her. "I never knew you had a cat," Tara said. "You've got a dog, and cats and dogs don't usually get along."

Sinda nodded but kept descending the stairs. "You're right. Sparky's not the least bit fond of Panther, and I'm quite sure the cat returns his feelings. I try to keep them separated as much as possible." By now they were in the hallway, and Sinda began calling, "Here, kitty, kitty!"

"When did you get a cat?" Glen asked, moving toward Sinda.

"A few days ago. One of my customers is moving. She can't take Panther along, so I adopted him." She drew in a deep breath. "Since I'm having some trouble, I thought having a cat might be a good idea."

Glen slipped his arm around Sinda's waist, and she found the gesture comforting yet a bit disarming. "Trouble? What kind of trouble are you having?"

"I'll explain it all later," she said, moving away from Glen. "Right now

I need to find that cat." Sinda stepped into the living room and called, "Panther! Come, kitty, kitty!"

Glen turned to Tara. "You're good with cats. Why don't you see if you can help?"

Tara shook her head and gave him an imploring look. "We need to get out of this house!"

"Tara Mae Olsen, would you quit being so melodramatic? Sinda needs our help, and it's the neighborly thing—"

Tara shook her head. "I just want to go home."

"We'll go as soon as we've helped Sinda solve her problem."

Sinda offered Glen a grateful smile. How could the man be so helpful and kind? Was it all an act, or did Glen Olsen really want to help?

Chapter Twelve

A green-eyed ebony cat streaked through the living room with the speed of lightning. "That was Panther," Sinda announced.

"I sure hope he won't fight with Jake," Tara mumbled.

"You're fast on your feet, Tara. Go after him!" Glen pointed to the staircase where Panther had bounded.

Tara scrambled after the cat, and Glen followed Sinda to the kitchen. Five minutes later Tara came running in, holding tightly to the cat, its ears lying flat against its head in irritation.

Sinda had been sitting beside Glen at the table, drinking a cup of coffee, and just as he reached for her hand, Tara marched across the room and dropped Panther into her lap.

"You found him!" Sinda exclaimed. "Where was he?"

"Hiding inside a box in that room full of junk." Tara gave her ponytail a flip and scrunched up her nose.

Glen's forehead wrinkled as he looked at his daughter. "I hope you didn't disturb anything."

Tara flopped into a chair. "Nothing except the dumb old cat."

"Now that he's been found, let's put him to work." Sinda stood up and hurried to the basement door. Glen and Tara followed. She placed Panther on the first step and gave him a little nudge. "Go get 'em, boy!" Sinda slammed the door. "That should take care of our little basement ghosts."

"You're sending a cat to chase ghosts?" Tara's eyes were wide, and her mouth hung slightly open.

"Panther's on a mouse hunt," Sinda explained, moving back toward the kitchen.

Tara was right on her heels. "Mice? You think there are mice in the basement?"

Sinda nodded. "I told you that before. I think the jumping doll leg was a lively mouse who has taken up residence in the box of doll parts. You probably frightened him, and when he jumped, it caused the doll leg to go flying."

Glen nodded. "In an old house like this, it's not uncommon to find a few mice scurrying around. We don't want them overrunning the place, though, so I think we should set some traps."

Sinda leaned against the cupboard. "That might help, but I'd rather let the cat take care of things naturally. I don't want to take the chance of either Sparky or Panther getting their noses caught in a trap."

"Or their tails," Tara added. Her gaze shifted to her father. "Remember when Jake got his tail caught in a mouse trap? That was awful!"

Glen held up his hands. "Okay, ladies. . .I get the point. We'll forget about setting any traps." He pulled Tara to his side and gave her a squeeze. "Guess what?"

She shrugged. "What?"

"Last Sunday, when Sinda came to our house for dinner, she invited us to eat at her place this Sunday." Glen smiled and winked at Sinda. "Now we get to try out some of her cooking."

Sinda was surprised Glen hadn't told his daughter about her dinner invitation until now, and the troubled look on Tara's face told Sinda all she needed to know. The child was not happy about this bit of news. *What have I done now?* she silently moaned.

It had been raining all morning, and Sinda could see out the kitchen window where the water was running off the roof like it was being released from a dam. "We do need the rain, but now new gutters will have to be put up. Another job for poor, overworked Glen. Is there no end to the work needing to be done around this old place?" She groaned. "I can't believe I invited the Olsens over for dinner today." Tara didn't want to come, and when he'd phoned last night, Glen had once more tried to convince Sinda to go to church with them. As much as she enjoyed Glen's company, she couldn't go. The last time she'd gone to church. . .

Sinda turned away from the window and grabbed her recipe for scalloped potatoes from the cupboard. *I will not allow myself to think about the past today. Thinking about it won't change a thing, and it will only cause me more pain.* She wiped a stray hair away from her face and moaned. "Why don't children get to choose their parents? Life is so unfair."

Sinda heard a knock on the front door and hurried to the hall mirror to check her appearance. She was wearing her hair up in a French roll and had chosen to wear a beige, short-sleeved cotton dress that just touched her ankles. The prim and proper look was a far cry from her normal ponytail and cutoffs.

Sinda's hands trembled as she opened the door. Glen smiled and gave her an approving nod. "You look nice today." He was dressed in a pair of navy blue slacks and a light blue cotton shirt, which made his indigo eyes seem even more intense than usual. He handed Sinda a plate of chocolate chip cookies and a bouquet of miniature red roses.

"Thank you, they're lovely." She opened the door wider, bidding him entrance. "Where's Tara?"

"She'll be here soon. She couldn't decide whether to stay in her church clothes or change into something more comfortable."

"Why don't you put the cookies on the kitchen counter? I'll find a vase for these beauties and use them as our centerpiece. I bought some lemon sherbet the other day, so the cookies should go well with that." Sinda knew she was babbling, but she seemed unable to stop herself. *If Glen would only quit staring at me, I might not feel as nervous as a baby robin being chased by a cat.*

"What's for dinner?" Glen asked, lifting his dark eyebrows and sniffing the air. "Something smells pretty good."

"Nothing fancy. Just scalloped potatoes."

"I'm sure they'll be great." He cleared his throat a few times, as though he might be trying to work up the courage to say something more. "I— uh—have a question for you."

"What is it?" she asked as she filled the vase with water.

Glen moved slowly toward Sinda. Her mouth went dry, and she swallowed so hard she almost choked. *What's he doing? I hope he's not. . .*

He took the vase from her hands and placed it on the counter. Then he pulled her into his arms. "My question is, how come you're so beautiful?"

Before Sinda could open her mouth to reply, his lips captured hers. The unexpected kiss left her weak in the knees and fighting for breath. When it ended, she pulled back slightly, gazing up at his handsome face. She pressed her head against his shoulder, breathing in the masculine scent of his subtle aftershave. She could feel the steady beat of Glen's heart against her ear, and she closed her eyes, feeling relaxed and safe in his embrace. Safer than she'd felt in a long time. What had happened to her resolve to keep her neighbor at arm's length? It was fading faster than a photograph left out in the sun, and she seemed powerless to stop it.

"I haven't felt this way about any woman since Connie died," Glen whispered. "I realize we haven't known each other very long, but I find myself thinking about you all the time." He lifted her chin with one hand, bent his head, and captured her mouth again.

How long the kiss might have lasted, Sinda would never know, for a shrill voice sliced through the air like a razor blade. "Dad, what are you doing?"

Glen pulled away first. He seemed almost in a daze as he stared at his daughter with a blank look on his face. Several awkward seconds ticked by, then he shook his head, as though coming out of a trance. "Tara, how'd you get here?"

"I walked. We live next door, remember?"

Glen's eyelids closed partway, and he shook his finger at Tara. "Don't get smart with me, young lady! I meant, why didn't you knock? You don't just walk into someone's house. I've taught you better manners than that."

Tara blinked several times, and Sinda wondered if the child was going to cry. "I did knock. Nobody answered, but since you were already here, I tried the door. It was open, so I thought it was okay to come in. Then I found you. . . . " Tara touched her lips with the tips of her fingers and grimaced. "That was really gross, Dad."

Sinda reached up with shaky fingers and brushed her own trembling lips. *What can I say or do to help ease this tension?*

Glen moved away from her and knelt in front of his daughter. "Sinda and I are both adults, and if we want to share a kiss, it shouldn't concern you."

Tara's eyes were wide, and she waved her hands in the air. "Why not? Dad, can't you see that Sinda's got you—"

Glen held up one hand. "That will be enough, Tara. I want you to apologize to Sinda for being so rude."

"It's okay." Sinda spoke softly, hoping to calm Glen down. From the angry scowl on his face, she was afraid he might be about to slap his daughter. She couldn't stand to witness such a scene, and she'd do almost anything to stop it from happening. Sinda touched Glen on the shoulder. "We didn't hear her knock, so she did the only thing she could think to do."

He stood up and put his arm around Sinda, but his gaze was fixed on Tara. "I'm glad Sinda is kind enough to forgive you, but you do need to apologize for your behavior," he said in a more subdued tone of voice.

Tara hung her head. "I–I'm sorry for coming into your house without being invited." She glanced up at Sinda, and tears shimmered in her dark eyes.

Sinda had the sudden urge to wrap the child in her arms and offer comfort, but she was sure it would not be appreciated. Tara obviously didn't like her, and she didn't think there was anything she could do to change that fact.

"I don't know about the rest of you, but I'm hungry," Glen said, changing the subject and breaking into Sinda's thoughts. "Is dinner ready yet?"

Sinda nodded. "I think so." She moved away from Glen and busied herself at the stove. *Inviting my neighbors to dinner was a terrible mistake, and it must never happen again.*

Chapter Thirteen

T here's only one way to get Glen Olsen out of my mind," Sinda fumed, "and that's to keep busy."

She was alone in the doll hospital, working on an antique bisque doll. Panther, who was sleeping under the table, meowed softly, as though in response to her grumbling.

In spite of her determination not to think about Glen, Sinda's thoughts swirled around in her head like a blender running at full speed. It had been four weeks since she'd had Glen and Tara over for dinner, and during those four weeks she'd been miserable.

Sinda swallowed hard and fought the urge to give in to her tears. Glen had called her after he'd gone home that night, apologizing for Tara's behavior and suggesting that they try dinner the following Sunday at his place. When Sinda told him she didn't want to see him anymore, he seemed confused. She'd even said she didn't want him doing any more work on her house, and he had argued about that as well. Sinda knew having Glen around would be too much temptation, and she might weaken and agree to go out with him again. Or worse yet, let him kiss her again. Of course her decision meant she would either have to do all her own home repairs or pay someone else to do them. Until business picked up and she had a steady cash flow, she would forget about all repairs that weren't absolutely necessary.

Sinda could still hear Glen's final words before she'd hung up the phone that night. "I care about you, Sinda, and I really want to help."

She'd almost weakened, but an image of her mother had jumped into her mind. There was no future for her and Glen, so why lead him on? And even if her past wasn't working against her, Tara certainly was!

The telephone rang, and Sinda's mind snapped back to the present. She reached for it, thankful that she'd remembered to bring the cordless phone downstairs this time. "Sinda's Doll Hospital." Her eyebrows shot up. "You want to run a story about me in your newspaper? I—I guess it would be all right. Yes, I'd like it to be a human interest story too." *That would no doubt be good for my business.*

Several minutes later she hung up the phone, having agreed to let a reporter from the *Daily Herald* interview her the following morning. She hoped it was the right decision.

The interview with the newspaper columnist went better than Sinda had expected, but she was relieved when he and his photographer said they had all they needed and left her house shortly before noon. Even though she knew the article they planned to print about her doll hospital would be good for business, Sinda had some reservations about having so much attention drawn to her. She'd always tried to stay out of the limelight, and during her childhood none of her friends except Carol had been invited to her home. Carol had only come over a few times, and that was always whenever Sinda's father was gone.

Thinking about her friend reminded Sinda that Carol had promised to come over after work today and help her paint the kitchen cabinets. After lunch she would go to the nearest hardware store and buy some paint.

Sinda knew Glen probably could paint the cabinets much faster and probably a whole lot neater than she or Carol, but she couldn't ask for his help. . .not after his daughter had seen them kissing and thrown such a fit. No matter how much it pained her, she had to keep her distance.

Glen paced back and forth in front of the counter at the hardware store, waiting for his brother to finish with a customer. He'd been promising himself for the last several weeks to repaint the barbecue and had decided to stop by Phil's Hardware on the way home from work and pick up what he needed for the project. He hoped to have several barbecues this summer and was getting a late start. *Too bad they won't include Sinda Shull,* he fumed inwardly. *I know the woman likes me, and she's just being stubborn, refusing to see me or even let me continue with the repairs on her home. If only there were some way I could convince her that my jealous daughter will eventually come*

around. I know Sinda has some issues she needs to resolve, but that's even more reason I should keep seeing her. I might be able to help.

"Hey, big brother, it's good to see you!"

Glen turned toward Phil, who was finally finished with his customer. He grabbed his brother in a bear hug. "It's good to see you too. It's been awhile, huh?"

Phil swiped a hand across his bearded chin and frowned. "I'll say. Where have you been keeping yourself, anyway?"

Glen was tempted to tell Phil about his new neighbor, and that up until a few weeks ago, he'd been helping Sinda with some repairs on her rambling old house, but he thought better of it. Phil was a confirmed bachelor, and whenever he discovered that Glen had dated any woman, Phil bombarded him with a bunch of wisecracks and unwanted advice.

"I've been busy." Glen nodded at Phil. "What's new in your life?"

Phil shrugged, and his blue eyes twinkled. "Until a few minutes ago, nothing was new."

Glen's interest was piqued. "What's that supposed to mean?"

"I've met the woman of my dreams," Phil said, running his fingers through his curly black hair. "She came in awhile ago, looking for some paint, and it was love at first sight."

Glen chuckled. How many times had he heard his goofy brother say he'd found the perfect woman, only to drop her flat when he became bored? Glen was sure this latest attraction would be no different than the others had been.

"You're not going to say anything?" Phil asked expectantly.

Glen shrugged his shoulders. "What would you like me to say?"

Phil wiggled his dark, bushy eyebrows, and Glen had a vision of his kid brother as an enormous teddy bear. "How about, 'Wow, brother, that's great. When do I get to meet this woman of your dreams?'"

"Okay, okay," Glen said, laughing. "When do I get to meet her?"

Phil turned his hands palm up. "Maybe you already have. She's your next-door neighbor."

Glen felt his jaw drop. "Sinda Shull?"

Phil nodded. "Like I said, she came in looking for some paint for her kitchen, and we got to talking. She told me she wants a new screen for her back door, and since the size she needs is out of stock, I promised to order one today and deliver it to her house as soon as it comes in." He smiled triumphantly. "That's how I got her address and discovered she lives next door to you. Small world, isn't it?"

"Too small if you ask me," Glen mumbled as he moved toward the front door.

"Hey, where are you going?"

"Home. Tara's probably starving, and I need to get dinner started."

"But you never said what you came in for."

Glen hunched his shoulders and offered his brother a halfhearted wave. "I came by for some heat-resistant paint, but it can wait. See you later, Phil." He left the hardware store feeling like someone had punched him in the stomach. Not only had Sinda decided to do some painting without his help, but she'd gone to his brother's store to buy the paint. As if that wasn't bad enough, Phil suddenly had a big crush on a woman he didn't even know, and he was obviously looking forward to delivering Sinda's new screen door. Glen loved his little brother, but he cared too much for Sinda to let her be taken in by Phil the Pill. He would do whatever it took to prevent her from being hurt. Trouble was, with her refusing to see him, he didn't have a clue what he could do other than pray. "That's it," he muttered under his breath. "I'll pray for answers until they come."

Tara let out a low whistle. "Wow! Take a look at this, Dad!"

"What is it?" Glen asked as he continued to chop mushrooms for the omelet he was making.

"Our weirdo neighbor lady made the newspaper. Listen to what it says: 'Doll Doctor Has Heavy Caseload.'" Tara stifled a giggle behind the paper. "Pretty impressive, huh?"

Glen wiped his hands on a paper towel and sauntered over to the kitchen table. "Let me see that." He snatched the newspaper out of Tara's hands. "I want you to stop referring to Sinda as 'our weirdo neighbor lady.' She's not weird!" He was still upset over the conversation he'd had with Phil the day before, and he didn't need anything else to get riled about.

Tara shook her head. "She plays with dolls, Dad. Don't you think that's kinda weird?"

"No, I don't, and how many times must I remind you what the Bible says about loving our neighbor?"

Tara shrugged. "I know, but—"

"Sinda is kind, sensitive, and reserved." Glen frowned. "And she doesn't play with dolls; she repairs them." His eyes quickly scanned the article about Sinda Shull who'd recently opened a doll hospital in the basement of her home. The story went on to say that almost any doll, no matter how old or badly damaged, could be repaired by an expert such as Doll Doctor Shull. There was a picture of Sinda sitting at her workbench, sanding a wooden doll head.

"She looks great," Glen murmured.

Tara groaned. "Where's Sinda been lately? I haven't seen her since I finished my punishment in her creepy basement. She hasn't been around making eyes at you, and it makes me wonder what's up."

Methodically, Glen pulled on his left earlobe. He knew exactly how long it had been since he'd last talked to Sinda. He'd seen her a few times out in the yard, but whenever he tried to make conversation, she always concocted some lame excuse to go back inside. Just when he and Sinda seemed to be getting closer, she'd pulled away. He didn't like this hot and cold stuff. *Well, maybe it's for the best. Even though Sinda says she's a Christian, she doesn't want anything to do with church. It might be better for all concerned if I bow out graciously.*

He shook his head, hoping to clear away the troubling thoughts. Who was he kidding? He didn't want to let Sinda walk out of his life. She was afraid of something, and it was probably more than concern over Tara's reaction to their relationship. Besides, he had to protect Sinda from his little brother. Phil might look like a teddy bear, but he acted more like a grizzly bear.

"Dad, are you listening to me?"

Glen lifted both elbows and flexed his shoulders as he stretched, then dropped the newspaper to the table. "What were you saying?"

"I asked about Sinda. Why do you think she hasn't been around lately?"

"I'm sure she's been busy." He pointed to the newspaper. "That article even says so."

"I guess a lot of people have broken dolls, huh?"

Glen gave a noncommittal grunt, thinking of the doll he'd given Sinda to repair. He wondered if she would still make good on it, even though she'd changed her mind and wouldn't allow him to do any more repairs on her house. If she did finish repairing it, he would gladly pay her whatever it cost.

"I'm sure happy I don't have to help in that doll hospital anymore." Tara looked at him pointedly. "It was awful!"

"I thought you liked fixing broken dolls."

"It was okay at first, but that house is creepy and full of strange noises. Besides, I don't like Sinda. She's w— I mean, different."

"God created each of us differently," Glen said patiently. "The world would be a boring place if we were all alike."

Tara scrunched up her nose. "Sinda is way different."

"Are you sure you aren't jealous?" Glen asked, taking a seat at the table.

"Why would I be?"

He raised his eyebrows. "Maybe you're envious of the attention I've shown Sinda."

"You can't help yourself because she's got you hypnotized with those green cat's eyes."

"Don't start with that again."

Tara held up both hands. "Okay, okay. I'm just glad Sinda hasn't been hanging around. I'm happy you're not going over there anymore, either."

"It's your fault I'm not," Glen blurted without thinking.

Tara flinched, making him feel like a rotten father. "What do you mean, it's my fault?"

"One of the reasons—probably the main one—Sinda won't see me anymore, is because she thinks you don't like her."

"She's right about that," Tara muttered. "I'm glad she's not around anymore."

"Tara Mae Olsen, that's an awful thing to say!" He leveled her with a look he hoped would make her realize the seriousness of the situation. "In the book of Proverbs we are told that he who despises his neighbor, sins."

"I don't despise Sinda, Dad. It's just that I know she's after you." Tara grabbed hold of his shirtsleeve. "She's trying to win you over with compliments and flirty looks."

"Flirty looks? What would a little girl know about flirty looks?"

She grinned at him. "I'm not a baby, you know."

Glen smiled, in spite of his irritation. "That's right, you're not." He patted the top of her head. "So try not to act like one."

Chapter Fourteen

As Glen knelt on the patio to begin scraping the rusted paint off his barbecue, he heard a noisy vehicle pull into Sinda's driveway. He straightened, rubbed the kinks out of his back, and moved casually around the side of the house. He didn't want to be seen or have anyone get the idea he was spying, so he crouched down by his front porch and peeked into Sinda's yard. It was just as he feared. . .a truck bearing the name PHIL'S HARDWARE was parked in her driveway, and Phil the Pill was climbing down from the driver's seat. Glen watched as his brother went around to the back of the pickup and withdrew a screen door. He whistled as he walked toward Sinda's front door, and it was all Glen could do to keep from jumping up, dashing through the gate, and grabbing Phil by the shirttail.

That would be ridiculous, Glen reprimanded himself. *It's a free country, and my brother's only doing his job. If Sinda ordered the screen door, Phil has every right to deliver it.*

"Why don't you use my binoculars, Dad?"

Glen whirled around at the sound of his daughter's voice. "Tara, you scared me! Why are you sneaking up on me like that?"

Tara snickered. "It looks like you were spying on someone." She shook her head and clicked her tongue. "Is it Sinda?"

Glen stood up straight and faced his daughter. "I wasn't spying on Sinda."

"Who then?"

"Uncle Phil."

Tara's forehead wrinkled. "Huh?"

Glen took Tara by the arm and led her around back, so they wouldn't be overheard. "I heard a vehicle pull into Sinda's driveway, and I thought I recognized the sound of Uncle Phil's truck. So, I went around front to check it out, and sure enough, he's delivering a new screen door to Sinda."

"That's good. Her old one was about to fall."

Glen opened his mouth to comment, but Tara cut him off. "Why don't we go over and tell Uncle Phil hello? We haven't seen him in ages."

He smiled. For once Tara had a good idea, and since this was her idea, Glen had a legitimate excuse to see Sinda.

Sinda came upstairs at the sound of a truck in her driveway, then peeked out the living room window. "Ah, my screen door has arrived." She hurried to open the front door, and Phil from Phil's Hardware met her on the porch. He leaned the screen door against the side of the house and grinned. "Where do you want this beauty?"

"Around back, please."

Phil hoisted it again like it weighed no more than a feather and stepped off the porch. Sinda followed.

"You got anyone lined up to install this?" Phil asked when they reached the backyard.

Install it? Sinda hadn't even thought about how she would replace her old screen with the new one. She gnawed on her lower lip as she contemplated the problem. "I guess I could try to put it up myself." Even as the words slipped off her tongue, Sinda realized it was a bad idea. She knew as much about putting up a screen door as a child understood the mechanics of driving a car.

"I'd be happy to install it for you," Phil offered as he set it down, leaning it against the porch railing. "In fact, I've got my helper working at the store all afternoon, so I could do it now if you like."

"How much would you charge?"

Phil shrugged his broad shoulders and gave her a lopsided grin. "Tell you what, I'll put up the door while I work up the nerve to ask you out to dinner."

Sinda swallowed hard. "Dinner?"

"Yeah, maybe some beer and pizza. I know this great place—"

She held up her hand. "I don't drink alcoholic beverages. I also don't go out with men I hardly know." *Except Glen Olsen,* her conscience reminded. *You went out with Glen a few weeks after you met.*

Phil took a step toward Sinda. "We introduced ourselves when you came into my store the other day, and sharing dinner would give us a chance to get better acquainted." He winked at her, and she was about to reply when Glen and Tara came bounding into the yard.

"Hey, brother, I heard the unmistakable rumble of your truck and thought I'd come over and say hi." Glen gave Phil a hearty slap on the back, then he turned to face Sinda.

She eyed him curiously. "You and Phil are brothers?" Except for the dark hair and blue eyes, the two men didn't look anything alike. Glen was slender and clean-shaven while Phil was stocky and sported a full beard. He also had a cocky attitude, which was the total opposite of Glen.

Before Glen could answer Sinda's question, Tara spoke up. "Uncle Phil's Dad's little brother." She looked up at her uncle and gave his loose shirttail a good yank. "How come you haven't been over to see us in such a long time?"

"Guess I've been too busy to socialize," Phil said, tugging on Tara's ponytail in response. His gaze swung back to Sinda, and he gave her another flirtatious wink. "I'm hoping to remedy that now that I've met your beautiful new neighbor." He glanced at his brother, and Sinda noticed that Glen wasn't smiling. In fact, he looked downright irritated.

"I plan to install Sinda's new screen door, then she's going out to dinner with me," Phil remarked with a smirk.

Sinda opened her mouth, but she never got a word out. "Is that so?" Glen interrupted. "Don't you have a store to run?"

Phil tucked his thumbs inside his jeans pockets and rocked back and forth on his heels. "Gabe's workin' for me all day, so I can spare a few minutes to put up Sinda's door." He reached out and grabbed hold of the screen, still leaning against the porch railing.

Before he could take a step, Glen seized the door and jerked it right out of Phil's hands. "Sinda hired me to do some repairs on her house in exchange for—" Glen paused and glanced down at his daughter. "Uh, I mean—I agreed to help her out, so putting up the screen door is my job."

Phil looked at Sinda, then back at Glen. "She said she had nobody to install the screen, and I volunteered."

"Is that a fact?"

Phil nodded and reached for the screen door.

Sinda wasn't sure what she should do or say. Glen and Phil were arguing over who would complete the task, but she had a feeling the tug-of-war had more to do with her than it did the door. She'd never had two men fight for her attention before, and it was a bit unnerving.

"I've got an idea," Tara interjected. "Dad, why don't you and Uncle Phil both put Sinda's screen door up? That way the job will get done twice as fast."

Glen shrugged. "I guess we could do that."

Phil nodded. "You know what they say—four hands are better than two."

"I think that's 'two heads are better than one,' Uncle Phil." Tara giggled and jabbed her uncle in the ribs.

He chortled. "Yeah, whatever."

A thought popped into Sinda's head, and she wondered why the idea hadn't come to her sooner. "I'll appreciate the help no matter who sets the screen door in place, but I won't be going out with anyone. I've got some work to do. So if you men will excuse me, I'm going downstairs to my workshop." With that, she stepped into the house and closed the door.

It was another warm Saturday, and Glen was outside mowing his lawn. He waved at Tara, who was across the street visiting her friend Penny, then he stopped to fill the mower with gas. A bloodcurdling scream, which sounded like it had come from Sinda's house, halted his actions.

Sinda's terrier, Sparky, was yapping through the fence, and Glen turned his head in that direction. Maybe Sinda had come face-to-face with an intruder. She might be hurt and in need of his help. *Maybe that goofy brother of mine is back, and he's bugging Sinda to go out with him again.*

With no further thought, Glen tore open the gate and raced into Sinda's backyard, nearly tripping over the black dog. There was another shrill scream, and Glen was sure it was coming from Sinda's basement. He made a dash for the door and gave the handle a firm yank. It didn't budge. "Must be locked," he muttered. He pounded on the door, calling out Sinda's name.

The door flew open, and Sinda threw herself into his arms. Glen felt like his heart had jumped right into his throat. Something was terribly wrong. "What is it? What happened down there?"

"I think Tara may be right about this spooky old house being haunted," she said with a deep moan.

Glen held her at arm's length as he studied her tear-streaked face. Sinda's deadpan expression and quivering lower lip told him how serious she was. *At least my bear of a brother wasn't the reason for her panic.* "Tell me what happened," he said as he took hold of her trembling hand.

She hiccuped. "A doll head. I saw a doll head."

"You screamed loud enough to wake a sleeping hound dog, and you're telling me it was just a doll head that scared you?" Glen knew women were prone to hysterics, but this was ridiculous.

"It was in my freezer," Sinda whimpered. "I found a vinyl doll head in the freezer."

Glen stood there several seconds, trying to digest this strange piece of information. He could understand what a shock it would be to open the freezer, fully intending to retrieve a package of meat, and discover a doll head staring back at him instead. "Someone's probably playing a trick on you." Glen's thoughts went immediately to his daughter, even though Tara hadn't been working in Sinda's doll hospital for several weeks. Unless she planted it there on her last day. "How long has it been since you opened the freezer?"

She shrugged. "A week—maybe two."

"Are you sure? It hasn't been any longer?"

"I think I took some ice cream out last Saturday." She nodded and swiped her hand across her chin. "Yes, that's the last time I opened it."

"And there was no doll head then?"

"I'm sure there wasn't."

A feeling of relief washed over Glen. He didn't see how it could have been Tara. He led Sinda into the basement. "Is the doll head still in the freezer?"

"Yes. When I first saw it, I screamed and slammed the door. Then I thought I must have been seeing things, so I opened the freezer again, but it was still there." She leaned heavily against him and drew in a shuddering breath. "I heard someone pounding on the basement door, and when I opened it and saw you, I kind of fell apart."

And right into my arms, Glen thought with a wry smile. At least something good came out of this whole weird experience. "Why don't you show me the doll?" he suggested.

Sinda gripped Glen's hand tightly as she led the way to the utility room. "Would you mind opening the freezer? I don't think I have the strength."

Glen grasped the handle and jerked the freezer door open. A round head with brown painted hair and bright blue eyes stared back at him. It was so creepy he almost let out a yelp himself. He reached inside to remove the icy-cold doll head. "Looks a little chilly, doesn't it?"

"I've been looking everywhere for that!" Sinda exclaimed. "It and several other doll parts have been missing for a few weeks."

Glen scratched the back of his head. "Hmm. . .sounds like a bit of a mystery to me. Maybe we should put Detective Tara Mae Olsen on the case. She'd love something as weird as this to sink her teeth into."

Sinda was obviously not amused by his comment. She was scared to death, and it showed clearly on her ashen face. Glen placed the doll head on top of the dryer and drew her into his arms. It felt so right to hold her like this. Too bad she didn't realize how good they could be for each other.

"Glen—"

"Sinda—"

Glen chuckled. "Go ahead."

"No, you first."

"I know there has to be a simple answer to this whole thing."

She looked up at him expectantly. "What could it be?"

He shrugged. "I don't know. Do you think you could have accidentally put the head into the freezer? I've done some pretty strange things when I'm preoccupied." He grinned. "Like putting dishwasher soap in the refrigerator instead of the cupboard."

She gave him a weak smile. "I know everyone is absentminded at times, but I don't even remember picking the doll head up, much less putting it in the freezer. Besides, what about the other missing doll parts?"

Glen frowned. "Maybe you misplaced them. I do that with my car keys a lot."

"You think I'm getting forgetful in my old age?"

"Hardly," he said with a wink. "Seriously, though, even if I'm not sure what's going on with the doll parts, I don't want anything to happen to our friendship." He brushed her cheek with the back of his hand. "I know you said you didn't want to see me anymore, but I'm hoping you'll reconsider. Please don't let Tara's resistance be a deciding factor."

Sinda licked her lips. "I want to see you, Glen, but it's not a good idea."

"Why not?"

"There are things in my past that prevent me from making a commitment to you—or any other man."

His eyebrows arched. "Are you trying to tell me that you lied about not being married?"

"No, of course not! I'm as single as any woman could be."

"And you're a Christian?"

Sinda nodded. "I am, but—"

"Then what's the problem?" Glen's finger curved under her trembling chin, and she met his gaze with a look that went straight to his heart. He felt as if her pain was his, and he wondered what he could do to help ease her discomfort. Instinctively, he bent his head to kiss her. When they broke away, he whispered, "I don't care about your past, Sinda. If you're a Christian, and you care for me, that's all that counts. We can work through any problems you have from your past." He kissed the tip of her nose. "No matter what you say, I'm not giving up on you. So there!"

Chapter Fifteen

"Where do we go from here?" Sinda asked Glen as she took a chair directly across from him.

Glen rapped his knuckles on the kitchen table and looked thoughtful. "I want to get to the bottom of the missing doll parts, but first I think we need to figure out some way to get our relationship back on track."

"I let you put up my screen door," she reminded.

"I'm talking about our personal relationship."

A film of tears obscured her vision. "But, Glen—"

He held up one hand. "I know. You have secrets from your past and can't make any kind of commitment."

She nodded in response and clasped her hands around her knees to keep them from shaking.

"We all have things from our past that we'd like to forget," he said softly. "But God doesn't want us to dwell on the past. So why don't we pray about this, then we'll deal with one problem at a time." He paused and flicked a crumb off the table. "I think it might help to talk about what's troubling you before we pray."

She counted on her fingers. "Lost doll parts. . .a vinyl head in the freezer. . . how's that for starters?"

He nodded. "We'll take care of that in good time, but right now we need to deal with the reason you won't allow me into your life."

Sinda wiped away the unwanted tears she felt on her cheeks and avoided his gaze. Silence wove around her, filling up the space between them. "I–I haven't dated much, and I've never been in love. Even the thought of it scares me." She swallowed hard. "I'm not sure I could ever love a man, so there's no point in leading you on."

"What are you afraid of, Sinda?"

"I'm afraid of love. I'm afraid of being hurt."

Glen's thumb stroked the top of her hand, and her skin tingled with each feathery touch. "Who are you angry with?" he coaxed.

Sinda jerked her hand away. Glen was treading on dangerous territory now. "What makes you think I'm angry?"

He leaned forward and studied her intently. "It's written all over your face. I hear it in the tone of your voice."

"Your daughter thinks she's a detective, and now you're moonlighting as a psychologist," she said sarcastically.

"I'm only trying to help, but I can't if you won't let me."

Sinda's nerves were tight like a rubber band. Angry, troubled thoughts tumbled around in her head, and she stared off into space. She wanted to run, to hide, and never have to deal with her pain. "My mother! I'm angry with my mother!" Sinda's hand went instinctively to her mouth. She hadn't meant to say that. It wasn't for Glen to know.

Glen seemed unaffected by her outrage. "What did your mother do?" he prompted.

Sinda sniffed deeply. She'd already let the cat out of the bag, so she may as well get the rest off her chest. "She left my father when I was ten years old."

"Left him? You mean she died?"

Sinda shook her head, swallowing back the pain and humiliation. "She walked out."

"Was there another man involved?"

A shuddering sigh escaped Sinda's trembling lips, and she was powerless to stop it. "No!" She gulped in a deep breath. "At least, I don't think so. She left us a note, but it didn't explain her reason for abandoning us. Her message said only that she was going and would never come back. There was no other explanation—not even an apology." Sinda picked at an imaginary piece of fuzz on her peach-colored T-shirt. "Mother was there when I went to bed one night, and she was gone the next morning when I awoke."

Glen reached for her hand again, and this time she didn't pull away. "I'm so sorry, Sinda."

"My father was devastated by her betrayal, and he. . ." Her voice trailed off. How could she explain about Dad? She'd never fully understood him herself.

"I'm sure it must have been hard on both you and your father," Glen acknowledged. "If you're ready, I'd like to pray now, then we can talk some more."

She shrugged. "I–I guess so."

With her hand held firmly in his, Sinda bowed her head. "Dear Lord," Glen prayed, "Sinda has some pain from her past that needs to be healed. We know You are the Great Physician and it's within Your power to heal physically and emotionally. Please touch Sinda's heart and let her feel Your presence. Help us get to the bottom of the missing doll parts, and we thank You in advance for Your answers. Amen."

When Sinda opened her eyes, she was able to offer Glen a brief smile. She felt a bit better after his beseeching prayer. It was a relief to have him know some of her past, and it was comforting to sit with him here in her kitchen. "Whenever anyone asks about Mother, I sort of leave the impression that she died," she said with a shrug of her shoulders. "To me she is dead. I hate what she did to Dad."

"To your dad?" Glen exclaimed. "What about what she did to you? Have you ever dealt with that?"

Sinda shook her head. "I try not to think about it. Dad was all I had, and until he died, I devoted my whole life to him." She gulped and tried to regain her composure. "I hadn't thought about Mother in years. Not until that stupid trunk arrived. It was hers, but I thought Dad threw it out after she left."

"Have you looked through it yet? It might help heal some of your pain."

Sinda jumped up and began pacing the floor. "I still can't find a key that fits the lock. My lawyer said Dad wanted me to have the trunk, but he didn't give him a key."

"I'm sure the lock can be broken. I'd be happy to do it for you," Glen offered.

Sinda stopped pacing and turned to face him. "I'm not sure I want to look at her things. I've spent most of my life trying to forget my mother. She wanted out of our lives and never made any effort to contact us, so why should I care about anything that belonged to her?"

"I'll stay with you. We can deal with this together."

"What about the missing doll parts?" Sinda grasped the back of a chair and grimaced. "I thought we were going to get to the bottom of that problem."

He nodded. "We are, but right now I think you should look through the trunk."

She held up her hands in defeat. "Okay, let's get this over with."

Sinda clicked on the overhead light in the storage room upstairs, and the bulky trunk came into view. She couldn't believe she'd actually told Glen the story of how Mother had abandoned her and Dad. It was a secret she'd promised never to share with anyone. Even her best friend Carol didn't know the truth. *Glen Olsen must have a powerful effect on me.*

Glen knelt beside the trunk and studied the lock. "I'd better go home and get a hacksaw." He glanced up at Sinda. "Unless you have one."

She shook her head. "I don't think so. After Dad died, I sold most of his tools. All I kept were the basics—a hammer, screwdriver, and a few other small items."

"Okay. I'll be back in a flash." Glen stood up. Her face lifted to meet his gaze, and she wanted to melt in the warmth of his sapphire-blue eyes. "If you're nervous about being here alone, you're welcome to come along," he said, giving her shoulder a gentle squeeze.

"I'll be okay—as long as I stay away from the basement."

Glen dropped a kiss to her forehead, then he was gone. She stared down at the trunk and, giving her thoughts free rein, an image of her mother came to mind. Sinda closed her eyes, trying to shut out the vision, but her mother's face, so much like her own, was as clear as the antique crystal vase sitting on her fireplace mantel.

"You did this to me, Mother," Sinda sobbed. "Why couldn't you let the past stay in the past?" She trembled. Was there something wrong with her? Hadn't Dad accused her of being just like Mother? Hadn't he told her that if she didn't exercise control over her emotions, she'd end up hurting some poor unsuspecting man, the way Mother had hurt him?

In spite of the pain he'd often inflicted upon her, Sinda's heart ached for her dad. He'd been the victim of his wife's abandonment. Marla Shull had given no thought to anyone but herself, leaving him to care for their only child. *What a heartless thing to do,* Sinda thought bitterly. *Mother couldn't have felt any love for me, or you, either, Dad. You don't walk out on someone you love.*

Sinda leaned over and fingered the lock on the trunk. "You made Dad the way he was, Mother, and I'm the one who suffered for it." *If only I hadn't been so much like you. If only. . .*

The prayer Glen prayed earlier replayed itself in her mind. It seemed like a genuine prayer—a plea to God for help. Dad's prayers always seemed genuine too—at least those he prayed at church meetings.

Sinda thought about the last time she'd gone to church. It was the night before Dad's heart attack, and they'd gone to a revival service. She would never forget the sight of her father kneeling at the altar during the close of the meeting. Had it been for show, like all the other times, or was Dad truly repentant for his sins?

Her mind took her back to the evening before the revival, when she and Dad had argued about the steak she'd fixed for dinner. He said it was overly done, and she'd tried to explain that the oven was too hot and needed repairing. She could still see the hostility on Dad's face when his hand connected to the side of her head. She could feel the pain and humiliation as she rushed to her room in tears.

That night at church, with Dad lying prostrate before the wooden altar, Sinda had been convinced that his display of emotions was only for attention, and at that moment, she vowed never to step inside another church. There were hypocrites there, and even those who weren't didn't seem able to discern when someone was physically and emotionally abusing their daughter. Whenever Dad walked into the sanctuary, he put on his "Mr. Christian" mask, but it fell off the moment they returned home.

Sinda hated her father's cruel treatment and hypocrisy at church, but she hated herself even more. After all, it was because she reminded him so much of her mother that Dad treated her the way he did.

Glen entered the room again, carrying a small hacksaw, and Sinda was thankful for the interruption. She'd spent enough time reliving the past and its painful memories.

"It's time to go to work," Glen announced. He knelt beside the trunk and quickly put the saw to good use. A few minutes later the lock snapped in two and fell to the floor with a thud.

Sinda took a deep breath to steady her nerves, and Glen moved aside. "You can open it now."

She knelt in front of the trunk, grasped the handle, and slowly opened the lid. There were a few items of clothing on top—a faded bridal veil, several lace handkerchiefs, and a delicate satin christening gown with a matching bonnet. Sinda fingered the soft material, remembering pictures that proved it had been her own. She moved the clothes aside and continued to explore.

"Would you rather be alone?" Glen asked, offering her a sympathetic smile.

She gazed at him through her pain and confusion. "No, please stay. I need the moral support."

He reached out and touched her arm. "I'll be here as long as you need me."

There was a small, green velvet box underneath the clothes. Sinda opened it, revealing several pieces of jewelry she recognized as her mother's. She placed the jewelry box and the clothes on a chair, then carried on with her search through the trunk. A few seconds later, she pulled out an old photo album. "There's probably a lot of pictures in here, and I'd like to look at them. Maybe we should go downstairs where it's more comfortable."

Glen shrugged. "Tara's spending the day with her friend across the street, so you've got me all to yourself."

"Let's go to the living room." She stood, then moved quickly toward the door.

They sat on the couch for over an hour, going through the album and talking about Sinda's childhood before her mother walked out.

"Your mother was a beautiful woman," Glen remarked. "You look a lot like her."

"I do have her green eyes and auburn hair," Sinda agreed. She drew in a deep breath and let it out in a rush. "Dad used to say I had her personality too."

"I'm sure he meant it as a compliment."

Sinda snapped the album shut, nearly catching his fingers inside. "He didn't mean it that way at all! He meant it as a warning. He used to tell me that if I wasn't careful, I'd end up wrecking some poor man's life the way Mother ruined his."

"You didn't believe him, I hope."

She bit down hard on her bottom lip, until she tasted blood. "I had no reason not to."

Glen took her hand and gave it a gentle squeeze. " 'Who can discern their own errors? Forgive my hidden faults,' " he said softly.

She tipped her head to one side. "What?"

"It's a quote from the book of Psalms," he explained, "and it means—"

"Never mind," she said, cutting him off. She placed the album on the coffee table and stood up. "I've had enough reminiscing for one day. I'd really like to look for those missing doll parts."

"Let's start in the basement," Glen suggested.

She was glad he hadn't kept prying into her past. There was too much pain there to deal with right now.

Glen led the way, and when they reached their destination, Sinda turned on a light in the room where she worked. "As you can see," she said, motioning with her hand, "I keep the dolls that come in for repairs on the shelf marked EMERGENCY ROOM."

Glen whistled. "Pretty impressive!"

"I use the metal table in the center of the room to do the work, then when a doll is done, I place it over there." She pointed to a shelf labeled RECOVERY ROOM.

"What about the parts and supplies you use for repairing? Where do you keep those?"

"Right there." She indicated another row of shelves on the opposite wall.

Glen nodded. "Are the missing pieces from a particular doll patient or from your supply of parts?"

"From my supply. Why do you ask?"

"Isn't it possible that you've already used the missing parts to repair some doll? Maybe you forgot which ones you used and thought they were still in a box. It could be that they're not really missing at all."

"There's just one flaw in your theory, Glen."

"What's that?"

"I keep good track of my inventory. To have three or four different parts missing at the same time doesn't add up."

Glen shrugged his shoulders. "It was only an idea."

"And let's not forget about that doll head in the freezer," Sinda reminded.

"How could I? It even gave me the creeps." He clapped his hands together. "Let's get to work. Those parts have to be down here someplace."

Chapter Sixteen

The search for the missing doll parts turned up nothing. Glen was a bit frustrated, but Sinda seemed to be filled with despair. They'd given up for the day and left the basement for the comfort of her living room, and now Glen sat on the couch with his arm draped across her shoulders. "I'm sorry we didn't find anything. I can't figure it out."

Sinda lifted her head slightly and looked at him. "It's not your fault."

"We still have no doll parts, and from the way you're looking at me, I'd say I haven't done much to help alleviate your fears."

"Just having you here has helped."

They sat in silence for a while, then Glen came up with a plan. "Since being down in the basement makes you so uptight, why not let me come over and give you a hand?"

Her forehead wrinkled. "Doing what?"

"Repairing dolls. I'm sure there's something I can do to help."

"Are you teasing me?"

He saw the skepticism in her squinted eyes and shook his head. "Who knows, it might even prove to be kind of fun."

"Oh Glen," Sinda said shakily, "that's such a sweet offer, but—"

"I can come over every evening for a few hours, and on the Saturdays I'm not on my mail route."

"I couldn't let you do that."

"Why not? Are you afraid I'll make your doll patients even sicker?" he asked with a grin.

"It's not that. I'm sure you'd do fine, but you've got your own life. You have responsibilities to your daughter."

"Maybe Tara could tag along," he suggested.

"You two have better things to do than repair dolls and hold my shaking hand. Just because I'm acting like a big chicken doesn't mean you have to babysit me." Sinda paused as she slid her tongue across her lower lip. "Besides, you can't always be down there with me."

"Why not? I'd gladly spend my free time helping if it would make you feel better."

"I go to the basement for lots of things that don't involve doll repairing," she reminded him. "My washer and dryer are down there, and so is my freezer."

Glen lifted Sinda's chin with his thumb. "I think I'm falling in love with you, and I believe God brought you to Elmwood for a purpose," he said, changing the subject.

She opened her mouth to say something, but he touched her lips with the tips of his fingers and whispered, "If we give this relationship a chance, we might even have a future together."

Sinda sat up straight, her back rigid, and her lips set in a thin line. "We can't have a future together, Glen. I can't love you."

"Can't, or won't?"

She averted his steady gaze. "I want to love you, but I can't. My life is all mixed up, and my past would always be in our way. Please don't pressure me."

The depth of sadness he saw reflected in her green eyes made his stomach clench, and he nodded in mock defeat. "I'll drop the subject." *For now, anyway.*

It had been three days since Sinda found the doll head in the freezer, and three days since Glen had declared his feelings for her. He'd phoned several times, and he'd come over twice to see how she was doing. She'd assured him that everything was fine, but it was a lie. How could anything be fine when she had doll parts unaccounted for and love burning in her heart for a man with whom she could never have a future?

Sinda had only been to the basement twice in the last three days. Once to retrieve clothes from the dryer, and another time to bring up a doll that needed some work. She planned to put the finishing touches on the painted face while working at her kitchen table. She knew she couldn't keep it up forever, but for now, until her nerves settled down, she'd do more of the doll repairs upstairs, only going to the basement to get necessary items or do laundry.

A Girl Scout leader had called yesterday, wanting to bring her troop to the doll hospital as a field trip. Sinda turned her down, saying she was too busy right now. The truth was, the idea of having a bunch of inquisitive girls roaming around her basement would have been too much to handle.

In spite of Sinda's emotional state, she had managed to go to a local swap meet this morning where she'd sold a few antiques and picked up some old doll parts. She'd even met with two new customers who wanted dolls restored before Christmas.

Her chores were done for the day now, and she stood in the spare bedroom, prepared to check out the rest of the contents of her mother's trunk. She glanced around the room. Everything was exactly as she'd left it on Saturday. The jewelry box and items of clothing were still on the chair. The trunk lid was closed, though no longer locked.

She ground her teeth together and opened the lid. Did she really want to do this? An inner voice seemed to be urging her on. With trembling hands she withdrew a white Bible, which had her mother's name engraved in gold letters on the front cover. A burgundy bookmark hung partway out, and Sinda opened it to the marked page. "Psalm 19:12. 'Who can discern their own errors? Forgive my hidden faults,'" she read aloud. She could hardly believe it was the same verse Glen had quoted to her the other day. "Mother must have felt guilty about something," she muttered. *Was Glen trying to tell me that I shouldn't feel guilty about anything, or was he referring to Dad? God knows, he had plenty to feel guilty about, but he always made me feel remorseful because I reminded him of Mother.*

Sinda closed the Bible and placed it on the chair next to the jewelry box and clothes. She reached inside the trunk and withdrew a small, black diary. It was fastened with a miniature padlock, but Sinda knew she could easily pry it open.

She went downstairs to the kitchen and took a pair of needle-nosed pliers from a drawer, then dropped to a seat at the table. In short order she had the lock open. *Would this be considered an invasion of privacy?* she wondered. *How could it be? Mother's gone, and after what she did to Dad and me, I have every right to read it.*

She opened the diary to the first entry, dated October 30, just a few days after Sinda's third birthday. With one hand cupped under her chin, she began to read.

Dear Diary:
Today I received some wonderful news. A visit to the doctor confirmed
my suspicions—I'm pregnant again. The baby is due the middle of
April. It will be nice for Sinda to have a sibling. Another child might
be good for our marriage too. William was thrilled with the news. He
wants a boy this time.

Sinda felt a headache coming on, and she began to rub her forehead in slow, circular motions. "Mother was pregnant when I was three years old? I'm an only child. What happened to the baby?"
She read on, finding the next entry dated several months later.

Dear Diary:
Christmas is behind us for another year. This was probably one of the
happiest holidays we've ever had. We had friends over for dinner,
and all William could talk about was the child we're expecting in the
spring. Sometimes my husband can be a bit harsh, but I'm hoping our
baby will soften his heart.

The pain in Sinda's head escalated, and she wondered if she should quit reading and go to bed. A part of her wanted to escape from the past, but another part needed to know what happened to the child her mother had carried—the one her father hoped was a boy; so she read on.

Dear Diary:
My heart feels as though it is breaking in two. A terrible thing
happened, and I wonder if I'll ever recover from the pain. I gave birth
to William Shull Jr. one week ago, but he lived only three days, never
leaving the confines of his tiny incubator. The child was born two
months prematurely, and William is inconsolable. He blames me for
the baby's death and says I did too much during my pregnancy. He's

convinced that if I'd rested more the child would not have come early.

Sinda covered her mouth with her hand as she choked on a sob. She'd had a baby brother! A child she'd never met and had no memory of. That in itself was painful, but the stark reality of her father wanting a son and blaming her mother for denying him the right was a terrible blow. She wrapped her arms around her stomach and bent into the pain. "Could this have been the reason Mother left?" she moaned. As the thought began to take hold, she reminded herself that she'd been ten years old when her mother abandoned them. That was seven years after William Jr. died. There had to be some other reason Mother had gone. Sinda was sure her only hope of discovering the truth lay in her mother's diary. She would get to the bottom of it, even if it took all night!

Sinda read the diary until the early morning hours, but the impact of her mother's final entry had been too much to bear. She'd fallen asleep on the couch, with the diary draped across her chest.

A resonant pounding roused her from a deep sleep. The diary fell to the floor as she clambered off the couch and staggered to the front door in a stupor. She wasn't aware that she'd spent the night in her blue jeans and sweatshirt, or that her eyes were bloodshot and her hair a disheveled mess until she glanced at her reflection in the hall mirror.

She opened the door and was surprised to see Glen standing on the front porch with a desperate look on his face. "Glen, what is it?"

His forehead wrinkled. "I need a favor, but I can see by looking at you that you're probably not the best one to ask."

"I didn't sleep well last night," she stated flatly.

"I'm sorry. Why didn't you call?"

She shrugged. "I'm fine now. What do you need?"

"A babysitter."

"What?" She stared at him blankly, trying to force the cobwebs out of her muddled brain.

"I need someone to watch Tara," Glen explained. "Mrs. Mayer phoned early this morning. She's sick with the flu."

"Won't Tara be in school all day?"

Glen shook his head. "She's off for the summer."

"Oh, I forgot." Sinda ran her fingers through her tangled hair, wishing she hadn't answered the door. "There's no point in you losing a whole day's pay. Send Tara over."

"I would have asked Penny's mother, Gwen, but they're on vacation at the beach this week. So if you're sure it wouldn't be too much of an inconvenience, I'd really appreciate your help today."

Of course it was inconvenient, but she would do it. Glen had done her plenty of favors, so turnabout was fair play. "It's fine. I had a bad night, but it won't keep me from watching Tara."

Glen's worried expression seemed to relax. "Thanks so much, Sinda." He touched her shoulder lightly. "How about coming over for supper tonight? I'll make my famous pasta, and I could fix a Caesar salad to go with it."

She reached up to rub the side of her unwashed face. "You're not obligated to cook for me, Glen. After walking your mail route all day you shouldn't have to come home and cook for me, anyway. Why don't you come over here tonight? I'll do the cooking."

"Are you sure you don't mind?"

She pushed an irritating lock of hair away from her face. "Positive."

He grinned. "You're wonderful. I'll send Tara over right away."

Glen leaned toward Sinda, and she thought he might be about to kiss her. She pulled quickly away when she remembered she hadn't yet brushed her teeth. "No problem. See you later."

He hesitated a moment, then with a wave of his hand, Glen turned and left. Sinda closed the door with a sigh, wishing she had time to shower and change before Tara arrived. A quick trip to the bathroom to wash her face and run a brush through her unruly curls was all she was able to manage before she heard another loud knock.

When Sinda opened the door Tara thrust a piece of paper into her hand. "Dad told me to come over here for the day and said I was supposed to give you this." The child was wearing a white blouse under a pair of green overalls, and she held a silver skateboard under the other arm.

Sinda motioned her inside and glanced at the document. It was a form giving Sinda permission to authorize emergency medical care for Tara. Great. "Uh, I'd rather you not do any skateboarding today."

Tara frowned. "Why not? I skateboard all the time."

"I know. I've watched you out front, and you've taken a few spills. You're in my care today, so I won't be responsible for you getting hurt."

Tara ambled into the living room and flopped onto the couch, wrapping her arms tightly around the skateboard, as though it were some kind of lifeline. "You're not my mother, you know. I don't have to do what you say."

Sinda felt her irritation begin to mount. She'd discovered some terrible things yesterday, spent a restless night on the couch, had been awakened by a desperate man, and now this? She was near the end of her rope, and one more good tug would probably cause it to snap right in two. She clenched her teeth and leveled Tara with what she hoped was a look of authority. "Your dad asked me to watch you today. This is my house, and I'll make the decisions. Is that clear?"

Tara nodded and dropped the skateboard to the floor. "What am I supposed to do all day?"

"Maybe we can work on some dolls." Sinda feigned a smile. "You did such a good job helping before."

Tara shrugged. "I never did anything that great. Besides, dolls are for kids."

"No, they're not," Sinda countered. "Lots of grown women, and even some men, collect dolls. Some are worth a lot of money. As you well know, many of the ones I repair are for collectors and antique dealers."

"I saw your picture in the paper a few weeks ago," Tara said, changing the subject. "That must have been really great for business."

Sinda nodded. "It was good advertisement. Several people have brought in dolls they want restored for Christmas."

"Christmas is a long ways off."

"Some dolls need lots of work. It takes time to repair them."

Tara wrinkled her nose. "People give away old dolls as presents?"

"Often a parent or grandparent will have a doll from their childhood that they want to pass on to a younger family member." Sinda took a seat in the overstuffed chair directly across from Tara. *I wonder if the girl knows anything about the doll her father asked me to fix.* "Did your mother have any dolls?" she casually questioned.

The child shrugged her shoulders. "I wouldn't know. I was only a year old when she died. I thought you knew that."

Sinda felt her face flush. Of course she knew it, but she wasn't about to tell Tara why she was fishing for information. Learning whether she knew about the doll wasn't all she planned to fish for, either. Since she had Tara alone for the day, maybe she could ask her some questions that would give an accurate picture of the way Glen was at home, when no one could see if his mask of Christianity had slipped or not.

"All I have are some pictures to prove that my mother even existed," Tara went on to say. "To tell you the truth, I don't feel like I ever had a mother."

"I know what you mean," Sinda said softly. "As I told you before, I lost my mother when I was young."

Tara didn't seem to be listening anymore. She was looking at something lying on the floor next to her skateboard. She reached down to pick it up. "What's this—some kind of diary?"

Sinda jumped up. "Give me that!" She snatched the book away so quickly that Tara's hand flew up, and she nearly slapped herself in the face.

"Hey, what'd you do that for? I wasn't gonna hurt the dumb thing!"

Sinda snapped the cover shut and held it close to her throbbing chest.

"What's in there?" Tara squinted dramatically. "Some deep, dark secrets from your past?"

"It's none of your business! Diaries are someone's private thoughts, and this one is not for snoopy little girls!" Sinda bolted for the door. "I'm going upstairs to take a shower. You can watch TV if you like." She stormed up the steps, painfully aware that it was going to be a very long day.

Chapter Seventeen

It was almost six o'clock when Glen arrived at Sinda's for supper. Her hair was piled up on her head in loose curls, and she was wearing a long, rust-colored skirt with a soft beige blouse.

Glen gave a low whistle when she opened the door. "You look great!"

She smiled and felt the heat of a blush creep up the back of her neck. "A far cry from the mess that greeted you at the door this morning, huh?" Sinda was feeling a bit friendlier toward Glen this evening. After questioning Tara today about her dad, she'd learned that he had never been physically abusive. If anything, Glen was sometimes too permissive, which explained why Tara got away with being so sassy.

Glen reached for her hand. "I know you don't always sleep in your clothes. Can you tell me about it now?"

"Not this minute." Sinda motioned toward the living room where Tara sat, two feet from the TV set.

Glen nodded. "You're right. Little pitchers have big ears, and mine probably holds a world record." He followed Sinda into the kitchen. "What's on the menu?"

"Lasagna." She opened the oven door to take a peek at its progress.

He sniffed the air appreciatively. "It smells terrific."

"I hope it's fit to eat," she said. "I found the recipe in a magazine, and it said not to precook the noodles, so I can only hope it'll be all right."

"Even if the noodles turn out chewy as rubber bands, I won't care." Glen's voice dropped to a whisper, and he moved closer. "Have you been praying about us?"

Sinda edged away from him, until her hip smacked the edge of the cupboard. "Ouch!"

He pulled her quickly into his arms. "Are you okay?"

She tried to push away, but her backside was pressed against the cupboard, and she had no place else to go. Her heartbeat picked up speed, and her mind became a clouded haze as he bent to kiss her. *Glen is a great dad; Tara said so today. Glen is a good neighbor; his actions have proven it to be so. Glen is a wonderful kisser. . .*

"No! No kissing!"

Glen and Sinda both whirled to face Tara.

"Young lady, that's enough!" Glen's face was red as a cherry, and a vein on the side of his neck bulged slightly.

Tara lifted her chin defiantly. "Can we go home now?"

"No, we certainly cannot go home! I just got here, and Sinda's worked hard to fix us a nice supper. We're going to sit down and enjoy the meal, just like any normal family."

What does a normal family look like? Sinda wondered. Appearances had always been so important to her father. She and Dad used to look like the picture of happiness, and she was sure everyone at their church had thought they were content. *If they'd only known what went on in our home.*

Tara's reply broke into Sinda's troubling thoughts. "We're not a family. I mean, we are, but Sinda's not part of it."

"I'm hoping she will be someday," Glen announced.

Sinda's mouth dropped open, and Tara began to cry. "Don't you love me anymore, Dad?"

Glen left Sinda's side and bent down to wrap his arms around Tara. "Of course I love you, but I also love Sinda."

"Why?" Tara wailed. "Why do you love her?"

Glen glanced over at Sinda, and she gripped the edge of the cupboard for support. "Sinda is a beautiful, sweet lady," he said, nodding toward her.

Sinda's ears were burning. Glen was telling Tara things she had no right to hear. Especially when they weren't true. She wasn't sweet. She had bitterness in her heart and wasn't able to trust. Besides, even if Glen was all he appeared to be, and even if she were able to set her fear of hurting him aside, Tara was still an issue. The child didn't like sharing her father, and Sinda was sure Tara would never accept the fact that Glen was in love with her. There was no future for her and Glen. Not now, not ever.

Sinda pulled back the covers and crawled into bed as a low groan escaped her lips. The last twenty-four hours had felt like the longest in history—her history, at least. It had begun with the reading of her mother's Bible and diary. Next, her day had been interrupted and rearranged when Glen showed up on her doorstep needing a babysitter for his inquisitive child. Then Tara had taken up most of her day with nosey questions and a bad attitude. The final straw came in the kitchen, where Glen professed his love for her in front of Tara. The child's predictable reaction nearly ruined dinner, even if the lasagna had turned out well. Glen and Tara went home shortly after the meal, and Sinda had been grateful. At least she wasn't forced to tell Glen what was troubling her so much that she'd slept on the couch in her clothes last night.

Sinda tucked the sheet under her chin and shifted her body to the right, then the left, trying to find a comfortable position. "I can't have a serious relationship with Glen, no matter how much my heart cries for it."

Sinda had never known the heady feeling of being in love before, and even though she found it exhilarating, she couldn't succumb to it. She was scared of marriage. She'd spent her whole life afraid of her father, blocking out his verbal and physical abuses by telling herself that even if he was doing wrong, she deserved it because she was like her mother. She'd convinced herself that Dad was the way he was because of the pain Mother had inflicted on him. Sinda had vacillated between blaming her mother, her father, and even herself. She knew the truth now, though—her mother's diary had finally brought everything into focus.

Sinda turned her head to the right, and her gaze came to rest on the diary, lying on the bedside table. She was thankful Tara hadn't read any of it. She reached out and grabbed it, thumbing through several pages, forcing herself to read her mother's final words one more time.

Dear Diary:
William and I had another argument. He continues to blame me for the death of our son, even though it's been two years. He wishes we'd never married and says even the sight of me makes him sick.

"Were you sickened by the sight of me, Dad?" Sinda whispered into the night. She sniffed deeply and forced herself to read on.

What did I do to cause William to feel such animosity? He even said he and Sinda would be better off without me. I love my daughter, and I can't bear to think of leaving her. Besides, where would I go? How would I support myself? I have no relatives to turn to, and no money of my own. William handles all the finances. I'm only allowed enough cash for household expenses. If I need personal things or clothes for Sinda, I have to make an itemized list, then he decides how much I'll be allowed to spend. William makes good money at his accounting firm, yet he acts as though we are paupers.

Sinda felt a knot form in her stomach as she tried to visualize her mother begging for money. The poor woman must have had no self-esteem. *Of course, I had no self-esteem when Dad was alive, either. If I had, I'd have left home and made a life of my own. Instead, I felt obligated to take care of Dad and try to make up for what Mother did to him.* Tears slipped from her eyes and landed on the next entry.

Dear Diary:
William's abuse has escalated. Last night, during another heated argument, he hit me. I didn't see it coming in time, so the blow landed on my jaw. It left an ugly bruise, and this morning I can barely open my mouth.

Thankfully, Sinda was asleep when it happened. I hope she never discovers the awful truth about her father. She seems devoted to him, and he to her.

A sob ripped from Sinda's throat, and tears coursed down her cheeks. "It's true, Mother. My loyalty was always with Dad. I did everything he told me to do. I remember hearing the two of you arguing, but I refused to accept what was really happening." She drew in a deep breath and turned to the last entry in her mother's diary.

Dear Diary:

I know what I must do, and it's breaking my heart. It's been seven years since William Jr.'s death, yet I've been reminded of it nearly every day. My husband won't let me forget, nor will he quit laying the blame at my feet. He's become more and more physically abusive, and I fear for my life. William gave me an ultimatum last night. He said I must move out of our house and leave Sinda with him.

I've become William's enemy, and it seems as if he wants it that way. I've tried to reestablish what we once had, but he's built a wall of indifference and hatred around himself. I've seen a counselor and even suggested that we try to have another baby, but he won't hear of it. He says I had my chance and failed. He insists that I take on a new identity and begin another life. One that won't include my precious little girl. He says that I have no other choice, and if I refuse, he'll tell Sinda I killed her baby brother. She's too young to understand. I'm afraid she would side with her father.

He said that if I don't leave, he will force me to watch while he doles out my punishments to Sinda. After suffering years of his abuse, I know well what William is capable of doing. I would do anything to protect our daughter.

Sinda's throat felt constricted, and it became difficult to swallow. "Oh Mother, why didn't you tell me the truth? Or why didn't you at least take me with you? You left me with a bitter, angry man." She shook her head slowly. She'd practically idolized her father when she was a child, and even if her mother had told the truth, she wouldn't have believed it. Dad had said everything was Mother's fault, and Sinda had accepted it as fact.

"I didn't see the truth because I didn't want to," she moaned. "Dad was more of a hypocrite than I'd ever begun to imagine!" She blinked away her tears, as she continued to read.

I've decided I must go in the morning, before Sinda wakes up. I'll leave a note on the kitchen table, stating only that I'm leaving and will never return. God forgive me for not having the courage to stand up to William. I have no family living nearby, and I don't even know if I can support myself. Taking Sinda with me would be a selfish thing to do. As much as I'll miss her, I know she will be better off with her father.

Sinda drew in a shuddering breath and tried to free her mind of the agonizing pain that held her in its grasp. "Dad used to tell me I would end up like you, Mother. I only dated a few times, and never more than once with the same man. Dad convinced me that, should I ever marry, I'd end up hurting my husband the way you hurt him." She covered her face with her hands and sobbed. Like mother, like daughter. Her father's accusing words rang in her head as she rocked back and forth, clutching a pillow to her chest. She'd lost so much. If only she'd been able to see through her father's charade. If she could just go back and change the past. Was it possible that Dad really had repented that night at the revival service? Why had he told Alex Masters to see that Sinda was given her mother's trunk? Could Dad have been trying to make restitution?

Sinda knew that only God could have seen what was in her father's heart. What mattered now was what she planned to do with her future. She hadn't known Glen very long, but in the short time they'd been together, she knew one thing for certain. She loved him as much as she was capable of loving anyone.

Chapter Eighteen

Sinda awoke the following morning feeling groggy and disoriented. A barrage of troublesome dreams had left her mind in a jumble. She forced herself to shower and change into a pair of blue jeans and a white T-shirt. There were several dolls that needed to be finished, and she knew staying busy would be the best remedy for her negative thoughts and self-pity.

She and Tara had done some work in the basement yesterday. Since nothing unusual had happened, she'd talked herself into going back down there again today. She had to conquer her fears, and facing them head-on was the only way.

After breakfast Sinda cleaned up the kitchen, made a few phone calls to customers, balanced her checkbook, took out the garbage, fed the dog and cat, and watered all her houseplants. By the time she finished her chores, it was noon and she was ready for lunch. This gave her an excuse to put off going to the basement awhile longer.

Panther rubbed against Sinda's leg as she stood at the kitchen sink, peeling a carrot to add to her shrimp salad. The cat purred softly when she lifted her foot to rub the top of his sleek head with the toe of her sneaker. "Would you like to go downstairs with me?" she murmured.

The feline meowed and turned so she could rub the other side of his body. Sinda was glad Panther had come to live with her. He'd already proven to be quite the mouser. No more strange noises in the basement, and no more jumping doll parts! Sinda had been hoping her two pets would become friends, but so far it didn't appear as if that would happen. She tried to keep them separated as much as possible, alternating Sparky and Panther from the house to the yard. She probably should find another home for one of them, but right now she had more pressing matters to worry about. The first one—to get some dolls ready to go home.

A short time later, Sinda flicked the basement light on and proceeded into the doll hospital. She had little enthusiasm, but at least she was going to get something accomplished.

Sinda knew she'd become good at her craft, but on days like today she had little energy, limited confidence in her abilities, and no feeling of self-worth. In fact, she wondered if her life had any meaning at all. Where would she be living and what would she be doing twenty years from now? Would she still be here in this old house, stringing dolls, gluing on synthetic wigs, and pining for a love she could never have? Except for Carol, she had no real friends, although Glen wanted to be her friend. In fact, he wanted more than friendship.

Before she abandoned me and Dad, I thought Mother and I were friends, Sinda thought wistfully. She massaged her forehead with the tips of her fingers, hoping to halt the troubling thoughts. *I wonder if Mother's still alive. It's been almost twenty-three years since she left. Would it be a mistake to try to look for her after all this time?*

"Maybe I'm not her only daughter. If Mother took on another identity, she might have gotten married again and could even have a whole new family by now. She's probably forgotten she ever had a daughter named Sinda." She moaned and shook her head. "And what would I say if I found her?"

As intriguing as the idea was, because of Dad, Sinda felt sure her mother would want nothing to do with her. Mother no doubt thought Sinda was on his side. After all, during the time her mother had been living with them, Sinda and her father had been close. *Does Mother even know that Dad is dead?*

Sinda pushed all thoughts of her mother aside and forced her mind to focus on the Raggedy Ann doll, whose face was missing its black button eyes. In short order she completed the job of sewing on new eyes, then she went to work on an old composition baby doll. One leg was missing, so Sinda rummaged for the part in a box marked COMPOSITION DOLL LEGS. She searched thoroughly, knowing there had been a match the last time she looked.

"I can't figure it out," she fumed. "I showed Mrs. Allen the leg I'd be using as a replacement the day she brought the doll in. Where could it be?"

Thinking she might have taken it out earlier and placed it somewhere, Sinda looked on all the shelves and through every box of composition parts. When she still couldn't locate the leg, she set the doll aside to work on something else.

Another doll needed a new wig. Her old one was made of mohair and had been badly moth-eaten. Sinda opened the top drawer of an old dresser used exclusively for doll wigs. She knew the right size and color would be there because she'd recently received an order from one of her suppliers. She searched through every package of wigs, but couldn't find the one she needed. "I don't understand this!" She slammed the drawer shut with such force it caused the drawer below to fly open.

Sinda gasped. Wedged between two boxes of open-and-close eyes was a vinyl doll arm. It was the one she'd been looking for the other day, when Glen helped her search for missing doll parts. "What in the world is going on?"

Icy fingers of fear crept up her spine as she closed the drawer then opened the one below. She kept stringing-cord in several sizes here, along with wooden neck buttons used on the older bisque dolls. Lying in the middle of a coil of elastic cord was a composition doll arm. It was also one she had been looking for.

"I've got to get out of here!" Sinda banged the drawer shut and bolted for the stairs. A few minutes later, she stood in the kitchen, willing her heartbeat to return to a normal, steady rhythm. She wiped her clammy hands on the front of her jeans and sank wearily into a chair. Leaning both elbows on the table, Sinda let her head fall forward into her hands.

Several minutes later, she lifted her head and glanced at the clock above the refrigerator. It was only three o'clock. Glen wouldn't be home for at least two hours. Sinda shook her head. *Why am I thinking of him?*

"Maybe a nap will help," Sinda mumbled. She left the kitchen and curled up on the couch in the living room, with Panther lying at her feet.

For the first half hour, sleep eluded her. Fears and troubled thoughts hissed at her like corn popping over hot coals. *Help me, Lord. Please help me.* The words exploded in her head, and she realized that she was praying. Maybe she hadn't strayed as far from the Lord as she'd thought.

Maybe He did still care about her.

When Sinda finally fell asleep, her thoughts mingled with her dreams and she could no longer distinguish between what was real and what wasn't.

Glen...

Tara...

Missing dolls...

Mother...

Sinda was awakened to the resonating chime of the grandfather clock, letting her know it was half past five. She sat up, yawned, and stretched like a cat. "Some little nap we took, huh, Panther?" The cat didn't budge, so she left him alone on the couch.

Her stomach rumbled as she plodded toward the kitchen. "I think I'd better have something to eat."

Her nerves were a bit steadier now, though she still felt physically fatigued and mentally drained. Some nourishment would hopefully recharge her batteries and get her thinking clearly.

Sinda opened the refrigerator to get some milk for the makings of clam chowder. She picked up the carton and halted. Her world was spinning out of control. With a piercing wail, she dropped the milk to the floor, turned, and rushed out the back door.

Glen was standing at the stove frying lamb chops for supper when he heard a sharp rapping on the door. Knowing Tara was engrossed in her favorite TV show in the living room, he turned the burner down and went to see who it was.

When he opened the door, startling green eyes flashed with obvious fear, and Sinda practically fell into his arms. He held her for several seconds, letting her wet the front of his T-shirt with her tears. When he could stand it no longer, Glen pulled back slightly. "What is it? Why are you crying?"

"I think I'm going crazy!" Sinda shifted her weight from one foot to the other, and he noticed how badly she was trembling.

"Come, have a seat at the table." Glen led Sinda to the kitchen, offered her a chair, then handed her a napkin. "Dry your eyes, take a deep breath, and tell me what has you so upset."

"Remember the missing doll parts we hunted for the other day?" she asked, her voice quivering.

He nodded and sat down beside her.

"I found some of them today."

"That's great! See, I told you not to worry."

She grasped his arm. "It's not great! I found the parts accidentally—in some really weird places!"

She went on to give him the details, and he listened quietly until he thought she was finished. "I still don't see why you think you're going crazy. We all misplace things. The other day I lost my car keys again, and Tara found them lying on the living room floor."

"It's not the same thing. I haven't even told you the worst part."

"There's more?"

She lowered her gaze to the table. "I was about to fix some chowder for supper, and when I opened the refrigerator to take out the milk, I found a doll body—one that's also been missing." She sucked in her lower lip. "It wasn't there earlier when I fixed lunch. Do you see now why I think I'm losing my mind?"

"I'm sure there has to be some logical explanation," he said with an assurance he didn't really feel.

She looked at him hopefully. "What do you think it is?"

He reached for her hand and gave it a gentle squeeze. "I don't know."

She hung her head dejectedly, and it pulled at his heartstrings. What was there about this woman that made him want to protect her? Was it the tilt of her head, that cute little nose, those gorgeous green eyes, her soft auburn hair? Or was it Sinda's vulnerability that touched the core of Glen's being? Had God sent her to him, or was it the other way around? Perhaps they needed each other more than either of them realized.

Glen shook his thoughts aside and focused on Sinda's immediate need. "Why don't you stay here for supper? Afterward, we'll go back to your house, and I'll help you look for more doll parts, or at least some clues that might tell us something about what's been going on."

Sinda raised her head. "Thanks, but I have to tell you, I don't have much hope of finding anything."

He studied her face a few seconds. Her smile was the saddest one he'd ever seen. It nearly broke his heart to see her suffering like this.

Prayer. That's what they both needed now. Lots and lots of prayer.

Chapter Nineteen

"Why can't I come too?" Tara whined after Glen informed her that he was going over to Sinda's house.

"Because you have dishes to do."

"There aren't that many," she argued. "I could do them when we get back."

Since when is Tara so anxious to go to Sinda's? Glen wondered. *She's got to be up to something.* He pointed to the sink. "I want you to do the dishes now, Tara."

Tara's lower lip protruded. "Please, Dad."

"Pouting will not help."

"Maybe we could use some help on this case," Sinda suggested. "After all, Tara has been practicing to be a detective."

The child jumped up and down excitedly. "A case? What kind of case are we on?"

"We are not on any case," Glen answered firmly. "I am going to help Sinda look for a few things she's misplaced." He turned so only Sinda could see his face, and he held one finger to his lips. When she nodded, he faced Tara again. "If we run into problems we can't handle, I'll call you."

"Promise?"

"I said so, didn't I?"

Before the child could reply, Glen grabbed Sinda by the hand and led her out the back door.

"Are you sure you have time for this?" Sinda asked when they reached her back porch.

"I'll always make time for you." Glen's answer was followed by a quick kiss.

"I wish you wouldn't do that."

He wrapped his arms around her. "You mean this?" When he bestowed

416

her with another kiss, he noticed she was blushing.

"I think we'd better go inside. Our neighbors might get the wrong idea." Sinda opened the back door and motioned toward her kitchen floor. "Excuse the mess. When I saw the doll body in the refrigerator, I dropped a carton of milk. I was so scared, I just ran out the door." She grabbed some paper towels, then dropped to her knees.

Glen skirted around her, heading for the refrigerator. Sure enough, there was a pink doll body lying on the top shelf. He reached inside and pulled it out, hardly batting an eyelash over this latest phenomenon.

"Be careful with that," Sinda cautioned. "It's quite valuable."

He carried it gingerly across the room and placed it on the table.

She stood up and moved to his side. "So what do you think?"

Glen drew in a deep breath. "I'd say someone is playing a pretty mean trick on you, and I've got a good idea who that someone might be."

"You do?" She clutched his arm as though her life depended on it. "Who is it, Glen? Who could be hiding my doll parts?"

"My daughter."

Sinda's eyes widened. "You think Tara did it?"

"She's the only one with opportunity or motive."

"You make it sound as though she's some kind of a criminal."

He shrugged. "I wouldn't put it quite like that, but Tara does resent you. I think finding out I'm in love with you might have pushed her over the edge." He cleared his throat a few times. "Now you know why I didn't want her coming over here yet. I needed to discuss this with you in private." He wiped his forehead with the back of his hand. "Of course, she is the only one who can help us find the rest of the missing doll parts."

Sinda stood there, slowly shaking her head. "But how? When could she have done all this?"

"When she was helping you repair dolls," he answered. "She was here for several hours at a time, then again when you kept her while Mrs. Mayer was sick."

Sinda pulled out a chair at the table and almost fell into it. "I did catch her nosing around the place a few times, while she was helping out with the dolls." She clicked her tongue. "I can't believe Tara would do something so cruel."

"Was she ever alone? Were you out of her sight long enough for her to hide the parts?"

"Several times, but—"

Glen snapped his fingers. "Case solved!" He pulled out the chair next to Sinda and took a seat.

"It's not as simple as you might think," Sinda said, toying with a strand of her hair.

"It seems like an open-and-shut case to me. The only thing left to do is have a little heart-to-heart talk with that daughter of mine."

She touched his arm. "Tara was not in my house today, Glen."

"So?"

"She couldn't have put the bisque doll in my refrigerator."

Glen squeezed his eyes shut, praying for guidance as he tried to put the pieces of the puzzle together. "Maybe she did it yesterday."

Sinda shook her head. "The doll wasn't there before my nap. Tara hasn't been here today, and neither has anyone else."

Glen's forehead wrinkled. "I'll tell you what I think."

"What's that?"

"I think the doll body was in the refrigerator earlier, and you just didn't see it."

"I don't think so," she argued. "If it had been there, I'm sure I would have noticed."

He pursed his lips. "I'm convinced that Tara has something to do with this. She could have come over here while you were taking your nap. Was the back door unlocked?"

Sinda shrugged her shoulders. "I don't know. I usually lock it, but it's possible that I forgot after I took out the garbage."

"If the door was unlocked, Tara could have come inside, crept down to the basement, picked up the doll body, and put it in your refrigerator." Glen turned his hands palms up. "It makes perfect sense to me. Tara's jealous and she's taking it out on you."

Sinda's body sagged with obvious relief, and she gave him a wide smile. "Glen Olsen, you're beginning to sound more like a detective than your nosey daughter." She emitted a small sigh. "If you're right about this, and Tara is responsible, what do we do now?"

He stood up. "I'm going to call my detective daughter on the phone and tell her to get over here right now."

"Could you wait awhile on that?"

"What for?"

"I'd like to discuss a few other things. That is, if you have the time to listen."

Glen chuckled in response to her question. "For you, I have all the time in the world."

Sinda handed Glen a glass of iced tea as they took a seat on the couch in her living room. She was about to bare her soul, because she couldn't carry the pain any longer. Her nerves were shot, her confidence gone, and she was afraid she might be close to a complete mental breakdown. "You know that old trunk of my mother's?" she asked as she pushed a stack of magazines aside and set her glass down on the coffee table.

Glen nodded.

"I looked through the rest of it the other day, and I found her Bible, as well as an old diary."

"Have you read any of it?"

Her eyes filled with unwanted tears. "All of it."

"I assume the content was upsetting?"

Sinda reached for her glass and took a sip of tea before answering. "Terribly upsetting."

"Is that what you wanted to talk about?"

She swallowed hard and nodded. "Remember when I told you that Mother left when I was ten years old?"

"I remember."

"Her diary revealed some things I didn't know before. Some alarming things." Sinda paused and licked her lips. "Mother didn't leave because she wanted to. She was forced to go."

Glen's eyebrows shot up. "Forced? How so?"

"When I was three years old, Mother had a baby boy, but he was born prematurely and died a few days later. If not for that diary, I would never have known I'd even had a brother." Tears coursed down Sinda's cheeks, and she wiped them away with the back of her hand. "Dad blamed Mother for the death of the baby."

Glen frowned as he set his glass of tea down on the table. "I don't understand. How could your mother be held accountable for a premature baby dying?"

"As far as I can tell, she wasn't responsible. Her diary says Dad accused her of doing too much while she was pregnant. He hounded her about it for years—even to the point of verbal and physical abuse."

"Your dad must have wanted a son badly to be so bitter and hostile. I think he needed professional help."

Sinda closed her eyes and drew in a deep breath. "He took me to church every Sunday and claimed to be a Christian."

"Just because someone goes to church doesn't make him a Christian. Christianity is a relationship with God." Glen flexed his fingers. "Far too many people go to church only for show."

She nodded in agreement. "I was shocked to learn it was Dad's blackmailing scheme that drove Mother away." Sinda choked back the sob rising in her throat.

Glen's eyes clouded with obvious confusion. "Blackmailing?"

Sinda set her glass down on the coffee table and stood up. She began to pace the length of the room. "Apparently Dad demanded that Mother move away and take on a new identity. He threatened to tell me that she'd killed my baby brother if she didn't." She hung her head. "He also threatened to hurt me."

When Glen stood up and guided her to stand in front of the fireplace, she leaned her head against his arm. "I can't believe I was so taken in by his lies. If I had only known the truth."

"You were just a child. Children usually believe what their parents tell them, whether it's right or wrong."

Sinda's eyes pooled with a fresh set of tears. "I grew up thinking I was just like my mother, and Dad reminded me of it nearly every day."

Glen quickly embraced her. "You can't let the words of a bitter, hateful man control your life. God created you, and He gave you the ability to love and be loved."

"I can't," she sobbed. "After what Dad did, I can never trust another man."

Glen kissed her forehead. "You can trust me."

"I wish it were that simple."

"It can be. Let me help you, Sinda. Let me show you how much I care."

She moved away from him. "I need more time. I need to work through all the things I've just learned. Dad pretended to be such a good Christian, all the while blaming Mother for everything. He was abusive to her, and as much as I hate to admit it, there were times when he abused me." She shuddered. "It was not normal discipline, Glen, but hair pulling, smacks across the face, a belt that could connect most anywhere on my body, and once, he even choked me."

Glen's eyes darkened. "I'm beginning to understand your reluctance to let me get close," he said, resting his forehead against hers. "I'm so sorry for all you've been through."

She sniffed deeply. "I've never discussed this with anyone. Our family secrets were well hidden. No one knew how controlling Dad could be." The strength drained from Sinda's legs, and she dropped into a nearby chair. "I covered for him because I thought everything was Mother's fault. If she hadn't gone, he might have been kinder. If I hadn't reminded him of her, maybe. . ." Her voice trailed off, and she closed her eyes against the pain.

Glen snorted. "Each of us is responsible for our own actions, and not all men are like your father." He moved to stand behind her, then began to knead the kinks from her shoulders and neck. "You've been through so much and discovered a lot in the last few days."

She shivered involuntarily. "There's still the matter of the missing doll parts. The mystery hasn't been solved yet, and until it is. . ."

"It will be solved soon," Glen said with assurance. "By the end of this evening, we'll have some answers."

Chapter Twenty

When Tara arrived at Sinda's, she was wearing a satisfied smile, but Glen glared at her, and it quickly faded.

"What's wrong, Dad? I thought you called me over to help solve a case."

He ushered Tara into the living room and motioned her to take a seat, then he joined Sinda on the couch.

"What's up?" Tara asked, dropping into the antique rocker.

Seconds of uneasy silence ticked by, then Glen glanced at Sinda. "Do you want to tell her or shall I?"

She shrugged. "She's your daughter."

Glen leaned forward, raked his fingers through his hair, then stared at Tara accusingly. "Sinda has some doll parts that are missing. Would you care to tell us where they are?"

Tara rapped her fingers on the arm of the chair. "Where were they last seen?"

Glen jumped up and moved swiftly across the room. "Don't play coy with me, young lady. You know perfectly well where they were last seen. Tell us where they are now!"

Tara's mouth dropped open, and her eyes widened. "You think I took some doll parts?"

"Didn't you?"

She shook her head.

"Come on, Tara! This has gone on long enough! Sinda needs those parts, and I want you to tell her where they are!"

Feeling a sudden need to protect Tara from her father's wrath, Sinda stood up and knelt in front of the child's chair. Even if Glen wasn't going to strike his daughter, he was yelling, and that upset her. "We're not mad at you, Tara," she said softly.

"Speak for yourself!" Glen shouted.

Tara looked up at her father, and her eyes filled with tears. "I haven't done anything wrong, and I don't know a thing about any missing doll parts."

"Are you saying you haven't hidden doll parts in some rather unusual places?" Sinda asked.

"Like maybe a freezer or the refrigerator?" Glen interjected.

Tara's mouth was set in a thin line. "I don't know what you're talking about."

"Tara Mae Olsen, I'm warning you. . . ."

"Maybe she's telling the truth," Sinda interjected.

Glen shook his head. "She has to be the guilty party. She's the only one with a motive."

"What kind of motive would I have?" Tara asked shakily.

"Do you really have to ask? You're jealous of Sinda, and you're trying to scare her away with ghost stories and disappearing doll parts."

Sinda looked the child full in the face. "Please believe me, I'm not trying to come between you and your father."

Tara glared back at her. "I think you've got him hypnotized into believing he loves you."

Glen held up his hands. "See, what'd I tell you? She hid those doll parts out of spite!" He gave Tara another warning look. "Are you going to show us where they are or not?"

The child squared her shoulders. "I can't, because I don't know."

"I believe her, Glen," Sinda said as she pulled herself to her feet.

"Well, I don't, and if she doesn't confess, she's going to be punished!"

Sinda flinched. She closed her eyes, trying to dispel the vision of her father coming at her with his belt. *"You're a bad girl—just like your mother, and you deserve to be punished."* Dad's angry words echoed in Sinda's head, as though he were standing right beside her. She cupped her hands against her ears, hoping to drown out the past.

Sinda felt Glen's hand touch her shoulder. "I'm sorry. I'm a little upset with my daughter right now, but I shouldn't be snapping at you."

When Sinda made no reply, he added, "It's okay. No one's going to get hurt." He gave Tara an icy stare. "Even if they do deserve to be spanked."

Tara shrugged, apparently unconvinced of the possibility of being taken over her father's knee. "I can't make you believe me, but I am a good detective. So if you'd like my help solving this mystery, I'm at your service."

Sinda offered the child what she hoped was a reassuring smile. "We appreciate that."

"Where do we start?" Tara asked eagerly.

"I think we should wait until tomorrow," Glen said. "It's getting late, and we'll all function better after a good night's rest."

Sinda gulped. "You might be able to get a good night's rest, but I sure won't. I haven't slept well in weeks. Not since this whole frightening mess started."

"I've got an idea. Tara and I can spend the night over here," Glen suggested. "That way you won't be alone."

Before Sinda could respond, Tara grabbed her father's arm and begged, "You've got to be kidding!"

Glen brushed her hand aside. "I'm completely serious. You can sleep upstairs in one of Sinda's spare rooms, and I'll sleep down here on the couch." He smiled at Sinda. "Since tomorrow's my day off, and Tara's on summer vacation, we can sleep in if we like. I'll fix us a hearty breakfast, and afterward we'll turn this house upside down until we find all those doll parts. How's that sound?"

It sounded wonderful to Sinda, but she hated to admit it. "I–I couldn't put you out like that, Glen."

"I'm more than happy to stay." He glanced down at Tara, who stood by his side with a frown on her face. "Let's think of this as an adventure. Who knows, it could even prove to be fun."

Sinda sat on the edge of her bed with her mother's diary in her lap. She blinked against the tide of tears that had begun to spill over. *Mother, if you are still alive, where are you now? Do you ever think of me? Have you tried to get in touch with me?* She didn't know why she kept running this over and over in her mind, or why it seemed so important to her now. She glanced at the diary again and knew the reason. *Mother didn't leave because she wanted to. She left because she was afraid of Dad. She thought he would turn me against*

her, and she was right, that's exactly what happened. Thoughts of her father's betrayal seemed to be just under the surface of her mind, like an itch needing to be scratched, and she groaned.

Throughout her youth, Sinda's resentment toward her mother had festered. It wasn't anger she was feeling now, though. It was sadness and a deep sense of loss, but she knew there was no going back. What was in the past was history. She would have to find the strength to forgive both of her parents and move on with her life.

She snapped off the light by her bed and collapsed against the pillow. What she needed now was a long talk with her heavenly Father, followed by a good night's sleep.

Glen punched his pillow for the third time and tried to find a comfortable position on the narrow couch he was using as a bed. He hoped they would find some answers to the doll mystery soon. Sinda needed to feel safe in her own home. He didn't relish the idea of making her living room a permanent bedroom every night, either. He gave the pillow one more jab and decided he could tough it for one night.

Glen fought sleep for several hours, and just as he was dozing off, a strange noise jolted him awake. He glanced at the grandfather clock across the room, noting that it was one in the morning. He sat up and swung his legs over the edge of the couch. His body felt stiff and unyielding as he attempted to stretch his limbs. He listened intently but heard no more noises. Since he was already awake, he decided to get a drink of water.

Glen entered the kitchen and was about to turn on the faucet at the sink when he heard the basement door open and click shut. He whirled around in time to see Sinda walk into the room. He hadn't turned on the light, so he could only make out her outline, but it was obvious that she was wearing a long nightgown. She padded across the room in her bare feet. It looked like she was holding something in her hands.

Glen squinted, trying to make out what it was. "Sinda? What are you doing?"

She made no reply as she bent to open the oven door.

"You're not planning to do any middle-of-the-night baking, I hope," he teased.

When she still didn't answer, he snapped on the overhead light. "What on earth?" Sinda was putting a vinyl doll leg into the oven! He moved in for a closer look, watching in fascination as she closed the oven door and turned to leave.

Glen followed her through the hallway. She opened the door that led to the basement and descended the stairs in the dark. Afraid she might fall, he turned on the light over the stairwell and followed.

Sinda walked slowly and deliberately into the doll hospital, apparently unaware of his presence. Glen watched in amazement as she pulled one of the boxes from a shelf and retrieved a small composition arm. She set the box on her workbench, turned, and made her way back to the stairs. When she reached the top, she headed toward the next flight of steps.

Glen stayed close behind, holding his breath as Sinda entered the guest room where Tara lay sleeping.

Sinda walked over to the dresser, bent down, and opened the bottom drawer, then placed the doll arm inside. When she banged the drawer shut, Tara bolted upright in bed. "Who's there?"

"It's me, Tara," Glen whispered. "Me and Sinda."

Tara snapped on the light by her bed. "What's going on, Dad? What are you doing in my room in the middle of the night?"

"Go back to sleep. I'll explain everything in the morning." Glen took Sinda's hand and led her toward the door.

"Wait a minute!" Tara called. "If something weird's going on, I want to know about it! After all, I was forced to spend the night in this creepy house, and I'm supposed to be helping you solve a big mystery."

Glen nodded. "You do deserve an explanation, but now's not the time. I need to get Sinda back to her own room."

"What's she doing in here again?"

Glen's forehead wrinkled. "Again? What do you mean?"

"She was in here earlier. I asked what she wanted, but she didn't answer. She walked over to the window, stood there a few minutes, then left. It was really creepy, Dad."

Sinda stood there, staring off into space and holding Glen's hand as though she didn't have a care in the world. Glen glanced over at her before he spoke to Tara again. "I think Sinda's been sleepwalking," he whispered. "I found her in the kitchen, then followed her to the basement."

"What was she doing down there?"

"Getting a doll part. She put one in the oven, and just now she placed a doll arm in that drawer." He pointed to the dresser and frowned.

"How weird!" Tara exclaimed. She nodded her head toward Sinda. "Just look at her. She's staring off into space like she doesn't know where she is."

"She doesn't," Glen said. "She has no idea what she's done, or even that she's out of her bed."

"Then wake her up."

"I don't think that's a good idea. I heard somewhere that waking a sleepwalker might cause them some kind of emotional trauma." He glanced at Sinda again, feeling a deep sense of concern. "I don't know if it's true or not, but to be on the safe side, I think I'll wait and tell her in the morning."

Suddenly Sinda began swaying back and forth, hollering, "Oh, my head! It hurts so bad!"

Glen held her steady, afraid she might topple to the floor.

She blinked several times, then looked right at him. "Glen? What are you doing in my room?"

"This isn't your room," he answered. "It's the guest room."

Sinda's face was a mask of confusion. "I'm in the guest room?"

He nodded. "I followed you here. You were sleepwalking."

Sinda sat at the kitchen table, holding a cup of hot chocolate in one hand. "I still can't believe I'm the one responsible for all those missing doll parts." She looked over at Glen, who sat in the chair beside her. "Do you think I'm losing my mind?"

He reached out and took hold of her free hand. "No, but I believe you're deeply troubled about that diary you found in your mother's trunk."

Sinda feigned a smile. "I don't think I've ever walked in my sleep before. In fact, the doll parts didn't turn up missing until that stupid trunk arrived. Maybe that's when all the sleepwalking began."

She saw Glen glance at the clock across the room. It was nearly two in the morning. Tara was back in bed, but Sinda needed to talk, so Glen had suggested they come to the kitchen for hot chocolate.

"Sinda," Glen said hesitantly, "I know you're upset about your recent discoveries, and I think maybe your subconscious has chosen to deal with it in a rather unusual way."

Sinda blew on her cocoa before taking a tentative sip. "I'll bet there are doll parts hidden all over this house. How am I ever going to make it stop happening?" A sickening wave of dread flowed through her. She looked at Glen, hoping he could give her some answers. "I can't go on living like this. Doll repairing and selling antiques is my livelihood. I can't keep losing doll parts or wandering around the house at all hours of the night like a raving lunatic."

"You're not a lunatic," Glen said softly. "I think the best thing for you to do is try to put the past behind you and start looking to the future."

"The future?" she shot back. "Do I even have a future?"

A tear trickled down her cheek, and Glen dried it with his thumb. "Of course you have a future. One with me, I hope."

Sinda rested her head on his shoulder and a low moan escaped her lips. "I only wish it were that simple."

"It can be," he whispered.

She lifted her head. "You have a spirited daughter to raise, Glen. Do you really want to take on the responsibility of babysitting your neurotic neighbor?"

Glen graced her with a tender smile. "It would give me nothing but pleasure."

"What about Tara?"

"What about her?"

"She doesn't like me. And this discovery won't help."

Glen leaned over and gently kissed her. "She'll grow to love you as much as I do." He wiggled his eyebrows. "Well, maybe not quite that much."

Sinda smiled in spite of her nagging doubts. She glanced at the clock again. "I've kept you up half the night. I'm sorry for causing so much trouble."

"I'd do it all over if you'd promise to think about a future with me," he said.

She studied him intently, realizing he had a much softer heart than she'd ever imagined. "You're serious, aren't you?"

"Couldn't be more serious." He drew her into his arms. "I don't want to rush you into a relationship you're not ready for."

"Thanks," she murmured. "I've still got a lot of things to work out."

"I'm here if you need me, and when the time's right, I hope to make you my wife."

Her eyes filled with tears. "You'd be willing to marry a crazy sleep-walker who can't deal with her past?"

He snickered. "I'm not worried about that. I think as you begin to trust God fully and let Him help you work through the pain, there'll be no need for your nightly treks."

"I hope you're right, Glen," she murmured. "I really hope you're right."

Chapter Twenty-One

For the next several weeks, things went better. Sinda was able to locate most of the missing doll parts, her sleepwalking had lessened, and Tara, though reluctantly, did seem a bit more resigned to the fact that Glen and Sinda planned to keep seeing one another. Sinda and Glen had gone to a couple of yard sales, and they'd even taken Tara on a picnic at the lake. They had also started praying regularly and studying the Bible together several evenings a week.

Sinda's biggest hurdle came when she agreed to attend church with the Olsens on the first Sunday of August. Today would be the first time she'd been in church since her father died, and just the thought of it set her nerves on edge. Would she fit in? Would the memory of Dad and his hypocrisy keep her from worshiping God?

She stood in front of the living room window, waiting for Glen to pick her up, and when she closed her eyes briefly, she could see her father sitting in his church pew with a pious look on his face. "How could I have been so blind? I knew how harsh Dad was with me. Every sharp word. . .every physical blow. . . Why didn't I realize he'd been the same way with Mother? Why did I blame her for his actions?"

A knock on the front door drew Sinda away from the window. Glen was waiting. It was time to go to church.

Sinda glanced over at Glen, then past him to Tara, who sat on his other side. He was smiling and nodding at the pastor's words. An occasional "Amen" would escape his lips. Was Glen really all he seemed to be? How could she be sure he wasn't merely pretending to be a good Christian, the way her father had? Could she ever learn to fully trust again?

"God's Word says, 'Don't worry about anything; instead, pray about

everything. Tell God what you need, and thank him for all he has done.'"
Pastor Benton's quote from Philippians 4:6 rocked Sinda to her soul. She'd
spent so many years worrying about everything, praying about little, and
never thanking God for the answers she'd received to those prayers she
had uttered. Hadn't it been God, working through Glen, who showed her
the facts regarding the missing doll parts? Hadn't she learned the truth
about her mother because God allowed her the opportunity to read that
diary?

The pastor's next words resounded in her head like the gong of her
grandfather clock. "In Hebrews 11:1 we are told that faith is being sure of
what we hope for and certain of what we do not see. The sixth verse of the
same chapter reminds us that without faith it's impossible to please God."
Pastor Benton looked out at the congregation. "How is your faith today?
Are you sure of God's love? Have you put your hope in Him? Are you
certain of the things which you cannot see?"

Sinda knew her faith had been weak for a long time. She'd allowed
her father's deceit and abusive ways to poison her mind and cloud her
judgment. She couldn't trust men because she hadn't been trusting the
Lord.

As though he sensed her confusion, Glen reached over and gave her
hand a gentle squeeze. She smiled and clasped his fingers in response. It
was time to leave the past behind. Sinda was ready to look to the future
and begin to trust again. She felt an overwhelming sense of gratitude
to God.

The pungent, spicy smell of Glen's homemade barbecue sauce simmering
in the Crock-Pot permeated the air as Sinda and Glen entered his kitchen
after church. Tara was out in the living room watching TV, and Sinda was
glad they could be alone for a few minutes. "Need help with anything?"
she asked.

He nodded toward the nearest cupboard. "I guess you can set out some
paper plates and cups while I start forming the hamburger patties and get
the chicken out of the refrigerator."

Glen headed for the refrigerator, and Sinda moved toward the cupboard he'd indicated. They collided somewhere in the middle of the room, and Glen quickly wrapped his arms around her. "Hey, I could get used to this kind of thing," he murmured.

She smiled up at him. "You think so?"

"Does this answer your question?" He bent his head, and his lips eagerly sought hers. The kiss only lasted a few seconds because they were interrupted by a deep voice.

"Ah-ha! So this is how you spend your Sunday afternoons!"

Sinda pulled away and turned to see Glen's brother standing inside the kitchen doorway, arms folded across his broad chest and a smirk on his bearded face.

"Phil! How'd you get in here?" Glen asked, brushing his fingers across his lips.

"I came to the front door, and Tara let me in. The kid said you were fixing hamburgers and chicken to put on the grill, but it looks to me like you were having dessert." Phil chuckled and winked at Sinda. Her face flamed, and she turned away.

"If you'd been in church this morning I might have asked you to join our barbecue," Glen said in a none-too-friendly tone.

The day Phil delivered her screen door Sinda had noticed the tension between the brothers, and she'd wondered what caused it. After hearing Glen's comment about church, she surmised that the problem could be about Phil's lack of interest in spiritual things.

"I was forced to go to Sunday school every day until I moved out of Mom and Dad's house, so I'm not about to spend all my Sundays sitting on hard pews, listening to doom and gloom from a pastor who should have retired ten years ago," Phil said with a sweeping gesture.

Glen made no comment, but when Sinda chanced a peek at him, she saw that his face was flushed.

Phil sniffed the air. "Something sure smells good. How about inviting me to join your little barbecue, even if I was a bad boy and skipped church this morning?"

Glen marched over to the cupboard and withdrew a glass pitcher and a jar of pre-mixed tea. He handed it to Phil. "Here, if you're going to join us, you may as well make yourself useful."

∞

As Glen flipped burgers on the grill, then checked the chicken on the rack above, he felt a trickle of sweat roll down his forehead and land on his nose. It was a warm day, and the barbecue was certainly hot enough to make a man perspire, but he knew the reason he felt so hot was because he was irritated about his brother joining them for lunch. Ever since Phil had shown up unannounced, he'd been hanging around Sinda, bombarding her with stupid jokes, and dropping hints about taking her out sometime. If Glen hadn't been trying to be a good Christian witness, he'd have booted his brother right out the garden gate.

Tara seemed to be enjoying her uncle's company, but Glen wondered if she was really glad to see Uncle Phil—or was she delighting in the fact that he was keeping Sinda away from her dad?

The meat was done, and Glen was about to tell his guests they could sit at the picnic table when he saw Sinda move toward the gate that separated their backyards. Was she leaving? Had she had all she could take of Phil the Pill?

He set the platter of chicken and burgers on the table and followed her. "Sinda, where are you going?"

She turned to face him. "I think I heard a car pull into my driveway. I'd better see who it is."

"I'll come with you," Glen offered.

She eyed him curiously. "Don't you want to stay and entertain your brother?"

"Phil's a big boy. He can take care of himself until we get back."

She shrugged, opened the gate, and Glen followed her around front. A sporty red car was parked in Sinda's driveway, and an attractive woman with short blond hair was heading toward the house.

"Carol!" Sinda waved. "What are you doing here?"

"I stopped by to see if you wanted to go to the mall, and maybe stop by my favorite pizza place for something to eat afterward."

"Actually, I was next door, about to sink my teeth into a juicy piece of barbecued chicken." Sinda gave Glen a quick glance, then swung her gaze back to her friend. "I guess you two haven't met."

"Not in person, but if this is the handsome mailman I've heard so much about, then I feel like I already know you," Carol announced.

Glen bit back the laughter bubbling in his throat. So Sinda had been talking about him. He smiled at Carol and extended his hand. "I'm Glen Olsen."

"Carol Riggins. It's nice to finally meet you."

"Carol and I have been friends since we were children," Sinda said. "Carol went to college while I stayed home repairing dolls and catering to my dad. Shortly after her graduation she moved from Seattle to Elmwood, and she's been after me to move here ever since."

"I'm glad you were finally persuaded," Glen said, placing his hand against the small of Sinda's back.

Carol started moving toward her car. "I should probably get going. The mall will only be open until six, and I don't want to keep you from your barbecue."

"Why don't you join us?" Sinda turned to face Glen. "You wouldn't mind one more at the table, would you?"

"I've got plenty of everything so you're more than welcome, Carol," he eagerly agreed.

Carol smiled. "I appreciate the offer, and I gladly accept."

A few minutes later Carol and Phil had been introduced, and everyone was seated at the picnic table. Glen said the blessing, then passed the plate of barbecued chicken to his guests.

Sinda bit into a juicy drumstick and smacked her lips. "Umm. . .this is delicious."

"Dad can cook just about anything and make it taste great," Tara put in.

"He certainly did a good job with this," Carol agreed. "Everything from the potato salad to the baked beans tastes wonderful." She giggled and poked Sinda in the ribs with her elbow. "Don't look any deeper, 'cause this one's a keeper."

Sinda smiled and nodded. She couldn't agree more.

"Dad, where's the mustard?"

"Oops, I must have forgotten to set it out. Guess you'll have to run inside and get the bottle out of the refrigerator."

Tara frowned. "How come I always have to do everything?"

"You don't have to do everything, Tara." Glen pointed toward the house.

Sinda jumped up. "I'll get the mustard."

"That's not necessary, Sinda," Glen said quickly.

Sinda held up one hand. "It's okay. I'm happy to go."

Once inside the house, Sinda went immediately to the kitchen and retrieved a squeeze bottle of mustard from the refrigerator. *At least there aren't any doll parts in here,* she thought ruefully. She closed the door and moved over to the window that overlooked the backyard. She didn't see Glen sitting beside Tara anymore and figured he'd probably gone back to the barbecue for more meat. Much to her surprise, Carol had moved from her spot and was now seated beside Phil.

Sinda smiled. "Maybe Phil's found another interest. That should take some of the pressure off me. Guess Carol showing up was a good thing."

"You're right, it was. Now I don't have to share you with my woman-crazy brother for the rest of the day."

Sinda whirled around at the sound of Glen's voice. She clasped her hand against her mouth. "Glen, I didn't hear you come in!"

He grinned, and her heart skipped a beat. "I thought you might need help finding the ketchup."

"It's mustard," she said, holding up the bottle.

"Oh, right." Glen moved slowly toward her, and Sinda could hear the echo of her heartbeat hammering in her ears.

Glen bent his head to kiss her, and she melted into his embrace. "I want to marry you, Sinda Shull," he murmured.

She licked her lips and offered him a faint smile. "I—I don't know what to say, Glen."

He gave her a crooked smile. "How about, 'Yes, I'd be happy to marry you'?"

She studied his handsome face, but before she could open her mouth to respond, there was a high-pitched scream, followed by, "Dad, you can't marry Sinda!"

Sinda and Glen both turned to face Tara. Her face was bright red, and her eyes were mere slits. "Can you give me one good reason why I shouldn't marry her?" Glen asked.

Tara marched across the room and stopped in front of her father. "Yes, I can."

Sinda knelt next to Tara. "Listen, Tara, I—"

"Dad's gotten along fine without a wife for nine whole years, and he doesn't need one now!" Tara shouted. "Especially not some sleepwalking, doll-collecting weirdo!"

A muscle in Glen's jaw quivered. "Tara Mae Olsen, you apologize to Sinda this minute!"

"It's okay, Glen," Sinda said, standing up again. "She needs more time."

Tara stomped her foot. "I don't need more time. I do not want a mother, and Dad doesn't need a wife!" She pivoted on her heel and bolted for the hall door, slamming it with such force that the WELCOME plaque fell off the wall and toppled to the floor.

Glen cleared his throat. "That sure went well."

Sinda's eyes filled with unwanted tears. "We'd better face the facts, Glen. It's not going to work for us. Tara isn't going to accept me."

He shrugged. "I think she's simply jealous. I'm sure she'll calm down and listen to reason."

Sinda dropped her gaze to the floor. "What if that never happens?"

He gave her shoulder a gentle squeeze, but she could see a look of defeat written on his face. "Guess I'll have to deal with it."

"Sorry about the barbecue being ruined, but I think I'd better go home so you can get things straightened out with Tara."

"I'll talk to her and try to help her understand."

Sinda blinked back her tears of frustration. She doubted that anything Glen had to say would penetrate Tara's wall of defense. She hated to admit it, but there was no future for her and Glen Olsen. Just when she'd made peace with God and had begun to trust, the rug was being yanked out from under her. Would she ever know real joy? Was it even possible to experience the kind of love God planned for a man and a woman?

Chapter Twenty-Two

Glen found Tara in her room, lying across the bed, crying as if her heart were breaking. He approached her slowly. "Tara, I need you to listen to me."

"Go away."

"I'm in love with Sinda. Won't you try to understand?" He took a seat on the edge of her bed and reached out to gently touch her back.

She jerked away. "Do you love her more than me?"

"Of course not. I love her in a different way, that's all." Glen sighed deeply. "It's been nine years since your mother died, and—"

Tara sat up suddenly. "Did you love her?"

"Connie?"

Her only reply was a curt nod.

"Of course I loved her. When she died, I thought I'd never recover, but God was good, and He filled my life with you."

She sniffed deeply. "Then how come I'm not enough for you now?"

Several seconds passed, as Glen tried to come up with an answer that might make sense to his distraught daughter. "God's plan was for a man to have a wife," he said softly. "I've waited a long time to find someone I could love enough to want for my wife."

Tara jumped up and stalked over to the window. She stood there, looking out at Sinda's house. "If you marry her, it'll never be the same."

"Tara, I know—"

She reeled around to face him. "I could never love Sinda."

How could he choose between Sinda and his daughter? He was in love with Sinda, but Tara was his only child. Until Tara calmed down and they worked through her jealousy, he'd have to keep Sinda Shull at arm's length. He hoped she would understand, but could he ask her to wait?

Sinda moped around the house for the next several weeks, unable to get much work done or even fix a decent meal. She'd heard from Carol, with news that she and Phil had gone bowling. This should have brought her joy, since it obviously meant Phil's interest had shifted from her to Carol. However, Glen had called too, informing her that he'd tried to reason with Tara, but it was to no avail. The child wouldn't accept the prospect of their marriage. Sinda understood, but the question foremost on her mind was what to do with the rest of her life. Even though Glen had tried to convince her that Tara would come around someday, she knew in her heart that their romance was over.

As she stood there staring out the living room window, Sinda caught a glimpse of the man she loved leaving for his mail route. She'd never meant to fall in love, and every encounter with Glen was something she both dreaded and anticipated. How could she stand seeing him like this, knowing they had no future together? Each time they met and uttered a casual greeting, a part of her heart crumbled a bit more. Sinda wanted to jerk the front door open and call out to Glen, but she knew it would be a mistake. She couldn't live here any longer, hoping, praying things would change. She wasn't growing younger, and she had no desire to wait around until Tara matured.

"The best thing I can do is move out of this house and get as far away from Elmwood as possible," she muttered. As soon as she had some breakfast, Sinda planned to phone the Realtor. *"No point putting off until tomorrow what you can do today."* Her father's favorite expression rang in her ears. This time, however, she would do it because it was the only way, not because it was something Dad would have expected.

It was nearly noon when Sinda called the Realtor's office, but she was informed that the Realtor who'd sold her the house was on vacation and wouldn't be back for two weeks. Sinda could either call someone else or wait.

"Guess a few more weeks won't matter," she muttered as she hung up the phone. "It will give me a chance to spruce the place up a bit so it looks more appealing to any prospective buyers."

Sinda left the kitchen and went out front to do some weeding. The flower beds were in terrible shape, and she knew a thorough going over should help. Dropping to her knees, with a shovel in her hand, Sinda filled her mind with determination. She glanced up when she heard laughter. Tara and her friend Penny were skateboarding on the sidewalk in front of her place. They had made some kind of crazy ramp out of plywood and a bucket. Penny waved, but Tara didn't even look her way.

A pang of regret stabbed Sinda's heart as she was reminded of how much she had lost. Not only had she been forced to give Glen up, but she'd been cheated out of having a stepdaughter. If only she and Tara could have become friends.

Sinda thrust the shovel into the damp soil, forcing her thoughts back to the job at hand. It would do no good to think about the what-ifs.

A verse of scripture she'd read that morning popped into her mind, and she recited it. " 'And we know that in all things God works for the good of those who love him, who have been called according to his purpose,' Romans 8:28." Surely God had something good planned for her. It simply wasn't going to be here, in this neighborhood, in the town where Glen Olsen lived. She'd have to move on with her life, even if it meant going back to Seattle, where she was born and raised.

Another thought came to mind. If she did go home, maybe she could discover the whereabouts of her mother. Perhaps she was still living in Seattle. Sinda knew she was grasping at straws, but in her present condition, she needed something to hang on to.

She grabbed a handful of weeds and gave them a yank. It felt good to take her frustrations out on the neglected flower bed. Half an hour later, she'd finished up one bed and was about to move to another when she heard a scream.

Her head snapped up. Sparky, who'd been lying peacefully at her side, ran toward the fence, barking frantically.

Sinda scrambled to her feet and followed the dog. She was surprised to see Tara sprawled on the sidewalk. Her skateboard was tipped on its side, a few feet away.

With no hesitation, Sinda jerked the gate open and hurried down the steps. Tara's friend Penny was standing over Tara, sobbing hysterically. "I only gave her a little push down the ramp, and I didn't mean for her to get hurt."

Sinda moved Penny gently aside and knelt next to Tara. Her eyes were shut, and she was moaning. "What is it, Tara? Where are you hurt?" She couldn't see any blood, yet it was obvious from the agonized expression on the young girl's face that she was in a great deal of pain.

When Tara spoke, her words came out in a whisper. "My head. . .my arm. . .they hurt." She opened her eyes, then squeezed them shut again.

Sinda's mouth went dry. One look at the girl's swollen, distorted-looking wrist told her it was most likely broken. She knew how to put broken dolls back together, but she didn't know the first thing about giving first aid to an injured child. Sinda looked up at Penny, who was still whimpering. "Penny, go tell Tara's babysitter to call 911. Tell her I think Tara has a broken arm and could have a concussion."

"Tara's staying at my house this week while her dad's at work."

"Then ask your mother to call for help."

Penny muttered something about it being all her fault, then she bolted across the street. Sinda leaned closer to Tara. "It's going to be okay. The paramedics will be here soon."

"Don't leave me," Tara wailed. "Please don't go."

An onslaught of tears rolled down the child's pale cheek, and Sinda wiped them away. "I won't leave you, honey, I promise."

As Sinda began to pace the length of the hospital waiting room, the numbness she'd felt earlier began to wear off. Penny's mother offered to call the post office to see if they could track Glen down, and Sinda had been allowed to ride with Tara in the ambulance. Once Glen arrived, Sinda had taken a seat in the waiting room.

She had just picked up a magazine when a nurse stepped to her side. "Are you Tara Olsen's babysitter?"

"I'm their next-door neighbor. Why do you ask?"

"Tara asked me to come get you," the nurse said. "She wants both you and her dad to be there when the doctor sets the bone."

The room began to spin, and Sinda closed her eyes for a moment, hoping to right her world again.

"The X-rays confirmed she broke her wrist," the nurse explained.

"Does she have a concussion?"

The nurse shook her head. "She's one lucky girl. I've seen some skate-board accidents that left the victim in much worse shape. Kids sure don't know the meaning of the word *careful*." She patted Sinda's arm in a motherly fashion. "It's a good thing you were there when it happened."

"I was only doing the neighborly thing," Sinda said absently. Her brain felt like it was on overload. Tara's wrist was broken, the doctor was about to set it, and the child wanted her to be there.

Sinda squared her shoulders and followed the nurse down the hall.

Chapter Twenty-Three

It was the last Saturday of October, and today was Sinda's thirty-third birthday. She found it hard to believe how much her life had changed in the last few months. Everything wasn't perfect as far as her emotional state, but thanks to God's love and Glen's friendship, she was beginning to heal. She was confident that the days ahead held great promise.

As Sinda checked her appearance in the full-length mirror on the back of her bedroom door, her thoughts began to drift. *I wish you were here to share in my joy, Mother. If only things had been different between you and Dad. I wish. . .*

There was a soft knock on the door, and she was grateful for the interruption. There was no point in dwelling on the past again. Not today. "Come in," she called.

Tara, dressed in a full-length pale yellow gown and matching slippers, entered the room. Her hair was left long, but pulled away from her face with a cluster of yellow and white ribbons holding it at the back of her head.

"You look beautiful," Sinda murmured. "Just like a flower in your mother's garden."

"Thanks. You look pretty too," the child replied.

Sinda glanced back at the mirror. She was wearing an ivory-colored full-length satin gown, detailed with tiny pearls sewn into the bodice. Her hair, piled on top of her head, was covered with a filmy veil held in place by a ring of miniature peach-colored carnations. "I'm glad you agreed to be my maid of honor. It means a lot to me," she said, moving away from the mirror.

Tara's cheeks flamed. "I suppose since you're gonna be my stepmom, we should try to help each other out." The child sniffed deeply, and Sinda wondered if she might be about to cry. "Like you did the day I broke my wrist. After all, I am supposed to love my neighbor."

Sinda reached for Tara's hand, glad that the cast was off now and the wrist had healed so nicely. "Your dad loves you very much. That's not going to change because he's marrying me." She swallowed hard, hoping to hold back the wall of tears threatening to spill over. "I love you, Tara, and I'll never do anything to come between you and your father. I hope you'll give me the chance to prove that." Sinda blotted the tears rolling down her cheeks with her lace handkerchief. "I've always been more comfortable with dolls than I have with people, but I'm going to try hard to be a good wife to your dad, and I really want to be your friend."

Tara's lower lip quivered slightly. "Am I supposed to call you Mom now?"

Sinda shook her head. "Sinda will be fine."

"I know it was dumb, but for a while I thought you had Dad under some kind of spell." Tara gave Sinda an unexpected grin. "I'm sure glad you didn't talk Dad into living in this old house."

"My house will work out well for my business, but your house is a much nicer place to live." Sinda smiled. "And Sparky is getting along quite well at Carol's." She bent down and pulled a cardboard box from under the bed.

"What's in there?" Tara asked, taking a step closer.

"Something for you." Sinda placed the box on top of the bed and nodded toward Tara. "Go ahead, open it."

Tara lifted the lid, her dark eyes filled with wonder as she pulled out the restored antique doll. "It's beautiful. Was it yours?"

Sinda shook her head. "It was your grandmother's doll, and your mother wanted you to have it. It needed some repairs, so your dad brought it to me several months ago. We've been saving it for just the right time."

Tara's eyes pooled with tears as she stroked the doll's delicate, porcelain face. "I'll take good care of it."

Sinda slipped her arm around Tara's shoulders, and when the child didn't pull away, she whispered a prayer of thanks. There was another knock, and she called, "Come in."

The door opened, and Carol poked her head inside. "You two about ready? I think the groom is going to have a nervous breakdown if we don't get this show on the road." She chuckled. "No show—the groom might go."

Tara giggled as she moved away from Sinda. "Should we be mean and make Dad wait?"

Sinda shook her head. "I want to start this marriage off on the right foot. No lies, no secrets, and no tricks." She extended her hand toward Tara. "Ready?"

"Ready as I'll ever be," the child answered as she slipped her hand into Sinda's.

The ladies descended the stairs, and Sinda scanned her living room, decorated with bouquets of autumn flowers and candles in shades of yellow and orange. *Some might think this an odd place for a wedding,* Sinda thought with a smile, *but I wanted my marriage to begin in the house where I learned what trust and true love really mean.*

As her gaze left the decorations, Sinda spotted her groom, dressed in a stunning black tux, standing in front of the fireplace. He looked so handsome. The minister stood on one side of Glen, and Phil stood on the other side. Tara and Carol had joined the bridal party and stood to the right of the men. Beside Sinda's friend was a petite older woman with short auburn hair, streaked with gray. Her green eyes shimmered in the candlelight, and her smile looked so familiar. Sinda swallowed against the knot that had lodged in her throat. *No, it couldn't be.* "Mother?" she mouthed.

The woman nodded, tears pooling in her eyes, and her chin trembled as she smiled.

But how? When? Sinda, so full of questions, took her place beside Glen. She looked at her mother, then back at Glen, hoping for some answers.

"I'll tell you about it after the ceremony," he whispered.

Sinda could hardly contain herself. Here she was standing in the living room of her rambling old house, about to marry the most wonderful man in the world, and her mother was here to witness the joyful event. It was too much to comprehend.

Feeling as if she were in a daze, Sinda tried to focus on the pastor's words about marriage and the responsibilities of a husband and wife. She'd spent her whole life wondering if all men were alike, and now, as she repeated her vows, Sinda's heart swelled with a joy she'd never known. Glen sealed their love with a kiss, and she found comfort in the warmth of his arms.

As soon as the minister announced, "I now present to you Mr. and Mrs. Glen Olsen," Glen grasped Sinda's hand, and they moved to the back of the room to greet their guests.

Sinda's mother was the last one through the receiving line, and she and Sinda clung to each other and wept. "How did you find me?" Sinda asked through her tears.

Her mother looked over at Glen. "I didn't. Your groom found me."

Sinda cast a questioning look at her husband. "How? When? Where?"

He lifted her chin so she was gazing into his eyes. "I hired a detective, and he found your mother living in Spokane, where she'd moved several years ago. She didn't know your father was dead or that you'd moved away."

Sinda turned to look at her mother again, and her vision clouded with tears. "How come you never came to see me?"

Clutching Sinda's arm, she replied, "Your father threatened to hurt you if I did. He was an angry, confused man, and I was afraid to stand up to him for fear of what he might do." She sniffed deeply. "Even though William filed for divorce, I never remarried. In order to support myself, I took a job as a maid at a local hotel. I never missed any of your school or church programs."

Sinda's eyebrows furrowed. "How did you manage to see my programs and not show yourself?"

Her mother dropped her gaze to the floor. "I wore a wig and dark glasses. Nobody recognized me, not even your father." She shook her head slowly. "I never stopped loving you or praying for you, Sinda. Please believe me, I had your best interest at heart."

Sinda was tempted to tell her mother that living with an abusive father could not have been the best thing for her, but she realized with regret that her mother had no idea Dad had mistreated her—no one else ever had. *It doesn't matter now*, Sinda mused. *I have Mother back again, and I'm thankful to God for that.* Through a sheen of tears, she smiled at Glen. "You're remarkable, and I love you so much."

He bent his head and kissed her so tenderly she thought she would drown in his love. "I wanted to give you a combined birthday and wedding present—something you would never forget." Then, taking Sinda's hand in his left hand, and her mother's hand in his right hand, he announced, "I thought it was the neighborly thing to do."

New York Times bestselling and award-winning author Wanda E. Brunstetter is one of the founders of the Amish fiction genre. She has written more than 100 books translated into four languages. With over 11 million copies sold, Wanda's stories consistently earn spots on the nation's most prestigious bestseller lists and have received numerous awards.

Wanda's ancestors were part of the Anabaptist faith, and her novels are based on personal research intended to accurately portray the Amish way of life. Her books are well-read and trusted by many Amish, who credit her for giving readers a deeper understanding of the Amish people and their customs.

When Wanda visits her Amish friends, she finds herself drawn to their peaceful lifestyle, sincerity, and close family ties. Wanda enjoys photography, ventriloquism, gardening, bird-watching, beachcombing, and time spent with her family. She and her husband, Richard, have been blessed with two grown children, six grandchildren, and two great-grandchildren.

To learn more about Wanda, visit her website at www.wanda brunstetter.com.

More from Wanda Brunstetter!

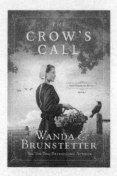

The Crow's Call Now Available!

When Vernon King, his son, and son-in-law are involved in a terrible accident, three women are left to cope with their deaths, as they become the sole providers of the family they have left. The women's only income must come from the family greenhouse, but someone seems to be trying to force them out of business.

Amy King has just lost her father and brother, and her mother needs her to help run the family's greenhouse. It doesn't seem fair to ask her to leave a job she loves, when there is still a sister and brother to help. But Sylvia is also grieving for her husband while left to raise three children, and Henry, just out of school, is saddled with all the jobs his father and older brother used to do. As Amy assumes her new role, she also asks Jared Riehl to put their courtship on hold. When things become even more stressful at the greenhouse, will Amy crumble under the pressure?

Paperback / 978-1-64352-021-6 / $15.99

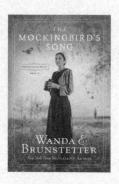

The Mockingbird's Song (Book 2) Releasing August 2020!

Sylvia has been nearly paralyzed with grief and anxiety since the tragic death of her husband, father, and brother in a traffic accident. She tries to help in the family's greenhouse while caring for her two young children, but she prefers not to have to deal with customers. Her mother's own grief causes her to hover over her children and grandchildren, and Sylvia seeks a diversion. She takes up birdwatching and soon meets an Amish man who teaches her about local birds. But Sylvia's mother doesn't trust Dennis Weaver, and as the relationship sours, mysterious attacks on the greenhouse start up again.

Paperback / 978-1-64352-231-9 / $15.99